Y0-BSR-526

Under the Rim

Damon A. Burris

Goatee Graphics
San Francisco, California

Under the Rim

By Damon A. Burris

Published by:
Goatee Graphics, LLC
PO Box 591840
San Francisco, CA 94159-1840

http://www.undertherimbook.com
http://www.beardedbooks.com

Contact by email
undertherimbook@yahoo.com

Copyright © Damon A. Burris, 2006
All right reserved. No part of this book may be reproduced or transmitted in any form or by any means, electronic or mechanical, including photo-copying, recording or by any information storage and retrieval system, without written permission from the author, except for the inclusion of brief quotations in review.

The Library of Congress has cataloged this edition as follows:

ISBN 0-9657257-1-5

Library of Congress Control Number: 2005932370

Printed in the United States of America

Contents

Contents cont.

For Tracy, Maya, and Nigel.
My past, present, and future,
(not respectively).

Basketball Court

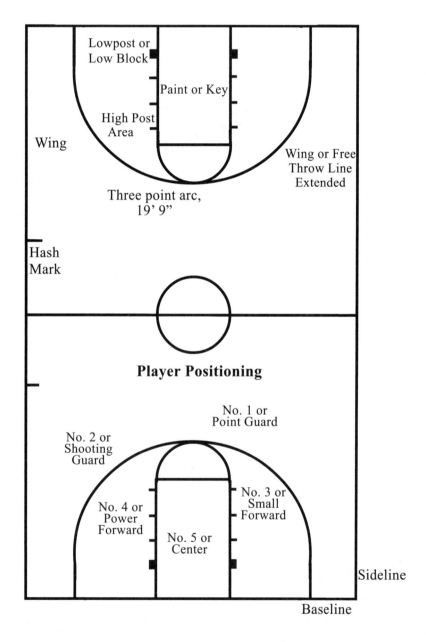

Lowpost or Low Block

Paint or Key

High Post Area

Wing

Wing or Free Throw Line Extended

Three point arc, 19' 9"

Hash Mark

Player Positioning

No. 1 or Point Guard

No. 2 or Shooting Guard

No. 3 or Small Forward

No. 4 or Power Forward

No. 5 or Center

Sideline

Baseline

Chapter 1

Back in the Game

May First, 1996

Lonnie Delaney needed this one to come through. She stood tapping her feet impatiently while waiting to meet the athletic director at Del Mar University. She hoped it would be her final interview for the head coach position of the women's basketball team. Since the resume frenzy at the Final Four, she had already interviewed for fifteen other head coaching jobs and had been rejected each time. Lonnie was hopeful because this was the first time she had been asked back for a second interview. She was anxious because vacancies were filling quickly; there wouldn't be many more opportunities.

Del Mar's Hall of Champions was impressive: mahogany paneling, brass accents, marble floor, quilted leather chairs, crystal chandeliers, faux fireplace. Eight-foot-high glass trophy cases circled the perimeter of the hall. The room was large enough for 300 boosters, their outsized postgraduate egos, their trophy wives, and most importantly, their checkbooks. The room made you want to give money. It felt successful.

Lonnie examined the trophy cases filled with the athletic lore of Del Mar University's eight NCAA championship teams. She stared at the pictures of the jubilant players during their shining moments of glory. It reminded her of her own triumphs as a player and later as a coach. She took in the ornately framed team photos and the retired numbers from the baseball, basketball, and swim teams.

"Is that? No... Those are swim trunks?!"

Why not retire a Speedo?

Lonnie's smile slowly faded. The trophies made her think about what it had taken for her to win a championship: the perseverance, the commitment–the divorce. She had never been good at moderation. Once she made the commitment to win the NCAA championship, virtually everything else, even her marriage, became secondary. What surprised her was how easily she had allowed it to atrophy and eventually die.

Four years ago she had coached the Ohio State women's basketball team to win the 1992 NCAA women's national championship. The same night, after she hoisted the trophy and cut down the nets, she was served her divorce papers in the locker room. Her husband, watching on television, had wanted to make a point. He had always had a wicked sense of humor.

Three years later, Lonnie had gone from championship coach to divorcee to be totally out–to become the director of a shelter for battered women. It all seemed like a lifetime ago. Though memories of her marriage had faded, Lonnie still missed coaching basketball. For a while, the thought was unsettling, she never really got over it. She touched the NCAA championship ring on her left ring finger. People often mistook it for a unique wedding ring and it was–of sorts.

"Can't take that away from me," she mumbled to herself.

"Take what?" asked Forrest Haneline, Del Mar's athletic director. He had approached silently and did a good job of scaring Lonnie. "Oh, I'm sorry," he said smiling. "You were staring like you've never seen one before, and we both know that's not the case."

"...Not again. Not this close," she said.

"Then you should go to the beach more often," Haneline said.

"No, the trophy. Not the... come on. I was looking at the faces in the photos."

He gave a big exaggerated wink and "okay" sign with his thumb and index finger.

Forrest Haneline, class of '72, had the George Hamilton-dipped-in-bronze thing down. No small feat, living in San Francisco where it's often a foggy 57 degrees in July. Haneline had made his money in police, and fireman badges. A bottom-line guy, he had started as a salesman, later bought the company, and combined local badge makers into one national company. He figured if the same strategy could work for Vince McMahon with professional wrestling and H. Wayne Huizinga with garbage, video rentals, and cars, it could work for him. But Haneline's first love was sports.

"So, do I have the job?" Lonnie asked, getting right to the point, as usual. Haneline didn't answer, he instead made small talk as they walked to his office.

While Forrest was making himself a cup of tea, Lonnie noticed the brass sign hanging behind Forrest's desk. "He with the most gold makes the most sense."

Lonnie said, "I don't want you to get the wrong impression. I'm very appreciative of this opportunity."

Haneline nodded. "You'd be starting off with a clean slate here Lonnie. We need someone who can show these girls how to win..."

"...Girls?" Lonnie questioned, arching a brow.

"I mean young ladies," Forrest corrected.

There was an awkward silence as he sipped his tea, thinking. Forrest wasn't quite convinced about Lonnie's priorities. She had raised a lot of hell at The Ohio State. Plus, the tea wasn't to his liking.

"I wasn't your first choice was I?" Lonnie asked, as though reading his thoughts. "I heard you interviewed Tracy Hilliard but she turned you guys down, said she wanted to keep coaching high school."

Forrest didn't like Lonnie Delaney's tone. He figured he was doing her a favor just by interviewing her. In his estimation, she had a lot of nerve for someone who couldn't find a coaching job for three years.

In terms of women's basketball, they both knew Del Mar was a third-tier program at best. It was light years from the elite power-houses; Tennessee, Stanford, Connecticut, or Duke–programs that competed every year for the national championship. Third-tier schools, so-called "mid-majors" like Del Mar, were either stepping stones for rising stars on their way to coaching major programs or a place where a coach who would never be ready for the big time could earn a nice living in relative obscurity, getting paid to coach a game kids play.

"I'll be honest," Haneline said. "When I saw you at the Final Four you were working at a Goddamn women's shelter. Don't get me wrong. It's noble work. Hell, we need people to do that kind of thing. But it isn't coaching basketball or else you wouldn't have been passing out your resume like breath mints."

Lonnie Delaney braced herself.

Haneline continued, "So, no you weren't my first choice. But you are my stopgap. I fired Satcher because she lost control of the team and I haven't been able to convince a top Division I coach to come here. But remember, Lonnie, this is an opportunity for you to get back in the game." Forrest paused dramatically, checking his hair in his reflection in a picture on his desk. A few moments later he turned back to Lonnie, waiting expectantly. "The job is yours for $55,000 a year." He smiled as if to hide the fact he hadn't cut $25,000 off her last coaching salary.

Lonnie took a deep breath. "You've got to be kidding, $55,000?" Haneline continued, "It's simply supply and demand."

"I haven't fallen that far."

"After what you did at Ohio State? It's a buyers' market for what you're selling." He pushed his tea away.

"We won two national championships."

"And what about the other stuff?" Forrest said.

"I got divorced, so what," Lonnie said.

"I wasn't talking about that, but now that you mention it..."

"I don't see what my divorce has to do with—what other stuff?"

"All the crap you pulled at Ohio Sate, I don't care if you won five championships in a row, we both know you're lucky to be sitting here."

They both knew he had a point. It wasn't the best way to start, but he had to make sure she knew who was the boss. Haneline figured the athletic director at The Ohio State lost control of her somewhere along the line and he wasn't going to make the same mistake.

"Tea?" he asked.

Haneline didn't hold grudges; he said his piece and moved on. He passed her a cup, then waited for an apology. Something like, "I'm sorry, sir... I was out of line, sir. It won't happen again, sir..."

Instead Lonnie said, "Thank you, Mr. Haneline." Then took her cup.

It was inappropriately obstinate in light of her weak bargaining position. Haneline wasn't fooled. His wife had said almost those exact same chilling words, "Thank you Forrest," right before she filed for divorce. She fought him tooth and nail on everything, including the kids, and eventually cleaned him out like raisin bran with an enema chaser. He would keep a sharp eye on Lonnie Delaney.

"I have a tough assignment for you, but it's the kind of thing that could move the women's program forward."

Lonnie was relieved to finally talk about basketball.

"I want you to convince Tamika Hightower to commit to playing here."

Lonnie shook her head. "Why would a player of that caliber

come here?... I mean, with all due respect," Lonnie finished.

"Let's just say I got word, given all her issues, that we might be the best she can do," Haneline said enigmatically. "In a sense you two have that in common."

"Del Mar? I read about her all the way back in Ohio," Lonnie shook her head again.

"She'll come."

"Why?"

"Because you, my dear, are a winner." Haneline steepled his fingers, resting his elbows on his crossed knee. "You won two Olympic gold medals, coached two national championship teams, fell just short of winning three in a row, and... you graduated 100% of your players."

"99 percent," she said. "One player didn't graduate. I really let her down by not–."

"–Anyway, this girl, Hightower is kind of 'on the fringe,' if you know what I mean. But if she's smart, she'll come here because you have a track record for making sure your players graduate. All 99 percent of them."

"Okay." Lonnie answered, figuring it was best to hold her tongue around Forrest Haneline.

They stood up and shook hands. "Now that that's settled, there is another matter."

"I need to make a phone call," Lonnie said, gathering her bag.

"It can wait," he said.

Lonnie put her bag on her shoulder and looked at him. "I know what you're going to say. Don't worry, I'm completely on board. There won't be any problems."

A steely-eyed Forrest Haneline said, "Well, I want this to be perfectly clear just in case I need to fire you."

September First

"Follow the traffic signs. They tell you when to stop and when to go. I know you hate listening to me, especially when I'm right. Just follow the traffic signs. They'll let you know," her father said.

"Okay. Daddy."

"No, promise me. Promise you'll watch the signals. I won't be able to bail you out if you're careless."

"I promise."

"As long as you do that, you'll be fine," he said, even though experience clouded his confidence in her. Monet could sense it.

"... I know you hate listening to me," her father said.

"Especially when you're right... right?" Monet said.

"Moments like these remind me what a good job we did raising you."

"I love you daddy."

"I love you too, sweetheart."

Monet ended the call and continued her cross-country drive. It had been five months since she had gotten a call from Lonnie Delaney, her freshman coach at Ohio State, with a request for her to come and play for her at Del Mar University in San Francisco. It was out of the blue, but she had eagerly accepted.

Monet had given herself three weeks to drive from her hometown, Columbus, Ohio, to San Francisco, giving herself plenty of time to stop along the way to work out at local gyms and play some pickup games. "Basketball across America," she called it.

During the trip, she played Hoosiers in Gary, broad shouldered guys in Chicago, Cheeseheads in Milwaukee, Lakers in Minneapolis, Cornhuskers in Lincoln, Cowboys in Cheyenne, and Mormons in Salt Lake City.

Guys generally avoid choosing a woman to play with them. If they chose her, they always put the shortest and least athletic guy on Monet. More disrespect came when, just before the game began, the guy guarding Monet was instructed to double-team off of her and help on defense and leave Monet open. Monet resisted the temptation to say, "It's your boy who's gonna need help." Boy, did he ever. Assists, treys, and fearless defense were Monet's trademark. Had them wondering who was that tall woman who was killin' 'em? It wasn't long before they were double-teaming Monet. That's the ultimate compliment.

After her team beat all comers, mainly because of Monet, she always made a point of thanking the guy who chose her to be on his team. His smile was always priceless, like buying America Online stock in 1989 when it was just $2.00 a share.

Back on the road, Monet thought about her social life in general and boyfriends in particular. She had only two serious boyfriends in college and was heartbroken over her high school sweetheart. None of them were really her type. All the other guys she dated were just something to do. Jocks and nerds. She always got the sense guys were trying to prove something by dating the best female athlete in the school. Not that having fifty boyfriends would

have been better, but two boyfriends in four years of college was
pathetic, like she had the cooties.

She took a moment for a little self-assessment. Monet McCasner
was six foot one. Creamed coffee skin. Excellent posture. Firm
athletic body, but attractive, not one of those bruisers. Confident,
yet still good to others. Yes, independent. Proud to be Black. Loves
sports.

What's not to like? She chuckled to herself. *Guy's are such
idiots.*

Still, she promised herself she would get and keep a boyfriend
this school year, despite the troubling fact that she was moving to
San Francisco but, she reminded herself, any guy she considered
would have to like women only.

Monet had traveled a lot for a twenty year old. Odd cities when
you listed them all together: Knoxville, Tennessee; College Station,
Texas; Chapel Hill, North Carolina; South Bend, Indiana; Lafayette,
Louisiana; Palo Alto, California; and Storrs, Connecticut. Not much
for tourism, but if you were looking for top of the line women's
college basketball cities, it was a murderers' row.

The year Monet played for Lonnie Delaney at Ohio State was
supposed to be a rebuilding year. But Monet, a freshman, in 1992
guided the Buckeyes to the championship game where they lost to
Tennessee and her high school rival, Jamila Jetter. Monet thought
it was going to be the beginning of a great college career with regular Final Four appearances. That is, until Lonnie Delaney's contract wasn't renewed.

After Coach Delaney left The Ohio State University
Monet's college career nose-dived. She transferred to Ohio University where she couldn't get her team into the Mid-American
Conference tournament, let alone the NCAAs. When things couldn't
get worse, she blew out her knee in October 1995 and redshirted
her last year. That was it. She was on schedule to graduate and
wasn't going to play her last year of eligibility until Lonnie Delaney
called the following April. It was a long shot but she saw it as her
last chance to win something before she graduated. If any coach
could lead her to a championship it was Coach Delaney.

     *   *   *   *

Lonnie Delaney was waiting in the parking lot when Monet drove up in her 1986 Honda CRX. It's the least you should do when your all-time favorite player, in her last year of eligibility, changes schools and drives clear across the country to play for you. They met each other with open arms.

"When I got the job, I almost didn't call you. I really didn't think you'd come," Lonnie said.

"And how would you have explained it if I saw you on ESPN2 Coach?"

Lonnie Delaney took a moment to look her over. "Look at you, all grown up. No more braces. You put on a few pounds."

"Fifteen."

"Took my advice," Lonnie said.

"Took me three years," Monet said.

"Three years, fifteen pounds,"

"All muscle."

"I see."

"Now, I'm a match up problem," Monet said, beaming from ear to ear.

"Too big for the guards–." Lonnie said.

"–And too quick for the forwards," they said together.

Monet understood Lonnie. Lonnie's yelling and berating didn't bother Monet because she trusted her knowledge and she knew Lonnie was a winner. Lonnie felt a special connection to Monet because they were so much alike. When Monet was a freshman at Ohio State Lonnie marveled at how similar their experiences were during their formative years. They had had the same problems with condescending boys when they played sport and jealous cheerleading girls after they finished. They had never taken the time to master the art of makeup application or walking gracefully in three-inch heels. Even their individual first kisses were disasters. It was uncanny.

"You still pronouncing your name like the French painter?" Lonnie asked.

"My mother hates it. I told her just because we live in the midwest doesn't mean everything has to be so damn phonetic."

"And I see you still have the tattoo on you leg that looks like a brier patch."

"Thorns come with love. But they also protect the heart, which is love."

"Relax it isn't permanently on my skin," Lonnie said, with a disproving sigh. She never understood the need to permanently record things on your skin.

Monet had had only four bags and two boxes in the back of her car. Lonnie helped her carry them to her dorm room. Monet asked, "Did you and Mr. Hawkins ever get back together?"

Lonnie didn't answer while she carried one of Monet's boxes. "I think about him now more than I ever did when were married."

"Sending divorce papers to the locker room the night you won the national championship was wrong."

"My mother told me 'Don't you give up your husband for that silly game.' I hadn't thought much of it at the time. But I guess she was right."

"I would get married every October if I could win the national championship and get a divorce on the same night," Monet said.

"You say that now," Lonnie said, giving Monet a look.

"So, what do we really have here?" Monet asked, changing the subject.

"I'm not sure really. Four returning seniors and I got Tamika Hightower to play here," Lonnie said, with a grin.

"Who's that?"

"Listen to you. You sound like a senior. Tamika was a high school All-American."

"So what's she doing coming here?"

"She had some issues with her grades and a few other things."

"Oh." Monet smiled. "Sounds like she's ... a *project*."

Lonnie said, "You know it wasn't that long ago when you were a lanky high school All-American freshman trying to prove yourself, too."

"And look what happened, right out of the box I took you to the finals," Monet laughed.

"Aren't you the one who's always complaining about being taller than the power forwards?"

"Hey, what happened to Williamson?" Monet said.

"Lucreshia Williamson?"

"Yeah, isn't she the only one keeping you from having a 100 percent graduation rate?"

"I tried to get her to finish even when I wasn't coaching."

"I know, you hounded that girl to get her degree."

"I didn't *hound* her," Lonnie corrected. "She was so close. She was just barely hanging on during the season. I thought about dismissing her from the team so she could concentrate on getting her grades because you knew once it was over..." Lonnie said.

"Yeah, but we needed her when My'esha hurt her knee! We wouldn't have gotten to the Finals without her."

"I've never had a player that hated school so much... God, I wish things had worked out differently."

"What's she doing now?"

"I don't know about now, but I saw her a couple of times in the shelter. It wasn't pretty..." Lonnie said sighing deeply. One of her coaching regrets had been not getting Lucreshia graduated and in a good job. It broke her heart to see her in a shelter. "You pick up any bad habits playing for the Bobcats?"

"No."

"We'll see."

"You put Tennessee on the schedule," Monet said.

"Pat and I have always been friendly. And I figured you had a score to settle with Jetter and the Volunteers."

"Damn right."

"We're going to show this program how to win," Lonnie said.

"I know it might be unrealistic, but I want a ring," Monet said.

"I've only got one year to do it, myself. They only gave me a one-year deal."

"That's it? That ain't cool, coach."

The headline read "Another Attack by Stinky Foiled."

Monet read the student newspaper while standing alone in the middle of her dorm room. She still had a few things to bring up. Her roommate, Shirlie Torretta, had already moved in, but was standing in a long line trying to register for a class whose professor was a lenient grader. She wanted to graduate *cum laude* and figured it could make a difference.

In between paragraphs Monet looked around the room. You can tell a lot about people by what they hang on their walls. Thankfully, she hadn't been paired with a dopey freshman. There were no posters of kittens, NSYNC, or the Backstreet Boys. Whew!

"A female freshman was attacked as she walked home from a party. Police believe the assailant was Stinky, who has been linked to seven sexual assaults at Del Mar University, University of San Francisco, and San Francisco State..."

There were the Greek letters, Sigma Xi, everywhere. On the walls, on book covers, pencils, even engraved in a sterling silver picture frame. Everything was meticulously placed. "What a cute family," Monet said, impressed with the wholesomeness and the height of everyone in the photo. She sat down at Shirlie's desk and continued to read.

"...The freshman, name withheld, thwarted her assailant by defecating on herself..."

Fight fire with fire. Monet thought, marveling at the young woman's ingenuity.

The Sigma Xi coaster made Monet pause: Only the most retentive of college students used coasters. For God's sake, at school no one cares about the damage condensation would cause to a coffee table.

Coasters notwithstanding, the more Monet looked around, the more she liked her roommate, mainly because she had to be at least a junior. Monet was a *soror* of Delta Sigma Theta herself. So she figured she wouldn't have to deal with a homesick freshman crying about missing some loser boyfriend back home. A soror knows how to share and knows when she's overstepping her bounds. She would know that "Shut up already about the boyfriend!" wasn't a personal attack but a request to get a grip. You can't have that conversation with a sniveling homesick freshman with kittens on her wall.

"...The assailant received his moniker because of his affinity for cheap cologne, often mixing two and three at a time..."

Isn't that lovely!

Monet heard the key in the door and quickly jumped to her side of the dorm room.

At first Shirlie didn't see Monet, who watched her come in and close the door. If Monet hadn't cleared her throat, Shirlie might have missed her.

"Oh, hi," Shirlie said.

Shirlie Torretta was a big girl, at 6 ft 5and solid. Her hair was pulled back into a no-nonsense ponytail

They introduced themselves.

"What made you come from Ohio to play with coach?" Shirlie asked.

"Coach Delaney is a winner," Monet answered as if that was enough.

Shirlie sighed, "Well, we haven't done much of that lately–win that is."

"Well, whatever you've got to offer the team she'll find it and use it. All you gotta do is want to win."

"When I was a freshman, I was like, 'Yeah, lets do it.' I'm not gonna play overseas or play on the Olympic team. Right now, my priority is to graduate Cum Laude and get into Stanford Medical School."

There's one person I won't pass the ball to in crunch time.

Monet turned to her suitcase on the bed.

The first things she unpacked were her two basketballs, the indoor Spalding and the suede outdoor Nike. In the small space of their dorm room she spun the ball on her finger, quick dribbled twice, juked once with a shoulder fake, put the ball back through her legs, and did a crossover dribble that bounced off her down turned shin, back through her legs, and back up to a spinning ball on her index finger. All of it lightning fast.

Shirlie was impressed. "A power forward with handles, we could use that."

"I play the point."

"Roxy plays point." At six-five, Shirlie was the starting center. She wasn't used to looking point guards almost in the eye. "Aren't you a little tall to play the point? What're you, five-eleven?"

"Six-one," Monet answered, drawing herself up.

"I hope you can shoot because we already have a point guard."

"I play point and only the point."

Everything about Tamika Hightower was ghetto. The way she talked in loud, profanity-laced slang. The way she walked, shoulders hunched, more dude than dame. The way she dressed; she showed up on a college recruiting trip in tight three-quarter leopard jeans, long-sleeve T-shirt trimmed in faux fur, and full-length leather coat with her hair in finger waves. She even had "Ghetto Bitch" tattooed on the right side of her neck. Tamika was so ghetto she appalled even girls from the ghetto. Ghetto sensibilities notwith-standing, Tamika was also one of the best high school power forwards in the state.

She had just finished unpacking when her roommate, Sonja Mortensen, walked into the dorm room struggling with her luggage. She dropped everything with a sigh. Tamika looked at her askance, didn't offer any help.

"You must be Ti...Timikoh?" Sonja asked.

"It's Tam-ee-kah," she answered.

"Your friends call you Meek, eh?" Sonja offered, she was thin but bubbly with a thick Minnesota accent.

"No! And you better not start either. Where you from?"

"The land of ten thousand lakes."

"Montana?"

"Gosh no, that's Big Sky country," she said, with more annoying cheerfulness.

"Wisconsin."

"Cheesehead? Nooo. I'll give you one more guess."

Tamika didn't like the geography quiz, especially on such short notice, and mistook Sonja's cheerfulness for superiority. Tamika would be damned if she was going to spend the whole year with someone quizzing her about subjects she didn't know or care to know anything about.

"Just forget it. And it's Tamika. *Get it right now,* 'cause I 'ain't gonna be correctin' you all year."

"Okie dokie. So, where *are you* from?" Sonja asked, playing it safe.

"Oakland."

"Oh, right here in the Golden State."

"Don't start wit' that state shit again!"

"I was just–."

"–Yeah? Well, I ain't tryin' to hear it."

They were really hitting it off.

Sonja meticulously unpacked her bags in silence. The Golden State comment having blown up in her face, she was reluctant to say anything that might offend her new roommate. She was already anxious and this was just the first five minutes. She had nine months to go.

Tamika was fascinated by her roommate. She was as thin as a rail and meticulous. Sonja put everything in a particular place, checked then double-checked it for location, purpose, and efficiency. The clock radio had to go on the night stand, not on the shelf at the top of her bed. She even closed her eyes and pretended to be drowsy. After that, Sonja separated her clothes by type and color in descending shades, whites bled into striped whites, which bled into light blues, into dark blues, into solid reds, into pastels and stripes, and so on.

"You know, you moved that bottle of hair gel four times," Tamika said. Thinking great, a neat freak.

"See there, been away from home all of twelve hours and I'm already a spaz." Sonja laughed.

"Five pairs. *Five* pairs of running shoes!" Tamika said, thinking she was a spaz long before she left Minnesota.

"One is for off road. Another pair for sprints. By the way, do you know where the track is?... Never mind. I rotate these two for medium distances. This pair is for really long runs. I can't wait to do a fun run under the Golden Gate Bridge. How much do you run?"

"Oh boy. Don't ask this fool any questions," Tamika thought, especially about geography.

"Only enough for one pair of shoes," Tamika finally answered. Even though Tamika had decided not to ask Sonja any questions, she had to ask her one more. "Whassup wit' all the modeling' pictures on the wall?"

"This is totally unnecessary." Roxy said, scanning the crowded room.

The huge weight room was filled with athletes from most of Del Mar's sports teams. The weight room had six complete sets of weight stations; dumbbells, curl bars, leg press, and row machines. The works, times six. Women congregated in the first station because every time a female entered the room they set off a ripple effect of turning muscle heads to check them out. Men, but some women too. There was less commotion when women stayed in the first station. It was better for everyone's concentration.

The women's basketball team entered in ones and twos. Clio hovered over Roxy as she attempted to bench press the 45-pound bar.

"Where are you on your list?" Clio asked.

"Finished curls, rows, and military press. Still gotta do legs and calves."

"Are we supposed to lift the number on this card?" Kendra asked, reracking her dumbbells.

"Duh, that's what personalizes the program," said Clio, the team's verbal dart thrower. Clio at 5'11" was of slender build and brown skin. Clio kept the team loose with her quick wit. She also carved up her teammates when they stepped out of line. She looked down at Roxy, "You gotta lift more than just the bar." She added two five-pound plates to the 45-pound bar.

"This body wasn't made to get hard and buffed," Roxy said.

"Yeah, you leave that up to all the guys you go out with," Clio joked. "You heard anything about the new coach?"

Kendra answered between sets. "I also heard she's big on eyes."

"Eyes?" Roxy said, straining to push up the bar.

"Yeah, makes you look her in the eyes."

That's weird, isn't it?" Clio said, walking over and standing inches from Kendra's face. "Look into my eyes. You're getting sleepy. Sleeeepy. Sleeeeeeeeepy."

"Will... you... take... these... off?" Roxy huffed, straining to lift the weight with her quivering arms.

"Look what you almost made me do." Clio said, trying not to laugh. "We could'uv killed her."

Roxy tried to do another rep but her arms refused.

"Another crop of transfers to whip into shape. I'm gettin' good at this," Roxy said.

Roxy Davidson was the team's unquestioned leader. She had Machiavellian instincts. A corporate raider at heart, she knew how to build coalitions, lie in wait, then blind-side her opponents with overwhelming numbers. How else could a freshman be named team captain over six returning seniors. She relied on Kendra, Clio, and Shirlie to help her wield influence over the team. Together they were called the Big Four.

Individually, Roxy, Clio, Kendra, and Shirlie were good players. They just hadn't been taught the discipline needed to become winners. None of them had won anything on any level. Since Roxy's teams never won, keeping everyone in line during the season was her badge of honor. Playing mother hen had become more important to her than winning.

Del Mar was unique in that it didn't have at least one lesbian player on the basketball roster. Roxy didn't like lesbians so she sabotaged prospective recruits who even dressed androgynously. She made sure they felt uncomfortable on their recuiting visits. She wanted the team to heterosexual. During Roxy's sophomore year she fabricated so many stories about the last lesbian senior, the girl suddenly quit because she couldn't take the mental abuse any longer. It was the last coach's inability to control the Big Four, Roxy in particular, that got her fired.

"Can't we just play basketball? We've only got one more year together," Kendra said. Kendra was, 6'2", with dark brown skin and a Bob haircut. She used her size and her feigned bad attitude to intimidate people, especially new recruits. She was the muscle of the Big Four, but she was getting tired of playing the heavy for Roxy all the time.

Shirlie, Monet, and Tamika entered the weight room.

"Ladies and gentlemen, and now, your NEW Lady Runnin' Rhiiii'nooooos..." Clio announced, imitating their public address announcer.

Roxy, Clio, and Kendra high-fived Shirlie.

"Monet, Tamika, this is Clio, Roxy, and Kendra." Shirlie introduced everyone.

Roxy got right to it. "So which one of you is gonna get me some bottled water?"

Monet and Shirlie didn't break stride toward the weight rack.

"Well?" Roxy insisted.

"Don't look at me; I'm a fifth year senior, I've gone through that crap already," Monet said.

Sonja and Tamika looked at each other. "You gots to be joking," Tamika said.

"We don't tell jokes to freshmen until *after* they become sophomores," Clio said.

"Matter of fact, who else wants water?" Roxy added.

The whole team and a couple of guys from a nearby weight station raised their hands.

"Make that a dozen; the bottled water cart for athletes is behind that door over there... What's your hand up for?" Roxy said to Jennifer, another freshman.

"I want some water, too," Jennifer said.

Roxy, Shirlie, Kendra, and Clio all laughed.

"Freshmen get their own water."

"Those zany freshman, you never know what they're gonna say next," Clio laughed.

"Be glad you're not the one playing fetch," Kendra said.

Tamika didn't know these women and resented being told what to do. The fact that she could kick all of their asses made her pause, but she fetched the water anyway.

"Freshmen are the best," Shirlie said, watching Jennifer and Sonja avoiding eye contact, not wanting to run any more errands.

Monet settled under the bench press bar. Roxy watched closely from the side. Monet easily pushed up eight quick reps, added 20 more pounds and completed another set of eight. Roxy, Kendra, Clio, and even Shirlie were amazed.

"I never met an All-American before," Clio said circling closely.

"And what's up with the tattoo?" Kendra asked.

"The thorns protect the heart—never mind," Monet said.

Monet stood still, looking forward, indulging the scrutiny, then she flinched, and Clio nearly jumped out of her skin.

"See over there, that's Del Mar's first four-year captain," Clio said, pointing to Roxy while giving her a high five.

"Hasn't happened yet," Roxy said. "As long as the freshmen don't get any *bright ideas.*" She gave Sonja and Jennifer the evil eye. Again, they cowered on cue. Freshman were made to be abused.

"I was the captain at Ohio State," Monet said. Not one to be intimidated. "And at Ohio University."

The entire team turned to see Roxy's reaction. She ignored it. "Where's my water?" Roxy said. "Damn Freshman."

Monet finished three sets on the bench press, four counting the warm-up set she did with Roxy's weight on the bar. She then moved on to leg presses.

Roxy nodded and gave Clio the signal.

"So, what position do you play?" Clio asked innocently.

"You know I play the point," Monet answered, cool and confident, anticipating the ambush. "I'm sure Big Shirlie told you already. Might be a problem for some of you." She was looking directly at Roxy, who was doing leg presses at the time.

"What are you looking at me for?" Roxy asked.

Yeah, keep playing dumb. Monet thought, then said, "Won the Big Ten with me on the point. Got to the finals with me on the point..."

"Where you choked on the last shot," Roxy said, shrugging her shoulders when everyone looked her way. Oops. "Just thought I'd mention that too since we're talking about history."

A couple of guys in a nearby station whispered among themselves–cat fight brewing.

Clio said, "Well, around here–."

"–Roxy plays the point. You can play two or three. Kendra plays the three and four spot, Shirlie plays the five." Monet interrupted

Clio continued, "Right. So you'll play the–."

"The point," Monet said.

"The two," Clio said.

"I play point and only the point," Monet countered.

"What're you? Five-eleven?"

"Six-one. What is it with you people in California? Can't tell how tall people are?"

"Why aren't you playing three or four? Small or power forward?" Kendra asked.

"Because I play the point. In the Magic Johnson mold of big point guards."

"I've seen Magic play. Honey, you're no Magic Johnson," Roxy said, getting up from the leg press.

Keep talkin', see if your mouth is that smart when I'm kicking your ass on the court.

"Your right, you haven't," Monet said.

Monet moved from underneath the bench press and went to the dumbbell rack. Roxy pretended to look for her towel and went over to grab some dumbbells to curl next to Monet. They stood in front of the mirror, curling. At five-eight, Roxy was average height for a point guard. Standing next to Monet she was a water bug.

Everyone paused, then went back to their exercise regimens while keeping an eye on Roxy and Monet. Roxy started with five-pound dumbbells. But when Monet picked up a pair of fifteens, Roxy gulped, then replaced the fives with fifteens from another station. One almost dropped on her foot when she jerked to pick it up. Monet and Roxy lifted the dumbbells from their waists to their chins. They went at it, side by side, curl for curl, for two reps, sizing up each other's resolve. Egos were on the line.

After the third rep, Monet's curls were still smooth, under control. It was Roxy who struggled to bring each dumbbell up from her waist. Straining. Making childbirth faces. Two reps and she was done. She nearly dropped the weights on her foot again trying to return them to the rack.

Everyone stepped back to watch Monet work out.

Clio nudged Shirlie. "What kind of woman curls 15-pounds dumbbells?"

"A virago," Shirlie said, showing off her pre-med vocabulary.

"Sounds contagious."

"We'll see now, won't we?"

   *   *   *   *

She hated to lose.

Monet McCasner didn't know it at the time. During the summer before entering the sixth grade, instead of going to summer camp Monet stayed home and played sports every day with the kids in the neighborhood. Her friends noticed the change immediately. By the time school started she was more interested in playing sports with the boys than talking about boys who played sports, a preoccupation of her girlfriends.

After each recess the boys chose an MVP for that recess, they squawked about it as they lined up. The girls talked about the benefits of clear nail polish versus clear nail polish with sparkles. Monet was tired of nail polish discussions and wanted to be the first female recess MVP.

"I'm gonna play football with the boys during lunch," Monet said.

"Ewwwww."

"You know you'll grow hair on your lip if you play with boys too much," Leslie said. She was the Sergeant at Arms and Keeper of Records for the future of traditional femininity, probably because her mother was a proud cookie-baking-husband-catering stay-at-home mom.

"I'm gonna be the MVP," Monet repeated.

It was the beginning of the year so the boys in her class only knew Monet as the girl who beats everyone in tetherball. She approached the game as they were choosing sides.

"I wanna play." Monet said to no one in particular.

"Yeah, right." Rebuffed Billy Willmont, the class bully.

Monet stood her ground. She did a quick count and realized she was thirteenth. They chose teams and not surprisingly she did not get drafted.

"You're out," Billy said.

Monet just stood there, frozen, not knowing what to do. She couldn't play, the teams wouldn't be even. But she didn't want to make the humiliating walk of shame back to her friends either.

"Hey, Tetherball. We're gonna play football now," Bill said.

"So."

"So move."

"You guys suck," she said, to the group, Billy Willmont in particular. Not very ladylike but substituting anger for disappointment seemed like a good idea, felt better too.

Then from the heavens came a voice. *"Randy Raven report to the office. Randy Raven report to the office,"* said Mrs. Bibby over the loudspeaker.

Just like that, odd numbers became her best friend. Begrudgingly the boys let Monet play. Billy Willmont was not pleased at all, but what could he do, six on six was better than five on five football.

Monet knew about how much Billy hated losing. The only thing Billy hated more than losing was being shown up. Once, in a Little League game he froze on a curve ball. Called strike three. The pitcher giggled as the infielders tossed the ball around. Billy played short-stop. The next inning, when the pitcher tried to stretch a single into a double, Billy tagged him so hard in the face he knocked out 4 teeth.

Monet knew the "bashed-in-teeth" story but she had other plans. She remembered how her father had taught her to stand up to bullies. Stand up to them and they usually fold. That's what Monet wanted to do, beat Billy. Beat him and rub his nose in it.

She was in her element; she loved to play in the sunshine. The boys didn't expect much from Monet, but what they got was a playmaker. Monet ran post patterns, buttonhooks, and even a double reverse, all for touchdowns.

A frustrated Billy paid her the ultimate compliment by switching to guard Monet himself to make sure she didn't score any more touchdowns.

Last play. Monet faked a buttonhook and went long. Billy bit on the fake and tried to recover. Monet made an over the shoulder catch but with 20 yards to go Billy was closing fast and he had the angle. Knowing she couldn't outrun him, she put on the brakes and sidestepped Billy's outstretched arms as he tried to make the two-handed touch tackle. He missed and fell to the ground. Monet walked in for the winning touchdown to the cheers of her teammates.

After recess, Monet was celebrated as the lunch recess Most Valuable Player. She basked in the post-lunch lineup chatter. "A girl won the lunch recess MVP by beating Billy Willmont." This day would be remembered... until next week.

As she was being cheered, Brenda rolled her eyes at Monet, jealous of all the attention she was receiving.

A giant was awakened in Monet that day.

Some kids play games for fun. Some kids play to win. For Monet, the fun was in the winning.

In the months to come, the more she played against Billy the more she wanted to kick his ass and rub his nose in his own superiority over girls. She made it her mission to represent Girl Power.

Billy never figured out that playing against a girl would always be a lose-lose proposition. As long as he felt girls were inferior, he would feel more agony in defeat and the thrill of victory would never be as sweet.

Monet liked that most of all.

Chapter 2

Chivalry vs. Self-reliance

September Twenty-first

"Hit the cutoff man!"

The Red Sox were losing, as usual, to the Yankees. Dan Cantrell sat three stools down from an impeccably dressed woman yelling at the television set in a bar at the San Francisco International Airport. She was tall, he was tall. They both liked baseball. He was traveling on business, she looked like she was traveling on business. They had a lot in common.

He thought about approaching her, but her short hair and forceful manner made him hesitate. This *was* San Francisco. Dan had just moved from Kansas and was having trouble distinguishing women who liked women from the women who liked men. He waited, looking for signs of heterosexuality.

"Forget the double play. Play in for the squeeze!"

Who is this woman? He thought, liking her athletic build and mop-top blond hair.

Dan made his move.

"I've been sitting next to you for 20 minutes. You know you can tell a lot about someone by the way they watch a baseball game."

"Like not to disturb them," Lonnie said, without looking away from the game.

Mayday! Mayday! Mayday!

Lonnie was about to dismiss him when she saw his reflection in the mirror behind the bar, between the liquor bottles.

He was cute. Very cute.

"Tell you what, let me buy you a drink–." Dan said.

"–I'm drinking water–."

"–Of your choice." Thinking fast. He added, "I'm something of a student of people. Let me tell you some things about you and if I get something wrong–."

"You mean when," Lonnie countered, turning her face to him.
"Just like that?"
"Yeah."
"And you'll go away."
"Yeah, but you gotta be truthful, don't just blow me off."
"Why not?" she asked.
This was going to be tough. But she didn't exactly say "no" so Dan proceeded. He would know where he stood in a few seconds.
"Well, you certainly welcome people with open arms," he said, trying for an ironic laugh. It worked, a little. "And you're an optimist."
"I'm a Red Sox fan. I have to be optimistic."
"Comes in handy after 78 years of futility."
"Exactly," she said, smiling.
Whew.
"One of these years it's going to be our year. Why not this one?" she said.
"Ya know, Sisyphus thought one day he would finally roll that boulder to the top of the hill, but there were forces working against him that were much bigger."
"The Curse of the Bambino."
"You said it, not me," Dan nodded, so far so good.
"When we finally win the World Series the streets will be paved with gold."
"And there'll be world peace. But, there's a difference between being optimistic and being delusional," he said.
"You calling me delusional?" she said, halfway serious.
"I'm calling you a Red Sox fan. Is that the same thing?"
"What else you got?" she asked looking at him and not the game. She gave him a grin of encouragement.
"You're a Red Sox fan, so you're loyal. Probably make someone a good wife," he said.
"For a minute you were on a roll."
"I don't see a ring."
"Divorced actually."
"Nice. I mean..."
"It's okay, I know what you mean," she said.
"You just a baseball fan?"
"Actually, I prefer pick and rolls to suicide squeezes."
Dan was impressed. "Not many women know whether balls

are stuffed or blown up. Let alone can talk strategy in two different sports. Didn't your parents warn you not to show off your sports knowledge to total strangers?" he asked.

When the announcer came on, Lonnie shushed him. They both looked up at the television set.

"The answer to the AFLAC Olympic trivia question is Teresa Edwards. Edwards won three gold medals in Los Angeles, Barcelona, and Atlanta and a bronze medal from Seoul," said the television announcer.

"I played with her on two of those teams."

"You have two gold medals?" Dan asked, disbelieving.

"Yup."

"For basketball."

"You don't believe me?" she asked arching a brow.

"No, it's not that..." Dan sat there going through his memory of female athletes from the eighties. This lady didn't come to mind. "Who are you?"

"A lady who knows whether balls are stuffed or blown up," Lonnie said, with a wry grin.

Well, well, well.

"Okay, tell me this, since you have all the answers." He paused for dramatic effect. "How deep would the ocean be if there weren't any sponges?" Lonnie smiled, then laughed out loud, getting it. "So what's a woman with great sports knowledge and a terrific sense of humor–."

"–And two gold medals."

"And two gold medals, doing now?" he asked, impressed.

"I coach."

"Coach what?"

"Basketball. I coach women's basketball," Lonnie answered, looking at her watch. She'd lost track of time and had to hurry to catch her flight.

"Leaving? You can't leave."

"Sorry, I have a flight to catch, maybe you do too."

"But I have more questions," he said.

She smiled again, a good sign. "Okay then, ask, quickly," she said.

"How did the Egyptians make the Pyramids? Who shot John Kennedy? What's your name?"

"Leverage, Oswald, and Delaney, Lonnie Delaney." They shook hands. Firm grip, not one of those dead fish handshakes. Dan liked confident women.

"In that order, or is leverage your first or your last name?" Dan said. She smiled again.

"It was really nice talking to you. Maybe I'll see you again," she said.

"Last question. Where do you coach?"

Before leaving she pointed to the Sporting Green section of the *San Francisco Chronicle* on the bar. A headline below the fold read, *The Long Road Back for Del Mar's New Women's Basketball Coach.*

As she walked away, he yelled, "Dan, my name is Dan Cantrell."

Ray Riddick, a player on the Del Mar men's basketball team hammed it up for a professional photographer as he sat in a huge vat of basketballs. It was one of those high-concept photos *Sports Illustrated* puts together every year for the College Preview edition.

When Shirlie stopped to watch, a distracted Monet walked right into her, Tamika bumped into Monet, then Sonja bumped into Tamika–a Three Stooges domino effect. The entire staff stopped and struggled to suppress their giggles. The photographer was not amused.

Monet whispered, "That's–."

"Ray Riddick," Shirlie said, indifferently.

"He's much cuter in person than on TV," Monet said.

"Look but don't touch. He's strictly on safari," Shirlie added.

"Don't you hate guys like that?" Sonja said.

"Especially when they're fine," Monet said.

Ray Riddick had grown up across the bay in West Oakland. Poverty was rampant in his neighborhood. His friends took the shortcut out of slinging rocks to make the big money fast and easy. They never made it out of the neighborhood, just took long vacations to their second homes in Santa Rita jail and San Quentin State Penitentiary. Ray chose the long scenic route. He played basketball, but his mother made sure school was a priority. He wanted to go to a public high school with his street corner buddies, but his mother insisted that he attend St. Mary's College High School in Berkeley instead of McClymonds in Oakland. He'd begged, but his mother didn't care that it was the alma mater of Bill Russell and Frank Robinson and categorically rejected his argument that as a future Hall of Famer he needed to go where past Hall of Famers had gone to high school. His mother sent him to St. Mary's because 97% of all their graduates go to college. She was serious about giving her only child the best opportunity to succeed. She sacrificed considerably to make it happen. So she was very angry during his sophomore year when his grades fell dramatically. She not only prevented him from playing basketball in the winter, she made him sign up for the St. Mary's drama program, yearbook, and poetry club as extracurricular replacements. Restricted from playing basketball but with plenty of time on his hands, Ray discovered photography, bebop jazz, and the poetry of Langston Hughes.

Shirlie, Monet, Tamika, and Sonja stood there admiring Ray's flexing biceps as he hammed it up for the photographer. They had forgotten they were on their way to the weight room.

"Couple more balls over here," the photographer said, directing his assistants. "And someone close the door over there. I got glare."

"What's this for?" Monet asked.

"S.I."

"*Sports Illustrated?*"

"Ray's got a good shot at the cover of the preview issue."

When Ray saw Monet, there was instant attraction. He winked. But because of Shirlie's warning, Monet pretended not to see him.

"One day that's gonna be me on the cover," Tamika said.

"Shhhh." One of the assistants had come over to them. "He has ears like a bat."

"Ladies, I don't mind you hanging out, but you gotta be quiet. You're distracting Ray over here," the photographer said, bringing everything to a complete stop.

The photographer instructed Ray to flex his biceps for the photo. Going for a little beefcake. He certainly knew what he was doing because it stopped Monet, Sonja, and Tamika in their tracks. Shirlie stood watching them with her arms crossed.

Shirlie led her teammates out of the arena. Shirlie rolled her eyes at Ray as they walked past the photo shoot. Being team players, Monet and Tamika rolled their eyes too.

September Twenty-third, Monday

Lonnie Delaney ran to catch up with Forrest Haneline and the men's basketball coach, Clint Warlich, in the hallway of the athletic department.

"Forrest."

"Dutch. Please, call me Dutch."

"I saw the men's media guide in the Sports Information Office. Full color, very nice," she said to Warlich. "By the way, any idea when ours will be ready?"

It was a good question. The media guides are the tomes of everything related to each of the 18 Del Mar sports teams. They are produced by the athletic department's Sports Information Office and used by newspapers, television, and radio. Media guides don't include anything nefarious. Never anything juicy; like the number of ghostwritten term papers, frequency of marijuana use (medical or recreational), misdemeanor crimes dismissed, or each player's actual under-the-table income.

"Did you ask Pete?" Forrest Haneline asked.

"Yeah. He said something about a Heisman media blitz, but I didn't know what that had to do with our media guide."

"Probably just backed up."

"He said something about November."

"Yeah, and?"

"Isn't that a little late? I mean isn't the whole point of having a media guide to give it to the media before the start of the season In case they want to do a story or just have current information."

"Talk to the Sports Information Director," Haneline said, impatient to move on.

Lonnie knew it was very early in the year to start putting on the pressure, especially after her promise to try to fit in. She was pressing hard, but the double standard of how men and womn are treated always made her angry. When Lonnie got angry she made things happen. She turned to Warlich. "When did you get yours?"

"Two weeks ago," he said, nonchalantly.

Lonnie Delaney winced inside but kept her composure. "This might be a long shot, but what is the possibility of getting us a radio contract?" Lonnie asked.

"Who do you mean by us?" Forrest Haneline said.

"Us, the women's team."

Haneline and Warlich chuckled.

"Lady, you've got a helluva imagination. Out of six million people in the Bay Area we can't get more than 300 to come to a women's game. What makes you think a radio station would want to broadcast the Del Mar women's games?"

"Which is why if the game were on the air, the fans might become more familiar with the team and want to see the games they are listening to."

"This isn't Columbus, Ohio. There's more things to do than focus on Rhino sports. Let's review the sports broadcasting landscape just for fall and winter. The Forty-niners, Raiders, Warriors, and Sharks all have radio contracts," Haneline ticked each one of his fingers while he counted; each sports team a little piggy. "That's four pro teams. On the college level, Cal and Stanford have radio contracts for football and men's basketball." He was up to eight piggies. "USF, San Jose State, St. Mary's, and Santa Clara men's basketball teams don't even have radio contracts and there's not one women's team with a radio contract." Twelve piggies. "So how do you expect me to convince a program director to dedicate two and one half hours of his airtime to women's basketball when there are men's programs that don't have radio coverage?"

"With coverage comes interest, with interest comes attendance."

"You got it backwards. Attendance proves you have interest, radio people only care about showing their advertisers people will be listening if they advertise during a program. If there's no people in the seats, it's a good bet there won't be anyone listening.

"Give it up already," Warlich said.

"So that's a no?" Lonnie asked.

Haneline wanted to say it meant "hell no." Instead he shook his head silently. "Speaking of people listening, I remember reading somewhere that you taught a Women's Studies class."

"Yes, I have a Ph.D. in Women's History, but my specialty is gender politics."

"What's political about gender?" Warlich asked, honestly clueless.

Lonnie Delaney answered his question by turning her attention back to Haneline. Warlich didn't like the snub.

Haneline said, "Barbara Keating, the professor who teaches one of those women's classes has taken ill and the Dean asked if I would ask you to fill in. He must have seen your bio."

"What kind of illness?"

"Breast cancer, I think. I think she caught it early though. So, can you do it?"

She nodded. It was short notice but she could wing it for a couple of weeks to give her some time to develop a curriculum.

"Jim, that reminds me, the booster's banquet has been moved to the Hall of Champions." Haneline said to Warlich.

"It's gettin' bigger and bigger every year."

"You just keep winning games and wwwwooooooosssssshhhhh!"

Haneline angled his flat palm up and extended his arm up as if it was a golf ball taking off on the 18th tee. Clint Warlich was in his third year of coaching the men's basketball team. Del Mar had won the national championship by beating Arkansas. The head coach Danville Hogue retired the following week. Warlich teams had performed well in the tournament when he was Creighton, so Haneline hired him with hopes of continuing the winning tradition at Del Mar. Under Warlich, however, Del Mar had never advanced past the second round even though most of the players from the national championship team were still playing for Del Mar. Warlich was a good recruiter but a terrible game tactician.

Haneline said to Warlich, "Remember, a loss in the second round of the NCAA tournament pays five times as much as the winner of the NIT. So, no underachieving this year–."

"–What time should we be there?" Lonnie asked.

Haneline and Clint Warlich looked at each other and then at Lonnie. They didn't have to say it, it was written on their faces. "Who invited you?"

Lonnie said, "You did say basketball banquet, right?"

Monet was lost. She had just finished her weight training program for the day and had gone to see Coach Delaney but she wasn't in her office.

She stood in the hallway trying to remember which way to the bookstore. She took one step left, then turned around and took two right. It was like watching someone teach themselves how to drive a stick shift. Once she got her bearings she turned around and... collided with a guy running down the hallway. Her books scattered across the floor along with her pencils and pens. It was a scholastic explosion.

Monet sat on the floor in a daze. "You need to watch where the hell you're..." Before looking into Ray's eyes. "Going... Hi."

She was still dazed when Ray pulled her to her feet and put his hand on her back to steady her, but she leaned into him and his hand grazed her behind. It cleared her head like smelling salts. Angry, Monet threw a wild openhanded swing. Ray ducked. Monet slipped and fell again.

"I hope boxing is on your class schedule." Ray said surveying the damage strewn about the hallway. "And driver's ed."

"I think the words you're looking for are 'Excuse me,'" Monet said. He offered his hand again, she hesitated but accepted it anyway.

"My bad. I was running down the hallway to–."

"–Don't you know not to run in the hallway?" she said.

"I saw you standing there. I was going to run past you. All of a sudden you turned and WHAM!" The loud noise startled Monet. "My name is..." Ray was still holding her hand. She immediately noticed the diamonds in his National Championship ring. She had never seen a player's ring this close before. Feeling mischievous, he raised her hand to his lips... "Ray Riddick. The pleasure is yours." And kissed *his own hand.*

Monet snatched her hand from him.

"Here, let me help you with that," Ray said, chuckling to himself.

"Thanks, but I don't do well around egomaniacs."

Ray wasn't quite an egomaniac, but he had acquired an incurable case of entitlement since becoming a "can't miss" basketball player in the fifth grade. Being a future NBA lottery pick also made him very popular with the ladies, which cemented the foundation he needed to be so filled with himself.

Out of nowhere he said, "Please allow me to assist you, 'Tis noble for a man to help a woman in need of his assistance... Shakespeare," he said.

"Shakespeare never said that," Monet said.

Ray paused then grinned, "Are these words not worthy of my most dutiful execution? These words, wellborn in deed and aristocracy, appealing to a man's highest calling–the aid of a woman."

"Wha–."

"I'm practicing for an assignment for my Classic Thespians class," Ray said. Ray wanted to become an actor because he figured show business would be the only career where he could maintain an equal number of sycophants after his professional basketball career was over.

"Oooohh. Shakespeare," Monet said. She paused, squinting, still trying to catch up.

"It would be an honor to assist you in the retrieval of your scholarly utensils," he said.

"I got it, thanks."

He's got to be kidding.

"Milady, do not discount this act, however small, between me and you, man and woman... pencil and book. For when it is combined in the Cosmos with other deeds, between other men and other women, the accumulation of these deeds could surely bring to bear an impact so profound its reverberations will be felt from the very hounds of hell!... to the glorious footsteps... of God."

"Isn't that a little over the top."

"You think? I mean, be ye mad, *woman*? I offer you shelter from the storm!"

"You're offering to pick up the books, *you knocked out of my hand!* And to be honest with you, I really don't want your help."

"Your words are like bile in the marrow of my bones, piercing my heart like a surgeon's blade–."

"–They didn't have surgeons back then," she said.

"I know," Ray said, dropping out of character.

"Well, if you're going to talk like that don't you think you need to be occupationally correct?"

"I was going to say... See, you made me lose my train of thought."

Whenever Ray made a new female acquaintance he amused himself with this kind of nuttiness. He was never mean-spirited, but the never-ending onslaught of women had made him cynical about their real intentions. He knew he was a Baby Daddy target. With child support for an NBA player starting from $6,000 per month, getting pregnant would be like winning the lottery for an unscrupulous woman, but with much better odds. So, Ray tested the fortitude of women with shenanigans. If they put up with a lot, it immediately gave him an advantage in the relationship.

Monet was having none of it. She began picking up her belongings.

"Here, let me help you with that," Ray said.

"I said I don't need your help," Monet said.

"Here we go, another Post-Feminista."

"Post-Fema what?"

"Post-Feminista. Not a Fema-Nazi, like that dumb ass Rush Limbaugh."

"Feminista. I'm afraid to ask what it means," she said.

"Remember the Sandanistas in El Salvador? In 1982. Never mind."

"Are you calling me a communist?"

"Worse. Women like you are–."

"–You don't even know me."

"Last couple of quarters I've been taking women's history classes, which is really like taking classes in woe-is-me. Actually you're more of a Third Wave Feminist," Ray said.

"Who are you calling a feminist?" Monet asked.

"You."

"Oh no."

"Methinks she doth protesteth too much. Now that's Shakespeare!" Ray said.

She looked at him blankly, making sure not to acknowledge the correct context or his handsome face. "It's protest, not protesteth."

"Methinks she doth protest too much. Not bad huh?" Ray said trying again, eyebrows arching for approval.

Monet said, "Maybe your groupies hang on every word you say..."

"Groupies?! Fans, they're called fans."

"And stop with the Shakespeare?" she said.

"I told you I'm taking a classic acting class, what do you think?" 'Methinks she doth protest too much.'"

"Don't give up basketball."

"You gotta give a brotha credit, I used it in the right context."

"By calling me a feminist?"

"You were born in the mid-70s, right? That makes you a daughter of the feminist movement but without the hairy legs and bad attitude. Sprinkle in some man-hating and a dash of lesbianism, TBD on that one. And what have you got? A Post-feminista."

"What's TBD?"

"To be determined."

"On what?"

"On the lesbian thing. But maybe. Do you wear boxers or briefs?" he said.

"What?"

"Sometimes they wear—never mind."

Monet kept her composure. She didn't want to feed into his little game. "It bothers guys like you when a woman has her own thing and can get it done by herself."

Ray started folk singing. "All weee are saaaaying. Is give peeeennnis a chance." He was cracking himself up. Seeing the disapproval on her face, he eased up. "Here, let me help you pick up your stuff."

"I said I don't want your help," Monet said, snatching a book out of his hand.

"Why not?"

"Because a woman's self-reliance is a fortress no man can take credit for building," Monet said.

"Nice. Who said that?"

"I did."

"See. Post-feminista."

Monet turned her back to him to pick up her things, but he ignored her wishes. She turned around and noticed him helping anyway.

"What are you doing?"

"Helping. What does it look like?" he said. "You're taking Keating. I'm taking that class too."

"You're taking The Body Politic? It's a women's studies class. And stop picking up my stuff," she said.

"I know. She's an easy grader. Guaranteed 'A,' but that's not why I'm taking it," Ray said.

"Keating isn't teaching it. You'd know that if you went to the bookstore... Will you stop?"

"So who's teaching it now?"

"I don't know. Stop...picking up...my stuff!"

As Ray reached for a book Monet kicked it away from him.

"You can't help someone when they don't want it," Monet said.

"Sure I can."

"No, you can't."

He tried again to pick up a book. Again she kicked it out of his reach. Reach, kick. Reach, kick. Reach kick.

"You know what I like about you already?" he said smiling. "You're not used to not getting what you want."

He was right.

Monet took it as a challenge to stop him from helping her. She boxed him out perfectly. Her back to his front, circling, in a dance of keep away. Bill Russell would have been proud. They circled around in an erotically funny dance of keep-away. Chivalry and female self-reliance hung in the balance.

When Forrest Haneline, Clint Warlich, and Lonnie Delaney turned the corner, Monet and Ray's dance came to an embarrassing halt. They stood frozen together, her butt squarely in his crotch.

The trio paused then continued down the hallway. Don't see that every day in the athletic department. Before turning the corner, Clint Warlich looked back and said, "Ray! You had better box out better than that during the season."

Chapter 3

Born on Third Base

September Twenty-fourth

Monet was late for the first day of class. Not good. Coach Delaney would not tolerate one of her players being late for her class.

She ran down the hallway; then stopped at the door to compose herself taking three deep breaths before stepping inside. The class was full. Lonnie stared at her as Monet avoided eye contact and looked for an open seat.

There was one seat, all the way in the back. The second to the last seat in the aisle. As she walked back to the open desk, Ray, Mr. Self Important, waved his hand like he was hailing a cab.

Great. Mr. Obnoxious.

For a feminist history class there were a lot of football and basketball players in attendance. The scheduled professor had a reputation for being an easy grader which resuscitated students on the cusp of academic disqualification. The Dean of the History department had even complained, wanting to limit the class to history majors. Knowing the Body Politic—Women's Global Fight for Self Determination and others like it helped keep athletes eligible, the Chancellor ignored her protests.

Monet tried not to look at Ray as she walked to her seat but she couldn't help it, he was still waving.

"What are you doing here?" she asked, standing in front of him.

"I go to school here," he said, playfully.

God, he could be obnoxious.

When she sat down, she took a long look at his huge National Championship ring. She wanted one.

"If I sit here, are you going to bother me all quarter?"

"Depends."

Lonnie stopped writing on the board, and came to stand in front of the class. "As many of you may know, Professor Keating has taken ill. In her place, I will be teaching this course, 'The Body Politic–Women's Global Fight for Self Determination.'" She then wrote it on the chalkboard. "You are all invited to stay. However, if you are looking for the generous grading distinguishing Professor Keating's class you probably should drop the class."

It was a jailbreak. By the time the class settled down only 25 of the original 63 students remained in the class. All of the students who left were players from a men's sports team. Only Ray and three football players remained.

Lonnie turned to the class. "I was just asked to teach this course, so I don't have a syllabus yet. But before the rest of you get up and leave..." She wrote, "Feminine Mystique." Lonnie turned to face the class and said, "What does this term describe?"

Silence.

"This was the term that described your grandmothers' unfulfilled lives as housewives. It's what started the second women's movement in the sixties and seventies."

Lonnie stared out at blank faces.

"How 'bout this?"

She wrote "1920."

Silence.

"Isn't that the year Great Depression started?"

"No, that was 1929. Remember, this isn't an economics class. It's a political science class. Anyone else? 1920. Anyone?"

"Paris, Olympics."

"No, that year it was in Antwerp, Belgium," Lonnie said.

Lonnie erased "1920" then wrote, "Elizabeth Cady Stanton."

Silence; then she wrote "Feminist" on the chalkboard.

"What does that word mean to any of you?"

Amidst the class grumbling, Ray, of all people, took the first crack.

"Feminist. Pants wearing', man-hatin', hairy leg havin', Birkenstock wearin', abortion rights fightin', equal rights supportin', all-sex-is-rape thinkin'..." The class sat in stunned silence. "Should I go on?"

"You've said quite a lot already," Lonnie Delaney said.

"I forgot homely," Ray smiled.

Lonnie said, "Funny thing is, except for that last comment, I agree with you." Now she had the class' attention.

"Some guys fear a feminine planet," Sarah Barksdale said, with a little edge. Ironically, Ray's definition fit her perfectly.

"I did say man-hating, didn't I?" Ray said.

Lonnie interrupted, "–Perception is often reality, regardless of whether it's true or not. Although he brings up an interesting question, do you have to be good-looking, feminine, *a babe,* as what's your name?" She pointed to Ray.

"Ray Riddick."

"As Ray put it, can you be a babe and still be a feminist? Because people are usually so caught up in the label they can't see when the label they are trying to avoid still applies to them."

"Isn't that called *denial?*" Ray chimed in enjoying the moment.

"It is," Lonnie answered. "It may come as a surprise, well maybe not to the black students who know that as late as 1964 black people in the South were routinely denied the right to vote. Which brings us back to 1920. To answer the question about 1920, that was the year women started voting in this country."

"So how did they, uh, how were they, uh, represented?" a student asked.

"They were represented by their husbands," Lonnie said.

"Their husbands!?" said one student.

"Oh, hell no," said another student.

"Cool, two votes," said an offensive lineman who was as big as two people already.

"We'd have to vote together then... or something," said Sarah.

"First you had to have a husband," Ray said, loud enough to be heard by Sarah. She gave him a cutting look which made him chuckle, then shiver in mock terror of her scary feminist glare.

Lonnie ignored him and continued. "Gender politics. Some of you might say, 'What's political about gender?' Well, wherever there are policies to be made and when those policies affect one gender but are created, written, and decided largely by the other gender, gender politics becomes a real battleground.

"Which brings us to the body politic as it relates to this course. First of all it's not some governing body of elected officials. The body politic is you. It's your body, not just how you vote but your voice, your political action. It's not just your body, but who decides who gets to touch it and under what circumstances. It's for you to realize politicians and judges decide what *they* will allow *you* to do with *your body* and what *they* will not permit others to do to *your body* even with *your* consent. If that doesn't alarm you– these decisions are being made all around you, every day."

"Where?"

Lonnie walked around her desk and perched on the edge. "Wherever the legal system defines the morality of a society. Unlike places where religious doctrine guides the legal system–places like Afghanistan, Iran, and other Muslim nations. In other countries, it's the political process that creates and shapes the legal system which shapes the morality of our society. So, it should bother you that in our political system 85 percent of politicians are men. It should bother you not because they are men but because those same men are making decisions that directly affect and are specific to women when they have never spent one day *being* a woman. So, who do you think is better suited to represent the interests of women in the political and legal process?"

"Women," Sarah quickly added.

Lonnie nodded. "Make no mistake. The body is political and the stakes are high. Reproductive rights, domestic violence laws, voting rights, health care, sexual harassment laws, child labor laws, these laws didn't just materialize. Those rights were born out of the daily injustices against your mothers and grandmothers. Most of those laws didn't exist forty years ago. And I'll be honest with you, your generation takes them for granted.

"The *Feminine Mystique*, 1920, *Roe v. Wade*. You should know the significance of these milestones. Maybe you're not interested, but you should still know this stuff as well as you know Lincoln freed the slaves and Washington was our first president. Now, I'm not saying that women in your generation don't appreciate the sacrifices other people have made. My problem with your generation is–to use a baseball analogy–that you were born on third base and you don't know who hit the triple to get you there."

Ray passed a note to Monet. "When I think of freedom, I think C-cups."

Monet responded, "With any luck that'll be your grade for this class."

"You're a freedom-fighting feminista, what size is your freedom?" Ray looked over her shoulder and down her shirt.

"Why are you still here?" Monet wrote back.

"I gotta keep an eye on you feminista insurgents."

"Why do you care? You'll just marry some bimbo with fake tits anyway."

"I don't want to wake up one morning and find women ruling the earth, like some bad remake of *Planet of the Apes*," he scribbled.

"Ah-ha. Someone *is afraid* of a feminine planet." They continued passing the note back and forth.

"Someone has to infiltrate in order to find out what you women are up to, before it's too late."

"What's that supposed to mean?"

"You heard the lady. If you feminists had your way, everything would be 'degenderized'," Ray wrote.

"De-genderized, is that a word?" she wrote back.

"You know what I mean. Women always want what guys have. Why can't there be guy stuff and girl stuff?" Ray wrote.

"Professor Delaney is the women's basketball coach."

"For real?"

"Yes, aren't you glad you stayed?" Monet wrote.

"Shhhh. I'd be able to get more out of this class if you'd stop passing me notes... Yeah, I'm glad. Just don't tell my fans." Ray wrote.

Maybe this guy wasn't so bad.

"Tell you what, I'll write some facts about women's history in this country and you tell me whether each is true or false," Lonnie said.

Again, she had the class' undivided attention.

"1974, *New York Times* finally stops separating classified employment ads by gender. True or false?"

Most of the class raised their hands for "False."

"True, it was common practice at newspapers across the country to separate jobs by gender, with teachers, nurses, and secretaries in the women's section, and managers, firemen, and police officers in the men's section... Okay, true or false, in 1965 could a married woman get a loan in her own name?"

"True."

"False, women were routinely denied real estate and business loans if they applied without their husbands as cosigners, really the principals. If you were single, as Mr. Riddick correctly stated, you were expected to go get a husband first."

The class grumbled at that.

"Next one. In the 1960's and 70's was bra burning a national phenomenon?"

"There is no way women were burning their $50 bra and panty sets from Victoria's Secret!" one student said.

"There was no Victoria's Secret back then," another corrected.

"Oh man, I would love to have been there for that," a cornerback whispered to Ray.

"Yeah, until you see your mother and all her baggy breasted friends bouncing around. You sure you want to see that? Your mother is at least fifty, right?" Ray said. "Well, not back then she wasn't."

The cornerback frowned at the thought.

Lonnie continued, "Actually, it's not true. In 1968, women were protesting the Miss America Beauty Pageant in Atlantic City. The Miss America pageant symbolized that women were merely ornaments, pretty things to be admired. A group of women protested that women should be treated as people of substance. So outside of the pageant, the protesting women threw 'instruments of torture' into a garbage can; things that made them more visually appealing, makeup, girdles, and bras. Afterward, they were going to set them on fire in protest but chose not to because it was a fire hazard. The Atlantic City Boardwalk is made of wood. So, later, it was the *New York Times* that referred to 'bra-burning' in one of its editorials as if it had actually happened when it didn't. The media latched on and ran with it, erroneously starting an urban myth in their effort to succinctly encapsulate the women's movement..."

Everyone nodded collectively thinking the same thing, "I never knew that."

Mbika Njai was the student sitting in front of Monet, "Excuse me. I forgot my pen. Do you have an extra?"

Monet gave her a strange look, "It's the first day of class," then smiled and passed her a pen.

Mbika was from Kenya. She was tall and athletic. She had grown up playing soccer, but had started playing basketball while living in a small apartment in Alphabet City on the lower East Side of Manhattan. She had left her native Kenya several weeks before she was to have been married. She was sixteen–an old woman.

Mbika finished high school in New York, then moved to San Francisco to study nursing, a perfectly acceptable female profession by African standards. Later, she found that Americans were more accepting of women becoming doctors than they were in Kenya where women were expected to have more subordinate professional roles. Mbika was no rebel, but she questioned why she should have to curb her ambition just because she was female. One doesn't have anything to do with the other, she thought. Western-trained doctors were highly regarded in her country. But in Kenya her gender would be in direct conflict with her professional status, even as a western-trained doctor.

Mbika turned around in her desk, "You play on the bahsket-bahll team, yes?"

Monet nodded.

"I want to play on the bahsket-bahll team."

"Well, it's not that simple. First you gotta be able to play and even then there has to be a spot."

"But I am a goot player," Mbika said.

"Doesn't matter."

"What you mean, doesn't matter? Coach would keep the best players, no?"

"There might not be room on the team because of the scholarship players," Monet said.

"They pay your fees for playing bahsket-bahll?" Mbika asked.

"Yes."

"What about football? I play football berry goot too."

"Only men play football."

"No, 'day have a football team here, women play."

"Trust me there aren't any women playing football."

"Ahhh, yes," Mbika said, insisting.

"Ahhh... no."

"But I see them practice. Running and kicking."

"You mean soccer."

"Yes, I mean soccer," Mbika chuckled. "You Americans, the whole world calls it football, but you–."

"It's taken. The word football is taken," Monet said.

"Football has been around much longer than your American soccer–."

"–You mean football."

"Football. It doesn't matter. I don't like football anyway," Mbika said.

"Football or soccer? You know what? Nevermind."

Mbika said, "Coach see me play, see me play bahsket-bahll, not football, she make room for me." Mbika had learned to be persistent from her time in New York; it drove her mother crazy when they talked on the phone. "What are those Americans doing to you?" her mother was fond of saying.

"When do you play?" she asked Monet.

"Practice doesn't even start for another three weeks. But we're gonna play today. You should come."

"Okay, I will come. I will come to show you I can play."

"Not me. The coach."

"First, I will show you." Mbika knew the coach would find out somehow.

"Maybe she'll have a walk-on tryout?" Monet said.

"What is that?"

"That's where people who don't have scholarships, like you, can try out for the team."

"Will they play?" Mbika asked.

"Sometimes," Monet said.

"Yes. If that is how it is done. I will do this walk-on tryout. Then, we shall see."

September Twenty-fifth

Monet sat next to Sonja along with the rest of the women's team while the men played their pickup games. The arena was empty except for the players.

Ray dazzled them with his smooth and accurate jump shot. There was no doubt about his future. Each time he hit a shot from three-point range he smiled and winked at Monet. It made her want to figure out a way she could irritate him on command. She needed something. Sitting there and rolling her eyes wasn't getting the job done.

"These guys know how to play," Sonja said.

"They're really athletic."

"No, I mean watch." Sonja analyzed the game as it unfolded. "Here comes the weak side pick, back cut, defended well, second option, screen-roll, show and recover, nice, back it out to set up a... Princeton backdoor. Lay-up... Now that's basketball."

"That's what I'm talkin' about!" Monet was amazed at the freshman's basketball IQ. Monet put her fist out. Sonja bopped the top with her own, giving her a pound.

Roxy sat off to the side with Clio, Shirlie, and Kendra. They watched the men play, but were more focused on watching the men than on watching the men play.

"I love shirts and skins," Roxy said.

"But only if the hot ones are skins," Clio said.

"Yeah, get the rest of them in the weight room," Kendra said.

"Tell 'em, 'You're shirts until you fill out a bit'."

"You're makin' the skins look bad."

"Ummph, have to work extra hard to make Ray look bad."

"What's up with Chris Chamberlain?" Kendra asked Roxy.

"He's still fine."

"You mean he still has a girlfriend," Clio said.

"Tch. I don't see 'Cornerback Chris.' All I see are basketball players with their shirts off," Roxy said.

"That's game point. Ask 'em to play another game," Clio said smiling.

"You know, maybe if you had a boyfriend, you wouldn't have to do so much window-shopping."

They laughed at Clio, who had never made good decisions about guys.

As the men walked off the court, the women milled about to get ready to play. On her way to the court Monet passed Ray. Ray's grin challenged Monet to top his performance. She gave him *that* look. *Stick around, you'll see.*

Roxy stood up from the bench bossing everyone around. "We gotta split 'em up evenly. So, I guess it's me, on the point, Clio, two, Monet, what, the three? Kendra, four, Shirlie five. Against..."

"I told you, I'm on the point," Monet said.

"You can't both play the point," Kendra stated the obvious.

Monet said, "Fine. Give me Sonja, Jennifer, and Tamika."

"All the freshman," Clio said.

Roxy huffed and shook her head. This was going to be easy. "Last year's starting five against freshman. You need one more."

A few moments earlier Mbika had sat down on the sideline.

"We'll take her."

"Who? Her?"

Mbika wasn't dressed like a basketball player, which is hard to do since there isn't much to hoop fashion. Mbika was wearing bright red Reeboks, the classic midcut shoe with the Velcro ankle straps millions of women wore at the beginning of the aerobic revolution in the early eighties. She wore the Green Nigerian national soccer shirt. Her shorts were a little too tight and ran a little too high by conventional hoop standards. To the delight of the men she had a nice little wedgie.

"You can have Jane Fonda," Roxy said.

Monet shot for outs and won. During the game Monet's voice could be heard above the bouncing balls. She was in total command of the game.

She directed. "Where you want it? Not there, deeper... That's your spot... If you want it there, you gotta fight for it... Use the bootie, use the bootie... That's what I'm talkin' 'bout."

She distributed. "Here you go, now go to work..."

She played defense. After a clean steal she looked at Roxy to mock her then streaked down the court for a lay-up. When she ran back on defense she told Roxy, "I picked you like a Safeway chicken." Had the fellas rollin'.

Monet had the game under control. "I got the rebound. Come on, run with me. Come on... Run with me. Fill the lane, girl... Watch it now, watch it... That's the way you finish."

Tamika was playing well against Kendra. Several times Tamika forced a bad shot, Monet reminded her gently to pass the ball.

"You see how I'm wearing her out, just kick it down to me big girl," Tamika said to Monet. In high school, Tamika was used to players deferring to her. Roxy's team went on a five-point run. Monet responded by not passing the ball to anyone. She single-handedly won the game by scoring the remainder of the points.

"So what's the difference between you taking all the shots and me taking shots?" Tamika asked Monet after the first game.

"I made all of mine. Because of that, we won," Monet said. "Don't worry I'll get you the ball."

Tamika didn't like being patronized, but as a power forward she would have to rely on the point guard to feed her the ball, so she kept quiet.

Monet was surprised by Mbika's basketball skill. She couldn't shoot worth a damn and she was utterly clueless on offense. But through her years of soccer she understood position defense and she was a tremendous athlete. Lonnie Delaney watched the game and saw that Monet and Mbika were the most athletic women on the court.

"You gotta get some real basketball shoes, girl; those Jenny Craig shoes ain't cuttin' it," Monet said to Mbika.

"'Deese are not goot?"

"They're good for something, just not basketball."

"No?"

"No."

"Okay, if I need other kinds of shoes, then I make arrangements and get them," Mbika said.

"Goot," Monet said.

Roxy took it upon herself to guard Monet. She was overmatched on offense. Monet was too strong for Roxy to get around and too tall to shoot over. Defensively, Monet had relegated Roxy to merely setting up other players and occasionally driving to the basket. After Monet blocked Roxy's fourth jump shot Roxy stopped shooting altogether. During the last game Monet relentlessly posted her up, pounding on Roxy not as a point guard but as a center. She scored effortlessly.

On one play she faked a drop off pass to Sonja, then crossover dribbled to her left; when Roxy blocked her path she spun back to her right, took two steps and could have made an easy lay-up but tossed the ball gently in the air for an alley-oop. Tamika caught it and laid it in. A low "Ooooooooooooooooo" came from the eight men on the sidelines.

Roxy was being embarrassed in front of the BMOCs of Del Mar. She tried playing Monet closer. But Monet was too big and too strong.

Monet waved everyone off and scored the last three points on Roxy, emphatically proving who was the better player. The games were never close (12-5, 12-2, and 12-4). Monet had served notice that there would be no tenured starting positions this season.

When Monet looked at Ray, he shook his head and said, "Yeah, you won today, but that doesn't make you a winner."

"Yeah, whatever."

Chapter 4

Niggers of the World

September Twenty-sixth
"Niggers."

"Excuse me," said an enormous African-American linebacker sitting in the back.

"Niggers. You know, niggers," Lonnie Delaney said, nonchalantly, leaving no doubt what she meant. "Today we are going to talk about the niggers among us."

The class rumbled with anxiety and confusion. Lonnie was, after all, a white woman.

"Words are powerful, aren't they?... Niggers." She said it again, taunting them with it. "Right now, how many of you are uncomfortable talking about niggers? I know the white students are." With good reason, because the black students were getting angry.

"Words, even this word, means different things to different people. Depends on the context, who's using it. A white man saying, 'Those dirty niggers' has a totally different meaning than one black man saying to another, 'Nigga, please.'"

Lonnie said, "Nigga please" with such soul a few of the black students smiled. It was like she knew–the way Bill Clinton, the first black president, knew–how to connect with black people.

"Words are powerful and impotent at the same time. In and of themselves they can do nothing more than describe or instruct. They only have power if we act on them. So, now that I have your attention, anyone want to explain to us what is a nigga?"

Silence.

"Come on don't be shy. What is a nigger? Who are the niggas among us? Anyone?"

Silence.

"Okay, I'll start. Niggas are the lowest of the low. They don't control their own bodies because they are prone to be murdered or jailed or beat up by the police. Niggas couldn't vote. Then they were prevented from voting. Then gerrymandering watered down their voting blocks."

"They're always on welfare," a nervous white student offered.

"Ahhh, someone willing to take a chance. Good. Anyone else? But you gotta use the word in a sentence because it helps to 369desensitize it, Lonnie said. The white student looked around at her black classmates, and used better judgment.

"We, uh, they, go to the worst schools," a black student said.

Lonnie continued, "Right. Niggas are deprived, tormented, tortured, and subjugated. Niggas live by the decisions made by people who claim they care, but their decisions prove they really don't understand niggas. Liberals and progressives think they are the champions of compassion but I ask you, can you really have someone's best interest at heart when you don't understand them?"

"So what's your point?"

"A voice from the back," Lonnie said. "I'm sorry I didn't hear you."

"I said what's your point? Because it seems to me all you're doing is pissing off all the black students. And for what?"

"I never said anything about black people. I'm talking about niggas. But you bring up a good point. See, I think there are niggas all over the world. Aborigines are the niggas of Australia."

"The niggas in the central valley of California are migrant workers from Mexico," a Latina said.

"Thank you... They call them Kafirs in South Africa," Lonnie said.

"Koreans in China," a Chinese student said.

"Chinese in Japan," a Japanese student said.

"Is what?" the African-American linebacker said.

"A nig-ger," said a diminutive Italian geek sitting next to the football player. The big fella squinted down at him, letting him know that despite the topic of discussion he still wasn't in a position to use the word in his presence. The geek froze and focused his eyes forward.

"Palestinians are the niggas of Israel," Ray said.

"Which is interesting, because Jews think they are the niggas of the world," Lonnie added. "Nigger is an ugly word. Not in and of itself. No word is intrinsically bad. The word nigger makes people uncomfortable here because of what people throughout American history have done to African-Americans. But African-Americans don't have a monopoly on genocide or persecution or even appalling treatment when you look around the world. And you don't have to go way back in history, just look around today. Niggers are people with less power, fewer assets, and less ability to protect themselves. And those people are being exploited right now in 1996, with no end in sight. Where is the outrage for them? Niggers... The word by itself is harmless, it's just a label. When I used it standing here before you no one lost their ability to vote, no one was denied a loan or was lynched. No one was harassed at the job, beaten up, or was denied the right to choose to have a baby."

Huh?

"It's understandable that the first thing that comes to mind when you think of the word nigger is an African-American. But what if I told you that, in India, a woman is routinely set on fire by her husband when his family wants more money from the bride's family? What if I told you domestic violence goes largely unpunished in many countries even when it's murder? That in some Muslim countries women are prohibited from being educated beyond their eighth birthday. That young girls in rural China are routinely sold into sexual slavery by their own parents. Given slavery, Jim Crow laws and then the voting obstacles in the 50s and 60s, during the last thirty years many African-Americans have enjoyed significant prosperity.

"But today, women around the world are still living tortured, defenseless lives. Being murdered by your husband's family is just as bad as being lynched by strangers. Being a slave in a cotton field is just as bad as being an eleven-year-old girl in a brothel. Maybe it's worse. But this isn't 1845, Jim Crow, or even pre-1920. Terrible, unspeakable things are happening to women right now. Today, in 1996.

"And that is why I say it is women who are the undisputed niggers of the world."

"Can you believe this?" Ray wrote to Monet.

"Uncomfortable?" was Monet's response.

"Nigga please," with a smiley face. "Where's she going with this?" Ray wrote.

"Don't know. But there might be a riot."

"I might throw the first rock," he wrote.

"She's tough. My first year she made all the freshman wear dresses or skirts on road trips."

"Even if I was a freshman I wouldn't wear a skirt," Ray wrote.

"Freshman on the basketball team, silly."

"So what?" Ray wrote.

"Our whole team was a bit mannish. I guess she wanted all the freshmen to start out wearing skirts as a sign of femininity."

"Mannish, you were probably the main one. Keep it real."

"Stop," Monet wrote.

"Bunch of tall, ass-kicking bruisers."

"I was used to wearing pants; skirts were way too girlie," Monet wrote.

"You female athletes run from that femininity huh?" Ray wrote.

"Shut up," Monet wrote.

"Don't tell anyone, but I am a lesbian trapped in man's body," Ray wrote.

"I'll have to remember that."

"Palestinians are the niggers of Israel," Ray said, participating in the class.

"Nice one," Monet wrote.

"I'm not just some dumb jock," Ray wrote back.

"Yes, you are, on many different levels."

"And you? Are you a lesbian trapped in woman's body?" he wrote.

"Nope."

"Prove it," he wrote.

Several minutes passed before she wrote him back.

"*And that is why I say it's women who are the undisputed niggers of the world,*" Lonnie said.

"I've felt that for a long time. Women get the short end," Monet wrote.

"Not when they're with me," Ray wrote.

"Shhhhhhh. She's giving out the assignment."

She didn't acknowledge his risqué message.

Lonnie had been thinking about an assignment to give to the class for several days. She didn't want to give weekly assignments because it would be too much work to grade the papers. She still wanted the class to have an impact that her students would never forget, maybe even inspire some of them to become advocates or community leaders.

"The assignment will be to write a 2,000 word essay on the treatment of women in another country. You also have to present

your report to the class. You can write about women in any country, but your oral report has to be in the first person."
The class looked around. There were roughly 22 students in the class. Too many for one report for each student. "Matter of fact, I'll group you into pairs." Lonnie Delaney said, looking at her watch. She needed to hurry.
From her podium she paired up the students by their seating locations; those sitting next to each other in class. If there was an odd number in a row, then the last person was paired with the nearest person in the last row of the next aisle. There were some groans about the pairings. Monet was sitting in front of Ray. Sure enough she was paired with him.
Damn.

Tamika and Sonja sat in their Writing Composition class. The professor started them off with the basics: her pet peeves and the bad habits of student writing she warned them to avoid if they wanted a decent grade. Things such as, when to use "which" versus "that." Write declarative sentences. She cautioned them, stating that while these rules were remedial they would serve them well in the future.
"Where are your books?" Sonja whispered, as she turned around.
"This is it?" Tamika said pointing to a sports magazine.
"Didn't you get your book money?"
"What book money?"
"I'll tell you later."
Sonja took meticulous notes while Tamika read about women basketball players overseas. Tamika looked up to the ceiling, deep in thought, trying to figure out how women basketball players in places like Israel, Germany, Russia, and France could make $150,000 a year, tax free, with free housing and limo service. Complicating the matter, she knew players in the American Basketball League and even in the proposed NBA sponsored women's league, the WNBA, would only make $50,000 a year. "How can playing professionally in the Ukraine be a better place for women than the United States?"
Tamika closed the *Sports Illustrated* magazine to gaze at Emmitt Smith on the cover. She wanted to be on the cover of before she graduated. "Graduate." She had to smile to herself about that one because she had no intention of graduating.

After class the students gathered their belongings, Tamika didn't have much.

"Don't expect to get my notes at the end of the quarter," Sonja said.

Tamika glared at Sonja, "Bitch, don't you ever..."

Everyone turned around. Tamika quelled her anger. She was upset until she realized there was nothing to be upset about. Sonja just stood there, angry about the fact she had to sleep in the same room with this crazy woman. "Sorry. But you ain't gonna *hafta* give me shit."

Sonja was learning that Tamika was more bark than bite. She realized that Tamika had apologized, in her own way. They walked out together.

"You do know we're gonna be tested on this, right?" Sonja said, just in case Tamika hadn't heard.

Tamika was nonchalant. "I got it all figured out. I'm gonna play here for three years, help build a national rep for this school being the 'Bomb'. Lead the nation in scoring and rebounding."

"How are you going to graduate if you don't take notes in class."

"Graduate? Girl, please. Who said anything about graduating?" Tamika said.

"Well, you gotta stay eligible to play," Sonja said.

"I just said I am going to lead the nation in scoring and rebounding," Tamika repeated. "Connect the damn dots."

Sonja shook her head.

"Oh, and you know my fourth year," Tamika continued.

"Your senior year."

"Whatever. That's an Olympic year, so you know I'm gonna play on the Olympic team, representin' the USA. Doin' my thang. By then, there will be a women's pro league. No doubt there'll be a bidding war."

"They're going to have a draft."

"Well there'll be a bidding war on who I'll sign with," Tamika said, undaunted.

"For?"

"My shoe contract."

Sonja looked at her, dumbfounded.

"Oh, I got it all figured out," Tamika said. "So, you keep takin' those notes."

"I see," Sonja said, but was really thinking what a nut she had for a roommate.

Sonja was a square, especially by Tamika's West Oakland standards. Being from Minnesota, she couldn't help it. Sonja was the third child of Mary and Olaf Mortensen, Olympic gymnasts. They had met at the 1976 Games in Montreal. She was from Minnesota, he was from that world gymnastic power–The Netherlands. When they met, Mary asked Olaf what a guy from Amsterdam was doing in the Summer Olympics. He said he hated the snow and wasn't blessed with the long legs needed to be a great cross country skier. Olaf placed dead last in his only event, the floor exercise. Mary was overrun by the Nadia Comaneci juggernaut.

They married shortly after the Olympics and moved to her native Minnesota. He wished she was from Florida, but moved to the United States anyway.

They didn't have a pedigree of winning medals at the Olympics, but that didn't stop Mary and Olaf from opening a gymnastics school in hopes of one day returning to the Olympics as coaches. None of their students amounted to much. Their only hope for Olympic glory lay in Olaf, Jr., Marjorie, and Sonja. Olaf Jr. and Marjorie were short, compact, and muscular, perfect for gymnastics except they were terribly clumsy. Olaf used to yell at Mary for giving him such clumsy children. She ignored him as only an American wife could.

Sonja could do the double backs and also be as graceful as a swan. Olaf and Mary thought they had a winner–until the eighth grade, when Sonja grew 5 inches to stand five-foot-eleven, 160 pounds, way too big to be a gymnast. They put her on a strict diet and an intense exercise program in hopes of making her the next Nadia. But there was no stopping Mother Nature.

After closing the gymnastics school, Olaf bought a trampoline and a basketball hoop. He figured he could make a little extra money by combining three sports: trampoline, basketball, and gymnastics. He would jump on a mini trampoline, do a couple of flips, and dunk the ball through the hoop. He saw the trick performed during halftime at a University of Minnesota basketball game while he was selling popcorn for extra money. Olaf remembered how the crowd went wild even though the guy kept missing the dunk. Olaf may have finished dead last at the Olympics, but he knew he could do a better job of dunking from a trampoline than that clown. He just needed a hook. He bought himself some purple tights, a gold cape, and a gold-sequined wrestler's mask. He painted some equestrian riding boots gold. He installed a basketball hoop to practice his routine. He called himself the Flying Dutchman. He thought it was original.

By the ninth grade Sonja had grown to six-one. She was still running, despite the fact her gymnastics career was over. She liked her body thin and sharp, not soft and rounded. When she entered the ninth grade, the girl's freshman basketball coach asked her to play on the team. She told him she didn't know anything about basketball.

He said, "Let me see you hold your arms up."

"No."

"Why not?"

"Because I didn't shave under my arms."

"Okay, then turn around... Now put your arms up... That's all you need to know."

"That's it?"

"There's a lot more. But you can't teach height. We practice at 4:00 after school. Can you come?"

"Yeah. Sure."

"Good! Oh, and Sonja?"

"Yeah."

"Before you come, shave. Basketball players hold their arms up a lot."

Her first year, Sonja was nothing more than a tree.

That summer, she studied the game and the great players who played it. Sonja was a technician at heart, believing that anything worth doing is worth doing perfectly. She practiced for hours on the industrial-strength hoop the Flying Dutchman had installed for himself in the backyard. Through hard work she made herself a very good basketball player.

*   *   *   *

"You know you my dog." Kyle Cameron said to Monet, while they stood in line at lunch at St. Ignatius.

They were friends, so she knew he meant it as a compliment, although the K-9 reference disturbed her. As a girl, once you allowed yourself to be called a dog, could "bitch" be far behind? *"Naw, you MY dog."* Monet said, trying to shift the emphasis from paws to the possessive. He didn't notice the reversal. *"You gonna eat your Cheez-its?"* he asked, on his way to helping himself.

She blocked his hand. *"Give me your pudding first,"* reaching over with her spoon. As she finished scooping the last of his pudding their eyes met with knowing grins. They were friends, "dogs" as they called it. And friends, at least on guy-friend terms, don't let friends just take things. You trade. Giving, like borrowing, is for girls and guys who get their lunch money taken. Monet understood that about boys. She was comfortable because she always knew where she stood with them. She knew how to protect herself by demanding respect. Eye for an eye. Pudding for Cheez-its.

Monet didn't share the same goal as many of her friends. The ultimate for them was to be a cheerleader. *"We have spirit,"* chants didn't appeal to her "life is a participation sport" credo. As she spent more time with boys her girlfriends drifted away.

Monet knew boys. Knew their code. Knew the peer pressure to be strong and confident–to be tough and act like a man. Boys weren't like girls because they didn't worry about feelings or appearances. They were like, well, babies, acting on pure impulse. See it, grab it. Think it, say it. See a weakness, exploit it. Need to talk about experience you don't have? Lie about it, but make sure the girl lives two time zones away, minimum.

Playing football and basketball with boys five days a week at recess revealed those kinds of insights. Their personalities surfaced when they played. On disputed calls, Bill Willmont always tried to talk louder than everyone, thinking volume equaled righteousness. Archie Thomas sucked his thumb when he was nervous. Tim Hannan was always cool. He could always avoid the pursuit, buy some time, and find the open receiver. The kid was cool, Joe Montana cool. Monet knew all their tendencies.

Monet was friends with all of them and she knew this made her girlfriends jealous. After a while, she took on some of their mannerisms. Her mother hated them–baggy pants, sitting with her legs wide open.

Monet also had access to all the cutest guys, which also made the other girls jealous. They only saw the good-natured side of boys–when they wanted something. Monet got to see the other side. She saw all the bad things boys do to each othe and they weren't pretty. Like the time Larry Hutchinson made Donald Lewis cry because he wouldn't stand up for his calls when he was fouled in basketball. Larry wanted Donald to fight Kenny Kemp, but he wouldn't. He wouldn't assert or defend himself which made him a coward, a girlie-boy. With stuff like that going on it was hard for Monet to like any of them more than just as friends. Besides, she knew that liking a boy when he knew she could beat him on a post pattern for a touchdown would complicate things.

Monet was thankful to be accepted as just a player. She liked competing against the best. The boys were the best competition. She was happy with the exchange.

Chapter 5

In the Room, But Not in the Game

September Twenty-seventh

The entire women's basketball team was crammed into the bathroom at the Arena. The team was scheduled to take individual head shots for the media guide at 6:00 PM but the players were rushing to get ready for the basketball reception by 8:00 PM. The team photo was taken after the head shots so they all had to stand around in their uniforms and wait. Someone should have caught the scheduling conflict; but, as usual, no one in the athletic department really cared that the women were over-scheduled. There was no way this would have happened to the men's team.

After the team photo, there was a mad dash to the locker room to change. Roxy and Monet were the first to sprint toward the exit. Monet had the lead through the arena tunnel, down the stairs, and through the underground tunnel. Roxy had cut down another hallway so Monet eased up a bit. As she ran up the stairs, into the locker room, past the showers, and through the maze of lockers she stopped in her tracks when she found Roxy standing at her locker changing her shirt. Roxy's eyes followed Monet but neither said a word. Monet huffed and went to her locker perplexed at how Roxy had beaten her to the locker room. She vowed to beat her next time.

They only had 30 minutes to change into formal wear, an impossible deadline for twelve women, especially since five minutes had to be spent getting to the lockers. Lonnie made it clear they could not be late.

Shirlie had to take a quick shower because she sweated profusely when she took more than ten running strides. She still had to worry about sweating through her blouse after she got dressed. "Anyone got any baby powder?"

The Lady Runnin' Rhinos were a smorgasbord of style. The seniors, Monet, Shirlie, Roxy, Clio, and Kendra all wore either pantsuits with pumps. Jennifer's outfit could have been torn out of the latest teen magazine. She wore burgundy corduroy bell bottoms, platform clogs, and a cardigan sweater. Sonja personified sensibility, wearing gabardine slacks, a chiffon blouse, cardigan sweater, and pumps. Tamika discovered new ways to shock and amaze with her ghetto-fabulous style: leather jacket, capri pants, and knee high denim boots. Sonja prayed Tamika's horrific taste in clothing wasn't contagious.

"I don't know why Coach be makin' us to wear heels," Tamika said.

Monet wasn't looking forward to walking in her two-inch heels either. She cursed herself for buying the shoes in the first place. It would have been easier to just fake it.

With a few minutes remaining and pressed for time, Roxy, Monet, Clio, Kendra, Sonja, and Shirlie were all crammed in front of the mirrors applying makeup.

Sonja stood in front of the mirror sucking in her cheeks.

"What are you doing?" Tamika asked.

"Do you think this sweater makes me look fat?"

"Girl, please. You weigh about this much." Tamika answered, snapping her fingers to show how much.

"I see you got your work boots on tonight, Tamika," Shirlie said laughing.

"Oh, you got jokes," Tamika said, dead serious. "You need to shut up 'cause your deodorant is letting you down." Roxy, Clio, and Kendra laughed at the wet patches forming under Shirlie's armpits. Sonja and Jennifer didn't dare laugh; they were still freshman. "Looks like you got them industrial strength armpits. The kind people don't clean, they evacuate."

"You couldn't spell evacuate to get your get-out-of-jail free card," Shirlie countered.

"Yeah, but I heard you were so funky as a kid 'yo momma used cleanser for baby powder."

We have a winner.

Everyone on the team made a mental note: When it comes to talking trash, don't mess with Tamika. The girl may dress like a hooker, but she will break you down?

Sonja and Kendra made room at the crowded mirror for Tamika.

Tamika tugged on the bottom of her leather jacket, turned left then right to make sure everything was in order. "That's what-I'm-talkin' 'bout," she said, nodding into the mirror, all proud. Kendra and Sonja looked at Tamika and then at each other. They puckered trying to stop themselves from laughing. Tamika was convinced she looked good; everyone else knew better.

Roxy and Monet stood side by side in the mirror applying their makeup. Roxy watched her technique, then gave advice out loud to no one in particular. "That lip color is all wrong... A brow wax wouldn't hurt... Isn't it time to clip those long-ass nose hairs?" Shirlie, Clio, and Kendra paused for a moment until they figured out Roxy was talking about Monet.

"You know a pedicure wouldn't hurt either," Roxy said, still talking into the mirror.

She's talkin' about me. Oh God, I hope I don't make myself look like a raccoon.

Like it or not, Monet found herself in the middle of a face-painting competition with Roxy. Given her skill level, the best that she could hope for was not to embarrass herself.

Roxy could feel Monet's apprehension with each tentative stroke of her sepia colored pillow pencil. It was the weakness Roxy was looking for in Monet who up until then had been impenetrable. For the past week, Monet had been demolishing Roxy on the court, and this was the perfect change of events she was looking for to swing the momentum of their burgeoning rivalry. Roxy was going to milk it. She was standing next to Monet. "Mirror, mirror on the wall. Who's the fairest one of all?"

When Lonnie entered the locker room they all applied their finishing touches, and closed their lockers and compacts, then headed for the exit. As they made the walk back to the Arena, Lonnie noticed how awkward some of her players looked walking in heels.

Roxy, Clio, and Kendra glided effortlessly, graceful as runway models. For her size and youth, Sonja walked with poise as well. It was Monet and Tamika who looked like men walking in women's shoes, wobbly, teetering with every step. Shoulders hunched, knees bent as they carefully placed one foot in front of the other.

Kendra said, "You got some tape?"

"For what?"

"Those two are gonna sprain their ankles before the night is over."

Roxy walked beside Monet. She knew Monet's competitive nature wouldn't allow her to lead. Every 50 feet Roxy increased her speed. Even with her longer legs Monet was at a disadvantage against Roxy's smooth confident strides in three-inch heels. Head up, back straight, shoulders square. Roxy nudged the pace faster, then faster. Lonnie and her assistant coaches giggled; that is, until Monet fell after turning her ankle. Lonnie Delaney saw an entire losing season flash before her eyes.

There were over 150 alumni and boosters milling about in the Hall of Champions. Food servers roamed about with trays of *hors d'oeuvres.*

The Hall of Champions was the first project Forrest Haneline initiated when he had taken the athletic director's position 10 years earlier. It had the highest priority, closely followed by the renovation and expansion of his own office. The Hall of Champions was the best way to make a tangible connection to the nebulous transaction of donating to the athletic program. Even Billy Joe Bivens, the head football coach, stopped by to show his support and glad hand with the alumni. Football and men's basketball were the big money earners for Del Mar's athletic program, so the two coaches never missed an opportunity to support the other's social functions with alumni and boosters. The more big names they had in the room, the better it would feel to give money. It worked like a charm. Donations to the athletic department remained 30% greater than before. The guy was good.

Ray didn't like to attend these receptions any more than his teammates. The whole affair had the forced jocularity of an adoption fair. A dog and pony show for "jock sniffers." Old men and women paying for the privilege of being around athletes, as if shaking hands and giving money were the keys to eternal youth. Ray called each encounter with a booster a "Money Shake" because after shaking hands crisp dollar bills would magically appear. The money made it bearable but no less awkward. Players knew these wealthy, mostly white people had an acute fear of big black men. They knew if it weren't for the fact they were going to the same university as the wealthy booster alumni, they wouldn't hesitate to call the police if any player was in their neighborhood after 6:00 PM.

Money can create strange acquaintances. The boosters had it, the players wanted it. Like strippers suppressing the contempt they have for the men to whom they give lap dances, booster money kept players on their best behavior during receptions.

Receptions were Ray's forte. He knew how to work a room.

He was always gracious even when their questions were idiotic. He always laughed at their corny off-putting jokes. He always looked them in the eye and smiled as they struggled to figure out how to mingle with a tall athletic black man. Sometimes Ray let them off the hook by talking about business news or national politics, showing them he wasn't just a guy who could get you 20 points and 10 rebounds. The secret to Ray's success was he was truly present with each person he met. It paid big dividends, $100 here, $300 there, each shake. It added up fast.

"Here's a little something, Ray; take your girlfriend out for a movie and a soda pop." The guy actually said "soda pop." As much as the concept of having *soda pop* belonged in the Smithsonian, Ray never rolled his eyes with contempt. His grandmother used to tell him, "Being nice don't cost a thing." The twist here was being nice actually earned him more money. In fact, sometimes he would get other players' money shakes simply because some of his teammates weren't particularly friendly to the grayhaired white men. Although, they did have fun flirting with their trophy wives. Ray would walk out of these receptions with $2500 cash in his pocket. And this was separate from the anonymous cash he received from them periodically by Federal Express.

Ray thought the women's team would decrease his take, but they had no effect. The boosters were there to shake hands with men, not women.

Tamika was standing behind a fake palm tree. She reached out and snatched an *hors d'oeuvre* from a tray as a server passed. Scared the hell out of him. He nearly dropped an entire tray of hot dogs wrapped in bacon. Only one fell to the floor. Tamika picked it up and popped it into her mouth. "You want one?" she asked Sonja, who appeared to be standing alone because she was standing next to Tamika who was standing behind a tree.

"No, thank you."

"Don't you ever eat?" Tamika said. "The hot dogs wrapped in bacon kinda reminds me of home."

"Is it the double helping of fat and cholesterol?"

"Yo' Momma never made you butter and syrup sandwiches or hamburgers on regular bread, huh?"

"Uh, no."

"Burgers be juicy. Bread be all gummy," Tamika said.

"And why are you standing behind that tree?" Sonja asked.

"Bet you ain't got nothin' like that in Minnesota."

"The thought of it makes me want to run ten miles," Sonja said.

"Hey, I wonder what Monet is looking at over there." Sonja scurried off glad to get away. Tamika's tales of fatty foods were making her nauseous.

Monet, Jennifer, and Sonja circled the room looking at the various pictures, NCAA trophies, plaques, and retired uniforms in the trophy cases. Monet was limping slightly.

"Hey, Monet look at this cool scarf," Jennifer said.

"Yeah, if you like wearing underwear on your head. That's some guy's swim trunks," Monet said.

"Eewwwwww..." Sonja said.

"That's why freshmen should be seen and not heard," Monet said. Lonnie approached Monet.

"Are you going to have walk-on tryouts this year?" Monet asked. "Because I know someone who might be able to help us out; actually she's in your class."

"Mbika Njai. Yeah, I've seen her play with you guys. Not bad, needs to learn the game," Lonnie said.

"But she's really athletic."

"True. Hey anyone know why Tamika is standing behind that tree?"

"She's probably embarrassed about her leopard top and capri pants."

"It's good camouflage on safari."

Lonnie went over to Tamika.

"There you are Tamika, I've been looking for you. You moved from the tree over there to the... tree over here."

"How long do we have to be here?" Tamika asked.

In response, Lonnie tapped her watch, then signaled "one more hour" just as Haneline called her over to be introduced to a booster.

Tamika sighed. She felt uncomfortable surrounded by all the affluence.

A rather short man, Victor Bitinour, approached Tamika just as Lonnie walked away. He popped up in front of Tamika as if knew he would need to have a quick conversation.

"You're Tamika Hightower, right?" he said, quickly putting on the charm.

"Yeah." She answered suspiciously, even though she noticed how he didn't snicker at her attire. Looked her right in the eye.

"I've watched your box scores for years," Victor said.

"I ain't played one minute of college ball yet."

"But you've been kickin' ass and taking names since your freshman year of high school."

"You been watching me that long?"

"McClymonds High. Then you went to Oakland Tech, right?"

"Yeah, but I didn't steal no car over there," looking around nervously.

"It's okay."

"No, really, I didn't."

"Hey, I'm not a federal agent... I do know you averaged a triple double every year since then. Am I right? Dropped fifty on Simi Valley for the CIS State championship at the Arco Arena back in March," Victor said.

Tamika was impressed. "Why you know so much about me?" Tamika asked.

Bitinour paused, "Because I know talent when I see it. And I can see it before anyone else does."

Tamika liked this guy.

"Tamika. Everyone needs someone to look out for their best interest, if you know what I mean," Victor said.

"Yeah, my momma."

"Professionally. Look out for *those* interests," nodding.

"Ahhhhhhh." Now Tamika was nodding. "So you're an agent?" Tamika blurted out.

"Shhhhhh," crossing his lips with is finger. "No, I'm not an agent."

"But you said..."

"I'm an attorney. I didn't say anything about being an agent! Jeez!" Victor said in a loud whisper as he looked around nervously. That was the kind of mistake that could get him blacklisted from future Del Mar receptions. The NCAA had strict rules against its athletes being involved with agents. College athletes are supposed to be amateurs.

Victor had started his law practice with several of his classmates right out of USC law school. They did everything from wills to tenant evictions and criminal law. Mostly, they chased ambulances because it paid the bills. The other three partners had become increasingly irritated with Victor because he preferred to party and go on long vacations rather than work at generating billable hours. Feeling the heat he promised them he would begin pulling his weight by becoming a sports agent.

Victor had a few friends who were agents. Aside from being

highly paid baby-sitters, agents did very little for their four percent share of a client's NBA contract. Victor figured all he had to do was find a few players who were destined to play professionally, "invest" in them while they were in college, then represent them when they were drafted and signed professional contracts. Of course, there was no guarantee the players would sign with the agent after their college eligibility was completed. But the right message, sent with the right 300-pound roughneck usually cleared up any misunderstandings.

Becoming a sports agent is a classic chicken-egg dilemma. Victor didn't have any clients and no first-round NBA player would allow him to represent him unless he had a few clients in his stable. So, Victor concentrated on Division II football players and mid-major men's basketball players. He scouted them, cultivated them, and then hoped one of them would get drafted and make a team. Tamika was under the radar because her grades had prevented her from going to a major program. With the ABL starting in a month and the WNBA on the horizon, she was worth the gamble. Victor was casting his net widely.

Across the room, Monet watched Ray and another player they called "Heat Check" chat up a few alumni; one was the Mayor of San Francisco. Sure enough, their conversation ended with a handshake filled with cash. Ray's hands were so large you couldn't see the money change hands unless you were watching closely. Monet had been alternating between watching Ray and Roxy, who was standing across the room. She walked up to Ray and Heat Check as the Mayor walked away. Ray and Heat Check were as giddy as two schoolgirls.

"... Shoo'bee da-bang, nephew!" Ray said to Heat Check, suggestively referring to something about the Mayor.

"Yep, shoo'bee da-bang," Heat Check replied. They stopped abruptly when Monet approached.

"You know, you shouldn't be starin' at a brotha when he's doin' his thang," Ray said. Heat Check didn't miss the opportunity to jump on the bandwagon with a bugged-eyed over-the-top look of surprise and disgust.

"The NCAA finds out about your *thang* and these little meet and greets will be a *thang* of the past," Monet said.

"Don't hate. Congratulate," Heat Check said, pushing the cash to the bottom of his pants pocket. "Shake." He pulled his hand out of his pocket and held out his palm. He looked inside of it like he made the money disappear. "It's empty; your eligibility is safe," A server passed by with a tray of chocolates. Ray grimaced. "I hate chocolate."

Monet took one, but when she saw Ray's face she took three more and quickly popped one in her mouth. It got the desired effect. "I see... you guys are... making out pretty well," she said, chomping on the viscous caramel center. Ray curled his upper lip.

"Wasn't that the mayor?" Monet asked.

"Yeah, he says he'd love for me to do an internship in his office. He knows I can't work," Ray said.

"So, what's up?"

"I don't know, but I'll go check him out."

"Hey, break 'em off," Heat Check said.

"Keepin' it real? It's all part of the hustle," Ray said to Monet.

"That's what happens when you hit the shot to win the championship," Heat Check said.

"Everybody wants to rub on me like a damn good luck charm," Ray said.

"Make 'em pay," Heat Check said.

"The guy's been trying to get me to go out with his daughter for two years. It pretty pathetic," Ray said.

"Who?" Monet asked.

"The mayor."

"Shut up!"

"Real talk," Ray said. "We'll see what he wants when I go see him. He knows I can't work during the season. But I'll bet his daughter is there when I go see him."

Heat Check said, "Just another fan. And fans gotta pay. Some pay with cash..." Ray joined in, "...and some pay with ass."

"That's real talk," Ray said, following up with a high five.

Monet noticed the ghetto abbreviations and third-person references that slipped into Ray's speech. It contradicted her first impression of Ray as an obnoxious egomaniac, who was obviously intelligent, maybe even well-read–as opposed to the garden variety ignoramus that he was acting like now. Intelligent assholes are at least charming.

Ray continued, "You know, this university makes a lot of money off of us and we don't see none of it. So, if some gray-haired guy who never played the game wants to slip a brotha a little cash so he can take his girl out for soda pop, a brotha ain't mad at ya."

"Take the girl too," Heat Check said.

"I don't know about all that. Hell just yesterday it came up"

"Who was it?" Heat Check asked.

"I forgot, but that ain't the point. Point is, without that pocket money things could have got embarrassing for a brotha."

"It cost what? A dollar," Monet said, on the verge of leaving.

"Somewhere around there. I kept the other $499 dollars he gave me just in case I needed a few soda pops myself," Ray said, with a smile and wink.

"Hey, what did you mean the other day when you said, 'You won, but you're not a winner.'" Monet asked.

"Nothing, I was just watching you play," Ray said, trying to avoid the topic.

"No, I really want to know." Monet stood there waiting for an answer. Ray sighed, knowing she wouldn't like what he had to say.

"You win games and you think you're a winner. But when the real chips are on the line, chances are, you won't come through."

Monet was outraged. "You've seen me play, what? Seven, maybe ten pickup games?"

"And your team won them all, so what? Winners win championships. Winning pickup games doesn't make you a winner. Winning the Big Ten conference doesn't even make you a winner."

"Preach, brotha, preach," Heat Check said.

Monet cut her eyes at Heat Check. Ray had a point, though Monet didn't like how he made it.

"You can still be a great player and still not be a champion. Four of the twelve players on the '92 Dream Team in Barcelona have not won championships, college or pro."

"Karl Malone," Heat Check said. "John Stockton."

"Chris Mullin. Charles Barkley. All of them are great players."

"All of them are Hall of famers."

"Christian Laettner is not getting into the Hall of Fame."

"Yeah, but he won two national championships at Duke."

"Hit that unbelievable shot against Kentucky. He'll always be The Man for that," Ray said, then turned to Monet. "The problem with your game is you don't do what winners do."

"How do you know?"

"See it in your game. You may not like it, but I know sometthing about winning. My freshman year we won the last game of the season. That's when I got this." Ray held up his hand and showed

Monet his diamond-crusted National Championship ring. "What happened your freshman year?"
That hurts.

From a corner in the Hall of Champions, Roxy, Clio, Kendra, and Shirlie were watching Monet and Ray.
"You think she likes him?" Kendra said.
"I warned her already, he's strictly on safari," Shirlie said. "So if she wants to be just another notch on his used condom–go ahead."
"He can paint some spots on me," Clio said.
Roxy was conspicuously silent.
"You see that? He winked at her," Kendra said.
"Damn, Monet, you don't have to show him all your teeth," Clio said.
"Yeah, well we'll see how long that lasts," Roxy said.
"Shut up. Remember, you like football players," Shirlie said.
Roxy had that look in her eyes already. She was going to beat Monet at something and this might be it. She knew it wouldn't be basketball related. Monet made that point crystal clear every day during their pickup games.
"I can have any of them, if I want," Roxy said. It was true.
Guys noticed Roxy. She had beautiful brown skin and shoulder length wavy hair. She was sexy. She was one of the few women on any of the sports teams who could be ultra feminine when she wished.
Roxy was the middle child between two older and two younger brothers. They never made concessions to her, so she learned to play for keeps, especially at the dinner table where quick reflexes and a convincing glare were at a premium. She couldn't compete with their physical strength and always lost in regular games of one-on-one or other games, so she learned to outsmart them. To make up for her comparatively diminutive size, she beat them in micro spinoff games which isolated certain parts of a sport. She beat her brothers regularly in *Around the World*, *H-O-R-S-E*, and *Make it Take It* which was probably why she gravitated toward basketball, rather than softball or volleyball. She loved to rub their noses in defeat, which always kept them coming back for more.
In high school, the parade of her brothers' girlfriends was endless. Dweebs, sluts, brainiacs, dope-heads, wannabe white girls, *actual* white girls–she saw them all. Her brothers were all good high school

athletes so they were very popular. She noted the different dating styles their girlfriends used during their relationships, then she asked her brothers how they felt about each one.

The brainiacs taught Roxy that being homely and completely devoid of style can still be sexy. Although, nerds in love can be a painful thing to watch. It's all subtext and binary inside jokes.

The dope-heads taught Roxy that guys really like women who are willing to let their inhibitions go. They certainly were a friendly lot. But being a dope-head required too much trust, since there would be times when you would be at their mercy. You'd need help getting home and that's when bad things happened. It's never a good idea to place your trust and dignity at the mercy of another dope-head who is only in charge because he is not as high as you.

Two of Roxy's brothers were particularly sadistic. They preyed specifically on the dope-heads with their sinister pranks. They proudly passed around photos of their "girlfriends" drugged up, semiconscious, and in a variety of revealing poses. This effectively inoculated Roxy against using illegal drugs.

The sluts taught Roxy about the double-edged sword of sex, having sex, and maintaining a good reputation. More sex, less respect. Early sex, less respect. Better to be a tease than a slut. A tease was still mysterious, a challenge for boys to search for just the right combination that would unlock her passion. Her brothers used to say the sluts always had a definite advantage over the teases, but Roxy noticed their "relationships" never lasted very long and they were never brought home to meet her parents. Their mother could sniff out a high school slut before she even rang the doorbell.

"Don't bring none of them hussies in my house."

Slut politics was one of the first no-win situations Roxy learned about being a woman. Boys spread rumors about her being a slut even when she didn't give in to their sexual desires. To make matters worse, girls reinforced those rumors because she was already friendly with lots of guys from sports. Slut politics was the reason Roxy couldn't wait to get the hell out of high school. Now a senior in college, Roxy controlled her own reputation. She indulged guys more often, but on her own terms and with her own pleasure in mind. She made it clear they had to deliver. Those who weren't as committed to her pleasure as much as their own were unceremoniously dismissed. She always made it a point to tell them why, and if they didn't take the news well, she spread the word among her girlfriends. She figured guys like that had to be stopped.

Surprisingly, it was her brother's Asian girlfriends who taught Roxy how to make a guy feel that he's the one in command while she got everything she wanted from him. Roxy saw how her brother's Asian and white girlfriends were willing to let him take credit for things they had suggested, turned down, thought better of, and even paid for. All for the sake of his ego. No way a sista was going for that. Credit would be given where credit was due.

"Feed the ego and you can work magic with men," Roxy's mother told her.

It was an effective strategy used by the successful girlfriends of her brothers. Roxy saw the pep in their step when they were together. Sure, the little hussy was just tasting a little jungle fruit before she went back to her home in the hills. But their dating strategy made sense in navigating the male ego, black or white.

Over the years Roxy had learned all the subtle skills of femininity. Given a little interest from a guy, she was confident she could attract any man she set her sights on. As she and her teammates watched Ray wink at Monet, Roxy was sure she could douse any flame there was between them.

Roxy was used to being the undisputed leader of the team. Now Monet was the best player. Roxy wasn't going to stand by and let some woman from the Horse Chestnut groves of Ohio just walk in and take over the team and the best guys, whether she liked Ray or not. This was about turf. Monet had to be stopped and Roxy had the angle.

Roxy walked past Ray. She purposely dropped her keys, knowing he would pick them up and get a good look at her when he stood up. The long whiff of her perfume was an extra bonus. It worked; he was smiling.

"Hope you don't handle the ball like you handle your keys," Ray said.

"They give the ball to the point guard because she handles the ball the best," she said suggestively.

"Ya heard!" Ray said, his interest piqued. "But isn't there's a new 6'1" point guard in town? You might not be the best."

"Depends on if you're talkin' about basketball."

"Yeah... I guess it does," Ray said, pondering the possibilities. They talked for several minutes. Roxy glanced over her shoulder at Monet then smiled at Ray. Monet could see his beaming smile from across the room.

Monet watched Roxy's every move from across the room. Roxy

had the poise of a much older woman. Monet noticed how Roxy looked them in the eye and how some guys couldn't handle it. Roxy's sensuality was confident, effortless, and fluid. Monet was more than a little envious.

How come I can't be that enticing? Look at her batting her eyes. Roxy had skills. Monet watched her, intent on decoding her feminine techniques. Two weeks after making her vow on Interstate 80 to improve her social life, Monet's social life had not improved.

Forrest Haneline thanked the alumni for attending the reception. He thanked the players for coming and enduring the alumni. He promised this year would be the best ever for Del Mar basketball. He was looking forward to adding more trophies to the cases. NCAA championship trophies.

Lonnie stood with her assistant coaches, Stephanie Foster and Renee Armitrage. Stephanie and Renee had been with Lonnie Delaney at The Ohio State University and had dropped everything to come to Del Mar with her.

"Nice speech," Lonnie said to Forrest Haneline as he walked through the crowd.

"Thank you. One thing about alumni, they want to feel like they are a part of the team."

"Like us?" Lonnie asked.

"Excuse me?" Haneline replied.

"We'd like to feel like we're a part of the team, too, since we actually are one of the teams in the athletic department."

"You're not going down that road again are you?"

"If the road leads to a media guide before the start of the season and a radio contract, why not?"

"You're dreaming about a radio contract."

"Dreaming and having a vision aren't the same thing," she said.

Haneline shook his head as he walked away. "What I don't understand is why you don't believe this isn't Columbus, Ohio."

Chapter 6

Quarters

October Fifth, 9:15 PM

Sonja answered the door. It was Jennifer. "You ready?"

"Where are we going?" Sonja asked, since it was a school night.

"I hear O'Grady's is cool–cheap beer and, of course, lots of cute college guys." She said it as if it were a big deal.

"Jennifer, this is college. Cute *college* guys are everywhere."

"*Riaaght, riaaght.*"

"And I don't know about you, but I haven't had three birthdays since last week," Sonja said.

"Common. It'll be fun. It's the last Saturday of the month."

"Did you celebrate the last Wednesday of the month like this?"

"You're a good Catholic girl. You know Saturday is the day to party so you'll have a good story to tell in confession on Sunday."

"We're not twenty-one," Sonja said.

"Don't worry, we'll get in," Jennifer finished.

They both looked over at Tamika who was lying on her back, fingers laced across her stomach, like Dracula.

"You wanna come?" Sonja asked.

"And hang out with a bunch of drunk ass squares," Tamika said with her eyes closed. "Uh, no thank you."

"Let's go," Jennifer said, quickly, before Tamika changed her mind.

"Sonja, your mom called."

"What did she say?"

Tamika continued, "Nothing. She asked if you were eating right. Something about 1500 canaries."

"Calories," Jennifer said.

"Canaries, calories, whatever."

"They're not the same thing."

"They're spelled the same," Tamika said.

Sonja rolled her eyes then nudged Jennifer to leave. Jennifer was excited about going out for the first time in the big city.

Jennifer Swilling was hot to trot for good reasons. One, she was a practicing Catholic away from her parents for the first time. Two, she had to make up for a lot of lost time.

Mildred and Herman Swilling modeled their four daughters' high school social lives on the Victorian era. They wanted them to avoid teen pregnancy and if that meant being draconian about their social lives, so be it. Their strategy was to keep their daughters' legs closed, or at least make it difficult to open them. They did that by setting up an impossible obstacle course that no high school boy would have the patience to endure. Add to that the fear of eternal damnation Catholics are famous for and you've got a recipe for virginity.

In Oroville, California, Jennifer's hometown, there weren't many employment or social opportunities. Jennifer's high school classmates knew they were destined to work in the lumber mills or go for the really big bucks at Wal-Mart, maybe even become a department manager. The community entrepreneurs had meth amphetamine labs in their basements while the adventurous joined the military. Teenage mothers had become a fad because the government's Assistance to Families with Dependent Children program would increase their monthly payments if they had more children. There was no incentive to work when they could sit at home, watch soap operas, and make just as much money as a full-time worker. It made, her dad, Herman, angry each time another one of Jennifer's classmates became pregnant.

"Damn welfare kids. Whatever happened to family values? Ronald Reagan ain't out of office eight good years and the whole country has gone crazy." That was usually enough to send the children running to another corner of the house, anything to get away from another sociopolitical lecture from their father with an eighth-grade education. "Look at the your mother and me. We got married. We was fruitful. Your mother was never good at math but we multiplied. Problem with you kids today, you're too smart for your own good. Got too many damn choices."

"Herman Swilling! Don't swear around the children," Mildred said.

"They hear ten times as bad at school, Millie, prob-ly from the teachers themselves. When I was a kid, we was happy to play kick the can. We'd kick it up the street to see what that tomato can would do next. Would it spin? Would it roll? Would it flip? Yep, good ole-fashion American entertainment. These kids today got, what's it called Millie?... *Space Invaders* and *Donkey Kong.* Sounds like a game they'd play in San Francisco, if you know what I mean." That was the enlightened paternal wisdom Jennifer was working with. She loved her parents, but she couldn't wait to get the hell out their house and Oroville.

It was because of her parents that Jennifer had never been kissed. Really kissed. Never experienced the head rush that comes with tasting someone else's tongue and slobber. She had never experienced a kiss where you have to wipe away the strings of saliva when you finally pull apart gasping for air. It was every high schooler's rite of passage, but not for Jennifer or her sisters. Not if their father could help it.

Each Sunday the Swilling clan went to St. Thomas' church. Sometimes during the week their mother carried them all to church again to light a candle and say a few Hail Marys for prevention's sake. The girls fought it, but later they all came to appreciate the value of good ole-fashioned Catholic guilt.

Herman Swilling's daughters ultimately fell into all the traps he was trying to get them to avoid. Victorian era dating rituals be damned. Not even the fear of Dante's Inferno prevented his two older daughters from having children by the local mullet heads working at Dairy Queen.

It was basketball that saved Jennifer from becoming just another teen mother. Teamwork made her feel as if she were part of something bigger than herself. Being physically fit made her fall in love with her body. Road games introduced her to other cities. Jennifer figured if cities like Sacramento, Chico, and Marysville could inspire her to want to see the world, her head would explode from the cultural diversity in San Francisco.

Now that Jennifer was 150 miles from her parents, she had to make up for lost time. There were boys to be kissed. It wouldn't take long to get to second base, maybe even round third. In fact, she was certain the albatross of her virginity would be gone by Halloween.

Jennifer and Sonja drove to O'Grady's on Geary Boulevard. It was the unofficial bar of Del Mar University students. The doorman was lenient about checking IDs and the beers were cheap. Perfect. They walked in with another 19 year old who was wearing a Del Mar football jersey which he knew was all the ID he'd ever need.

          *   *   *   *

"So, where are you going?" Monet asked Shirlie, as she brushed her hair.

"A couple of guys asked me and Clio out."

"That's cool."

"They seemed nice enough, but I wasn't going unless Clio went with the other guy," Shirlie said.

"They just asked you go out?" Monet said.

"Yeah."

"Just like that?"

"Yeah?" Shirlie stopped brushing her hair when it dawned on her. "What are you trying to say?"

"Nothing... They must be tall."

"Not really, five-eleven, kinda slim, one guy has a cute butt," said Shirlie, standing six foot five.

"And they just asked you out." Short nice guys never asked Monet out.

"You make it sound so impossible. I just gave 'em a little look."

"A little look."

"A little look. God, it's not *that* hard, remember, they're guys." Shirlie flashed a sly grin and that "little look" for Monet to see. She grabbed her keys and some money before she walked out. "Cinderella, don't wait up."

Monet lay on her bed staring up at the ceiling thinking about where she would go if she went on a date. It was a good question. She had not gone on one in a long time. She figured if she weren't going to keep the promise to herself to improve her love life, the least she should do was go to some museums and art galleries.

I haven't been to a museum or art gallery since I've been here. I definitely can't tell my father about that. Where's Wayman when you need him?

Wayman Samuels was the only boyfriend she had ever had who actually liked going to the museum.

Wayman The Art Appreciator. I miss that guy. He was the only one who could appreciate why Jackson Pollack's art was a statement on repetitive patterns of nature and not just expensive kindergarten art. He liked impressionist art. Can't say that about everyone, although he was totally wrong about Vincent Van Gogh being overrated. Sensitive and thoughtful. He was always making me think.

Monet smiled, thinking about Wayman. Then she remembered

how sensitive he was. The very thing that allowed him to appreciate art was the same thing that turned Monet off. The guy had no ego, no swagger, no "guyness." A good chick flick would make him make cry. *Terms of Endearment?* Forget about it. He even cried at the end of *Hoosiers* when the small town kids beat the heavily favored big city kids. That ended it.

I mean, damn, Man-up.

Monet knew one day he would have a great career, be a great husband and father, but he was also destined to order fu-fu drinks from Starbucks and need her shoulder to cry on more than she would need his. So, even though she loved Wayman's intelligence, his wit, his willingness to appreciate art, she refused to invest in their relationship. Eventually, the relationship atrophied and died from an acute case of "Not-Man-Enough."

Damn roughnecks! Yeah, they're fine. But they're never the sharpest tools in the shed. Sure as hell aren't going to set foot in a museum. Not with those guys. Egos always on the line. Can't take a joke. It never works with those guys. Maybe, coach was right; takes a special guy who won't be intimidated by being seen as Mr. Monet McCasner.

Monet smiled. She had gotten up and was staring at herself in the wall mirror. She rotated her hips to check out her behind.

Takes a lot to handle all this.

Monet felt the pressure. This was the last year of a college career that had been thrown horribly off track. She had spent her whole college career focused on the goal of winning a championship at the expense of her social life. And now she had to face the fact she probably wouldn't reach her goal of winning a championship, nor would she have had any meaningful relationships with men. She was determined to reach at least one of those goals; otherwise, she felt, her college career would be a disappointment.

Monet usually didn't go on many second dates with those good-looking roughnecks. She didn't help matters by insisting on steering first-date conversations around to her accomplishments after sitting through their soliloquies about themselves. Not being the center of attention usually proved too much for really good-looking guys or athletes. They just weren't used to listening. Her relationship with the really smart guys never worked out either because they knew they had their pick of women who were looking to get married.

Monet found that women who were agreeable and were willing

to keep their mouths shut made it difficult for women like herself. She figured it gave the impression they would be nagging wives. But an accommodating woman can be a quiet date today and still become a nagging wife tomorrow.

I don't care. I still like the way a roughneck can just gobble you up in his arms. I couldn't get that from that pencil-neck crybaby Wayman.

That manly, gobble-you-up presence covered up a lot of the deficiencies of roughneck men; their selfishness, lack of communication, even a little cluelessness. It was just frustrating for Monet to date guys who felt everything was always about them. Dating roughnecks was fulfilling but not comfortable. Dating "Art Appreciators," sensitive types, was far more comfortable but not as fulfilling.

Aaaggghhhhhhhhhh!

Where are all the guys who are sensitive with a strong undercurrent of "guyness"?

It wasn't as if Monet were on some mission to bring out the sensitive side of a brooding bad boy. He didn't have to be worldly, didn't need to know about Picasso, Renoir, or Sisley. He just needed to be open-minded. Strong, not physically, but mentally strong. He also needed to be self-assured enough to handle a tall, competitive, opinionated black woman, but smart enough to not be hung up by his sensitive side. It was a lot to hope for. The focus of most guys in college is convincing women to help them explore the sensitive side of their love muscle.

Monet stood at the mirror combing her hair; then she shook her head.

"A little look." Who was Shirlie kidding with her big goofy ass?

9:25 PM

O' Grady's was hoppin'.

"Where you going?" Jennifer asked. They had just sat down at the bar.

"To play pool."

"Do you know how to play pool?"

"No, but I see someone over there who's gonna give me lessons," Sonja said with a wink. Jennifer was in awe for moment.

"I'll come with–."

"–No."

"Why not?" Jennifer asked.

"I wanna work the room a little, then I'll come get you. You probably should start off slow anyway. You ever drink before?" Sonja said.

"Are you kidding? My parents would kill me," Jennifer said.

"Exactly. You need to take it one step at a time; go have a drink, nothing hard. Try a beer or something."

Jennifer wanted to check out Sonja's technique for picking up guys. She admired her confidence. Instead, she ordered a drink.

Sonja had figured that two giggly freshmen standing around a pool table would make them look conspicuously eighteen. By going alone she could at least act older. The pool table was a good place to start. She was a little nervous; after all, these were college men. Well, maybe not the hairy old guy with the leather jacket and wallet chained to his belt loop. But everyone else looked like they were in college.

Sonja had never gone this long without a boyfriend before, so she was hoping someone would step up and rescue her social life. Her last boyfriend had said a long, tearful good-bye the day she flew out of Minneapolis. Now she was feeling the pangs of emptiness that come when no one is calling you twelve times a day to say absolutely nothing. *What are you doing? Nothing, thinking about you. What are you doing? The same thing as you. Isn't that weird? Yeah, we are so right for each other.*

Sonja put her quarters on the table and announced she was next.

"You sure you know how to play?" the targeted cutie said, right on cue.

"I was just watching you from over there and it looked like fun," Sonja answered.

"You want some lessons?" said Thomas, the cutie.

Bingo.

Meanwhile, Jennifer waited for the bartender to take her order. She was going to order a Budweiser, something safe.

Chad Wilcox, sophomore and quarters player extraordinaire was waiting as well. "Hi."

Jennifer nodded and smiled.

Chad said, "My friend here has to go. And uhm, we were playing quarters. But like I said, my friend has to go and, uh, I was wondering if you would, uhh, like to play with me?"

"Sure. Is it hard to play."

"No, it's really easy. It's just bouncing a quarter off the bar into the glass. Whoever gets it into the glass can choose who has to drink."

"Whoa, that sounds hard," Jennifer said. "What do you have to drink?"

"Shot of tequila."

"I've never had tequila," Jennifer said.

"It'll be fun. Wait and see," Chad said.

Bing, bing, bing. Game over.

"Wow, you're good," Jennifer giggled. She had had to drink three shots of tequila and they were already starting to take affect.

Uh-oh is right! The first shot let her inhibitions go, the second and third made sure they wouldn't come back. Thumping music, alcohol, cute guys, it was a recipe for morning–after Catholic guilt. And for a practicing Catholic like Jennifer it meant a confession session was in her near future. Jennifer didn't care; she would deal with the guilt later.

The bartender had seen this setup before. Young freshman comes in, tries to drink with the big boys, and gets hammered. The fun was just beginning. With sinister intentions, the bartender played *I Touch Myself* on the jukebox to see if he could get something started. It worked like Simon Says. Before long, not only was Jennifer rubbing her legs and stomach to the beat but she had climbed up onto the bar and was gyrating around like a stripper. She had a funny little alcohol induced grin on her face. Her eyes were barely open and she was feeling no pain.

Oh, if Daddy could have seen his little girl!

Chad couldn't believe that his skill at bouncing a quarter into a glass would ever pay this kind of dividend. The bartender was in heaven. He alternated between taking drink orders and looking up Jennifer's skirt. It had a detrimental impact on his tips from the female patrons but it was worth the sacrifice. The catcalls finally brought Sonja and the pool players in from the other room. Sonja couldn't believe her eyes. No less than five guys were looking up Jennifer's skirt while she danced–still grinning.

Sonja rushed over.

"Hey, Sonja," Jennifer said, drunk and giggly, with a wiggly finger wave.

"Get down from there," Sonja yelled.

"Hey, what the..."

"C'mon, get down."

"We're leaving? We just got here," Jennifer said.

Chad, who had been looking up Jennifer's skirt, held out his hand to help her down off the bar. He was the only one at the bar willing to catch her if she fell. Chad was hoping to get one last look up her skirt. He definitely had the best seat in the house. Jennifer showed remarkable balance given her blood-alcohol level and was able to step down from the bar without falling. While they walked toward the exit she stumbled. On the way down she grabbed Chad's shirt to break her fall, ripping off every single button on his Ralph Lauren oxford shirt. She held on for dear life as he watched his buttons bounce away in eight different directions like albino roaches scurrying from the light. At least he still had the small buttons that kept his collar down.

"See! Let's go before you trip and undress someone else," Sonja said taking Jennifer's arm.

"It's cool," Chad said, his shirt open. He tried to look sexy, but his skinny chest couldn't pull it off.

Sonja said, "Yeah, I'll bet. I saw you. You just want to get more peeks up her skirt,"

"I... uh..."

"Yeah, busted.

"Yeah, but look how cute he is," Jennifer said, pawing at him gently with her finger tips. She squeezed the corners of his mouth together. "This is Chaaaad," Jennifer said, burping tequila into his face. Chad grimaced but held firm.

"Who's the party pooper?" Chad asked, trying to hold his breath and talk at the same time.

"The patty paper is Sony-a... Soy-a."

"It's Sonja. Chaaaaad. Just in case you thought I was a DVD or a salty dipping sauce," Sonja said.

"Sun-ya? Chad here is really good at quarters," Jennifer said. "I lost three, no, *four* times."

"It was just three," Chad said.

"What were you drinking?–."

"Beers–." Chad said, quick to respond.

"Te-kee'tha... Hey, that's your roommate's name," Jennifer said.

Sonja shot Chad the look of death. "God, I hope no one else from the school is here," Sonja said.

"Football player dude is here," Jennifer slurred, before she burped in Chad's face again.

"It's cool, there aren't that many people from school," Chad said. "Here, let me help you."

"Okay, let's go," Sonja said.

"See what a nice guy Chaaaad is. I like you Chad, you're nice. Nice Chad. Nice Chad. Look *at meeeeee*, I'm going home with nice nice Chad," Jennifer said.

Somehow, Chad was attracted to Jennifer despite her drunkenness and tequila breath. He wanted to make sure she got back to her dorm room safely. But if she did, he hoped she would remember how he drove her home, helped her to the dorm, propped her up in the elevator and finally got her into bed. Jennifer wouldn't remember any of it. Even though Chad conducted himself like a gentleman, he was sure to remember the color of her thong panties.

10:30 PM

Let's see.

Monet looked at herself in her dorm room mirror. She was assessing herself.

Guys like demure. How do you look demure?

She tilted her chin down then turned her chin a little to the right, then looked up at the mirror.

Nice.

She held the pose for a few seconds then sighed in frustration. Because she was six-one, most guys would be too short to get the full impact of Monet's eyes.

Here I am, a complex black woman, inquire within.

If she were standing, a guy would have to be six-five to get the full impact.

Ray is six-six, but he was obnoxious. Forget about him. Besides it's never a good idea to tailor your pickup strategy to suit one person.

She sat down and looked into a hand mirror, chin down, eyes up. Monet had not tried to look sexy in a mirror since she was 14 years old.

Hmmmm, now we're talkin'. That's nice. Okay, okay, I'll use that when I'm sitting down.

She stood in front of the mirror again and stared at her face, examining every pore. She was beautiful, but was convinced her nose was crooked, her ears were way too big and the mole just above the corner of her mouth had to go. Never mind that the same mark accented the world-class beauty of Cindy Crawford, Marilyn Monroe, and Madonna. Monet wasn't convinced in her own mind she was attractive–which is the single most important part of feeling attractive.

There was no way a guy who was five-eleven would ask a big geek like Shirlie out on a date. No way.

Monet was sinking into a pathetic abyss of delusional envy. She couldn't allow herself to believe in the dating success of her teammates. She had stooped to chiding a six-five woman for being asked out by a five-eleven man.

If a big geek like Shirlie can get asked out, where's my five-eight man?

She went back to practicing her "look."

Guys like women who look inviting. Inviting. Inviting. How do you look inviting?

She tried the head-turned-down-chin-up thing again but it still looked demure. She then tried it with a suggestive grin while craning her neck and pushing her left cheek forward. She even tried to do that Spock thing and raised one eyebrow. It wasn't exactly inviting. It looked more like a turtle with dirt in its eye.

Okay, Okay. Forget that one.

This time she squinted slightly, then winked.

Ah, ahhh? Now that was nice. But should I add the chin down looking up maneuver? No wait, I'll use this one when I'm standing face to face. I'll save the demure thing for when I'm sitting. What about a pucker, no, a pout?

She tried both ways but her pouts looked like mopes. She shook her head both times.

Forget the pout.

She thought about all the conversations she had had with her mother about men, and couldn't recall the one about how to attract a guy.

After a few more practices Monet was satisfied with her new looks; the Sitting Demure and the Standing Inviting Wink with a Spock finish. They were understated. Suggestive, but not sluty.

Perfect.

She thought of Ray. Looking in the mirror she said out loud, "You can't handle all this woman."

Chapter 7

Experience: The Best Teacher

October Seventh, 10:15 AM
Class: The Body Politic
The note read: "I hope you like dark chocolate." Ray reread it, then looked over his shoulder, grinning and nodding at the coed who sent it. He turned around and tapped his friend on the shoulder to gloat about it.

Monet watched the whole thing develop. She sent a note of her own. "I thought you hated chocolate?"

Ray winked at Monet. "Watch this."

Lonnie began the lecture, "A young girl, she's 15, in the tenth grade. She's stuck. She's got a big decision to make. She's pregnant. She's pregnant, but it's 1972–before *Roe v Wade*. *Roe v Wade*, depending on your point of view, legalized abortion and gave women reproductive freedom, or gave them the right to kill their unborn children.

"This ninth grader didn't care about government's place in the womb and didn't think it was murder to end her pregnancy. She was scared. She wanted to be the first person in her family to go to college and she thought having a baby, especially then, would prevent her from reaching her goal. You gotta remember. Back then, women were still expected just to get married and have children. This tenth grader wanted to go to college and start on a profession before settling down. All that was in jeopardy now.

"The guy, I mean the father, another teenager, was acting just as she expected. He denied it was his. Put the responsibility for contraception on her. Accused her of trying to ruin his life. He called her a leech, a gold digger. 'How could you do this to me?' He forgot he was there too.

"The idea of telling her God-fearing parents was out of the question.

"There wasn't much time, she had missed her period three weeks before. Each day that passed narrowed her options. She'd have to do something before her mother figured it out. Her mother already suspected something when she made a peanut butter and dill pickle sandwich.

"She was scared of the shame she would bring to her family if she had a baby. The finger-pointing and shaking heads would be too much to bear." Lonnie looked around the room before continuing.

"It was a difficult decision for her, but she made up her mind to end her pregnancy. That's when she really got scared."

"It was early January of 1973. The Supreme Court had heard each side in *Roe v Wade,* but they had not made a decision yet. There were no Planned Parenthood clinics in her hometown. Your family physician certainly wouldn't perform the procedure even though all doctors are trained in it. She'd heard the stories of kitchen tables, unsanitary needles, and probing hands between her legs. She was scared of being left for dead in a hotel room after paying $750 for the privilege. She was scared of being one of those women stumbling into a hospital emergency room bleeding from an abortion gone bad. She was in the predicament alone–all because she had been too scared to insist that Mr. How-could-you-do-this-to-me? wear a condom. The fear she felt now and the fear she felt about asking him to wear a condom didn't compare. Well, it was too late to insist that he wear one now.

"So how do you find someone with highly specialized training to perform an illegal service underground? Oh, and if things go wrong they would also be convicted of murder. It wouldn't be easy. It was sort of like asking around to find out who could process a ton of cocaine for medical purposes–not an easy question to ask.

"She asked her best friend, but the guy she referred her to gave her the creeps. He wanted $1000, payable up front, and a hotel room. She set everything up, but in the hotel he brought out some tools in a dirty towel. The tools didn't look dirty, but they didn't look sterile either. She backed out. He kept the money.

"She took a chance and confided in her aunt, who was a nurse. She referred her to a doctor who would do the procedure. When she called, he was matter-of-fact, but not cold. She needed to pay $750 up front, but he took the time to describe every aspect of the procedure.

"They met at her aunt's house. They did it on the kitchen table but only because it was the place with the best light. Her aunt held her hand while the doctor described the scrapes and pinches she would feel. It took thirty-five minutes, start to finish. No hangers, no ammonia, no knitting needles.

"Later that evening she woke up in a bed full of blood. Her aunt took her to the hospital where they stopped the bleeding. But as she lay there recuperating, the nurses were nasty to her. They knew. "She hated those nurses for judging her. They didn't know her. Didn't know her future and how this was the best decision for her. Their condemnation wouldn't help her raise her child. Wouldn't be there to provide financial and moral support.

"Back then, this was how most of the one million annual abortions were performed. There were many deaths related to abortions, mostly to women of color. While it wasn't legal and the circumstances were not the best, women found a way to take control and manage their reproduction themselves. Those days may not be far away again given how *Roe v Wade* is constantly being attacked and eroded." Lonnied turned to erase the chalkboard.

"Professor Delaney?"

"Yes."

"You never told us the name of the tenth grader."

Lonnie turned to face the class. Class was almost over.

"Her name was Lonnie Delaney."

Monet ran to catch up with Lonnie as she walked down the hallway after class. They walked in silence together for a few moments.

"Wow," Monet said breaking the silence.

Lonnie continued walking. They made it all the way to the Quad before she said, "There's a lot about me that would surprise you."

"The fact you can't cook didn't surprise me, coach," Monet said.

"That's different," Lonnie said.

"Tell that to your ex-husband, coach," Monet said. They continued their walk across campus. "You ever think about–."

"Sure."

"Well?" Monet said.

"I don't know. At the time I thought it would be the end of my life. Which was stupid because it would have just been the beginning of something different."

"But what are the chances you would have gone to college, played basketball, won two gold medals–seen the world. You probably would have been some secretary answering phones or a waitress taking orders–."

"–Easy."

"Sorry, Coach."

Lonnie sighed, "Maybe. Maybe not. When you're that young you don't know what you want. It's easy to say I wouldn't have been able to do this or that. I didn't go straight to college, I worked for a few years. Who's to say something bigger or better may have come along? Maybe my kid would have grown up to become the Governor of Ohio. Who knows?" They walked along again in silence.

"I would have done the same thing," Monet said.

"To some degree I regret it."

"Why?"

"It was selfish. Because the sum total of why we are here is not based on what you accomplish," Lonnie answered.

Monet said, "But Coach, would you say that if all you did was reproduce? You said so yourself in class, that's what the Feminine Mystique was all about. Women were boxed into reproducing, Supporting their husbands, and raising their children. It wasn't fulfilling. The second women's movement was about adding equality, accomplishment, and ambition to their own lives. You know, meaning."

"Nobody in this country looks at their life like that–in the macro," Lonnie said.

"Isn't that the difference between being in a First World country and a Third World country?"

"Because Third World women are too busy making it from day to day?"

"Too busy feeding ten kids."

"Believe me, they're pushing big ideas, and their children aren't holding them back. American and European women may have made more progress but they haven't cornered the market on feminism," Lonnie said.

"True that."

Lonnie and Monet walked toward her office through campus. Lonnie could tell Monet had more questions about her decision to abort her pregnancy but was reluctant to ask. She felt she owed Monet a more personal answer as to why she choose to have an abortion and not give her some high-minded feminist justification.

Lonnie paused and turned to Monet, "I was just fifteen. I was scared because all I wanted to do was pursue my dream to play basketball. I couldn't see myself doing it with a baby."

"What about your parents?"

"My parents would have been thrilled," Lonnie said. "That's what scared me. I wanted to go to college, travel, and play basketball. They would have said I needed to be home with my baby and they would have been right."

"Maybe you could have done both?"

"I didn't think so. Besides being ambitious requires selfishness."

"You told me that three years ago," Monet said.

"Plus, I was fifteen, which automatically made me selfish."

"You make it sound like, back then, being ambitious was a very heady concept for women."

"It was. Women wanted something more from life. It wasn't that being maternal was meaningless. Mothers make a significant contribution. But every society seems to want women to contribute by staying home and raising good kids. Well, my mother's generation was so bored they fought for the right to expand their contribution to society," Lonnie answered.

"It costs though."

Lonnie nodded, "Sure it does. Having options costs. Thing is people always want what they don't have. Talk to a hundred child-less professional women and 85 percent will tell you they want children. Talk to 100 full time mothers–."

"If you can find 100," Monet said.

"Seventy-five percent will tell you they want to work in some capacity. But they made those choices in their lives. And I made mine. I don't regret that," Lonnie Delaney said. "I don't know about you, but I'd rather have a choice than not."

"You know, a choice was made for me recently that I want to change–."

"–Forget it, I'm not switching you from Ray," Lonnie said, cutting her off at the pass.

"Why not?"

"I see you talking in class."

"He's getting on my nerves," Monet said.

"Then why are you passing notes?"

Monet blushed.

"I see how you look at him," Lonnie continued.

"So."

"You like him and–."

"–I do not."

"I may not have had a date in three years but I know the look of love when I see it," Lonnie said smiling.

"I can't believe you won't switch us," Monet changed the subject. "I'm listening to you, but I don't think that's what you want. What I hear is you saying 'Don't... Stop. Don't... Stop. Don't. Stop. Don't, stop. Don't stop!'"

October Thirteenth
During lunch break, Ray hung out with his teammates Flip Mode, Snag, and Heat Check in the Quad. They sat and watched the usual parade of humanity; jocks to geeks, nerds to goths.

"Damn, that girl is fine," Flip said. "Wait a minute. Wasn't that the same babe that was all in your grill the other day?"

"What babe *isn't* all up in my grill?" Ray said grinning.

Monet was passing by and joined them. "Whassup?"

"Chillin', takin' in the sights," Ray said.

"Yeah, I'll bet," Monet said.

"B.O.D., B.O.D.," Heat Check said, on yellow alert.

The fellas cringed. "Ain't no B.O.D."

Monet asked, "What does B.O.D mean?"

"Body of the day." Monet was sorry she asked.

"Yo, if you can't do a better job of bird doggin' then just don't say nothin'," Ray said. "Besides, I hit that already."

"Me too," Snag said. "I like it when they have learned to suppress their gag reflex."

"We're looking for new ones."

Monet said, "Please tell me you're not talking about what I think you're talking about?"

"The boom shocka-la-ka," Ray said, giving his boys a pound.

"That's disgusting."

"One man's bile is another man's meal," Heat Check said.

"Look at the bottom feeder flossin' the wisdom," Ray said. "I think if you just concentrated on the babes I turn down you might be able to get your groove on."

"I gets mine," Heat Check said.

"He can't get nothin' decent because his breath is always hummin'," Flip Mode said.

"I can smell your breath through your face," Snag said. Everyone doubled over in laughter.

"Cuz, you're a baller on the number three team in the country.

You can't let that kind of mojo go to waste on the but-her-faces you be chasin'," Ray said.

Eric Ueland, a nerdy junior who lived across the hall from Ray, approached the group. "Thanks, man, for the hookup at the Mayor's office."

"No sweat, dog," Ray said.

"What did he do?" Monet asked.

"Ray got me a meeting with the Mayor," Eric said.

"Really," Monet said, surprised.

"Me and Young E are always getting into arguments about politics. Lately, he's been sticking pictures of Reagan on my door."

"He's a tough one to convert, but there's still hope," Eric said. I'm not worried, his tax bracket will convert him to a Republican when he makes it to the NBA."

"Makes sense," Monet said, nodding.

"Eric's a poli-sci major and has a hard-on for that shit, so I called the mayor and I told him I'd like him to meet a friend of mine, that he really wants to do an internship and then I asked if he could find a spot for him. The mayor said, 'no sweat'," Ray said.

"Just like that."

"I told you his daughter wants to hook up with me."

"She don't need his help to do that," Flip Mode said.

"Naw, it's a little more serious than that," Ray said. "She *really* wants to hookup, like, long term. So, I figured, I may not need anything from the mayor but he can hookup my boy up–Boom! I'm gonna go with you just to make sure, aight!"

Eric nodded. A woman walking past winked at Ray. He winked back while Monet looked on.

"Shoo-be da-bang, nephew. Another satisfied customer," Ray said, winking at Monet, then slapping fives with his crew.

Ray's bravado and ghetto diction irritated Monet. "How does a guy who can quote Shakespeare one minute and–."

"–Whoa, whoa, whoa, whoa, whoa," Ray said.

Heat Check laughed. "Shakespeare. Oh okay, your girl here's got jokes."

"Better watch out man, she might start spreading rumors you're a premed major," Flip laughed.

"Or a straight A student."

"See what you did?" Ray said to Monet giving her a silencing look.

"I'll see you guys later," Monet said, fed up and happy to get away from them.

As she walked across the Quad, Monet decided this was going to be the first day of taking control of her social life. No man was safe. She was armed and dangerous, with a quiver full of Cupid's arrows; the sitting-demure stare, the standing squinty-eyed wink with a Spock finish, and a secret weapon she had thought of just the other night.

There weren't that many tall black male students at Del Mar, so a marginally qualified guy only passed by once every five minutes. If she broadened her market she'd have more options, but she wasn't ready to date non-black guys yet.

How about that guy? No, too short... And that one? Ughl, this is the fourth day in a row for that shirt... That one? Sooooo, not my type. Well. Pick one already.

It was presumptuous for Monet to think that someone could resist her Inviting and Demure looks, practiced or not. Monet was a ball player with a shooter's mentality. It never occurred to her that a guy might not be interested. Her motto: To be a great shooter, to be great at anything, you had to have confidence. Confidence breeds presumption.

She was setting her sights. She was locked and loaded to use the standing squinty eye with the Spock finish. *Be patient.* She told herself. That's when she spotted her target.

Captain, studious brotha dead ahead.

Range?

150 feet.

Take us there... Range?

One hundred feet and closing.

A group of brothas were walking to class through the Quad. Monet vaguely recognized them, especially the cute one on the end. Her confidence was surging. She was closing in. Being demure and inviting can wait. It was time for... The secret weapon... of Star Trek proportions.

Status report.

Six-three, I'd say 210 from here, but it's just a guess. Cute smile. One previous contact in the cafeteria; he said to avoid the omelets.

Captain, he's walking with a cluster.

Don't worry, we're only going after the one on the end. Range?

Eighty feet.

Captain, intercepting coed! He's stopping to talk.

His buddies kept walking.

Damn, we'll have to wait for her to clear.
Class is in five minutes.
I know. It's going to be close. Reduce speed, hold at seventy feet.
Aye, aye, holding at seventy.
Monet looked at her watch.
Captain, four minutes to class, we're not gonna to make it.
Maybe we should...
Hold your course, God Damn it! We're gonna wait for this interloper to clear out. Range?!
Seventy feet and holding.
Steady. Steady.
Captain, she's clear.
All ahead full.
Aye, aye, full power.
Range.
Fifty feet, thirty. Twenty.
Steady.
Ten, five.
Steady. Now!...
Monet collided with the unsuspecting guy. She caught him just right, a perfect cross check that sent him flying. Books, paper, and pens flew everywhere.
Captain, turns out he was five-ten, 165.
Uh-oh.
Uh, Captain?... He's pissed.
Monet's plan was to bump the guy and have that lead to a conversation. That was her secret weapon. It worked for Ray. She didn't factor into the equation that she might knock the guy into next week. After all, she was six-one and a solid 185 pounds. The collision left him in the awkward position of facing his friends who were definitely laughing at him and not with him. The only thing worse than being embarrassed in front of your friends is not being able to do anything about it. He thought it was an accident. Monet decided it would be better not to tell him she hit him on purpose.
Things went from bad to worse when Monet stood over him like Ali standing over Liston. His friends laughed. She offered to help him up. He scowled and tried to get up with as much poise as a man can muster after being knocked on his ass by woman. Needless to say, he was in no mood to talk. He quickly tried to gather his pencils along with his pride. Monet apologized and offered to help, but after he refused she stood there for a few

awkward moments, then walked away.

Captain, the secret weapon needs more testing.

Aye... But we have more arrows in Cupid's quiver.

There was only one priest hearing confessions at Our Lady of Lourdes Catholic church. Sonja walked around in small circles, waiting for her turn. She looked up at the cross then back down to her watch. She didn't have much time, she had just finished her four-mile after-practice run and had to be back on campus soon.

The confession was taking a long time. As she waited, Sonja lit a candle, prayed, and lit another candle. She wondered if impatience was one of the seven deadly sins. In her boredom, she tried to name all of them, but didn't get past lust and envy because those were the ones she was most guilty of.

The door opened and a teary-eyed Jennifer emerged. Oops! Sonja added impatience to her list of confessions.

Jennifer and Sonja acknowledged each other with little more than a "What's up?" chin up.

"That must have been a doozie?" Sonja said.

"I had to break it up into two parts. Part one was the bar," Jennifer said.

"The guy who helped me get you home, what's his name?"

"Chad."

"Chad, yeah that's it. He was really nice."

"That was part two."

"You didn't–."

"–No, 'course not... Well, not that night."

"When you weren't drunk."

"Right. He turned out to be really, really nice."

The priest heard their voices and cracked the door open to get a good look at Jennifer in the light. Her story had seriously challenged his commitment to celibacy. He mumbled to himself, "Kids today. I mean, my goodness."

"What else did you do?"

"I have to make amends with myself."

"That the worst. Why can't he just give us a few Hail Marys like when we were kids?"

"I know, making amends with myself makes me feel even more guilty."

They looked over their shoulders at the priest as he quickly closed the door.

"You probably got off easy," Sonja said.

Thirty-five women lined the baseline for walk-on tryouts. They must really love the game, because even if they make the team, walk-ons only play in winning blowouts. And even then, they only go into the game so the home audience can applaud the starters individually as they walk off the court with a minute remaining. Someone has to finish a blowout game. No reason to risk an injury to your scholarship players when there are walk-ons to trot out onto the court during garbage time. The only other time walk-ons play is when coaches use them to motivate the scholarship players.

Walk-ons are the boogiemen for collegiate players.

"Don't play hard and a walk-on's gonna git you. They're gonna take all your minutes, your shots, maybe even your girlfriend. Shhhhhh. Did you hear that?..."

Lonnie had three positions to fill. Division IA women's teams are allowed 15 scholarship positions while the men are only allowed to have 12. Lonnie would consider herself lucky if she was able to find one player out of this lot of thirty-five. She wasn't optimistic.

Before she started practice, Renee handed Coach Delaney a note. It was unusual to get a phone message on the court, so for a moment Lonnie thought it was an emergency. It turned out to be a message from Dan Cantrell, the man she had met at the airport. He was nice enough, fun to talk to, but Lonnie Delaney wasn't willing to give him any time during the season. He didn't know it, but interrupting her practice was not the way to get on her good side, although she liked his ingenuity and his sense of humor.

The message read, "Answer lady, there are only twenty-four hours in the day. If I sent you a broken clock that read eight o'clock would you make time for me one out of the two times the clock would have the correct time? AM or PM?–Dan." It made her smile but it wouldn't work. She balled up the note and tossed it into the wastebasket.

Mbika swayed from side to side, ready. Lonnie blew her whistle to get everyone's attention. Monet was sitting in the stands. She motioned to Mbika who had forgotten her basketball shoes and was standing in her old Jane Fonda Reeboks. She didn't have time to run to her dorm room so she asked Monet to lend her shoes. Monet didn't like the idea but handed them over anyway.

Mbika grew up playing soccer in Nigeria, but began playing basketball when her aunt smuggled her out of the country, with her mother's blessing, to go to New York. She was just 16. Basketball was an American sport; she played it to forget about her country. The tryout began with some fundamental drills. Three-man weave. Dribbling. Shooting. It was a nightmare. All the women had played girls' high school basketball. The reason none of them were playing college basketball became quickly apparent–they didn't have the talent. They were also dreadfully out of shape. By the third set of weaves all but a handful of them were completely exhausted. Lonnie hadn't even made them do any conditioning drills.

Mbika Njai stood out. She ran like a deer. Even though she didn't have great basketball footwork she had quick feet from playing soccer. She had an ugly but effective little eight-foot shot and, most importantly, she finished all her lay-ups. She wasn't the best player of all the women who were trying out, but Renee and Stephanie, the assistant coaches, could tell she had grit. They lobbied Lonnie Delaney to put her on the team. When the player Mbika was guarding scored on successive trips down the court, Mbika dug down and stopped her from scoring another basket for the remainder of the tryout. She was the kind of player Lonnie made room for on her teams. Hard-working role players.

Of the thirty-five women who lined the baseline for two days, only Mbika and Gina Giambi, a shy soft-spoken sophomore, made the team.

Gina had tried out for the team the previous year, but she was the last player who didn't make the cut. She was five-ten, an elongated fireplug of a woman with very long arms. In high school they had called her "Drags," because it looked like her knuckles would hit the floor when she walked. She was one of the better players at high school in San Mateo, California, but her league wasn't that good. This became evident when she played pickup games with the Del Mar women's players and they trounced her.

It was a struggle for Gina's mother to pay the tuition each quarter. She was the first person in their family to go college. Gina was always amazed by her mother's determination to make sure she would have a better life. From the time Gina had started kindergarten, her mother had worked two, sometimes three, jobs to send her to the best private schools. Her mother didn't have much time to spend with Gina. She spent most of her time working long hours or nursing her wounds from her physically abusive loser boyfriends. Gina had gotten used to the cycle; argue, fight, police response, reconciliation, or; argue, fight, hospital visit, reconciliation. At any rate, Gina accepted her mother's sacrifice and made sure she upheld her end by doing well in school. After a long discussion and her mother's blessing Gina chose Del Mar even though it was far more expensive than the University of California.

She wanted to study Hospitality Management and Del Mar had the best program on the West Coast. Her mother still had to supplement her education cost because her student loans and grants were maxed out. Gina didn't like the idea of mortgaging her future with student loans. She worked on her game during the summer months because she hoped to somehow get a scholarship; but it was a long shot to even make the team.

When it was announced that Mbika and Gina had made the cut, they sensed immediately from Coach Delaney there would be no celebration. After all, they had won only the right to practice and sit on the bench.

Chapter 8

Midnight Madness

October Fourteenth
Monet sent her Secret Weapon back to the lab after laying out the little guy in the Quad. It needed side impact adjustments to accommodate the diminutive man. Secret Weapon or not, she still didn't have any dating prospects and was getting tired of hanging out with women all the time. So, it was a pleasant surprise when Milton Worthy asked her out after class.

Milton was nerdy, but tall, with an affinity for argyles and athletic women. Since he was a nerd, the former suited him better than the latter. Milton was definitely an Art Appreciator. The argyle was a bad omen, but Monet still hoped that the confidence it took to ask her out was indicative of his high levels of "male presence."

Milton surprised Monet on their first date when he showed up wearing a sweat suit. It was out of character; Milton always wore college semiformal wear: loafers, khaki pants with argyle sweaters, and matching socks. If it was too hot for a sweater, his argyle socks always matched the color of his oxford shirt.

As he stood in the doorway waiting for Monet she asked, "What happened to the argyle?" He pulled up both of his pants legs revealing his ubiquitous socks.

"Oh... With Nikes... That's a nice look," she said, wishing she could roll her eyes without insulting him.

He smiled. "I figured we could do something you really like..."
Shopping on the first date?

"Play basketball," he said, before she could answer.
Ohhh. He thinks basketball is... Guys are such idiots.

"I guess," she said. "I mean it wouldn't be my first choice."

"It'll be fun," Milton said.

At the gym, Monet dribbled leisurely, she didn't want to get too sweaty especially if they were going out later. She was trying to be flexible by not chastising his choice. She shot a lazy 15-foot jump shot. Short. She noticed him turn to box out. She almost landed on him which made her mad because she didn't want to twist her ankle on a date. Milton rebounded the missed shot, cleared 15 feet then drove hard to the basket for a lay-up. Monet barely stepped into the paint to play defense.

"One," he said, pumped up.

Monet stood there standing near the baseline under the basket, hands on her hips.

This cat really thinks he's doing something.

Milton inbounded the ball and hit a lucky jump shot. The guy had the ugliest jump shot she'd ever seen, although Jamal Wilkes, Pervis Short, and Bill Cartwright would have been proud. As she fished the ball out of the net, she turned and watched him walk to the top of the key with this nerdy pimp strut. Like he was *the man*.

No he didn't.

Ray heard the thud of bouncing basketballs as he was leaving the weight room of the arena. He stood at the end of the tunnel and watched Monet play the geek. He stood back so he wouldn't be seen.

Monet had a decision to make.

I could let him win, boost his little ego or kick his ass and risk him never calling me again.

She would have let him win but the nerdy pimp stroll could not be tolerated.

"Ball up," she said.

Monet stole the ball, picked him clean, then proceeded to score on him every way possible. She beat Milton off the dribble. She scored on him in the post. She scored with jump shots. She scored with a jump-hook.

After Monet missed a shot, Milton grabbed the rebound then tried to drive to the hoop. But in his awkwardness he barreled into Monet knocking her over onto her back. Her head snapped back. Ray caught himself from running out to help her.

Monet dusted herself off. Tough first date. From that point on, Milton didn't score another point. He never even touched the ball except to retrieve it from under the net. The final score was 15-2. Monet sat with Milton as he caught his breath.

Ray smiled and ducked out of the arena before they saw him.

"You wanna go out and get something to eat?" she asked, being nice considering he knocked her off her feet.

"No, thank you, I have a physics exam I have to study for," he said. Milton couldn't even look at her. He was physically and mentally beaten. When she got up to leave he said, "What? No kiss?"

"Please. Win a game first," she said, without breaking stride. It cut him to the core. She knew his kind; all he wanted to do was beat her in a game so he could brag to his buddies that he beat Monet McCasner, the All-American.

Well, not this All-American.

"Aren't you tired of being broke?" Tamika asked.

"It's college. We're supposed to be broke," Sonja answered as she got ready to go to a frat party. Sonja's meticulousness amused Tamika. She sat watching her try on ensemble after ensemble.

"You said something about getting book money," Tamika said, after a few minutes.

"We've been in school for three weeks, and you didn't pick up your book money?"

"I didn't say I didn't pick it up. I cashed the check."

"You did buy books with it, right?"

"Yeah, that's them right over there," Tamika said.

The books were in pristine condition on her shelf. "But I thought I heard you say that we could sell them, and get our money back," Tamika said.

"Yeah, but that's at the end of the quarter, after you've read them."

"Hmmmm, what if you could rent them out or something, you know, cut out the middle man."

"Then that would make you a bookstore, and not a student-athlete."

Tamika's brain was working hard. "Not if you just focused on the most popular books, the ones everyone needs. There must be a way to make a little extra money off of books."

Sonja didn't answer to avoid being recruited as an accomplice.

"I ain't never been this broke."

"The NCAA likes it that way," Sonja said.

The phone rang. Sonja answered it, then held it out for Tamika.

"Who is it?" Tamika said.

"I don't know, it's a guy. An older guy."

Tamika took the phone, and rolled her eyes. "You're supposed to ask who it is... Whassup?... Oh, hi..." Tamika turned her back, and took a couple of steps away from Sonja. Sonja got the hint, and dug into her closet to look for something to wear to the party.

Victor Bitinour was just checking in with his potential clients. For Victor, Tamika was a safety, a player to have on his roster just in case all the others fell through. The women's professional leagues were still in their infancy, so there wasn't a market for her basketball talent yet. But if all his other players fell through, he would at least be able to say he had a player in the WNBA. Victor prided himself on being both prudent and ahead of the curve. That's why he was giving Tamika so much attention.

"...Thanks. You were here?... Yeah, I know... Hell yeah, I'm still interested... Well, I'll do my best...Okay, I'll talk to you later... Okay, bye."

Sonja listened to Tamika's conversation but couldn't tell what they were talking about.

October Fourteenth, 11:50 PM

College kids were jumping over themselves trying to get on national television. Dick Vitale, college basketball's biggest fan, was broadcasting in the middle of a six-foot-wide mosh pit. He was in the eye of the storm. The cameraman valiantly followed him as the frenzied college kids bumped into him, polished his bald head, and gave him the 'ole rabbit ears. Vitale was unflappable in his reporting.

"It's showtime baby! Midnight Madness. The start of the college basketball season. We're *live* in San Francisco at Del Mar University, where the Runnin' Rhinos are ranked number three in the country. This year Del Mar is flat out loaded with high flyers, and PTP'er, Ray Riddick. Look for them to march through the WCC. Coach Warlich's Runnin' Rhinos will be right there come tournament time. Indianapolis, baby, the Final Four!!! On the women's side, guess who emerged out of nowhere? I'll give you a hint: her freshman year she was an All-American, and led Ohio State to the 1992 championship game in Los Angeles. That's right, Monet McCasner! She's reunited with Coach Lonnie Delaney, and let me tell you something, they think they can get into the NCAA tournament this year. We're talkin' sleeper, baby! You talk about a great story. If the Lady Runnin' Rhinos can get to the Big Dance in her first year back coaching, it would be the feel-good story of the year. So, forget about the World Series! Forget about football and hockey! Forget about the college players of yesteryear playing in the NBA! It's time for the start of the most exciting sport in all the land— college basketball. And that's excitement with a capital E!"

The men's and women's teams trotted onto the basketball court in front of 15,225 screaming Runnin' Rhino fans. Both teams were dressed in their warm-up tear away pants, and shooting shirts. Home game uniforms underneath. Crimson trimming cream.

The men and women entered from opposite sides, and jogged around the court, meeting at half-court. Shortest to tallest. Being one of the tallest on the team, Monet ran in the rear with the forwards and centers. Roxy led the way because she was the shortest on the team. Monet didn't like the visual. People might think Roxy would be the starting point guard, the team leader. Monet had other plans.

Students held up signs hoping the ESPN cameras would put them on national television. "You can't beat horniness," read one sign.

Some students tried to lead a call-response chant. "We be horny yes we do; we are horny, how 'bout you!"

They couldn't get the cheer going, probably because of their improper use of a transitive verb. You'd expect that from high school kids but not at the college level. At any rate, they were too clever for family television programming. The director in the ESPN truck visually edited the content of every shot before going live with it. He steered away from the kids waving their middle fingers among other obscene gestures. He focused on foam fingers, unicorned face painters, and the occasional buxom coed. Amid all the chaos, one racy sign slipped through and was shown to one million late night viewers.

"Jennifer, How 'bout another Table Dance?"

"And now, your Del Mar University Ruuuunniin' Rhiiiiiinnooooos. For the women, at point guard, a senior and the only three time team captain in Del Mar history, Roxy Davidson."

As the team stood on the court waiting to be introduced, Shirlie was smiling from ear to ear. Monet thought she was amused by the sign, but after following her eyes realized she wasn't looking at anything in particular. She was just really, really happy. Inexplicably happy. The kind of happy where you had to ask, "What the hell are you so happy about?"

"They've been doing these Midnight Madness things since I've been here and this is the first time we've been invited to participate," Shirlie said.

The crowd gave the count down. "Five! Four! Three! Two! One!" The clock struck 12:00 AM. Basketball time! "Hoop! Hoop! Hoop! Hoop! Hoop!"

According to NCAA rules, college basketball teams may not start practicing before midnight, October 15th. Coaches used to start the first practice at their usual time–*that afternoon.*

In 1971, coach Lefty Driesell started practice at 12:01 AM as a motivational tool at the University of Maryland. "While other teams are sleeping we're taking the first steps toward winning a national championship," he'd tell his players. When other coaches learned what the Old Left-hander was doing, they started conducting their own midnight practices. Then ESPN started reporting live from different universities in each of the four time zones. What started as a simple motivational tool had become a college basketball phenomenon complete with satellite feeds, talking heads, and commercials. Only in America can people figure out a way to make money celebrating the first day of college basketball practice.

Forrest Haneline, Clint Warlich, the men's coach, and Lonnie Delaney stood on the sideline watching the players run through a lay-up drill. The screaming fans made it difficult to hear anything. A ferocious dunk by one of the men made it impossible.

"*Hear that. That's what it's all about!*" Haneline yelled at Coach Warlich standing to his left. "Crazed students, fawning alumni, national television, it all means..."

"What did you say?" Lonnie asked. It was so loud she had to nudge him to get his attention.

Haneline turned to her and rubbed his thumb over his index and middle finger.

"Oh..." She had no idea what the hell he was talking about, something about money.

Haneline was in heaven. "With that number three ranking, the sky's the limit." Haneline never turned to address Lonnie, so she spoke to him, more to give the appearance she was in on the conversation. Haneline said to Warlich, "We should do well in alumni donations and ticket sales."

"Well? We're gonna *sell out* every game. Just look at this crowd."

"We've got five games on CBS. We'll have to divide the proceeds with the rest of the WCC, but the exposure fuels the licensing sales."

Ray threw down an I-can't-believe-what-I-just-saw dunk. He bounced the ball about 8 feet high ran under it, jumped, caught the ball in midair, crossed it through his legs, brought it up and threw it down over his shoulder with the left hand after a half twist.

Lonnie waited for a break in the conversation. "Have you had a chance to call around to explore the possibility of getting us a radio contract?"

Haneline shook his head then turned back to Warlich.

Heat Check threw down a straight power dunk, pedestrian by any standard. The crowd raised nines, and tens. A couple of clever students turned their nine cards upside down, which caught on.

"Are we still doing the three-point contest? It's getting a little late," Lonnie said, still trying to get in on the conversation.

They all looked at their watches. It was 12:35 AM.

"You still wanna do it?" Warlich said to Lonnie Delaney.

"Yes, how 'bout your best against my best," she answered. "I have someone who could give your guy a run for his money."

"My guy is Ray. You got someone better than a future NBA lottery pick?"

"Tell you what, I'll bet you a week's worth of 6:00 AM practices that we win," Lonnie said, confidently.

"You got it," Warlich smiled.

Five minutes later, Lonnie had gathered the team together. "They challenged us to a three-point shooting contest."

Everyone perked up until Lonnie selected Monet to represent the women's team. Roxy and Clio wanted to shoot. As the players with the most seniority on the team they wanted to represent the team against the men.

Ray met Monet at midcourt. "You hear that?... My fans." He basked in the applause. "The Top Gun plaque will go nicely with the other three I already have."

"Only plaque you're gonna get tonight is on your teeth," Monet said, smiling broadly to the crowd.

"We'll see. I'm not one of those argyle-wearing geeks you can beat up on." He winked devilishly then swaggered off to his end of the court. It took a moment for Monet to realize he was referring to her date with Milton.

They each stood exactly nineteen feet, nine inches from the hoop. Three-point land. There were five racks of basketballs carrying five balls each, one on each baseline, two from the foul line extended, one rack from the top of the key. Each ball was worth one point, with the last ball painted crimson and cream. The "money ball" was worth three-points. They had 45 seconds. To shoot all the balls.

Monet was confident she could win, despite the underwhelming support of her teammates. She was really motivated to beat Ray now.

Lonnie had confidence in Monet. She knew a victory over Ray would be the perfect way to win over some fans, maybe get a few hundred to come watch the women play. They would come out to watch that tall point guard who had outshot Del Mar's surefire NBA lottery pick. Lonnie trusted Monet and wasn't about to let someone from last year's team screw up the opportunity to make a positive impression.

Monet looked back at Ray just before they started shooting. Ray put down the ball then strangled himself with both hands. He laughed at her before turning to inspect the balls on his rack.

She *really* had to win now.

Haneline was sitting alone at mid-court. Lonnie Delaney walked over to him. "I know this isn't the best time but as you can see I've got fourteen players and only twelve scholarships. I want to give my two walk-ons scholarships."

"Can't do it. Numbers," Haneline said.

"The NCAA allows 15 for women."

"Yeah, and only 12 for men."

"And so."

"We don't have two extra scholarships in the budget."

"But–."

"Not in the budget," Forrest Haneline said, ending the discussion.

Ready. Go! 45. 44. 43...

After the first rack Ray and Monet were tied. By the third rack Monet was leading by one point.

Fourth rack. Ray made only two of five, missing the money ball. As the crowd watched, they groaned with every one of their favorite's missed shots. Monet sensed the opportunity and made three of the first four shots, but she needed the money ball. She took a deep breath.

Shot. *Yesssss.*

They both ran to the fifth and final rack of balls. Monet had a commanding 16-11 lead. The way Ray was shooting, all Monet needed to do was make two or three shots and she would win. Lonnie winked at Warlich, confident Monet was going to win. Monet made only one of the first four. On the other court Ray had found his stroke. He made two, then three, then four shots in a row. A crescendo of crowd noise rose with every one of his made shots.

Monet needed to make the money ball. Nineteen-nine wasn't that far away. It was just one shot. She had done it thousands of times before. As she grabbed for her last shot she made sure everything was perfect; feet set, shoulders square, "take your time," elbow in, palm spread, release, follow through. Ray released his shot right after Monet. Both shots arched simultaneously. Leading only by two, Monet needed this shot to put the game out of reach. She could miss and still win, Ray could not. Monet's shot rattled in then out.

Ray's shot? *Ch-kh.*

Monet couldn't believe it. Everything was perfect. Her feet, elbow, shoulders, they were all perfect. But the ball didn't go in. She was pissed because she failed at taking that NBA-sized ego down a few notches. Surprisingly, Ray was a gracious winner. They shook hands at mid-court, like tennis players. He even presented her to the crowd so she could get her own share of the applause.

When he wanted to the guy could really turn on the charm.

Afterward, Monet walked over and slumped in her chair next to her teammates. She hated to lose. She always took it hard. Sonja and Tamika gave her a dap of support as she sat slumped in her chair. Roxy was still pissed about not being selected to shoot.

Down the sideline, Coach Warlich held out six fingers to Lonnie, then pretended to sleep on his praying hands.

It was going to be an early morning for the Lady Runnin' Rhinos.

Chapter 9

Crimson vs. Cream

October Fifteenth, **5:45 AM**

"What's up with this six in the morning practice?" Tamika complained.

Monet was reading the newspaper, killing time before heading to practice. She had finished reading the *Sporting Green and* was flipping through local news when she read that Stinky had attacked another college coed at San Francisco State. The article said the victim was on an athletic scholarship but did not state which team. Monet thought for a moment then read a story about voter registration. That's when she remembered she forgot to apply for an absentee ballot in Ohio.

Jennifer ran into the locker room and fell playfully into Sonja's lap, giggling, and panting.

"Get off of me," Sonja said, looking down at Jennifer's head which was in her lap.

"Awwwl... Why didn't you guys come to the Gamma Alpha party after Midnight Madness."

"Because it was one-thirty in the morning and we have six o'clock practice." Sonja said.

"Guess what we did?"

"Well, you didn't take a shower, that's for sure," Sonja said, pushing Jennifer onto the floor.

Monet said, "You guys better hurry up."

"We went over to the Lambda Nu sorority house then we TP'd the Beta Omega frat house across the street," Jennifer finished.

"You're just a freshman, you're not even part of the sorority," Clio said from across the room.

"I know, they were totally cool. So, of course the Betas got all bent out of shape to do something because, I mean, we *really* TP'd their house. You know what they did?... Go ahead guess..." Jennifer was up and changing her clothes. "Panty raid."

The entire team looked over. And sure enough, she wasn't wearing any.

"Oh... my... gawd," Sonja said, mortified.

"Isn't college the best," Jennifer laughed.

"The hot water's out again," Kendra said, peeking out from the row of face bowls. Last year's players groaned. They knew the drill.

"It'll warm up by the time practice ends. Hopefully, anyway."

"What's up with these early practices?" Jennifer asked, repeating Tamika's question.

"We've always had practice this early," Kendra answered.

"Every day?"

"Every day. The men have the gym from three to five and volleyball has it from six to eight. Morning's the only spot available that fits in with everyone's class schedule," Shirlie said to Tamika amidst the locker room chaos.

"Is the water going to warm up?" Tamika asked.

"That's a good question."

Clio, the jokester, walked up behind Jennifer. "Hey baby, can a sista get a table dance?"

"You see that sign last night?" Kendra asked.

"What sign?"

"Awww, you missed it."

"There was the Dick Vitale sign and the 'Nothing beats being horny' sign, then there was the 'Jennifer, Can I get a table dance?' sign."

"No way."

"Way!" Clio said, doing her best imitation of a valley girl, complete with hair flip.

"They kicked him out."

"Yeah. *After* he got on television, Angela saw it on ESPN in her dorm room."

Jennifer started freaking out. She didn't care about what her teammates thought, she was concerned that her father had seen it on ESPN. There would be hell to pay and, no doubt–confession. She certainly didn't think the events of one drunken night would get national exposure. For now, Jennifer remained silent.

Monet ignored the discussion altogether. She was still hurting from her loss to Ray in the three-point shootout.

Mbika tapped Monet on the shoulder. She had forgotten her team issued sports bra in her dorm room. She didn't have a replacement so she asked Monet. Just like her shoes she didn't have time to retrieve it so Monet lent her one, even though she was more than a little annoyed.

Kendra said to Monet, "Hey sharpshooter. You played for Coach before, what was it like?"

Looking up, Monet said, "Always look her in the eye."

"Huh?"

"You'll see. With Coach, it's not always about basketball... Oh, and be on time, for everything."

Everyone looked at the clock. It was at least a three-minute walk from their locker room in the student center to the arena and it was 5:50 AM already. End of conversation. Everyone hurried to make it to the arena on time.

Roxy strolled into the locker room.

"You better hurry, Coach won't like you being late for the first practice," Monet said, trying to be nice.

"It's just the first practice. That Midnight Madness crap didn't end until 1:15," Roxy said.

"Which means you didn't get to bed until, what, 4:00?" Clio asked gathering her things.

"I'm just tellin' you," Monet said, one last time. And with that she left. Roxy would learn soon enough that when Lonnie said 6:00 AM, she meant 6:00 AM.

All the players made it to the court on time, except Roxy, who was late by only one minute. Lonnie Delaney made her run two laps for every minute she was late for every player and coach on the team–thirty laps, due now. That got everyone's attention. Monet shrugged her shoulders at Roxy just before she started her laps.

Lonnie said, "Huddle up. I expect everyone to be on time. No excuses. Excuses are for the weak-minded. Oversleep, broken nails, PMS. You leave all that girlie shit in the locker room. From the moment you step on the court I expect you to be ready to play and giving 100 percent. The first thing we're gonna do is teach you how to play this game as a team. Together..." She stopped and looked around. "Where's Gina?"

"I'm here, coach," Gina said, in a mousy voice, stepping from behind Kendra.

"Stand someplace where I can see you. Okay, so where was I? Yes, together... And if all goes well, you'll begin to think like a team and if that goes well, you'll win like a team. I've watched your films from last year. Ladies, we have *a lot* of work to do." She stopped again. "Oh before I forget, Jennifer, what was that thing about a table dance last night?"

Everyone snickered as Jennifer turned red.

"You don't know what a table dance is, Coach? It's when..."

"I know what a table dance is, Clio, thank you. I mean, was it some fool trying to be funny–." Lonnie asked.

"–Or was it a regular customer," Clio added, laughing.

"Stop it Clio," Lonnie said. "Listen to me. This may sound corny, but people will only respect you if you respect yourself."

Roxy, Kendra, and Clio rolled their eyes at another coaching platitude. What is it about coaches and clichés? They all seem compelled to use the game as a metaphor to teach life lessons. When they ran out of metaphors they used analogies and similes to demonstrate the parallelisms of succeeding in basketball as a corollary to succeeding in life.

"Players understand when I say respect the university, respect your teammates, and respect your opponents. But, guess whom they always forget?"

There was a long silence so Monet answered, "Themselves."

"Right. If you don't respect yourself, no one else will." Lonnie turned and gave Jennifer a long hard look.

Roxy completed her laps and joined the huddle. The team went through Lonnie's base play. Roxy knew her starting position at point guard was in trouble when the guards separated from the centers and forwards and Monet was in her group.

The base play called for down picks from the high post, flare outs with backdoor cuts on one side, a weak-side pick to create a rotating three-point option. Simple.

In English, it meant the biggest players, the center and power forward, would start at the free throw line and come down the key to set screens for the shooting guard and small forward. The plan was to stand right next to or behind the defender, so when the offensive player made her move the screener would be in the defender's way–the down pick. The guard and forward would thoretically run to an open space near the sideline–the flare out. If that were open, they would have an uncontested 15-foot shot. If the defender got around the pick and overplayed the flare out, the guard could cut back to the hoop–the backdoor cut–and hopefully get a lay-up. And if none of those options materialized, after the pass to the sideline the point guard could set a screen; on the opposite side she'd pass the ball–weak-side pick–where the shooting guard or small forward would have an open three-point shot around the top of the key–rotating three-point option.

Down pick. Flare out. Backdoor. If there's nothing, weak side pick, kick it out for a three. Simple. And that was just the base play. Later, Lonnie would add drive and kicks, run outs, high post sets, pick and rolls, and that's not counting the individual moves players could create for themselves.

They practiced the play in individual groups, then came together as a team. The first time they ran it, the players caromed off each other like lottery balls.

"No, no, no," Lonnie said. They needed to go back to the basics. Lonnie made the team run three-man weaves. Run down the court, pass the ball, switch places with the receiver, pass the ball, repeat, until you get to the end of the court when whoever has the ball last shoots a lay-up. Fundamental basketball. It's the same weave that's taught to third-grade girls and practiced at every level of basketball, including the NBA.

Monet's threesome included Tamika and Sonja. They had flawless execution. Up and back, crisp passes, no dribbles, finished lay-up. Perfect. Roxy noticed how Lonnie looked at Monet when she ran the drill. Well-played basketball always put a little grin on Lonnie's face. "That's how you run a weave," she said, clapping her hands in that way-to-go coaching staccato.

Roxy ran the weave with her crew, Kendra and Clio. Their passes were sloppy and they missed the first lay-up–a cardinal sin. On the way back, Roxy passed to the wing too far out for Kendra to make the lay-up. She had to take three steps to make up the distance and make the lay-up.

Lonnie's mood changed quickly. "On a fast break, you have to either make that pass sooner or hold it so the defender has to come to you. The objective is to make the defender commit *before* making the pass. Pass too soon and the cutter will be in no-man's land and ripe for an offensive foul. Pass too late and there's no angle and it's easier for the defender to play two people at once. That could be a four point turnaround. Think about it. No lay-up, an offensive foul on the collision, and if they're in the bonus, free throws the other way. You got it?" Lonnie turned to Roxy. Make the defender commit so no one gets hurt. Do it again." They ran it again with better results.

Crimson jerseys versus cream–likely starters versus reserves, respectively. Crimson team: Monet point guard, Roxy shooting guard, Clio small forward, Kendra power forward, and Shirlie playing center. The cream team: Gina shooting guard, Mbika small forward, Tamika power forward, Sonja center. Down pick. Flare out. Backdoor. Opposite side pick. Kick it out for a three. It seemed so simple but their execution was still a mess. They looked like bumper cars.

On one play, Monet was set to take an open jump shot but when Roxy was open under the basket on a backdoor cut, Monet flicked a pass at the top of her jump. Roxy was wide open. But she turned her back to rebound the shot and the ball bounced off her head. Everyone froze after Lonnie's whistle.

"Monet, good pass. Roxy. You were wide open."

"I know, coach."

"You were open, but you gotta catch 'em with your hands, not your head. You gotta keep your head in the game."

"She is," Clio whispered to Kendra.

"Where's Gina?" Lonnie asked.

"Here I am coach," Gina whispered, stepping out from behind Big Shirlie.

They ran the pick and roll. The Crimson team, the likely starters, were on defense. Poor execution all around. The Cream team kept scoring on a jump shot over the top of the defense. Gina, who was playing offense, always shied away from setting a good solid pick. She looked more like a matador avoiding a charging bull. Even so, the offense kept scoring. Lonnie blew her whistle.

"Tamika, what is your assignment on defense?"

"Coach, shouldn't I stop the person I'm guarding from scoring?"

"Well that's true, but you're only half right. It's about team defense. Whether they score on Monet or Clio, they're still scoring against *us*. We're all trying to stop that, right? So, it really doesn't matter whether it's your man or someone else's man who scores."

*   *   *   *

Lonnie blew her whistle.

"Okay, two-minute break."

"Freshmen. I want Gatorade."

"I want water... and a towel."

Tamika, Sonja, Jennifer, Gina, and Mbika all turned to Lonnie. "You don't expect me to get it, do you?" she said.

They all put their heads down and fetched the upperclassmen's orders. The rest of the team sat down and relaxed. The break lasted five minutes.

It was only the first practice, and Monet was making a far better impression than Roxy. Roxy knew it, too. She still wasn't sure if Monet's pass that hit her in the head was malicious.

"The last thing we'll do today is free throws. Five in a row, but no one can leave until we're all done."

The drill proved to be more difficult than it sounded. Monet shot five and made five. Perfect form. Everyone eventually made five in a row, except Mbika. It didn't take long before she was the only one shooting. Everyone was getting impatient. They were tired. They smelled. They all wanted practice to end so they could shower and get on with the rest of the day. Mbika felt the pressure, which only made her miss more shots. Just when Lonnie Delaney was going to end practice. Roxy sucked her teeth and shook her head after Mbika missed another shot. Everyone started giggling.

Lonnie was livid. "Hey... *Hey*!!! Remember what we're trying to do here. We're one team, with one goal. No wonder you lost so many games last year. You don't support each other. The only way we'll be successful this year is if we do this together. You hear me? Together. Together, together, together. Since you're so bored waiting for your teammate to finish her shooting, I'll give you something to do while you wait. Start running until Mbika finishes."

When Lonnie Delaney blew her whistle the team reluctantly trudged off to run around the court.

The pressure on Mbika to make five shots in a row increased with every lap. As they passed, each player shot a cold look at Mbika, their tormentor. Scholarship players don't like to run for the mistakes of walk-ons. Mbika managed to make four shots in a row. The entire gym hoped she would make the fifth shot and put them out of their misery. Nope. Everyone exhaled, put their heads down and kept running. Mbika started at zero.

Mbika ended up shooting 115 free throws before making five in a row. Her teammates ran an extra 51 laps, three miles all totaled.

They were pissed.

Arena after practice, 8:15 AM

"Brown Nosers always have something to say in private," Roxy said to Clio and Kendra, as she watched Monet talk to Lonnie on the sideline after practice.

"You're just mad," Kendra said.

"Getting your butt kicked in practice will do that," Clio added.

"Those extra laps didn't help," Roxy said.

It was only 8:15 AM. Roxy was thinking of something sinister. Shirlie saw it in Roxy's eyes.

Monet walked back to the locker room alone. Ray was waiting for her in the hallway outside of the weight room.

"Good first practice," he said.

"Sure," Monet said.

"Kicked some butt. And that dime that bounced off Roxy's head had me rollin'."

Monet smiled.

I liked that one too.

"Yeah, she's pissed about that and a lot of other things she can't stop on the court," Monet said.

Ray said, "Watch out for her though. Kendra and Clio too. Real talk. They pull tricks."

"Yeah, okay. You going to work out?"

"Just finished. Been here since 5:45."

"Really."

"What? A brotha can't work on his game? Pound iron for thirty, handle the ball for fifteen, run stairs for fifteen, shoot for thirty. Every day by six o'clock. You wanna join me?"

"I'm a little busy at six," Monet said.

"Aight, then. Gotta hit my stairs," Ray said, as he trotted off.

"Real talk. Watch out for those three." As he turned around, he caught her looking at his behind.

Damn. He was fine.

"Uh... Hey, whas 'up?" she stammered.

Ray was grinning as he turned the corner.

In the locker room, a solemn Mbika sat at her locker as angry teammates passed by. She was on the verge of tears. She held out the sweaty sports bra she had borrowed. Monet waved her off, then turned to console her. "It's all right."

"Everybody hates me," Mbika said, sniveling. At the moment Monet couldn't argue with her.

"Just do us all a favor."

Mbika looked up, hopeful. "I should practice my free throws–."

"–You should practice *making* your free throws," Roxy said, as she stormed in, headed straight toward Mbika. Everyone stepped aside to give her plenty of room. "I don't know how you're gonna do it! I don't care how you do it! But I ain't gonna run extra laps 'cause a damn walk-on can't make five free throws."

Monet intervened. "Roxy she feels bad enough." Mbika tried to hold it together. Just as she opened her mouth to apologize Monet pushed a towel in her face then turned to Roxy. "Get to practice on time before you talk about running," Monet said.

"This is between me and Ma-Brick-a."

"It's Mbika," Mbika said, looking at Monet and then Roxy. She hadn't noticed the rising tension between them. "It's Mbika," still trying to get Roxy's attention. Monet stood up. "Umm, excuse me, it's..."

"Okay! She knows," Monet said, impatiently, eyes locked on Roxy.

"Stay out of it Monet," Roxy said. "In fact, you need to slow your roll or your season's gonna be one long nightmare."

Clio, Kendra, and Shirlie each looked at each other, knowing what that meant.

"Psshh, I've carried sorrier teams all by myself," Monet said.

That didn't come out right.

The entire team rightfully took it as an insult.

Just as Roxy took a step toward Monet the coaches entered the room. Everybody scattered.

Lonnie held up an embroidered basketball patch."Regarding the team captain. I don't want to just choose someone so next week we're going to vote for one."

Monet and Roxy exchanged glares.

Lonnie Delaney continued, "Every week and after every game I give out game balls to players who play well, support their teammates, or just work hard. Today's game balls go to Monet for working so hard and to Mbika for shooting terribly under pressure, but not giving up."

The team clapped halfheartedly, but only after Lonnie began clapping herself.

Jennifer turned on the shower. "Eeoooww, the water is still cold."

"It will warm up in another half hour," Kendra said. "Don't worry, you'll get used to it by December." They all undressed, showered, and changed so they could get to class.

Sonja put on her running shoes. "You are not going running?" Tamika asked.

"Yes, I am. Wanna come?"

"Girl, please."

*   *   *   *

Bill Willmont was spreading rumors that Monet liked girls. Liked girls in that way. To Billy, Monet was an affront to his budding male superiority which was having trouble taking root with all the school yard butt kicking he had endured from Monet. Using his boyhood adolescent logic he figured the worst thing you can call a boy is a sissy–a girl in effect. Billy figured, since Monet played ball just as good as any boy she would be vulnerable to the ridicule of liking girls. It was pathetically impotent slander.

It was Billy's sister, Sandra, who had to show her older brother a thing or two about character assassination. Never send in a boy to do a girl's job. Girls know how to strike at the core. She had her brother simply draw a picture of Monet with a mustache. That was it. They drew mustached characters on all of Monet's stuff; her lunch bag, her book covers, on her desk, little mustached Monets, even on her pencils. They were relentless.

Monet knew it was Sandra, but suffered in silence to avoid having the entire seventh and eighth grades turn against her.

Billy and Sandra got really good at it. Stick-figure Monets playing basketball–with a mustache. A stick-figure Monet head winking–with a mustache. A mustached Monet kissing another girl. When Monet tried to change book covers they just wrote inside the pages. She didn't know what to do.

It wasn't until her father innocently complimented her on her doodling that things changed. He noticed a well-drawn Monet rising for a dunk, arms and legs spread, like the Jordan logo–with a mustache. He encouraged her to keep up her art because her mustached-lady series expressed the frustration and duality of today's modern woman.

Monet broke down and cried.

Her father thought it was teenage angst. It wouldn't be the first time one of his compliments had made her cry. He didn't say anything else. He certainly didn't want to spoil her interest in art simply by liking it. After she told him what was going on at school he just shook his head.

"So what're you gonna do?" he said. Just like that, no emotion. No, "Aww sugar, let me fix it for you." No, "I'm gonna call the Willmonts and straighten this out."

"I don't know," she said.

He paused, then lowered his voice dramatically. "You gotta be willing to go your own way..."

"I do that."

"And not care what other people think. That's the hard part."
he said. _"Try that,"_ knowing his daughter's resolve, whoever was
tormenting her with stick figure art was going to be in big trouble.
Once Monet was armed with her father's wisdom, the Willmonts
became powerless. She even co-opted their taunting art by making
stick figures of herself that were far more creative. She showed
them to friends, who began making stick figures of themselves. Soon
all of the eighth graders of St. Ignatius elementary school were drawing   stick   figures   of   their   parents,   teachers,
athletes, politicians. It had become a way to express themselves
and their teen angst–Egyptian style.

Sandra and Billy tried other ways to make Monet feel bad, but
they had lost their power over her. Monet's confidence deflected
their feeble attempts like a superhero overpowering mere mortals.

Chapter 10

Eating With the Enemy

October Fifteenth
Class: The Body Politic
Mbika walked to the front of the class. By the time she was twelve she had lived through a civil war, survived famine prompted by her corrupt government, and even stared down a hungry lion when she got lost walking to school. Mbika had lived through the sort of experiences her classmates only watched on The Discovery Channel. As she stood at the podium her experience was written on her face.

"They held me down. I screamed for my mother. I knew she was in the other room, but she did not come. I was only thirteen years old but I was strong. I played soccer all the time. So, when they tried to open my legs, they couldn't. I held them closed. The old lady looked at her friend. She was helping her. She said, 'We are gonna need some help with this one. Go get her mother. Maybe she can calm her down.'

"They got my mother. I remember while I was laying there I felt so happy. My mother was going to save me. But my mother didn't save me. She told me I had to have the Cutting. I had to have the Cutting so I can get married one day. So my husband will know I am pure. It is our tradition. I must uphold my family's honor.

"I didn't care. I didn't want The Cutting. The knife didn't look clean. The old woman said it would be okay. I didn't believe her. All the women in my family have problems when they give birth. My mother's sisters say because of the Cutting the baby tears you down there. The skin is too... what did she say?.. She say the skin is too hard. It does not stretch.

"The old woman say, 'I am only going to cut here.' She pinched me down there to show me where. My legs were still closed. I kicked her. I didn't mean to, but it hurt when she did that. I did not want the Cutting. I wanted my mother to save me, but she didn't.

"'Such a silly girl,' the old woman said, rubbing her nose.

"I didn't care. I did not want the Cutting.

"I am from the Samburu tribe in Kenya. Since I left Kenya I learned that I am one of the lucky ones. It is different for different countries. In Nigeria, Kenya, Liberia, and Egypt about 43 percent of women have had the Cutting, but in Djibouti and Somalia it is as high as 97 percent.

"I am lucky because I only had the clitoridectomy; my clitoris was amputated. Some have the excision, when the clitoris and labia minora are removed. Worst of all is the infibulation. That is when after the excision of the clitoris and the labia minora, the labia majora are cut or scraped away to make raw skin, then they are held together until they heal, either by stitching the edges of the wound or by tying the legs together. As the wounds heal, scar tissue joins the labia and covers the urethra and most of the vaginal orifice, leaving only a small opening that's as small as a matchstick so you can pee and have your period. That is why the baby tears the skin. One of my mother's sisters died when she gave birth. In Somalia and Djibouti, almost all of the women have this type of cutting. They also get lots of infections because everything is so plugged up.

"The custom is supposed to reduce your desire to have sex. To keep you pure. After the Cutting, you don't want to have sex because it's painful. That is how women keep their family honor, by being pure, but why does honor have to be so painful?

"Why, I asked my mother, 'Why do I need this?' She said, 'To ensure our virtue. So you can get married. So you will be clean. Without the Cutting you are not clean and no man will marry you.'"

The class was a aghast. Mbika paused for a long time as they stared at her.

"Do not look at me like that. Do not judge me or my country for our traditions. In the West, you are hypocrites. In the United States, you are hypocrites. You think you know what's right for everyone around the world. In the West, they call the Cutting Female Genital Mutilation, but women here do the same thing, with their breast implants, their BOTOX and collagen, their liposuction. It's just a different kind of cutting. You think surgery will make you beautiful, that you can just take a pill and everything will be all right. What's the difference? Men here take Viagra. Well, the men in my country *do not need* Viagra. So don't judge me and my traditions," she said, looking around the room.

"When I have a child I do not want my daughter to have the Cutting and I will fight to the death to stop it. That's my story."

Lonnie had tears in her eyes when she said, "Thank you, Mbika."

After the oral reports, Lonnie silenced the class for five minutes. She wanted everyone to reflect on the stories with their eyes closed. After five minutes of silence she guided their thoughts by making vivid visual suggestions; dark rooms, unheard screams, excruciating pain, crushing fear, the relentless assault on their dignity with inexplicable traditions held by people who are supposed to protect you. She wanted her students to mentally trade places. It was the only way to make a connection. Then, just as she had taken them into the abyss of their imagination, Lonnie changed their view of these same women. She guided the class to see their bravery and courage to endure these horrific traditions, all for their family's honor or for the sake of their children.

November Third, 3:30 PM

It looked like Tamika was fast asleep when Sonja opened the door. She tried to close it quietly.

"Where you coming from? Tamika asked, opening her eyes. She was lying in state again.

"Running."

Tamika's eyes were still closed. "I can see that. Isn't it raining?"

"Yeah," Sonja said, giving her attitude.

Tamika sat up and gave her that girl-I-will-kick-your-ass-right-here-and-now look. Sonja froze for a moment until Tamika lay back on the bed. "How far this time?" Tamika asked.

"Just four miles."

"Four miles? After all that runnin' we did at practice. I took the rest of the day off just to recopulate," Tamika said.

"You mean recuperate."

"Whatever. To chill."

Changing the subject, Sonja said, "I was wondering why you didn't come to class."

"I was watching my soaps," Tamika answered.

Sonja looked at her watch. "What about class?"

"I'm sure they had it," Tamika answered. "If it's raining where'd you run?" Tamika switched the topic back.

"I didn't want to run outside, because it's raining. So, get this, I went to the Rec center. I figured it was open and they've got three full-size basketball courts in there, right? So, each sideline is 94 feet, each end line is 50 feet, plus the 3 feet in between, so that's..."

"Okay, okay, I got it."

"Multiply the sidelines by two, then the end lines by six, add twelve feet for the space in between the courts, and you got the circumference, I mean the distance around the edges. I was like, that's 500 feet–."

"–It's cool, I ain't that curious!" Tamika said, trying to slow her roll.

It was too late. Seemed like every time Tamika talked to Sonja she insisted on teaching her something new, first geography, now arithmetic. It was getting on Tamika's nerves.

"Like I said it was one of those 'Clear-Your-Head' runs," Sonja said.

"Tell me you don't name your runs?" Tamika said shaking her head.

"There's the Clear-Your-Head run, the Oh-My-God-My-Hips-Are-Exploding run."

Tamika looked at Sonja's boyish frame. "Girl, you ain't got no hips."

"You remember that guy I went out with the other night. We're out on a date, you know, hangin,' and he keeps looking at this girl. And she was really thin. But he kept looking at her. I was like, what's up with that? And he was like, nothing. But I totally busted him. I hate it when guys do that."

"Is this going somewhere?" Tamika asked, incapable of empathy.

"Uhm, do you think I look fat?"

"Girl, please. Your boney ass is so skinny I stopped taking deep breaths around you because I don't want your feet sticking out of my mouth."

"You're right. I am tall, I am strong," Sonja said, repeating her mantra.

"Your narrow ass could jump through a key hole," Tamika said. "Yo' Momma called; then ya daddy called, but I couldn't understand him."

"What did they say?"

"Yo Momma said, she'd call you back. But I don't know what ya Daddy was talkin' 'bout. '*Wat zij hebben gegten?*'"

"My dad's Dutch. He asked you, 'What has she been eating?'"

"Well, then he said, 'Gooten Plenty', I told him don't I know about no Good N' Plenty."

"He said, 'Goden ochtend,' good afternoon," Sonja said.

Sonja sat a grocery bag full of magazines on her desk, then began sifting through the pages. Tamika, pretending to be asleep, snuck peeks at her after she noticed Sonja wasn't reading the articles.

"You do your paper for English Comp?" Sonja asked, tossing a magazine aside and reaching for a new one.

"Nah, I can't think of nothing to write about."

"It's supposed to be about something you can't do without," Sonja said.

Sonja glanced through the fashion spreads, dog-eared her favorite pages, then looked through the entire magazine once more in case she had missed something.

"Yeah, well, I could do without writing a stupid ass paper on stuff I can't do without."

"You gotta turn in something," Sonja said, wisely not correcting Tamika's double negatives.

Sonja then ripped out her favorite pages from the magazine, set them aside and threw the remainder away, discarding $50.00 worth of magazines. Tamika gave up hope of ever understanding her roommate.

"What did you write about?" Tamika asked.

"My parents."

"How nice... Hey, I got a question for you. What's up with all the magazines?"

November Sixth

When women basketball players eat, they eat big. They are not salad and water women. Their bodies are machines that need to be fueled and maintained.

Clio had chicken, macaroni and cheese, mixed vegetables, and carrot cake piled high on *two plates*. That was firsts. For seconds, she had more vegetables, casserole, quiche, and a fruit ambrosia. She playfully bumped into Kendra in the buffet line. They grinned at each other.

"You gonna eat all that?"

"You know it, girl."

Monet ate five times as much as the typical "girl next door." You can eat big meals when you're in tune with your body and trust your ability to shape and mold it. Trust comes from two-hour practices, weight training, and even more running. Stubborn excess weight doesn't stand a chance.

"Is that all you're going to eat?" Jennifer said to Sonja.

"I don't feel so good."

"You don't look so good," Clio said, eyeing Sonja's bony frame.

"You think I look fat?" Sonja asked Jennifer.

"Are you kidding?" Jennifer said, taking such a big bite of her quiche that her cheeks bulged.

It was too much for Sonja, and she got up and ran to the rest room. Clio barely noticed.

"Why'd you do that?" Monet asked her.

"What?" Jennifer's mouth was still bulging with food.

"You never miss an opportunity, huh?"

"I'm just having fun, this is college, we're supposed to have fun."

"Didn't you try to steal Washington's mascot?" Shirlie asked.

"We would have fed him, taken him for long walks," Jennifer said with a mock defensive smirk.

"You TP'ed a frat house," Roxy said, from the other end of the table.

"Toilet paper *is* biodegradable, right? So, what's the big deal?" Jennifer said.

"You actually gave your underwear to a total stranger."

"It was a panty raid. C'mon now, what's the big deal over one pair of panties?"

By then Sonja had returned. She looked pale.

"Jennifer's on a rampage of fun."

"*Hellooooo*, it's college," Jennifer said.

"You tell them how you turned my room upside down?" Sonja said. "Litterally, upside down.

"Oh yeah. That was funny. Clothes, pictures, pens, chairs, books, everything. You have to admit when you first walked into your room it freaked you out."

"Why didn't you turn over Tamika's side," Tamika said.

"Because she knew better," Tamika said, shooting Jennifer a look.

"You guys forgot that I am the team Quarters champion. I can get you all drunk in 10 games," Jennifer said.

Gina sat quietly through the exchange.

"Slow down, frosh," Roxy said, from the other end of the table.

"Frosh?" Jennifer asked, turning to Roxy.

"Frosh. Freshman. Rookie. Which do you prefer? Save some fun for your sophomore year," Roxy said.

"The way she's going, may not be a sophomore year,"Shirlie said.

"Can't do everything that feels good," Clio said.

Jennifer dismissed their advice.

The Big Four; Roxy, Clio, Kendra, and Shirlie sat at the opposite end of the table from Monet and the coaches. Roxy and Monet exchanged glares every fifth bite.

"If I have to run one more lap because of those idiots..." Clio said.

"If I hear one more time about how 'fundamentally sound' a player Monet is," Roxy said.

"All I know is I better not lose my spot to a freshman," Kendra said, referring with a nod to Tamika.

"How'd we get this coach, anyway? It feels like we're playing on the men's team. All that damn running."

"Scared of getting in touch with your inner Y chromosome?" Clio asked.

Roxy whispered to Kendra and Shirlie, "You know we gotta do something about Monet."

Shirlie shook her head. After three years she was getting tired of conspiring with Roxy. "Every year it's someone new."

"That's easy for you to say, girl. You don't have someone trying to take your playing time," Kendra said.

"Yeah," said Clio, herself a tenuous starter.

Roxy said turning to Kendra, "Remember what we did to that chick from Contra Costa College? Thought she was going to come in here and run things."

"Oh man, we got her good. She never knew what hit her."

During a game, the foolhardy junior college transfer got on Roxy about not passing to her when she was open. Roxy responded by subtly and gradually freezing her out of games. It was diabolically carried out by Clio, Kendra, and Shirlie. They didn't abruptly stop passing her the ball but each of them took turns ignoring her when she was open then increased the number of missed passes by two each game. Her scoring average slowly dropped from 18 points per game down to 10 all the way down to six. She fell out of the starting lineup and didn't figure out the conspiracy until the last game of the season when she was reviewing the game videos from the entire season. She broke down and cried. She knew if she stayed at Del Mar she would never get the ball and if she transferred she'd lose a year of playing eligibility. Either way, it would be a year of wasted time. She transferred.

"I don't know about you but I'm tired of losing all the time," Shirlie said.

"We don't lose all the time," Roxy said.

"We lose a lot."

"We do not."

"We lose a lot more than we win," Clio said.

"Maybe we'd win more if you concentrated on playing basketball instead of concocting ways to protect your playing time. I thought we had a shot to win our conference last year," Shirlie said.

"We came in sixth."

"Exactly. So listen, we play 31 games this year. Fifteen non-league and sixteen league games. If we win our conference we get an automatic tournament bid."

"Tournament? You've been sniffing too many cadavers," Roxy said.

"If we win twenty games we're a shoo-in," Shirlie said, ignoring Roxy.

"Last year we were 8-24." Clio said.

"But if we only win eighteen games and don't win the conference then we'll be on the bubble and we'd have to beat at least one or two ranked teams. If we only win seventeen games then we'd have to beat at least three ranked teams and be playing well at the end of the season."

"We're playing Tennessee, Stanford, and UConn," Kendra said.

"We ain't gonna beat two of those three teams," Roxy said.

"Shirlie, what if we only win 16 games this year?" Clio asked.

"Then forget it."

"Not to change the subject but, why are you putting the moves on Ray?" Clio said to Roxy, changing the subject.

"I think he's cute," Roxy said.

"All of a sudden?" Kendra chimed in.

"All of a sudden after Monet got interested," Clio finished.

"Little Miss Rough-Around-The-Edges won't be able to keep up."

"Sort of like how you can't keep up with her on the basketball court?" Clio asked.

"Shut up," Roxy said.

"What about Chris?" Shirlie said, the voice of reason.

"He still has a girlfriend," Roxy said.

"So it's okay to squeeze between someone trying to make a love connection but not when they're already in love?" Shirlie asked.

Roxy said, "In the free market, it's finders keepers." Clio and Kendra gave her a high five. Shirlie rolled her eyes.

"Well, I think we could win it this year," Shirlie said, bringing the discussion back to the game.

"Win what, the NCAA championship?" Kendra asked.

"The WCC," Shirlie answered. "Don't get carried away."

"With who? The stork playing point guard, Ms. Minnesota Goodie Two Shoes and Ghetto Fabulous? Please. We're not gonna win any more games than last year," Roxy said.

"You guys got Coach Satcher fired because you wouldn't stop all that crap," Shirlie said, exhausted.

"Why is it our fault Mr. Haneline didn't renew her contract?" Roxy asked, shrugging innocently.

"You know what I mean. Aren't you tired of all this tension?" Shirlie asked.

"You're such a Libra, Shirlie," Clio said.

Roxy whispered to Shirlie, Kendra, and Clio. "All those in favor of protecting their playing time. Say aye."

Kendra, Clio, and Roxy murmured, "Aye."

"Looks like the ayes have it."

Lonnie, Renee, and Stephanie heard the voice vote but figured it was the seniors deciding which freshman would fetch desert.

The coaches were eating their meals at the opposite end of the table.

Lonnie said between bites, "I've been running around all week trying to get us a radio contract. I went to the sports station, three news stations, public radio, KISS, the Bone, NOW radio..."

"Kiss-the-bone-now?" Renee asked, shaking her head.

"No."

"What about the Spanish and Chinese stations?"

"I didn't think of that. I did get an appointment with the Christian station. I told them it would be good exposure to young women. But, he didn't go for it," Lonnie said.

"Probably because he thought young women should be having babies and not running around in shorts chasing a ball," Stephanie said.

"And sweating," Renee added. "Haneline make any calls?"

Lonnie answered "What do you think? So get this, I talked to Ed Mc Fadden, the dean of the Communications school. They have student broadcasters and I told him student broadcasts would be good training."

"Yeah."

"We didn't have to do all this when we were at Merle's, getting radio contracts." Lonnie Delaney started.

"Merle's?" Renee asked.

"What about Merle?" Lonnie replied.

"You said, when we were at Merle's," Stephanie said.

"No I didn't."

"You did. You said. You know what, never mind," Stephanie said, looking at Renee.

Renee and Stephanie, the assistant coaches, were former players on Lonnie's first championship team. They had been through a lot together. The championships, Lonnie's divorce, Renee's boyfriend turned stalker, and Stephanie's deranged cat. Lonnie was demanding of her assistant coaches. Renee and Stephanie started out as players who moved up to graduate assistants and then assistant coaches when other assistants quit.

Having been through so much together, Renee and Stephanie were used to Lonnie's odd habit of periodically inserting her ex-husband's name into the middle of conversations. It usually occurred when she referenced anything in Ohio. It was really noticeable during the times she missed him most. Ohio had been a happy time for Lonnie, so she thought. Her career was going well, and she won two NCAA championships. Lonnie loved her husband and had no reason to think he was unhappy. So, the divorce completely blind-sided her. In fact, she never really accepted the end of her marriage. To deal with the pain she threw herself completely into work; first, the women's shelter, now coaching.

Lonnie took a deep breath, "Well, I'm going to keep after Mc Fadden. He said he had a few students who would be great at play by play. He stopped laughing when I told him I wanted female announcers," Lonnie said.

"You're kidding, that's great," Renee laughed.

"He didn't think so. He said he'd think about it."

"He's bluffing."

"What if he talks to Haneline?"

"Let's just say I told him it wouldn't look good giving the job to a man when so many of them already work on football, men's basketball, and baseball broadcasts. This is the only women's sport that has a chance of developing a broadcast audience, most of which would be female. Why should they have to listen to a man describe a women's game?"

"What did he say to that?" Stephanie asked.

"'You have a point.' I just told him this was a good opportunity to put our program on the map with women because once word gets around that the Dean of Communication at Del Mar thinks outside the box more students, more *female* students, would consider coming to Del Mar instead of automatically going to Syracuse or San Francisco State," Lonnie said.

"So you made it his idea?" Stephanie said.

"I said it would serve his interests."

"And he went for it?" Renee asked.

"As if it were his own," Lonnie said, triumphantly smug.

"Sweet. Del Mar women's basketball is on the air," Renee smiled showing her dimples.

"I'm starting to worry about Tamika," Stephanie said. "She gets down on herself when she doesn't play perfectly."

"We might need to get her some therapy with all the bad habits we have to coach out of her," Lonnie said.

"Sonja is like that, too," Renee added.

"That girl knows the game, does all the little things," Stephanie said.

"Good footwork."

"Yeah, but her weight will prevent her being much of a presence in the paint. Too light," Lonnie said.

Lonnie pushed her plate away then, shaking her head, stood up to address the team. "This is going to be our best season yet. If we play as a team we will surprise a lot of people."

Monet had heard it all before, but it wasn't until Lonnie announced the results for captain that she looked up from her plate. Her heart sank when Lonnie announced that Roxy would be the team captain. Monet took no consolation in the fact the vote was very close. She was convinced now, more than ever, that she was playing with a bunch of losers.

Jennifer, barely listening, whispered in Sonja's ear. "You wanna double date tomorrow night?"

Chapter 11

Ray-nation

November Seventh

Thomas and Chad had never met before, but they had something in common. They had both met their girlfriends on the same night at O'Grady's back in October. Chad had helped Sonja carry a drunk Jennifer back to her dorm room. Moments before, Thomas had given Sonja pool lessons before she had had to rescue Jennifer.

The three of them stood outside of Sonja's door waiting for her to come out. Chad broke the silence, "I read in my psychology class that the sense of smell makes the most lasting impression."

"I read that somewhere too," Jennifer said.

Thomas said nothing.

"I wonder if you, you know, did something where, like, you blasted all five senses at the same time, would that something be marked permanently in your head?" Chad said.

"Like forever," Jennifer said.

"Things that make you go hmmmmmm," Chad said, his eye locked on Jennifer's.

Thomas rolled his eyes then knocked impatiently on Sonja's door. "Come on, let's go."

Double-dating is difficult because it's hard getting four people to agree on something to do. They all agreed to go to the movies, but Thomas and Chad couldn't agree on which movie to see. Thomas was adamant about seeing *Mortal Kombat* while Sonja and Jennifer wanted to see *My Best Friend's Wedding* for the third time. When Chad sided with the women, Thomas began to question his manhood.

"What kind of guy lets women choose the movie? Women will always choose chick flicks over action movies," Thomas said.

But what could Thomas say? He was outnumbered.

Sonja, Jennifer, and Chad spent the entire trip to the movie debating a basketball conundrum. Sonja posed the question, "Down three, with the ball, 20 seconds remaining. Do you shoot the three or take an open lay-up?"

Thomas, a football guy, said, "Shoot the three."

Sonja dismissed his strategy, "You take the lay-up and foul, because if they miss one free throw you should have four or five seconds to tie the game the next time down the court, which is a lot easier than making a three." Chad and Jennifer agreed again, making Thomas feel like an outsider.

For the entire night, Chad and Jennifer tested his memory theory. All during the course of the date they filled each other's five senses. They complimented the others' cologne. They fed each other popcorn and whispered in each other's ears. They stared into each other's eyes, held hands, and rubbed each other during the movie, discreetly placing a coat over their laps.

Thomas and Sonja held hands, but they had little to say to each other although Thomas was fully expecting to get lucky.

After the first movie, they snuck into *Men in Black.* Once they were sure the coast was clear, Thomas and Chad went out to buy popcorn and drinks.

"Dude, right-on for talking them into sneaking in," Thomas said. "I really didn't think you had the stones for it."

"What do you mean?"

"Dude, *My Best Friends Wedding*? That's chick flick stuff. How come you didn't want to see *Mortal Kombat,* or *Starship Troopers*?"

"Jennifer said she wanted to see Julia Roberts," Chad said.

"Dude, *Julia Roberts*?! I couldn't even get you to go for *Boogie Nights*," Thomas said.

"Who wants to see a movie about disco?"

"Dude, it's about porn. And porn is how you set the table for later. What kind of dude are you?"

"And have her be all uncomfortable," Chad said. Thomas just shook his head.

Thomas said, "Julia Roberts is hot though, but not as hot as Calista Flockhart. Okay, who's hotter Calista or Kate Moss."

"Those babes are all skinny as hell," Chad said.

"I know." Thomas' eyes glazed for a moment. "Hey, do you think Sonja is a little chunky? I mean, don't tell her or anything but, you know. What do you think?"

Before Chad could answer, a rail thin girl stood in line next to them. Thomas nudged Chad, "Dude, check it out. Now, *she's hot.*" While Thomas and Chad were getting popcorn, Sonja and Jennifer where sitting through the scene when the alien takes over the farmer's body. They looked at each other, totally grossed out. Whose idea was this?

Sonja leaned in close to Jennifer.

"Chad is so into you. You guys can't keep your hands off each other," Sonja said. "I don't feel that way about Thomas."

"Chad is sooo nice to me. He likes basketball, I play basketball. He likes *Buffy the Vampire Slayer.* I like *The Simpsons.* How cool is that? It's like we think so much alike, when we disagree, it's like arguing with yourself," Jennifer said.

"I had a boyfriend like that in high school, its was really weird because we ate our Reese's Peanut Butter Cups the exact same way. I was like, whoa."

"Chad totally gets me," Jennifer said.

"The way you change your mind."

"I know, really. But he's really fun, he took me down the crookedest street in the world."

"You know what? Thomas makes little comments about your weight," Jennifer said.

"I know," Sonja said, looking down at her hand.

"It's like he would like you more if you were thinner or something?"

"Do you think this sweater makes me look fat? My last boyfriend was the same way," Sonja said.

"I didn't even have a boyfriend in high school," Jennifer said.

"No way. What? Did you have like really bad acne or some kind of bad rash?"

"No. My parents wouldn't let us go on dates away from the house."

Back in line, Chad and Thomas had just finished picking up the popcorn and sodas. After his comment about the girl in line Chad said, "Don't do that."

"What?"

"Don't make comments about other babes when you're here with Sonja," Chad said, getting angry.

"Who're you, my mother?" Thomas asked, irritated.

"I'm just saying it's not right."

"Dude, we're out here, they're in there. I'm a big boy now,

I can do what I want," Thomas said, shaking his head. "*Psshh*, I'm going out with freakin' Mr. Rogers over here."

"I'm not here with you, I'm here with Jennifer. So don't get on my case because I respect my date even when she's not around."

"Like the night you met her and you were looking up her dress?" Chad got angry at himself after Thomas exposed his hypocrisy. Not wanting to face facts, Chad pushed Thomas. Thomas was quite a bit larger than Chad. When Thomas punched Chad in the eye, popcorn flew like confetti. They wrestled until a security guard separated them. Thomas glared at Chad and then left, deciding to ditch the whole date. He would talk with Sonja later.

Chad struggled with the security guard who wanted to throw him out of the theater. Chad finally got him to listen long enough to tell him he just wanted to tell his girlfriend they had to leave.

"Let me see your ticket," the security guard said, blocking his way.

"Uh, I just need to see my girlfriend."

"So, where's your ticket?... First, you get your ass kicked. Now you get busted sneaking into a movie. You're not having a good day are you?" Out of pity, he waved Chad into the movie. "You got thirty seconds and then I'm calling the police."

Chad ran into the theater. Sonja and Jennifer saw his swelling eye and asked, "What happened? Where is Thomas," as he rushed them out and drove them back to campus.

"Your boyfriend is an..." He couldn't make himself say it, but they got the idea.

At the dorm, Sonja went to her room. In Jennifer's room Chad told her what had happened. She consoled him, rubbing his head as he lay on her lap. It was still early in their relationship, but it felt like more than just infatuation.

As they lay on her bed, Chad said, "I can't show you now, but I have a surprise for you."

November Ninth

Tim Todd was reading his book of poems at A *Clean Well Lighted Place for Books* on Van Ness Avenue. It was an impossibly long name for a bookstore but at least it wasn't false advertising. Monet loved Todd's poetry–the realism, free-flowing prose, and whimsical humor.

Monet had been anticipating the book signing for three weeks. It came just in time. She had been so consumed with adjusting to

San Francisco, school, her bitchy teammates, and improving her social life that she had neglected the most important person, herself. She smiled and settled in for the first reading. As the crowd applauded, Monet turned to see a tall black man duck behind a bookshelf. He looked familiar.

No way.

Curious, she got up to investigate. "Excuse me," Monet said, as the guy hunched over the books on the bottom shelf. He didn't answer. She noticed the section, but he was shuffling through books way too fast to actually read the titles. "Excuse me."

He stood up quickly, eyes bugged out. "Yes."

"Ray! What are you doing here?... In the... homoerotic section," Monet said.

"Hey, you're right," he yelled, dropping the books. "*This isn't Home Improvement!* I told the guy Hoooome Improoove-ment. I can understand mistaking home for homo, but improvement doesn't sound anything like erotic?"

Ray was always the embodiment of cool. Monet had never seen him this fidgety. She liked seeing this other side of him.

"It's okay, I won't tell your fans I saw you at a poetry reading checking out..." She squinted to see the books on the bottom self. "The Magnum series." Ray frowned. "So what are you really doing here?"

Looking sheepish, Ray confessed that Tim Todd was one of his favorite poets, then caught himself and shrugged not wanting to reveal anything more about himself. "All right; well I'm out." He was still clearly uncomfortable. Monet couldn't tell if it was because he'd been busted at a poetry reading or in the homoerotic section. They were standing near the exit, Ray was moving toward the door.

"Where are you going? You'll miss the next poem."

"Yeah, still, I'm out. I'll check you later."

As Ray walked past the counter, Nigel the cashier said, "Ray, hey man."

"Hey, sup' yo'?"

"Dude, thanks for arranging for Sean Cantor at the *Chronicle* to talk with me. He read some of my stuff, and he gave me some good advice. Right on, dude."

"No problem, *dude*. I'm glad it worked out, Sean is cool people. Known him since my freshman year," Ray said. "But keep that on the under, along with those bad directions you gave me."

"Remember, when I asked you about Home Improvement?" Ray said, winking at the clueless cashier. He winked back, but Monet wasn't buying it.

Ray turned to Monet, "Hey, you wanna get something to eat?" Monet smiled, but made him wait for a moment so she wouldn't appear too eager. "Well... Okay."

"You like Moroccan food?"

They went to Pasha's, a Moroccan restaurant on Broadway. Moroccan food was quite exotic for a girl from Columbus, Ohio. Ray ordered their meals with confidence and even though she couldn't pronounce any of the dishes they were all very tasty. As they sat on the pillows sipping mint tea, Monet couldn't help but notice what an unexpectedly good time she was having with Ray. When the restaurant's belly dancer pulled him up to learn how to belly dance, he willingly went on stage. He wore the red fez hat with all the other tourists, then did a belly dance solo. What he lacked in flexibility he made up with enthusiasm. He received the loudest applause. Monet couldn't stop laughing at him.

I like this Ray. I just hope the Ray that's obnoxious, purposefully annoying, and checking out other women, doesn't show up.

Monet was pleasantly surprised when Ray didn't flirt with the two beautiful women sitting at the next table. He actually ignored them despite their best efforts to get his attention.

"What you did for the guy at the bookstore was really nice," Monet said.

"I've known Sean at the *Chronicle* since my freshman year. Nigel writes for his school newspaper, wants to be a sports writer. I just brought them together."

"Why didn't you want him to tell anyone?"

"Just want to keep stuff like that on the down-low. Been Gone and Gatorback–."

"–Who?"

"Some OG buddies from my neighborhood. They told me something I'll never forget. They said, 'Use your gifts so other people can ride on your coattails.' So, when someone tries to do something for me, I say 'okay' but you gotta give it to one of my boys."

"I'll bet some people get pissed," Monet said.

"Doesn't always work, but if I tell you, you can help me by helping this person over here, it's a way for me to see how genuine people are or are they just looking for something in return. Hell, I got the coach who recruited me to give my best friend in high school a full scholarship in order to get me to come here," Ray said.

"A full ride?" Monet asked.

"Tuition, room, board, books. The whole wop."

"Damn. That's $28,000."

"I just asked 'em how bad do you want me to come here? Because another school already said they would do it."

"And they said yes?"

"Yep, they didn't know I wanted to play here anyway. I just wanted to see how much I could get out of them... Don't tell me how much you love me, prove it to me."

"Damn."

"I was a high school senior, doin' it to 'em. Funny thing is my boy, Flip Mode, couldn't play a lick."

"You got that knucklehead a basketball scholarship?"

"And he was the twelfth man on our high school team."

"And they gave him a basketball scholarship?" Monet asked.

"Naw, they couldn't do that. They gave him a football scholarship. You can get lost on a football team; basketball is a little different.

"That is really nice," Monet said. "You know, the food here is great."

"Monet, I don't know much about much, but I know about two things; food and people," Ray said, sitting back from his finished meal.

"Then why don't you talk like this around your friends?" she asked.

"Like what?"

"You haven't cursed or made a misogynistic remark all night. You haven't even referred to yourself in the third person. What's up with that?" Monet said.

"Ain't nothing up with it. A brotha can't just chill?" he said smiling. "I see *you've* been gettin' after it lately; keep it real."

"What?"

"Argyle man. That guy you blasted in the quad," Ray said. "Looks like you're trying pretty hard to give it away. I guess you couldn't find any takers." Ray said.

"Shut up," Monet said, mortified that he'd seen them.

"You break him off?"

"No, I didn't *break him off*. I did beat his ass in hoop though," she said.

Ray shook his head in pity for the guy. "What kind of woman crushes a man's ego on the first date?"

"Hey, he was the one that wanted to play basketball on a first date," Monet said, not liking the turn the conversation had taken.

"How are you gonna make a love connection that way?" Ray said. "Make a brother jump through hoops to get some."

"First of all, playing basketball was his idea. And look who's talkin' about making people jump through hoops. Count Chocula. The guy that hates chocolate."

"Ohhhh that's right, you were there when that girl gave me that chocolate."

"Yeah, because you said you like it," Monet said, irritated.

"But I'm allergic."

"Right, but you still had that girl looking all over the city for this special chocolate. What's it called?"

"Hey, you gotta prove yourself before you get to the major leagues," Ray said, dismissing the thought.

"Major leagues? You're just a guy power trippin' in relationships so you can find some pushover to run up behind your ass."

For once, Ray had no response. Instead, he paid for dinner, then helped her up from her seat.

Ray then took her to the St. Francis Hotel. A nice way to see the city skyline is from its outdoor elevators. As they rode up Monet pressed herself against the elevator door. She was terrified.

Monet whispered, "You didn't say it was an outdoor elevator."

"But we're indoors," Ray said.

"Barely. The elevator is all glass–I'm afraid of heights!" she said feeling for the lobby button, too scared to locate it.

"Here, I'll get it."

"No!... Stop moving."

By then they were at the top floor. On the ride down, Ray resisted the urge to make the elevator stop at every floor.

"How was I supposed to know?" he asked.

"It's okay. Just stop talking until we get out," Monet said, starting to sweat.

"Isn't that cute? My strong, independent black woman is afraid of heights. Now I know how to get what I want from you. Take you to a glass outdoor elevator."

After descending to the lobby, they walked peacefully through Union Square, although Ray thought it odd that someone like Monet would be afraid of heights, especially given all the power she liked to wield in relationships–and said so.

"Don't start with the power thing again. It's you that wants someone to control, that's why you play all those damn mind games," she said.

"Women have all the control they will ever need, it's not my fault you don't use it," Ray said.

"What power?"

"Poo'nani power. The Boom Shaka-la-ka," Ray laughed.

Monet was insulted and didn't bother to answer.

Ray continued, "That's your problem right there. I read somewhere that the one that wants sex least is the one that has the most power in the relationship. From my experience–."

"Which I'm sure is a lot," Monet said.

"Real talk. That's why I set the ground rules early before I get to know 'em."

"Get to know 'em how?"

"You get to know a woman real well when you're intimate," Ray said, smiling.

"What intimacy?"

"Oh, there's some intimacy going on."

"Doing intimate things is not the same as being intimate," Monet corrected him.

"Baby, you gotta see what's out there."

"And that's all you see... What's out there." She stuck out her chest. Ray couldn't stop staring at her breasts. "See what I mean?"

"You started it. I don't just get with anyone, I have standards."

"Yeah, the standard is, say the pledge of allegiance to Ray-nation or you're out?"

"Ray-nation... I like it. Maybe you'll find yourself wanting to become a citizen," Ray smirked.

"You know there's more to relationships than... poo'nani."

"See, the jealousy always bubbles up," Ray said.

"Please. I ain't sacrificing my self-respect for anyone, not even you," Monet replied.

"Now look who's using ain't–."

Monet sighed. "These poor girls only do it because they know if they don't you won't be bothered with them. *Real talk?*"

"Real talk."

"Let me ask you a serious question?" Monet said.

"A serious question."

"Have you ever had a girlfriend?"

"Ray-nation would gladly expedite your applications, if you know what I mean?"

His answer stopped Monet cold.

She and Ray understood that their relationship was platonic. She'd indulged his comments, but this time he had crossed the line. Ray wanted to somehow make it right, but he didn't know how to apologize and still be cool. Apologizing felt too much like losing. His ego wouldn't allow it.

They rode back to the dorms in silence in Ray's car.

Ray walked Monet to her door in silence, still debating if he should apologize or not. This was uncharted territory for him.

"Uh, Please don't tell my fans about the..."

"It's cool." Monet paused for a moment at the door giving him one last chance to make it right.

"Uh... right on," Ray said.

Monet shook her head and closed the door in his face.

November Sixteenth, 6:55 PM

"Good evening, ladies and gentlemen. Welcome to the first ever broadcast of Lady Runnin' Rhinos basketball. Before we begin, I want to thank Lonnie Delaney for making these broadcasts possible and give a shout out to my girls at Gillson Hall. I'm Thalia Clark, doing the play by play. The Lady Rhinos are set to play the UC Santa Cruz Banana Slugs here at the Watering hole."

"Did you know that banana slugs are bisexual? I mean that they are both male and female."

"That's my partner Courtney Heinz, as in the ketchup, providing the game analysis. Courtney played high school basketball but never quite made it to the college level. She's assured me she knows the game, but we'll have to wait and see about that... Well, if you can hear the sound of my voice on the radio, our range is only ten blocks. You should come and watch the Lady Runnin' Rhinos play. There are plenty of great seats available, attendance is expected to be about 120."

"With 15,000 empty seats. They could sit next to the coach, maybe even get to play a few minutes," Courtney said.

Lonnie gathered her team together.

"Okay, lets play hard out there. We can only win if we play as a team. So, let's do it."

"TOGETHER." Tamika, Monet, Sonja, and Mbika were the only players who contributed to the cheer. Lonnie gave everyone the evil eye. It was a bad omen.

As the teams walked onto the court, Roxy flashed a sinister smile at Monet then made eye contact with Clio and a reluctant Shirlie.

Thalia Clark said, "The Rhinos start Monet McCasner at point guard, Roxy Davidson at shooting guard, Clio Wysinger at small forward, Tamika Hightower at power forward, and Shirlie Torretta at center... And the Rhinos win the tip. McCasner brings the ball up the court, signals for the play to begin."

On offense, Monet started the play by passing to Roxy who was supposed to pass it back to a cutting Monet. Monet was open, but she never received the pass. Instead Roxy passed it to Shirlie who made a smooth jump hook over the defender.

"That was a nice play but shouldn't Davidson have hit McCasner cutting to the basket?" Clark asked Heinz.

"Yep, she was wide open," Heinz said.

During the next six possessions, Monet started the play and each time she was open neither Clio, Shirlie, nor Roxy passed the ball back to her. Since different players missed making the pass to Monet, it was also deviously subtle. They either passed it among themselves or shot.

"With each missed shot or turnover, the Banana slugs came down and scored. With eight minutes remaining, the Banana slugs have gone on a 24 to 4 run. That's a twelve-point lead turned into a eight point deficit.

Monet knew what was going on. She also knew what to do. On the next four possessions she either shot the ball or passed it to Tamika. When Del Mar tied the score, the Banana slugs called time out, five minutes remained in the first half..

Monet felt vindicated. She had guided the team back. She expected her teammates to be thankful.

In the huddle, Lonnie said, "Nice job, Monet. But you're not hitting the open man..." As the starters returned to the floor, Lonnie pointed to Kendra. "You're in for Monet." Kendra pointed to herself. "Yes, you. Get in there."

Monet walked to the end of the bench. She was mad. "Why am I sitting Coach?"

As Kendra got up to walk to the scorer's table, Mbika saw it as an opportunity to support her teammate. She saw American football players, basketball players, and especially baseball players do it, so when Kendra passed Mbika she smacked her on her behind. Kendra eyes bugged out as she rubbed her behind and checked in at the scorer's table.

Lonnie walked over and knelt in front of Monet. "Never take over a game like that unless I give you permission." Lonnie walked back to her chair without waiting for Monet's response. Roxy loved it.

At half-time, the game was tied, 34-34.

Walking to the locker room, Monet stopped Lonnie with a hand on her arm. "Coach, you let Roxy and Clio miss all those passes, then when I bring us back, you take me out?" Lonnie stopped her cold with a scowl, before shrugging off her hand and continuing to the lockers.

Before the coaches entered the locker room, Tamika yelled at her teammates hands on hips, neck and head swaying. "I don't know what you guys got going on, but you better cut it out and get wit' the program before I have to whop some ass around here." Any other freshman would have been laughed at by the seniors, but they all knew Tamika was ghetto enough to ambush each and every one of them.

When Lonnie entered the locker room all eyes turned to her. "Ladies, we are going to do things my way around here. Anyone with different ideas can turn in her uniform right now. You don't have to like each other, but you'd better figure out how to play together," she said, looking directly at Monet and then Roxy.

She pointed to Kendra. "You're starting the second half."

The second half was very close. Each time the Rhinos made a run, the Banana Slugs countered with the oldest play in basketball, the pick and roll.

"Each time they have run the pick and roll they have scored. 40-34 Banana slugs," Clark said.

"What's surprising is they are running it against Tamika Hightower, one of the best players on the Rhino's roster," Clark said.

The Rhinos and Banana Slugs traded baskets virtually the entire second half. The Rhinos scored in a variety of ways; the Banana slugs scored almost exclusively with the pick and roll. With one minute remaining the Rhinos were up by two, 56-54. A stolen pass and then a traveling violation gave the ball back to the Banana Slugs.

"With five seconds remaining, the Banana Slugs are leading 58-56. The Rhinos call time out."

Lonnie designed the play for Monet to take the last shot. While she was explaining it to the team Roxy, Clio, and Shirlie exchanged conspiratorial looks.

"Hightower to inbound. Rhinos in a stack as they line for the inbound play. Looks like a soccer wall for a penalty kick. Tamika inbounds to Clio, four seconds, McCasner rolls around a double pick, three seconds, she's open at the top of the key. Two. Clio fakes and passes it to Roxy who's got a tough shot on the baseline. One. The shot is up."

BUZZER.

"No good! No good! And the UC Santa Cruz Banana Slugs defeat the Del Mar Lady Runnin' Rhinos by two, 58-56. What a heartbreaking loss for the Rhinos, who were bigger and more athletic but were not the better team here tonight," Clark said.

"That's why they play the games," Courtney Heinz said, finally.

"Tamika Hightower had a breakout game for a freshman, with 20 points and 15 rebounds. She keeps playing like that and she's going to be a star."

The team walked, dejected, back to the locker room after exchanging the obligatory high-fives with the Banana Slugs at midcourt.

It was silent in the locker room. Lonnie stormed in. She stood in the middle of the floor staring at each player in turn. Didn't blink once. Didn't say a word. Didn't have to. If someone dropped their head she barked, "Get your head up and look up at me!" Monet and Roxy glared at each other when they were sure Lonnie wasn't looking at them.

"We stunk tonight. I think some of you know why... Ego. Ego! Ego!!! Egos getting in the way! *I won't tolerate it!*" With that she left, slamming the door on the way out.

Once she was sure the coaches were gone, Clio said, "That wasn't so bad."

Shirlie grabbed Clio and whispered loudly in her ear, "I told you it wouldn't work."

"Shut up," Roxy said.

"I swear, yawl don't start doin' what the coaches say..." Tamika said.

Despite Tamika's bad reputation Roxy stood up and was going to put the freshman in her place, but Clio pulled her shirt from behind and she plopped back into her seat.

Monet sat at her locker, dejected. She slowly placed her uniform, socks, and underwear in a tagged mesh bag with her name and number on it. Taped to the inside of her locker was a photo of Magic Johnson blissfully hugging the Larry O'Brien NBA Championship trophy, in his rookie year when he did everything but the laundry. She stared at the photo which only made her think about what a long shot it would be for her to ever hold the NCAA championship trophy. She couldn't believe she came all the way from Ohio to play with these losers.

"Everybody up!" Lonnie had returned. "You heard me. Everybody up. And if you've taken off your uniform, put it back on. Be on the court in five minutes."

There were still 15 people in the area cleaning up, breaking down tables, and stacking chairs, when the team arrived in the Arena. Lonnie conducted a full-blown practice right there. It was hard enough dealing with losing to an inferior team. Now, they were going to practice 30 minutes after losing the game. The team was especially humiliated when the Lady Banana Slugs players walked through the Arena, after showering, on their way to their team bus.

"Get a good look, ladies," Lonnie said. "Get a good look at the team that did this to you. On second thought, when you go back to the locker room have a look in the mirror."

Jennifer, Mbika, Sonja, and Gina all had the same thought. "Who was she talking about?"

None of them had played a single minute.

*   *   *   *

"You're not wearing those baggy cargo pants and Nikes out to dinner with us. It's your father's birthday and you're not going out with us like that," Monet's mother said, arms crossed.

"What's wrong with this?" Monet asked.

"What's right with it? You look like you're going to work on the docks for one. It doesn't hurt to dress like a young lady every now and then, just to practice. What's the matter with the skirt you bought last week?"

"You bought."

"Of course I bought it-you don't have a job," Mrs. McCasner said.

"You picked it out, too. I don't want to wear a skirt and I don't have a top to wear with it, anyway."

"What happened to the blue silk top? You said you liked it when we bought the skirt?... When I bought the skirt." Monet took off the white Nike lows.

"No, not those shoes either," her mother said.

Her mother went into her closet and spread out two outfits on her bed. A skirt and blouse along with a knit dress. Heels required.

"Mom, do I have to go? Those shoes hurt my feet."

"If you practiced walking in them as much as you practiced your free throws, you would be as graceful as a swan."

"I really don't want to go."

"You're going. You know why? Because it's your father's birthday, and it doesn't hurt to dress and act like a lady sometimes. It's not gonna hurt you."

"Yeah, it's gonna hurt my feet."

"Sweetheart, if you want to play sports, be some kind of jock, fine, you can still be feminine. You should still be able to act like a lady when you have to. And just because you're feminine doesn't mean you can't still be competitive and play sports and all that."

"Yeah, Mom, but it's a lot of work."

Chapter 12

A Run From the Roses

November Sixteenth, 11:15 PM

"You know, you should go to the party," Sonja said to Tamika, who was lying on her bed.

"Why?" Tamika asked.

"Because everyone is going to be there."

"And..."

"And so you should, too, instead of lying around all the time."

"Why would I want to hang around a whole bunch of, what did you call them?"

"Frat boys?" Sonja said.

"Oh, the 'r' comes before the 'a' and not before the 't'."

"Ha, ha, ha, very funny."

"We just had a long ass practice *after* a game that we *lost*."

"Come on, it'll be fun."

"Aren't you tired? Oh yeah, you didn't play enough to get tired. Matter of fact, yo ass didn't play at all. Hell yeah, you wanna go out," Tamika said.

"That's not very nice. I did a run before the game, remember? Hey, why don't you wear your leopard jeans... but not the fur collared top okay?" Sonja asked.

"What's wrong with that?"

"It's just...it's too much, okay? It doesn't say."

"What *does* it say then?"

Skank, was the first word that popped into Sonja's mind, but she said, "It doesn't say, ya know, college. You're in college you should dress like it. Why don't you wear the basketball sweatshirt."

"With my leopard pants?"

"Well, no that really wouldn't go together either, but you gotta start somewhere. Look, the party is casual. You don't have to dress up. No pressure. See, I'm wearing a sweatshirt too."

"Like I want to go dressed up looking like someone from Minnesota. Halloween was two weeks ago," Tamika said.

"I just thought it would be good for you to come to the party with the rest of the team, but if you're gonna be mean..."

"Okay, I'll go," Tamika said, feeling a little guilty about coming down so hard on Sonja. "But ain't no way I'm gonna wear the same thing as you to a party."

This was a big sacrifice for Tamika. Her idea of a good time was *not* hanging around a bunch of drunken people. Going to a party with Sonja was a major concession. But she reminded herself that she needed to adjust to the college life. Tamika had to stay in school long enough for the ABL or WNBA to notice her. Then she could just play ball for a living.

"Is that boyfriend of yours going to be there?" Tamika asked.

"Yeah, we're meeting there."

"I'll help you see if he looks at any other skinny girls," Tamika said.

"How nice is that? See, we're gonna be best buds," Sonja said, meaning it.

Tamika and Sonja walked up the stairs to the Phi Nu Pi fraternity house. It was raging inside. They waited a few moments after knocking with the huge lion-faced knocker. When a door opened and a guy ran out screaming. Sonja and Tamika stepped aside just in time. He was being chased by two women with huge water guns. Sonja and Tamika stepped aside just in time, then looked at each other before stepping aside again to dodge another guy who was chasing the two women who were chasing the screaming guy. Sonja smiled, it reminded her of the frat party scene from every college movie she had ever seen. Tamika shook her head wondering if she'd made a mistake.

Sonja turned to Tamika and said, "And you wanted to stay home."

Tamika rolled her eyes, "One of those fools gets my hair wet and it's on."

The Phi Nu Pi house was huge. Seventy-five fraternity brothers lived there. It was known as the jock frat since most of the frat boys were football and baseball players. Eighty-five percent of the big brothers were white, but there were some African-Americans in the fold. The white guys were very WASPy without the Republican entitlement. Mostly, it was just a lot of guys enjoying the good fortune of being athletic, good looking, or both. At the Phi Nu Pi house, everyone felt welcome, which was why they threw the best parties.

When Tamika arrived in her skintight pants and leotard top, all heads turned. As cavalier as Tamika could be about what people thought of her, she became self-conscious about her outfit. She got mad at Sonja, despite the fact that she had tried to get her to wear something else. Sonja secretly hoped Tamika would ditch her so they both could have a good time, separately.

They stood in line for beer right behind Ray.

"Tough loss tonight," Ray said.

Tamika said, "Yeah, bitches trippin'. Not doin' what the coach say. I got mine though. 20 and 15."

"Cha-ching, that's what I'm talkin' 'bout," Ray said, giving her a pound.

"Hell yeah. Gonna drop 20 and 15 on that ass all season, regardless," Tamika said.

The beer line moved quickly. A coed passed by and copped a long feel on Ray's behind while he talked to Tamika. Surprised Tamika, especially when Ray just smiled.

"You always let strangers feel on your ass?" Tamika asked.

"She's not exactly a stranger," he said.

"Ray! Hey Ray! You da man, bro!" a drunken fraternity brother yelled from across the room.

Ray rolled his eyes as he approached. Ray was good-natured with the guy as he babbled on and on about the game-winning shot Ray had hit on Syracuse three years ago to win the national championship. Tamika noticed that Ray was guarded. He never took his eyes off the guy until he left.

Ray said, "You gotta watch your back with these cats. They'll come up and slap you five, maybe buy you a beer, but deep down they want to take you down a notch, brag to their friends they mopped up Ray Riddick."

"C'mon," Tamika said.

"Real talk. I used to think Charles Barkley was putting too much on it. But the Chuckster don't play."

"Throw that ass through a window in a minute, for *real*," Tamika said.

"Since my sophomore year, 'hella' cats have stepped up to me 'cause of some imaginary funk they created in their head. It always starts with 'You da man.' Then after five too many beers that beer courage gets goin'. Next thing you know his girlfriend is looking at a brother. Then the same guy's got a problem with me. 'You think you're hot shit, huh? Mr. B-Baller! Mr. NB-Aaayyy!' Like it's my fault his girl wants some California Black Snake."

Right on cue another fan approached, "Ray, you're the man!" Ray turned to fill up his beer cup. "Anyway. Good luck with the rest of the season." He toasted Tamika then walked off.

Tamika saw Monet and walked over to talk with her. "Hey, I wanted to ask you something about Sonja."

"Yeah."

"The girl stares into the mirror talking to herself. You know what I'm sayin'. Talkin' 'bout how she's got terrible skin."

"She has beautiful skin," Monet said.

"Well she doesn't see it that way. She sees zits or somethin'. Got pictures of models all over the wall. The whole room is a damn scrapbook. I thought I'd ask you because I thought it might be, you know, a thing," Tamika said.

"Yeah... No. I mean, I know what you're saying but I don't know what's going on with her."

Jennifer danced provocatively with Chad in the middle of the dance floor. She ground her hips into his crotch while he provided a firm foundation and enjoyed the view. Jennifer was loving the freedom of college. She could eat whatever she wanted, stay out late, study, not study, watch the soaps, order pizza at 1:30 in the morning, she could do anything she wanted. What Jennifer liked the most was the fact she could date whomever she wanted. Jennifer had been quiet and unassuming in high school. Now, she was on the dance floor dirty dancing with Chad. None of her old friends from Oroville would have recognized her.

Walking through the hallway, Monet bumped into Ray again. This time, it wasn't hard enough to knock her off her feet.

"Hey. Don't I know you?" Ray said. "Wait, I think I'm supposed to say, 'Excuse me here.'"

Monet smiled.

"Tough loss," he said.

"Yeah, we could have played a lot better."

"I was talking about the one you got Midnight Madness."

"No, you didn't bring up that ancient history."

"You know what they say happens when you don't know your history," Ray said.

"You really know how to get on my nerves," she said.

"Yeah, but I can flip the script and make you think. And that's what you dig about me," he said, with a grin.

Ray was distracted by two good-looking women *both* of whom were trying to get his attention.

"No, most of the time I think of you as a butt hole who's full of himself. Like now," Monet said, looking over her shoulder at the two coeds.

Motioning with his head, he instructed them to meet him in another room. He turned back to Monet distractedly. "I think you're right... Uhmmm, excuse me."

Monet was insulted.

I knew that guy from the restaurant was only temporary.

It didn't make sense, but compatibility is only as good as the most annoying personality trait of the other person. She liked the off-campus Ray, it was the on-campus Ray she disliked.

Ray walked over, put his arms around both coeds and escorted them to the dance floor.

Don't look. Don't look. Don't look.

Monet didn't want to give them the satisfaction. But she couldn't help it. She looked. All three of them caught her. Ray chuckled and squeezed the coeds a little tighter.

The three of them were gyrating on the dance floor. While looking at Monet, Ray put a little extra bump into his grind. The ladies took it to another level which made all the guys in the room jealous.

Damn, why did I do that?

Monet almost slapped herself on the forehead when Milton turned the corner. He was wearing a yellow, red, and blue argyle sweater with matching socks.

"Milton. Hi. You know you never called me after we played," Monet said.

"I told you I had a lab assignment."

"You said you had a test," Monet said.

He noticed the look in her eyes. "Everything okay?" genuinely concerned.

She was still thinking about Ray and the coeds. She smiled.

No, everything is not okay.

The DJ played *It Takes Two* by Rob Base. There was a collective rush to the dance floor. There were more men than women, but natural selection left Monet, Shirlie, Sonja, Tamika, and Kendra, all the six-footers, without dance partners. They watched as everyone else danced. Clio couldn't take it anymore. She grabbed Roxy, who held on to Shirlie to keep from falling, who pulled on Kendra to follow the crowd. Kendra grabbed Sonja, who grabbed Gina. Gina thought about pulling Tamika in but her ice-cold glare made her snatch her hand away. The tree-ladies made a conga line to the center of the dance floor.

One, two, three. Get loose.

Monet watched her teammates walk onto the dance floor. Milton just stood there.

"Milton."

"Yeah?"

"Do you want to dance?"

"Uh–"

"–Good." Monet grabbed him by the hand and led him to the dance floor.

Shirlie and Sonja didn't have much rhythm, but they tried to keep up. Kendra, Clio, and Monet went into a dance retrospective. Soon they were doing the Running Man, the Body Language, and the Cabbage Patch. Not many things are funnier than watching rhythmically challenged people attempt the Cabbage Patch. They were all flailing shoulders and arms.

Somebody say, "Oo-ah, oo-oo-ah..."

The female ballers were having fun dancing among themselves. They looked like redwoods in a forest of Christmas trees. There's something about women having fun by themselves that attracts men. The song had not ended before several guys tried to move in on the dance circle. When one tried to bump and grind his way into the circle, they just turned their backs and closed ranks in a perfectly executed team box out. They weren't going to let any guys in, not when they hadn't wanted to dance with them before.

As Monet danced with Milton, she watched Ray. It pissed her off that he had dismissed her for two bimbos, especially after their dinner outing. It aroused her competitive juices. Monet was determined to show him that she could attract men as well as he could attract women. While the two coeds dirty danced around Ray, Monet decided to do a little dirty dancing of her own with Milton.

At first, Ray barely noticed; the bimbos were doing a good job of diverting his attention. Monet saw some interest in his eyes when he saw her dancing with Milton. It wasn't jealousy, but it was interest. She would have preferred jealousy.

Jennifer had done so much dirty dancing with Chad that they had retired to a corner to lock lips and make out. Every so often Jennifer would pull Chad back to the dance floor. He was reluctant and put up a small fight. Given his lack of rhythm, he knew his limitations and that people would make fun of his dancing. But he loved indulging Jennifer's whims. To Jennifer, it was one of the many ways he showed how much he loved her.

Gina had no idea her social life would improve so dramatically just by being on the basketball team. No way she would have been able to go to a party with the beautiful people of Del Mar. She couldn't believe she was at the Phi Nu Pi house dancing with guys who were bona fide BMOCs.

Vince Fontainebleau knew a lot of Phi Nu Pi brothers. He was too strange to be a member. His teammates didn't know if it was because he was a place kicker or because he was from a small town in Appalachia with curiously close family lineage. Vince had a bit of a temper, but because he was only 5' 8" his football teammates didn't pay much attention to his cute little tirades. The main reason his teammates tolerated his water-jug-kicking tantrums was because in three years the guy had not missed one extra point and had made 95 percent of his field goals. Putting points on the board is how you win football games. Vince was as dependable as the law of gravity.

Vince relied on corny pickup lines because he didn't know any better. Virtually all of the players on the football team were popular with the ladies. Everyone, except Vince. He resented being ignored by women when so many less important teammates were being showered with female affection. Even though he was just a placekicker, he felt he was entitled to more female attention, so he sought women he could control.

There was something about Gina that made her stand out to Vince. He had learned how to spot a woman who would suit him in a crowd. He was attracted to her like a moth to a flame. He noticed Gina's deferential body language. He noticed that when someone passed she made room for them. She never stood her ground, insisting that they move around her. Vince also noticed that, even though it was a party, Gina allowed people to stand directly in front of her with their backs to her as if she wasn't there. And when she stood in a group talking with friends, she rarely added to the conversation. Individually, those things didn't amount to much, but collectively Gina was Vince's type. He made his move.

Gina couldn't believe her luck when Vince, the placekicker, wearing his game day jersey, sauntered up to her and said, "You wanna see my game balls?"

Did she ever!

Sonja talked with Thomas at the bottom of the grand staircase. She had forgiven him for leaving her on their double date. Sonja really liked Thomas, but he hadn't stopped checking out other women, usually very thin women, when they were out together.

After dancing together, Monet, and Milton went their separate ways. She decided to explore the frat house. From the patio, Monet could see the entire party, the backyard, the lounge, and a little of the dance floor. She watched people talking and nursing their beers in the backyard next to the pool. She saw Jennifer jump into the pool with her clothes on and then convince Chad to jump in with her. She watched Tamika shake her head at the pandemonium of the frat party, then watched her get fed up and leave. Monet was about to go into the lounge through the sliding glass doors when she saw Roxy talking with a good-looking guy wearing a football jersey. They were sitting on the couch in a dark lounge. Roxy didn't see Monet.

Jennifer and Chad came inside. They were still dripping wet. "Hey Monet, someone knows where they're keeping Stanford's mascot."

"The Christmas tree?"

"Yeah, we're gonna go see if we can borrow it." Jennifer made quotation marks with her fingers when she said "borrow it." "You wanna come?"

"Nah, I'm cool," Monet answered, as Jennifer and Chad bounded off leaving a water trail on the floor. She yelled after them, "You be careful, you crazy kids."

Monet stood alone. She watched the reaction of guys as they looked her over. They liked what they saw until they compared her height to their own. Monet watched for that moment when they decided to take a pass. It happened a lot. Then there were the really tall guys who thought they didn't have to put forth any effort simply because they were tall. Monet shot them down quickly.

Monet turned back to watch the party, glancing over at Roxy and a guy. It seemed that they were just acquaintances, maybe class-mates, until Roxy started putting the moves on him. Monet had an unobstructed view. Their flirting ran through her head like a horse race.

And they're off. First out of the gate are two fillies, Nice Eye Contact, *and* Undivided Attention. Male Ego *is right there.* Nice Eye Contact. Undivided Attention. *You're So Funny and* Sit A Little Closer *come around the outside as they hit the first furlong at the end of the couch.* Nice Eye Contact *is still right there driving the pace.*

*It's a three-horse race–*Nice Eye Contact, You're So Funny, *and* Touch My Hand. *The colt,* Male Ego, *is surging and feeling his oats.* Sit A Little Closer *is a distant memory replaced by* Touch My Hand.

And here comes You're The Man*!*

On the back stretch, You're The Man *is really responding.* Don't Say Anything Stupid *lingers just off the pace, in sixth place.*

As they enter the final turn it's Male Ego, Nice Eye Contact, Undivided Attention, You're So Funny, and Touch My Hand. Don't Say Anything Stupid *is positioned nicely as a spoiler.*

Don't Say Anything Stupid *makes a move.. He charges to take command of the race. The filly,* Undivided Attention *is fading along with* Nice Eye Contact. Touch My Hand *is a distant memory.*

Look at the long shot, Don't Say Anything Stupid*! He has grabbed this race by the throat, totally changing the momentum.* Shouldn't Have Said That *makes a move into the second place followed by* What The Hell?, You Want What? *and* Hell No. Undivided Attention, Nice Eye Contact, and You're So Funny *are nowhere to be found.*

And down the stretch they come! It's C'mon Baby. Hell No. C'mon Baby. Hell No. A*nd here comes* Flattery. *But* Flattery *is going nowhere.* C'mon Baby. Hell no. C'mon Baby. *And it's...* Hell No *at the wire.*

Monet started laughing as the guy quickly let go of Roxy's arm after she looked down at his hand and back up at him.

Man, she's good; in total control the whole time. I can do that.

Monet nodded to herself. She walked into a large room of the frat house that had been turned into a lovers' lounge. Ray was sitting on a stool at the bar while the two coeds, Buffy and Kirsten, competed for his attention. Monet stood off to the side, sneaking peeks at the amorous trio.

When Shirlie snuck up behind her. "Ooops, sorry, didn't mean to scare you...." She followed her eyes to Ray and the coeds. "...Or interrupt your fantasy."

Monet didn't answer.

"I told you before, he's trouble." They turned to look at the trio. "Guys like that, you can only keep their attention for 20 minutes." When Shirlie saw the glazed look on Monet's face she knew she was a goner. "All right, be hardheaded."

The dance floor emptied when a Dougie E. Fresh song was mixed out.

Milton stepped into the lounge; when he saw Monet he tried to duck out. Too late.

"Milton... So... Do you have a lot of friends in this fraternity?" Monet asked.

"A couple..."

Monet was half paying attention to Milton when she got the idea to make Ray jealous, using the techniques she saw Roxy using. *How hard could it be?*

"Hey, Milton. Thanks for dancing with me."

Monet didn't hear his response. She was focused on Ray and the bimbos. "Let's stand over here," she said, quickly reviewing all of Roxy's techniques in her mind, then guiding herself into a strategic position.

Close the gap. Give him your undivided attention. Touch his hand. Funny, make sure to laugh at his jokes.

"You know I love argyle," Monet said.

Milton said, "I've been busy studying, taking a full load this quarter, but I was thinking, maybe we could go out again, this time no basketball. I learned my lesson."

Monet chuckled heartily.

Good. Good. Wait, he's frowning. He thinks I'm laughing at him. Quick, touch his arm, now close the gap. Good. He's relaxing.

"It wasn't that big a deal," she said.

"Well, I don't want to get my ass kicked again," he said.

Look away, then right back into his eyes. Good. Now try the Spock finish.

She took another look at Ray, who was still holding court with the coeds. Milton was beginning to relax.

"So what's your major again?" Monet asked.

Good. Show you're interested.

"Engineering," Milton said.

"Isn't that a hard school to get into?" She moved even closer.

"Yeah, but I've always been pretty good at math. And I like building stuff. When I was kid I built a tree house in the backyard complete with electricity and running water. Used to do my homework and watch TV up there. My mother didn't get pissed until the building inspector came and said she needed a permit to have a tree house with a kitchen."

"How'd they find out?"

"I think the neighbors snitched me out after I told their son Kenny I wouldn't help him with his homework anymore."

Monet laughed right on cue. Milton loosened up, right on cue.

"Did you get in trouble?" pretending to hang on his every word.

"Not really. I just had to take everything down."

"Serves you right for not getting in fights and selling drugs at school like everyone else," she said, touching his arm. He laughed with her and looked down at his arm to confirm it was hers and not his own. He had never experienced such undivided attention from a woman before. A tent was rising in his pants.

Across the room, Ray noticed how things were heating up between Monet and Milton. Not to be outdone, he fondled Buffy, then Kirsten. Ray made sure to make eye contact with Monet. *Take that*, Monet thought. Out of nowhere Roxy walked up to Ray, whispered something in his ear and passed him a piece of paper. Buffy and Kirsten almost hissed at her, but let Roxy have the moment as long as she didn't stay too long. She was in and out.

Monet responded by touching Milton's arm and pulling him toward her. It was awkward because she didn't want to kiss him, just bring him closer. Milton was really heating up. Monet knew she was playing with fire when she saw the stiff bulge in his pants.

Mayday-Mayday-Mayday.

She excused herself to go to the ladies' room.

Ray pretended not to notice when she got up to leave. After a few minutes Milton, got up to search for her. Soon after that, Ray ditched the two bimbos to look for Monet.

Ray passed Milton in the hallway. After sizing him up he concluded there was no way Milton could be a threat. "Yo, where is that babe you were sitting with back there?" Ray said.

"Monet?" Milton asked.

"Yeah, her."

"I don't know. One of her teammates said she left."

"You guys aren't... you know?" Ray said.

"No, I can't be with a woman who can back me down in the paint and post me up."

Ray smiled before he left to look for Monet.

"Right on, brah," Ray said. "Hey, nice sweater."

*   *   *   *

November Seventeenth 1:55 AM

"Monet... Monet. Hold up," Ray said, running to catch up with her.

"Go away. I see enough of you in class," Monet said, annoyed.

"C'mon girl, wait up."

"What happened? Did the bimbos have last minute biology exams to study for?"

"First, you gotta be able to spell biology. What happened to Cardigan Man?"

She had to smile. "You mean Argyle Man... A cardigan is a long sleeve button up sweater."

"I'm sure he looks dumb as hell in both of them," Ray laughed.

"Don't say that. He's really nice," Monet said.

"C'mon, real talk?"

"Real talk."

"I saw the game tonight. You didn't believe me when I said–."

"When you basically called me a loser," Monet said.

"No. I didn't say you were a loser, I said you weren't a winner. Watching the game proved my point. What happened when Roxy and Shirlie stopped passing? You took over the game."

"And brought us back."

"But you gotta involve your teammates. Even if you don't like them–."

"–They don't like me."

"Doesn't matter. You're the point guard, the leader. It all starts with you. If you don't reach out to them, it's gonna be a long season," Ray said.

"It's already too long and I've only played one game with these losers."

"You came here to win. And as unrealistic as that idea is given who's on the team, I can guarantee you won't win if you don't convince your teammates to follow your lead," he said.

"Right."

"They should be lining up behind you. You and Lonnie are the only two who have gone to the finals."

"Right, so what am I supposed to do?" Monet said.

"How bad do you want it?" There was a long silence. "I learned my freshman year that there is a subtle part of winning that requires submission. You can't just take over every game situation every time."

"Jordan did it," she said.

"Yeah, but he didn't win until after he submitted to trusting his teammates–."

"–You've seen them. They drop passes, they don't finish–."

"–Jordan never would have gotten past the Celtics, the Pistons or the Lakers if he hadn't submitted to trusting his teammates. They have to carry some of the load. Hell, those three teams alone will end up with as many as eight Hall of Famers. Eight! Everyone talks about Jordan's will to win, but he had that extra gear because he didn't have to spend all his energy keeping the game close. Jordan can score and defend. But the championships only came after the trust and submission. You have to submit before your team will go to the next level. I'm telling you, I had the same problem."

Monet tried to sneak a peek at his Championship ring.

"Where's your ring?"

"I don't wear it around to parties. Someone sees it, gets a crazy idea; now we have a problem. Better to just leave it home," Ray said. "You know I lead the entire country in scoring out of high school."

"So, did I," she countered.

"Could you have entered the NBA draft?" Ray said.

"Why didn't you?" Monet asked.

"Moms wanted me to play it safe. Me, not knowing if I could really get down with grown ass men, coming straight out of high school. Looking back, I'm glad I didn't go. Everything turned out fine. I didn't get hurt, which was my biggest fear. We ended up winning a national championship. The money is always gonna be there," he said with a wink.

Money rolled her eyes. She thought about his advice about the team. As much as she wanted to disagree, he was right.

"Where are you going?" Ray asked

"Back to my room."

"The party just started," he said.

Monet continued down the sidewalk. "Well, if you're going to walk back, I know a shortcut through here." Monet hesitated when she saw how dark it was, not to mention the fact they would be trespassing. "C'mon', it's cold out here," he said.

"I hope you're not that stalker?"

"Did I look like the stalking type back at the party?"

"No, your hands were quite full," Monet said.

"Exactly."

Monet sped up the pace after they were on the other side of the block. "You know what I hate about women like that?" Monet said.

"Here it comes. Post-feminista philosophy," he said, bracing himself.

"Women like that make it harder for women like me."

"Harder to do what?"

"Oh, I don't know, go out with a guy and not feel like I gotta have sex with him to keep his attention."

"Don't blame the guy," Ray shrugged. "That's on you."

"You know what I mean," she said.

"If you like the guy, then what's the problem?" Ray asked.

"It's disrespectful. Take you for example."

"I gots to get mine," Ray said shrugging.

"Real talk... See, now you got me saying real talk," Monet said. "What's wrong with gettin' some?"

"There's no problem as long I say 'yes' after we go on the first date. If I say 'no', all of a sudden you can't find my phone number."

"Yeah, that's it, blame it on me. You blame men because you haven't figured out a way to keep a guy interested, like I said. Women have all the power and don't know what to do with it."

"What do you call it? Poo 'nani power?"

"That's what I'm talkin' 'bout. That Poo 'nani. But really it's a metaphor for the power to say 'yes'," Ray said, testing.

"Poo 'nani is a metaphor–."

"–For the power to say yes. You have to complete the thought otherwise it makes no sense."

"Where do you come up with this stuff?" Monet said, shaking her head. "*Poo 'nani* metaphors aside, I still shouldn't have to trade sex for companionship. Its like I'm holding myself hostage."

"Hostage. That's funny," Ray said.

"You don't know what you're missing."

"All the poo 'nani I get? I ain't missing much," he said.

"The meaningful cannot be created by the frequent," she said.

"The meaningful can't be created by the frequent. That's cute. The bad part is you don't know what you got down there. Poo 'nani is the most powerful thing on the planet. Real talk?"

"Yeah, a regular stealth superpower," Monet said, shaking her head.

"Let the women of Palestine and Israel stop givin' up the Boom Shaka-la-ka. Guaranteed, those guys would find a way to get along within 48 hours."

"Just like that!"

"You know how mellow cats get after a good one, get that silly looking grin on their face. You know... Well, maybe you don't know."

"I know how to play my position," she said. "Have you hollerin' for your momma."

"I don't know, you seem out of practice to me."

"Who said I was lonely?" Monet said.

Ray chuckled at her denial. "I was being nice. I could have said desperate."

"Just because I'm not going out having sex with people to increase my numbers doesn't make me desperate."

"Okay," Ray shrugged.

"No, really."

"Okaaay."

"I mean, intimacy, sex, those things are precious."

"I think you're putting it on a little thick? But believe me it's okay," Ray said.

"I just think it's an honor to, you know, have someone inside you. No, actually it's more important than that... What's more important than an honor?"

"A graduation," Ray said. "A graduation is more important than an honor," Ray said, then yelled to the heavens like a howling wolf, "HEAR YEE, HEAR YEE. FROM THIS DAY FORTH, IT WILL BE A COMMENCEMENT TO BE INSIDE MONET MCCASNER! HEAR YEE, HEAR YEE, IT'S A COMMENCE-MENT–"

"–Stop that!" she said.

Neighborhood dogs started barking and a couple of house lights turned on.

Monet stopped, looked at Ray incredulously, then continued walking. Ray followed behind. "How 'bout an arraignment? That's definitely more important than an honor." He looked down at his crotch. "ALL RISE..."

"Can you ever be serious?"

"That's another thing. You Feministas are too sensitive for your own good. You sound like my older sister with her spinster-ass. Always blaming other babes for going places she don't want to go. I told her, you ain't that sexy. So, you especially gotta get funky and take it there to keep a man."

"Where?"

"Here," pointing down, but being careful not to be offensive.

"I am not going to *take it there* to keep a man," Monet said.

"But you're the one complaining about the competition from Buffy and Kirsten back at the party."

"Thing One and Thing Two," Monet said.

"Their names are Buffy and Kirsten and like it or not, they're the competition. They *are* taking it there. Going the extra mile. Giving 110 percent. Leaving it all on the floor."

"You mean bed," she said.

"The bed, the floor, the bathroom, the hallway–."

"–Okay, okay, I got it. But they're stupid."

"They're willing to get a little funky. Get sick with it. That's what makes them sexy. Guys love that shit–I love that shit," Ray said.

"It's stupid to even try to keep a guy with just sex. And, being sexual doesn't make you sexy."

"Hmmmmmm." Ray thought about that one for moment. "You're right, it's not a good long-term strategy," Ray said.

"For who?" she said.

"For them and for me."

"Yeah right. You say that now," she said.

"I'm serious," he responded.

"Guys are such idiots. Take me, for example, I love sports, have my own money, my own car," Monet said.

"Maybe that's the problem. You don't treat a brotha right," Ray said.

"Anyway, I'm not asking him for anything other than to treat me right? If he does that, he won't have anything to worry about."

"Is that right?" Ray contemplated the possibilities before stealing a really good look at Monet's figure.

"Don't do that."

"What?"

"I hate when guys do that."

"What? Look?" Ray asked.

"You know, I wouldn't mind if you went back to the party. Back to Buffy and Kirsten, or Roxy or whomever else," Monet said. His antics had made her ambivalent.

"Oh, you saw that? I don't know what that was about. Roxy just came up, said a couple of things, and gave me her number."

"Maybe she wants to get in line–take a number." Monet was getting made, she could feel her face heating up. She stopped walking. "Guys like you, you think you're so in touch, but you're really afraid to open up. You know, I wish you *would* go back to the party."

That was a zinger. Ray paused for a moment letting Monet continue walking. He considered going back to the party to hook up with Buffy and Kirsten. Under normal circumstances it wouldn't be a hard choice.

"Let's see, guaranteed *menage a trois* versus convincing a feminist to do the nasty. Hmmmm, *menage a trois* or feminist. *Menage a trois*, feminist," he thought.

Ray surprised himself by choosing to walk Monet back to the dorms. After all, he could hook up with Thing One and Thing Two any time.

He saw a rose bush, but when he went to take a stem, he pricked his finger on a thorn. Monet looked back and saw Ray flinging his hand in pain. She smiled because she knew her tattoo was prophetic. He caught up to her and tried to give her the rose, but Monet wouldn't take it.

"Take it."

"No."

As they walked through campus, Ray sucked on his pricked finger. It was dark. Ray caught up and walked five feet behind Monet. When she stopped, he stopped. When she walked, he walked. For several minutes a campus police squad car watched the childish show unfold in front of them. When they reached the car the officers rolled down their windows.

"Miss. You okay?"

"Yeah, seems like I've attracted a stray. He's following me home."

The officer squinted. "Ray Riddick?"

Monet and Ray saw the confusion on the campus police officers' faces. Why would the campus BMOC go sniffing behind a woman who wasn't interested? Didn't make sense to these highly trained crime fighters. And who was this woman with the nerve to call Ray Riddick a stray? Since it was Ray, the star basketball player, future NBA first rounder, the officers let them continue.

After turning a corner Monet said, "What are you doing?"

"Walking you home."

"You can't – never mind."

"That was a cold shot, calling a brotha a stray dog like that."

"The dog part already fit," she said.

"And you just added the stray part," Ray said. "Here, I got you this."

"No, I'm not touching that thing," Monet smiled. "Like you said, it's not like you couldn't find someone to follow you home for the night. Keep it up and I'll tell all your fans you followed me home like a guy who couldn't get his mojo workin' as a member of the number three ranked team."

"Take it. See, it's that kind of attitude that keeps you from keeping a boyfriend. You're gonna take that rose as gift of my appreciation, whether you like it or not." he said.

Monet wanted to say something that was ladylike, yet so emasculating Ray would turn around and go back to the party. She couldn't think of anything so she did what any competitive independent woman would do; broke into a flat out sprint to the dorm. Ray gave chase, however, being cautious with the rose thorns slowed him down. They ran the last two blocks of fraternity row, past the business school, past the Watering Hole campus bar, past the student recreation center, and past the cafeteria.

They ran into the dorm tripping over themselves to push the elevator button. Monet's room was on the sixth floor. Ray bolted for the stairs. Monet looked up again at the elevator panel and chased after him.

Despite Ray's lead, Monet arrived at her door first. Ray arrived five seconds later. They stood in front of Monet's room, chests heaving and hands clasped behind their heads. Every few seconds they glanced at each other while they tried to catch a breath.

"God damn!... My girl's... got jets," Ray said, in between breaths.

"Don't tell me your feelings are hurt 'cause you lost to a woman?"

"No, but I didn't expect to get tripped coming up the stairs. Do I have a footprint on my back?"

"Let me see... nah, it's not bad..." Monet paused, then said, "That was nice."

"What? Me falling on my face or you stepping on my back?"

"You walking me home, silly."

"Racing you home," he said.

"Racing and losing."

"You won't tell my fans, will you?"

"I've got a better idea." Monet slowly closed the gap between them pushing him up against the wall across from her door. Both of their hearts were pounding from the run. Then she kissed him.

Ray said. "Whoa... I hadn't... thought... of that."

"Shhhh. You shouldn't talk with your mouth full," Monet said. When their lips unlocked, she looked deeply into Ray's eyes. "I really do appreciate you walking me home. Thanks for the rose." They were face-to-face, staring into each other's eyes. She closed his eyes with her hands. He smiled, mind racing. "Sexy enough?"she whispered. "Funky enough?"

She pulled him toward her by his belt loops, slow and gentle. She was the ultimate sensuous woman. Monet looked down the hall to make sure the coast was clear. He was expecting the best-case scenario with a happy ending right there in the hallway. She gently closed his eyes with her fingertips.

"No peeking... Knowing how much you like to win you're probably disappointed at losing the race," she said.

Smiling peacefully with his eyes closed, Ray said, "I'm pretty sure you tripped me."

Monet smiled. "Well, since I cheated, we need a tiebreaker."

"Huh? Tiebreaker. Yeah, okay," he said, just around the corner from ecstasy.

"Shhhh."

"Right. My fans."

While his eyes were still closed, Monet backed away from him. The look on his face, lips pursed, awaiting the next kiss, was priceless. He looked vulnerable and goofy. Monet could barely contain her laughter. His eyes were still closed. She pushed up against him, nuzzling his neck with her lips.

"Okay, a tiebreaker," she said in his ear before backing away.

"Yeah baby."

"Thanks for the race."

His eyes were still closed as she backed away. Ray opened them just in time to see Monet duck behind her door. Then she was gone. All that remained was the raging tent pole in his pants. He was about to knock on the door, but he stopped himself with his knuckles an inch from the door. It didn't happen often to Ray, but Monet had turned the tables. The only thing he could do was get the hell out of there with some of his dignity intact.

As he walked down the hallway, he thought about how the night could have ended with Buffy and Kirsten. He gambled and lost. Now, all he had to show for it were uncomfortably tight pockets.

Chapter 13

Persuasive Motivation

November Seventeenth, 7:00 AM
*4,997... Coach, I can make 'em. 4,998. I can make five thousand
free throws in a row. 4,999... But your teammates have been
running for the last nine hours... See, this is the last one, five thous...
Noooooooooo.*

Sonja had the same nightmare, the one where she is shooting
on an island court. Not only does she miss the 5000th shot, but the
ball rolls out of bounds and drops off a cliff. It's one thousand feet
down on all four sides. On the shore below, Gators and Terrapins
are being washed over with a Crimson Tide. It freaked her out.
She had the same dream over and over, but with different mascots,
depending on the conference. Being from Minnesota, some nights
Gophers, Badgers and Wolverines lurked at the bottom of the cliff.
Other nights it was Trojans, Bruins, and Sun Devils waiting for her
to miss that last free throw. It was awful. Her teammates had to
keep running while she started from zero.

"But I can't make five thousand in a row," she whimpered
pathetically to Lonnie in her sleep.

The same dream, over and over.

*Lonnie would say, "You can and you will Sonja. Or your
teammates will run... FOREVER. Ahhh Ha-ha-ha-ha-haaa!"
Lightning flashes from the distance would illuminate her face.*

*As Sonja began shooting the second set of five thousand free
throws, mascots would jump on huge trampolines from the shore
below. They waved signs and balloons to distract her. Up then
down, disappearing for ten seconds at a time then springing up just
in time to wave spaghetti balloons. Normal archrivals had a
common enemy–Sonja. Seminoles and Cowboys, Blue Devils and
Demon Deacons teamed up against Sonja. Chanting together,
"Ooga-chaka. Son-ja. Ooga-chaka. Son-ja. Ooga-chaka."*

They were waiting to take her into a fiery purgatory the second she missed. "Son-ja, Son-ja."

"Sonja. Sonja. Wake up. Sonja." Sonja opened her eyes to a face full of Lonnie Delaney.

"Aiiiiggggggghhh!"

"Sonja! Wake up."

"Yeah, wake up," Tamika said, groggily, climbing back into bed after letting in Coach Delaney.

"Good morning. You must have been having a bad dream... You wanna talk about it."

"Uhhh, no," Sonja said. "Coach?" Still groggy. "What time is it?"

"Seven."

"Uh-ohhh! I'm late," beginning to jump out of bed.

"Relax. It's Sunday. There's no practice today."

Sonja exhaled, still not making the connection. If she's not late for practice why is the coach in her dorm room at seven in the morning?

"The priests at Our Lady of Lourdes told me you've missed the last two Sunday masses," Lonnie said.

"Yeah, but..."

"I promised your parents if you went to mass at home, I would make sure you went to mass every Sunday your first quarter of the school year. Remember? So get up, you got twenty minutes to get ready."

"But..."

"Don't worry, you won't be alone, Jennifer is outside waiting for you." Jennifer stuck her head into the room, giggling and looking around Sonja's side of the room. She had pulled an all-nighter and was struggling to stay awake.

Sonja pulled her blankets over her head.

Lonnie snatched the blankets back as Sonja curled up into the fetal position. "Get up!" Lonnie was distracted by Sonja's side of the room. Everything was... upside down. Lonnie craned her neck, her head tilted downward as she tried to see the room right-side up. It was surreal, literally everything was upside down; pictures, cups, books, stickers, lamps, all of Sonja's modeling photos–everything. She heard Jennifer giggling behind her again.

There was a brief tug-o-war for a blanket between Lonnie and Sonja. It ended with Sonja being dragged to the floor clutching her blanket.

"Why is your room upside down?" Lonnie asked

Jennifer giggled again, "I did that last night, coach."

Lonnie smiled at the good clean college fun. She tilted her head again trying to look at the photos. "Okay then, Sonja, what's with all the pictures of models?"

November Eighteenth, Monday

Losing a game is not the worst part of losing. Practice after losing a game is the worst part of losing a game. – Monet McCasner

One by one they looked up at the wall clock in the locker room. It was 5:35 AM, far too early in the morning to feel this kind of anxiety. As each player went through their prepractice rituals, only the chatter of the early morning elderly swimmers could be heard from the far corners of the locker room.

"I wish I could have seen Sonja's room, all upside down," Clio laughed. "We got a freshmen with a sense of humor."

"I thought you guys were going to steal Stanford's mascot?"

"They got scared," Jennifer said. "But the night was too young to just go home so we, you know."

"You get Tamika, too?"

"They know better," Tamika said, rolling her eyes.

Roxy figured any coach that would make them practice immediately after a game was capable of all kinds of humiliation. She was right, Lonnie Delaney prided herself on being unpredictable, imaginative, and more than a little diabolical. Lonnie believed poor performance was an indication of poor preparation, which was the coach's responsibility. Lonnie Delaney took it personally if her team was not prepared. So, if the team ran out of gas, they ran more in practice to build their endurance. If they had a lackluster rebounding night, then two hour box out drills would follow. Only a poor shooting night was exempt from post-game practice rehabilitation–free throws excepted. Anyone can shoot poorly in a game.

When Lonnie entered the locker room, everyone froze. She was followed by a foul stench. Monet noticed that all of the coaches wore spearmint dabs under their noses. It made them look like blonde Charlie Chaplins and reminded her of the autopsy scene from *Silence of the Lambs*. Monet surveyed the scene and added it up.

Uh-oh. Angry coach, a bad loss, plus this awful smell.

Lonnie said, "Last game–we stunk. Anyone want to guess how badly?"

No one answered the rhetorical question.

"This badly!" Lonnie said, throwing the large duffle bag she'd been holding into the center of the room. The smell was overpowering. The duffel bag was filled with 14 nylon mesh sacks containing each player's unwashed uniform from the game two nights ago. The stench made everyone's eyes water.

"Find your uniform..." Lonnie ordered.

"Please don't say it. Please, please-please, please, please." Monet mumbled to herself, her eyes closed in prayer.

"...and put it on."

"Damn," Monet said, a little too loudly.

"Be on the floor in fifteen minutes. Oh, and ladies, don't even think of washing them in the face bowl or putting perfume on. Wear them as is... Where is Gina?..."

Gina stepped from behind Big Shirlie. "Here I am coach," she whispered.

The coaches left, but the stench remained. There was a collective exhale when Clio, the lookout, gave the all clear sign. The players rummaged through the pile and reluctantly got dressed. Sitting next to each other, Monet couldn't tell which was worse, smelling her own funk or smelling someone else's.

Kendra turned to Gina, "Why are you always standing behind people?"

Gina didn't answer. "Well, for today, don't stand so close to me."

As the team approached the court, they saw six men sitting on the sideline stretching and warming up and wearing Del Mar Runnin Rhinos Women's Basketball shirts.

"What are these guys doing here?" Sonja asked aloud.

"What's Chad doing here, Jennifer?" Gina asked.

Chad mouthed the word, "Surprise," to Jennifer.

Elite women's teams often practice against men. Men are generally faster, stronger, and thus perfect for practice competition for women. The men were proficient players, good high school players. They had lower status than walk-ons so it took a special kind of male ego to practice with women, knowing their efforts would never be seen and barely acknowledged. At least walk-ons can put on the uniform and sit at the end of the bench for games. These male "tackling dummies" can never receive anything more than a T-shirt, the maximum benefit allowed by the NCAA.

The men could play at full speed, but with a couple of exceptions. On a fast break they had to pull up for a jumpshot and not drive to the basket, thus avoiding any collisions with the smaller women. And they could not try to draw offensive fouls. They were encouraged to reach, grab, and hold, but in a basketball appropriate way. Anyone caught or accused of copping a feel would be kicked off the team or knocked out by one of the players.

Lonnie turned to face the team. "Ladies, these guys are here to help you improve your game."

It was bad enough they had to practice smelling themselves and their smelly teammates, at least everyone smelled equally bad. Now, they also had to practice with men. It was cruel, diabolically cruel.

"Last game we didn't pass the ball. So today we're going to learn how to pass."

Mbika was particularly enthusiastic. It was her first basketball game. Despite the results, she was thrilled to be on the team. She knew she would always be a role player, but she wanted to contribute to the team by being the team's best player-cheerleader. Every team has one, the player who greets everybody with a high five when they come out of the game, the one that tosses the water and passes the towels. She watched on television how football players congratulated, acknowledged, and pumped each other up. So, when the players broke the huddle, Mbika smacked Monet, Roxy, and Kendra on the behind and said, "Let's go, starters." The surprise gave them a chill and lifted them to their toes.

Lonnie proceeded to take the team through every conceivable passing drill; chest passes, bounce passes, lob passes, inbound passes, outlet passes, inlet passes, fast-break passes, backdoor passes, passes to the cutter, lead passes, and passes off the screen. They learned how to catch passes, how to shield passes, how to hold on to passes, and how to come to the ball so it couldn't be stolen from behind.

To really drive the point home, the players had to yell "We stink" every time Lonnie Delaney blew her whistle. Humiliating but effective. Lonnie knew from her psychology classes that the sense of smell is a most powerful reminder. Pavlov would have been proud. Monet made a point of staring at Roxy every time they had to repeat the "We stink" chant. In Monet's mind, it was all Roxy's fault.

When someone missed making a pass or dropped a pass, she and the person who was open had to stand back to back, twist, and hand each other the ball. If someone missed a second pass she and the player who was open had to sit down face to face, legs open, and do scissors stretches, one pulling the other toward her, then pass the ball one hundred times back and forth as they sat with their legs open. No one missed a third pass.

After forty-five minutes they started a normal practice.

Meanwhile, Lonnie's frustration with Tamika's defense was getting worse.

"No. No. No. Tamika!" Lonnie yelled. "You did the same thing during the game."

"I was taught to stay with my man," Tamika said defiantly.

"Maybe in high school that worked, but at the college level we play it the way it's supposed to be played. Show and recover. When your man is screening Monet's man, you have to step up two steps to here. That's the show. Even with the screener to stop the shot over the top."

"Then what about my man?" Tamika said.

"Monet will have her if she rolls, cuts to the basket. But if she doesn't then wait one second, which will allow Monet to step around the screen. But then you have to get back to your man. That's the recover. That's how you defend the oldest play in basketball. See?"

"Coach. Trust me my man ain't gonna score."

"But if she helps Monet's man score, then she's scoring against all of us, right? I mean that's what this is about, right? Stopping their team from scoring against our team?" Lonnie tried to reason with her.

"All I know is we won a state championship doing it the other way," Tamika said.

"Get out!" Lonnie yelled at Tamika. She'd had enough.

"What?"

"Get out. Get out of my practice until you want to play on this team. Go. Get out!" Lonnie yelled, turning her back on her.

Tamika was shocked as she headed off the court to the shower with the rest of the team staring at her.

Lonnie took the team through a series of drills, but she ended practice early. Their poor execution and utter lack of team cooperation was depressing her. The spearmint dabs were wearing out too. But before she dismissed the team each player had to make five free throws. Each time practice ended, Mbika felt the pressure to make her free throws. For the first time, when she couldn't make more than three in a row, the team rebounded her missed shots, offered encouraging words before every shot. Shaking her head, Lonnie finally dismissed the team but was happy to see they'd learned the importance of supporting each other.

As the players filed out. The coaches sat on the bleachers.

"Whew, please don't do that to them again," Renee said.

"I think we got the worst of it," Stephanie said, wrinkling her nose.

"Maybe kicking Tamika out wasn't such a good idea," Renee said, tentatively.

Lonnie turned to Renee, "Talk to me like that again and everyone will get kicked out. Do I need to remind you I've been playing and coaching this game before these women were even born."

"You don't have to convince me Lonnie. I'm just saying, players have changed," Renee said.

"How long have you, I mean, have we been out of coaching?" Stephanie said.

"Three years," Renee answered.

"But the game hasn't changed," Lonnie said.

"If the players have changed, then the game has changed. You can't yell at these kids and expect them to respect you just because you're the coach," Stephanie countered.

"The way to win never changes. Remember when you two played for me and we won it all? Remember how you complained? We didn't have a lot of talent on that team, but I've never had a group of women who were more committed to each other on the court."

"That *was* a great year," Renee admitted while Stephanie nodded.

"We just don't want you to make the same mistake as Petra Petitkovich, remember Petra?"

Lonnie nodded while rolling her eyes.

"Actually, we don't want to lose our jobs again," Stephanie said.

Renee said, "You know, five years ago a coach I really respected was speaking to a group of high school players and one girl asked the coach, 'What was the biggest mistake you made that cost your team a game?' The coach said, 'The mistakes that linger have nothing to do with winning or losing a game. What hurts ten times more than losing any game is realizing I didn't handle a player correctly...'"

Stephanie continued the quote. "...'There will always be wins and losses, bad coaching decisions, playing man to man when we should have switched to zone. That's nothing. That's basketball...'" Lonnie finished it, "'...Nothing hurts more than misreading what a kid needs; yelling when they needed a hug, or hugging them when what they really need is a kick in the ass.'" Lonnie turned to Renee. "I remember saying that."

"It's still the most important thing you taught me," Renee said.

"All we're saying is let's learn from our past mistakes," Stephanie said.

"So we can keep our jobs this time?" Renee said.

Billy Joe Bivens, the head football coach, entered the gym. "Hey Missy, tough loss to the Banana slugs," Bivens said, chuckling sarcastically.

"Yeah, it was a game we should have won," Lonnie admitted.

"I see y'all got a pretty tough schedule comin' up. Doin' lots of travelin'."

"We're playing the Lady Volunteers in a couple of weeks."

"Travel for you guys ain't too bad as long as you travel out of the state. If you play in California, it makes for a long weekend."

"Most of our games are in California," Lonnie said. She didn't know where he was going with the conversation.

"Yeah, I know. Anyway, I don't mind you flying on my dime, but y'all got to be ready if you're gonna play on television. Don't go embarrassing the school on national TV."

"When did the women's basketball team's road trips get on your dime?" Lonnie challenged.

"Excuse me?"

"You heard me."

Renee interrupted them, knowing it was about to get ugly. "Lonnie, you're going to be late for your conference call. Don't worry, coach Bivens. We'll be ready for the Volunteers." Both Renee and Stephanie whisked Lonnie Delaney off before she could say another word.

Lonnie was angry at Bivens and was getting angrier because she didn't have a chance to tell him what he needed to hear. "Stephanie, if you pull me away like that again–."

"Would it have been so hard to just smile and say we'll get 'em next time. Why can't you just say what you're supposed to say instead of looking for a fight all the time?" Renee asked.

"Did you hear what he said? Flying on his dime. We're not flying on his dime. His budget is three times the size of ours."

"Everything is not going to be equal," Stephanie was trying to calm her down, but the facts made Lonnie angrier.

"What's right is right. And more importantly, it's also the law," Lonnie said.

"Yelling at Bivens won't get them to gives us more resources or comply with Title IX," Renee said.

"The goal of Title IX was equal facilities for women when organizations receive federal funding. Oh, that guy makes me mad! So, we should just shut up and be happy? Be happy to be here–."

"Maybe tone it down a little," Stephanie suggested.

"Or set more modest goals," Renee added.

"Even though 'modest goals' means taking cold showers after practice, in an open locker room, while waiting until the end of the season to get our media guide. No, thank you. And then you want me to listen to that jackass tell me I'm flying on his dime."

"Please Lonnie, let's make it a goal to keep our jobs," Renee pleaded.

"It wouldn't hurt to get a few more gears, instead of just on and off," Stephanie said.

"On and off works," Lonnie Delaney said, crossing her arms.

"Three years ago, on and off got us all fired."

November Nineteenth, 10:00 AM

"I was talking with Coach Bivens about our upcoming schedule," Lonnie said to Forrest Haneline. They were sitting in his office.

"Yes," Haneline said, while wondering why would the football coach would be concerned about the women's basketball schedule.

"He said something curious, that we were traveling on his dime."

"That's ridiculous. He knows every team has their own budget. I'll talk with him," Haneline said.

"Thanks. You know I looked at our travel arrangements."

"Uh-oh, here it comes."

"We only get $20 for meal money while football players get $100," Lonnie Delaney said.

"C'mon Lonnie. Some of those guys weight 300 pounds."

"Why don't you base the per diem money on the weight of the player," she said.

"You know, sometimes I think you take this stuff too far."

"The basketball team gets $100 per day too."

"It's just meal money," Haneline said.

"And single rooms. Why do we have to double up? We took two vans over to our game at Hayward State; they took a chartered bus to Berkeley to play Cal," Lonnie Delaney said. "I mean how can you do this to the women's teams?"

"I have to take care of the big dogs because they take care of the rest of you."

"So that's what Bivens meant by traveling on his dime. His team flies down to play San Diego State and we have to drive when we play the San Diego Toreros?"

"You don't play them until–."

"I checked with Sandy. No wonder he said it's better for us if we play outside of California. That's probably the only time we'll get to get on a plane."

"Lonnie."

"Dutch. You've gotta change that. You can't expect my players to spend six-seven hours in a van and be ready to play a game let alone be ready to go to class when we get back. What kind of program is this?"

Haneline held up his hand, "Tell you what. You raise the money for airfare, you can fly. Get 250 paying customers to come to your game–do even better than that–get 1000 people to come to three of your games and you can fly the rest of the season. That's not so bad, right? That's only 700 more people."

November Nineteenth, 6:00 PM

Mail call. Monet plopped down on her bed to read her mail. Her mother said she was sending her a surprise. But knowing her mother she probably hadn't sent it yet.

Hmmmm, mom must have run out of her stationery to send me this brown recycled thing. No return address. This can't be from my mother.

Now, she was really curious. Monet opened the envelope and was speechless. The letter smelled bad.

The note read, "I've been watching you, watching you closely. Watching you play. Watching you eat. Watching you study. You're the number one player and I'm your number one fan. P.S. You shouldn't date losers who wear argyle." She was still staring at the letter when Ray knocked on the door and let himself in. She put it back in the envelope. He plopped onto her bed like he was at home. "Turn it to ESPN... Watch this... " He tuned in just in time to see the replay of a nasty dunk he threw down against Cal. "Posterized. By the number three ranked team in the nation. Now that's real." Monet watched, but didn't say anything.

"Hey, when do you want your rematch from Midnight Madness?" Ray asked. Monet didn't answer. "Don't wait and try to say I was avoiding you."

"I've been working on what you said. Subtly though," Monet said.

"You don't have time for all that. You guys are 1-3. The season's gonna get away from you."

"Yeah, you're right."

"I know you hate saying that. Just take it one step at a time... You know, I never did answer your question. If I had a girlfriend," Ray said.

"That was a hundred years ago."

"Well, I have," Ray said.

Monet imitated a bimbo, "Oh my Gawd, was she like, really, really beautiful, with lots of hair and beautifully painted toes? Did she like, always want to do what you wanted to do and somehow always said yes. And by the way, how great is that? And, oh my God, you guys must have made the cutest couple," Monet said.

"Seriously–."

"Seriously, did she bring you chocolate every day, or bring her friends over for a little, you know, boom-shaka-la-ka, while you switched talking between Shakespeare and Ebonics?"

"You know what I liked about her the most?" Ray said.

"Let me guess. Her big, bountiful, bodacious brains?"

"Excuse me. She was a very confident girl. Open-minded, not stubborn like some people I know. I loved that about her. Firm handshake. And a good kisser, not too reserved, but not too aggressive either. Wasn't shoving her tongue down my throat."

"Guys do that. Depth does not equal more passion," Monet said.

"I loved that girl."

"That's amazing. How did she get that far? She must have agreed to indentured servitude in Ray-nation," Monet said.

"Shopping."

"Shopping?"

"Shopping. She was smart with her money. She liked nice

things. Nothing extravagant. No $600 shoes, no $1200 dress that she had to buy to wear to some event when she already had a nice dress."

"That only works the same people won't be at the both fuctions., because I do that."

"That's what I'm talkin' about. I want someone who isn't gonna spend money like it's printed by the NBA."

"So what happened to your girlfriend?"

"I messed it up."

"Really, I never would have guessed that," Monet said, with heavy sarcasm.

"I should have listened to my mother."

"What did she say?"

"She said, 'Treat a girlfriend like your wife. That way when you do get married you will have had a lot of practice treating her right.'"

Monet looked at him incredulously stretched out on the bed. "Why won't brothas listen to their mommas?"

November Twentieth

Whoever delivered the stack of boxes to Lonnie's office was in a hurry because they had been dropped right in the middle of the floor where someone was assured of tripping over them. Lonnie opened one of the boxes, shaking her head as she flipped through one of the 500 freshly printed media guides. They were two months late.

Lonnie knew her team didn't have high priority with the athletic department. Men's basketball and football monopolized the majority of the Sports Information Department's resources.

The issue of equality in the athletic department was always on her mind. At what point does having low priority become unequal treatment or a violation of Title IX? When does being taken for granted become a form of discrimination? Keep in mind, merely being taken for granted might get you an apology, but proving charges of discrimination pays treble damages plus attorney's fees.

The media guides weren't for Lonnie, they were for the media— to help them write their stories about the players. They were useless sitting in Lonnie's office. The mere sight of them made Lonnie Delaney angrier, so she swiveled her chair and turned her back on them.

She took two more deep breaths to calm herself. She remembered the promise she had made to Haneline about being a team player, that she wouldn't cause any trouble, as she had done at The Ohio State. She thought long and hard about her integrity. Practicing what she preached so often to her players. But her anger was swelling–slowly, like a sprained ankle.

She wondered why *she* had to be so honorable. For what? So her team could be dismissed in every way imaginable. Or was she being honorable so she could keep her job? And isn't that just a nice justification for being a sellout? She had no answers.

Lonnie wanted to keep quiet, but Haneline was making it very difficult. She took three deep breaths this time and counted the ways she felt the women's athletic facilities were inferior to the men's. There were so many; the communal locker room and its cold showers, inferior travel accommodations, the thirty-five percent fewer female athletic scholarships, female teams got only a fifth as much meal money as that received by the men's basketball and football teams. The idea of more equitable practice times had been dismissed. To top it off, all the female coaches were paid up to 40 percent less than male coaches even when they were coaching the same sport.

Lonnie took four more deep breaths.

Producing the media guide two months late was bad enough. Delivering them to the coach instead of mailing them directly to the newspaper writers, television, and radio sports departments sent Lonnie over the edge. She had decided all the promises she made to Haneline at the beginning of the season were now null and void.

She picked up the phone and called Hooty Barneveld, the President of the West Coast Conference. They talked for 15 minutes about basketball, the Big Ten and her problems at The Ohio State University. After he had welcomed her and said he was confident she would be an asset to the WCC, Lonnie pounced. She asked if the conference had any rules for member schools to follow regarding media guides. He said they had to be distributed no later than two weeks before the season started. She then told him she had just received her team's media guide and that the media guides for Del Mar women's volleyball, gymnastics, and soccer had been delivered three weeks after their seasons began. She then thanked him for his time, said a few kind words and hung up. Done. It was just the leverage she needed without having to take legal action.

Ten minutes later, Haneline barged into Lonnie's office. She almost laughed out loud when he tripped over the media guides. She knew he would be upset. She didn't know it would take only ten minutes.

"What the hell are you doing?" he said, looking back at the boxes in the middle of her office.

"Excuse me?"

"I got a call from Hooty Barneveld, the president of the WCC. He tells me he got word that the media guides for the women's teams aren't getting out in time."

"I just got mine. They're right there."

Haneline looked down at the boxes. "How would he know that?"

Lonnie shrugged.

"You know what I'm talking about, Lonnie. How would he know the women's media guides are getting out after the season starts?"

"Hey, you guys do things differently out here on the west coast. I just called him to ask if there is a conference rule about media guides. In the Big 10 we did things a little more efficiently..."

"I don't care what you did in the Big 10."

"I'm sorry, I just thought it was a West Coast thing. You guys are more laid back out here," she said.

"Around here, we don't go to the media or the commissioner if there's a problem. If you have a problem with how things are run, you come talk to me. You got that?"

"I did, remember?" She had him there.

"Well, do you remember our conversation back in April, where you said you were on board. Then I listed all the things I didn't want to happen if I hired you."

"Yeah, it was right after you said you want this to be perfectly clear. Talking to the conference president wasn't on the list."

"How dare you? *How dare you!*"

"Don't you think you should be saying that to the Sport Information Director?" Lonnie said, totally calm.

"You must really hate coaching," Haneline said. His face was getting red despite his bronze tan.

Lonnie didn't answer. She knew where this was going.

"I know you probably think we're all a of bunch of chauvinists who could care less about women's athletics. One, it's not true. Two, we're doing a better job better than most," Haneline said.

"Well, from my perspective you're not following the Title IX statute. The facilities and resources are supposed to be equal for both men and women," Lonnie said.

"Lonnie, do us all a favor? Don't try to change us. Don't try to change the way we do things here. All you need to do is find your place in our family."

As Haneline turned to leave he tripped over the boxes again.

Chapter 14

Hooks

December First, 7:20 PM
"You have one saved message."
Tamika pushed the access code to the room voice mail.
Sent today, December 1st at 7:05 pm.
Tamika hadn't opened any of her textbooks in the eight weeks she had been at Del Mar. Finals were approaching. She wasn't worried about her grades. She had spoken to several football players who had told her not to worry as long as she kept her points and rebounds up.
Tamika plopped down on her bed and listened to the speakerphone.
"Hi Sonja. I'm totally psyched about being invited to the Tri Psi's mini rush party... Message saved. Sent today at 7:07 PM."
Sonja, I'm psyched. Are you psyched or what?... Message saved."
"Man that girl is a square," Tamika mumbled to herself.
Sonja keyed the door and came in.
"Whassup Sonja?" Tamika said.
"I am so psyched, guess what?"
"Uhmm, you got invited to the Bi-Tri's mini bike party?"
"Sort of, how'd you know?"
Tamika pointed to the speakerphone, which was still turned on. Sonja dropped her books on the bed and went to the mirror. "Can I ask you a question? Do you think I'm too heavy?"
"That's the fifth time you asked me that this week. Damn, do you want me to say. 'Yes, you're a fat cow.' Get it over with," Tamika said.
"I don't know. Thomas is always looking at these thin girls. Maybe I should be thinner. My dad was always trying to get me to lose weight so I could do gymnastics."

Tamika shook her head, "You're messed up and don't even know it. I don't know how that happened. You had everything you could want."

"That's not very nice... Hey, did you apologize to Coach yet?"

"For what?"

"For talking back, being insubordinate... You want me to go on?"

"I ain't apologizin'."

Sonja stood in the mirror looking at herself. "Well, when you don't get in the game when we play Tennessee on television, don't blame anyone but yourself."

That got Tamika's attention.

Sonja looked at her flat behind in the mirror. She pulled out her high school gymnastic leotard and pressed it against herself, "Maybe if I could get into this again."

"Girl, you care way too much about what people think."

Sonja wanted to say, "You should care more about how you dress in public." But she didn't dare say it out loud.

Sent today at 8:15 PM. Tamika, Victor Bitinour. Got your message. Just following up to see if you got it. I sent it on–on second thought–give me a call when you get this message. My number is 213-345... Message erased.

"Wasn't that the guy from the reception?" Sonja asked.

"Yeah, and...."

December Third

It was Friday night. The night Chris Chamberlain asked Monet to go out with him. Chris Chamberlain. Monet couldn't believe it. He was by far the best-looking guy on the football team. He was fast, he was strong, he was expected to be an early first-round pick in the NFL draft. With the ladies, his smile alone put him in the top five on campus. Sure, the guy had a little attitude, but wasn't that to be expected?

Monet had wondered what it would be like to go out with a guy like Chris. The guys she usually dated, the Milton types, Art Appreciators, always left her wishing they were something else. Chris' star power could illuminate a Monday night football game at Candlestick Park. Then, again, he had never heard of Langston Hughes, Renoir, or Salvador Dali.

Chris had said he would pick her up at 7:30. When he arrived at 8:15 Monet let him know being late wasn't okay. Keeping Ray's advice in mind, she was careful, tempering her displeasure so it wouldn't ruin the date. It was definitely a fine art. Like disputing a referee's call, say what you need to say then move on. Get in and get out. It was a bad omen when he shrugged. Monet was not the type to allow herself to be taken for granted.

In the dorm parking lot, Chris walked to his car to open the car door for Monet. Monet's car happened to be parked next to his and was facing out. She was still peeved about his nonchalance at being late, so she waited for him to open his door for her, then decided to unlocked the driver's side of her car. They both tried to open the doors at the same time. They stood there looking at each other.

Roxy happened to be looking out of her window. She saw Chris and Monet standing in the parking lot holding their doors open. Neither budged. Roxy liked Chris a lot, but had stayed away because he already had a girlfriend. At least, that's what she had thought. When she saw Monet and Chris in the parking lot, she called Clio, who called her friend the offensive lineman, who called a wide receiver, who confirmed that Chris was newly single. It took all of three minutes. During that time Roxy kept her eye on Monet and Chris. She had an idea.

Roxy made up some lame excuse to call Ray. She used all her feminine charm. But she balked when Ray tried to give her his usual gatekeeper assignments. She wasn't going for it.

Sometimes guys just won't cooperate.

In the parking lot, Chris stood holding his door open. "What are you doing?" he asked in a good-natured tone.

"I'm going to drive," Monet said.

"Stop playing!"

"I'm serious."

There was no way Chris Chamberlain was going to let Monet drive. If his friends caught him riding in the passenger seat with a woman, *on a date*, he would never hear the end of it. Monet knew this was a losing battle, but she wanted to make a point without ruining the night–take back some control of the date.

"Stop playin', we're gonna be late for the movie."

"Hmmmm, I wonder why?" That's all she really wanted to say. She could have said more, but the standoff was quickly turning into a test of will and she knew from experience it wouldn't end well. So, she locked her car door and got into Chris' car. She stopped herself from reaching over and unlocking his door, sending a subtle message how she felt the date was going.

During the ride over, all Chris talked about was himself. His game-winning catches, his draft prospects, his car, the music he liked, on and on. Chris, Chris-Chris, Chris, Chris.

So this is what it's like to date a guy with lots of options.

When Chris parked, Monet made a point of letting herself out of the car. She watched Chris hustle around the car only to find her standing patiently a few feet away.

As they walked, he closed the distance that separated them. He thought about trying to put his arm around Monet, but the vibe wasn't right. Maybe later, on the way back. He wasn't worried; he usually got his way with women.

At the restaurant, when he reached for the door Monet was already holding it open for him. He said, "After you," but Monet held out her palm instructing him to go first.

What could he say?

"Have you been here before?" Monet shook her head. "It's one of my favorite places," Chris said. Alumni own this place. "All you gotta do his tell them you play at Del Mar and they'll take car of you."

"So you brought me to a place where you can get free food?"

"No, it's not like that, but you know, they'll take care of you. It's good value," Chris said.

"Because its free," Monet said.

The *maitre d'* listened to their bickering as she guided them to their table. His eye brows arched when Monet purposely sat with her back to the wall so Chris would have to sit with his back to the restaurant. He prepared the waitress for a contentious meal at table seven. Monet watched Chris' face as he grudgingly sat down wondering if she knew she was sitting in the his seat–the position men usually sit on a date. He let it slide.

"The food here is really good. Here, let me order for you."

"No, that's okay," Monet said.

"I know what's really good here," Chris said.

"Yeah, but you don't know me and what I like."

What could he say?

Throughout dinner, Chris talked more about his favorite subject–himself. Halfway through the meal, Chris winked at Monet. She hoped it was his contact lens giving him trouble.

Monet and Chris each had a goal; Chris was trying to set up some kind of intimacy to end the night, while Monet started the date looking for companionship. The more competitive and testy their date became the more her plans transformed into foiling any of his plans that would lead to any kind of intimacy. The chess match went on all night. Monet reacted to Chris' moves while anticipating any traps four moves ahead.

Chris was on autopilot: Pick up girl. Drive. Open doors. Be civilized. Make her laugh. Talk about yourself. Be impressive. Go out to dinner. Emphasize your bright future in the NFL. Make googly eyes to set up a nightcap. Pay for dinner. Pay for the movie. Increase the body contact during the movie by touching her hand. Prompt her to do some touching of her own. Encourage "creative intimacy." After the movie, direct the conversation to erotic topics, sexy movies, sensual foods, hot actors she's attracted to. Lightly probe about her sexual ethics. Take her home. Go inside. Discuss more erotic topics. Make a move one level beyond the topic she was willing to discuss. Hit for the cycle: First base, second base, third base. Close the deal– home run.

Chris was on "make googly eyes."

When dinner arrived she caught herself tuning out yet another one of his autobiographical legends. When the heavily discounted bill arrived Chris grabbed it quickly without letting her see it. He was determined to pay for dinner at the very least. Monet saw it coming. She excused herself to use the ladies' room. She didn't have to go, but she was looking good that night and she wanted him to get a good look at what he would be missing later. She even put a little extra swivel in her hips for good measure. He noticed, all right.

She took a moment to figure out how much her meal had cost, then gave it directly to the waitress on her way back to their table. It wasn't until the waitress brought back Chris' change that he realized what Monet had done.

"You know you didn't have to do that. I said, 'I got it.'" He was irritated.

"I wouldn't want you to pay for a meal I didn't like," Monet said. *What could he said?*

They went to a movie, but once again Monet paid for her own ticket.

Their date touched all the bases. It was well choreographed but poorly executed. He was a future NFL draft pick, he thought he was charming, humorous, and good looking. It was Monet who didn't stick to the script. She paid for her own movie and meal. Her improvisation played the date to her strengths, which thwarted the obligation of intimate reciprocity Chris was trying to set up. Chris played the game out, hoping for a last minute checkmate–a kiss at the very least. You never know, she might get caught up in the aura of Chris Chamberlain. It had happened before. Not this time.

Their date didn't even end with a platonic handshake.

As Monet closed the door, Shirlie asked, "So how'd it go?"

Monet shrugged. "Typical."

"Really. I've heard good things about him. He just broke up with his girlfriend. You know Roxy is really hot for him."

"She can have him," Monet said.

Monet thought about making disparaging comments, but didn't see the point. Chris couldn't help who he was or the benefits he had come to expect from being a great football player. Monet decided *she* was just not going to be one of *his* fringe benefits.

Shirlie was right, too; she had heard good things about him– probably because that's all he ever talked about.

It was girls' night out. Gina, Jennifer, and Sonja were at O'Grady's. It was the only place they knew where they could buy beer without the hassle of getting ID'd.

"Next time, we're gonna tell you we're leaving at 6:30 so you can be ready by 8:00. You changed your clothes six times," Jennifer said to Sonja.

"I couldn't decide. The skirt wouldn't work with the sweater and the pants wouldn't work with the top I wanted to wear," Sonja said.

"Does it have to be perfect?"

Sonja didn't answer but the answer was yes.

"Tamika is right, you're way too anal," Jennifer said.

"Stop flirting with those guys," Gina said to Sonja.

"Okay, but when I get them to buy us a pitcher you can't have any."

"Hey, what did you tell Thomas?" Gina asked Sonja. "Something lame like, I'm in a study group and we're all getting together tonight at one girl's apartment."

"I didn't tell him anything," Sonja said.

"She didn't have to because he broke up with her," Jennifer added.

"Maybe you could say it a little louder," Sonja hissed. She wasn't doing a good job of hiding her disappointment.

"He still chasing stick figures?" Gina asked.

"He switched to exclamation marks," Jennifer said. "Stick figures had way too much booty."

"I'll have another boyfriend by the end of the week, watch," Sonja said.

"What did you tell Chad?" Gina asked Jennifer.

"I told him the girls were going out."

"Do you think these pants make me look fat?" Sonja asked.

"NO!" said Jennifer and Gina in unison.

"How did he take it? I mean, you guys are always together."

"Even in practice," Sonja said.

"It's still nice to go out without him once in a while. Look what I got." Jennifer showed them a new tribal tattoo she got just below the panty line on her back.

At that moment Chad walked up behind Jennifer and kissed her on the cheek. "Heeeey, I'm the only one who's supposed to see that."

"Hey, this is supposed to be girls' night out," Sonja said.

"Don't be mad, Sonja. Come here and let me give you a big hug." Chad said. Sonja recoiled. "OK then, what are you drinking? Let me buy you guys a pitcher." Chad was too good to be true. Jennifer hugged him for that.

Sonja asked Gina, "What about you, what did you tell Vince?"

"What is up with your roommate?" Gina asked Sonja, quickly changing the subject.

"Uhhh, that girl never studies. We have Writing Comp together, the professor caught Tamika reading *Sports Illustrated*."

"Ouch."

"How dumb is that?" Gina said.

"You mean how dumb is she?" Jennifer said.

"She's definitely not dumb, but she takes pride in being ignorant."

"Is there a difference?"

"She just sees herself playing basketball and isn't worried about anything else," Sonja said.

"Now that is dumb."

"It won't be if she takes it all the way to the bank. The ABL is playing now and the WNBA is starting up next summer."

"They aren't going to make any money. I hear the average salary is going to be about $50,000 a year."

"Ain't gonna get rich on that."

"$50,000 for three months of work? That ain't bad."

"Hey, Gina what did you tell Vince?" Sonja repeated.

"I just told him we were going out. I didn't tell him where. He gets kind of jealous."

Jennifer said, "I had a friend who had a really jealous boyfriend, but he was always snooping around and checking on her like she was his property. I hate that. Promise me you'll never check up on me like that, Chad."

Chad smiled, "OK, but what do you think I'm doing now?" Jennifer hadn't thought of that.

Gina said, "Hey, Vince isn't that bad."

"I hear he punches holes in the walls after a game if the ball doesn't go right through the middle."

"He hasn't missed all year." Sonja said.

"I mean right down the middle. Not left. Not right. He wants it to go dead center perfect," Gina said.

"He talks to himself."

"Yeah! I've heard him, too."

"Walkin' down the hallway talking to himself," Jennifer said. "Gina, you gotta find love where you find it but... Your boyfriend is a lunatic."

"He is not," Gina shook her head.

"Then why didn't you tell him where you were going?" Jennifer asked.

"Because I didn't know how to say it in a way that wouldn't upset him."

"Well you better think of a way now, because here he comes."

Gina was petrified. She was standing in the middle of the bar. There was no place to hide. Jennifer saw the anger in his eyes and the veins bulging in his neck.

"I thought you were studying," Vince said. Before Gina could answer Vince grabbed her arm firmly "Let's go."

"I'm not ready yet," Gina said.

"Excuse me."

"I said, I'm not ready yet."

Vince was keenly aware people were watching them. He whispered in her ear. "You know it makes me sad when you don't do what I tell you and I don't like it when we're not together. Let's go back to my place and order pizza. I'm buying."

Gina's smile put everyone at ease. Gina and Vince hugged, then left together.

*   *   *   *

"C'mon, we have to get started on our report," Ray said. He and Monet were sitting in a study lounge on her dormitory floor. "But this stuff is fascinating. Listen, did you know that in 1875 the Supreme Court decided that women were citizens under the 14th Amendment, but that citizenship didn't automatically mean women had the right to vote. It's right here in *Minor v. Happersett*."

"You must be talking about the same Supreme Court that allowed separate but equal facilities in *Plessy v. Ferguson*. That Supreme Court? Let me see that." Ray flipped to a totally different section of the book. "Look, New Zealand was the first country to grant women the right to vote. Norway was the first to allow women to stand for election, in 1907, but didn't give women the right to vote until 1913.

"That's backwards," Monet said. "Well, the Tennessee state legislature was one of the last to vote on the 19th Amendment allowing American women the right to vote."

"Switzerland didn't allow women to vote until 1971," Ray said.

"Big business didn't want it; even Frederick Douglass said, 'The right to vote should be given to black men before women.'"

"Freddy Afro was wrong on that one."

"You can't call Frederick Douglass, Freddy Afro."

"Why not?" Ray said, laughing at his irreverence.

"You just can't."

"Hey, Portugal didn't grant full women's voting rights until 1976."

"No way, 1976? Listen, so the Tennessee state legislature was divided right down the middle, right?"

"So."

"Tennessee was one of the last states to vote, and the last state needed to ratify the 19th Amendment. They needed 36 states, 3/4 of 48, but 12 states had already voted it down. So the youngest man in the legislature, Harry Burn, was the last man to vote. The vote was tied and he had indicated that he was going to vote it down. His one vote would decide if women would have the right to vote in the entire country."

"Damn, so what happened?" Ray said sarcastically.

"Shut up. He voted to approve, mainly because his mother wrote him a note telling him to be a 'good boy', and vote for women. See what happens when men listen to women! Just like that women won the right to vote on August 18, 1920. There were only two more states remaining that had yet to decide, so time was running out. Can you imagine how long it would have taken if he had voted no? It would have taken a couple more years to do it all over again, pass Congress, and then get 36 states to vote on it again."

Ray had thought about asking Monet about her date with Chris Chamberlain but decided it could wait.

December Tenth
Sonja was sitting in a hurdler's stretch when Tamika ran into the room and tripped over her.

"Owwwww."

"Did I get a FedEx package?" Tamika asked, hopping from left foot to right. She had to go the bathroom.

Sonja was rubbing her head. "Hello. Earth to rude ghetto girl." That got her attention. Tamika shot her a mean look. But it's hard to be intimidating when you have to pee. After two months, Tamika's mean looks no longer petrified Sonja, although they still made her uneasy.

Sonja pointed to the package on Tamika's bed.

"That's what I'm talkin' 'bout," she said, pouncing on the package. She opened it and smiled. She was careful not to remove the contents. She also couldn't wait any longer to answer nature's call. She tossed the package on the bed then jumped over Sonja.

Sonja thought about taking a peek. She wouldn't want Tamika to look at her mail, but she was too nosey to stop herself.

"Oh my God." There were at least ten $100 bills.

Sonja heard Tamika inserting the key in the door. She took a quick look at the sender. Victor Bitinour, Marina Del Rey, then put the package down.

Tamika returned with a big smile. She plopped herself on her bed. She realized there was no way she could tell if Sonja had looked at her package. She tried to read Sonja's face, but Sonja looked preoccupied.

Tamika went to pick up the FedEx package filled with cash before she had to explain what was in it. She thought she had picked it up by the top but actually had grabbed the bottom and the money fell to the floor. They looked at each other, not knowing what to say.

"Whoa!" Sonja said, trying to sound surprised.

"Yeah, well, you know, uh..."

"Who sent you all that money, eh?"

"I'm not sure," Tamika said, lying her ass off.

"Give me a break."

"I... I..."

"It's from a booster, huh?"

"Naw, a booster wouldn't give this much..."

"I mean, you don't have to answer if you don't want to," Sonja said. She liked watching Tamika squirm. "It's gotta be from a booster."

"I told you boosters don't give this much. It's from an agent."

"An agent!"

"Shhhhh!"

Sonja whispered even though they were the only two people in the room, "What are you doing with an agent?"

"I am not—officially."

"Isn't having an unofficial agent just like having an official one?" Sonja said.

"I haven't signed anything. *You* signed for the package."

"But your name's on it."

"I could say I never received it. It's all cash."

"Won't they come and break your arm or something?"

"It's not a loan. It's just a little... a little incentive to sign with him when I turn pro," Tamika said.

"You shouldn't take any money until you know there's actually gonna be a league beyond this year."

"Between the ABL and the WNBA there will be a league, trust me."

"Yeah, but the way you play screen-roll defense, you might not be playing in it," Sonja said.

"You sound like Coach. One thing is for sho', Tamika is gonna look out for Tamika."

"Well, while Tamika is taking care of Tamika, don't screw it up for the rest of us," Sonja said.

"That won't happen unless you-know-who finds out. At this point only three people know about the money, you, me, and my agent. And my agent and me aren't going to tell anybody."

Tamika didn't want to feel as if she had to be nicer to Sonja just to get her to keep her secret. So, she thought about something she could use to blackmail Sonja to makes things even. Tamika soon figured out that Sonja was too squeaky clean to have any secrets that needed keeping.

Sonja got up from her hurdlers' stretch, checked herself out in the mirror, then put on her running shoes.

"Going for a run, eh?" Tamika asked in her best Minnesotan accent.

*   *   *   *

During her freshman year in high school Monet had been the second best point guard in the nation for her age group. When she learned that she was second, she wanted to know who was number one. She learned that her name was Jamila Jetter and she hailed from Miami, Florida.

Monet would play against Jamila at AAU tournaments. She was good, but built in the classic short and quick point guard mold. She could penetrate, drop dimes, and had blinding handles.

Monet, on the other hand, was more of a basketball freak. She was already a shade under six feet tall which made her as tall as the center and power forwards but she had all the skills that Jamila and other point guards had. Being that tall meant she had more arrows in her basketball quiver. She could use her size to shoot over the top of shorter point guards or post them up in the paint.

The summer before Monet's and Jamila's senior year they met again at several AAU tournaments. In previous meetings they had played evenly. All the elite colleges were heavily recruiting them both. But Monet only wanted to go to Tennessee. For her it was Tennessee or nothing. She liked Ohio State because of Lonnie Delane made a great impression on her during the recruiting process. But Ohio State could never match Tennessee's storied women's basketball tradition.

Pat Summitt, the head coach of the Tennessee Lady Vols attended the last AAU tournament before letters of intent would be signed. It was crucial to play well. Unfortunately, through a numbers quirk, Summitt had only one scholarship available that year.

Jamila told Monet that Tennessee was her number one choice. One of the assistant coaches told Monet that they were interested in both of them but because they only had one scholarship, whomever played better at the camp would most likely get the scholarship offer. Monet didn't need any more motivation than that.

During the eight games they played during the camp neither of them gained a clear advantage. During their separate games Monet and Jamila had similar points and assists, the hallmark of a true point guard. Even though Monet consistently grabbed more rebounds, Jamila was considered a slightly better defender. It was inevitable that their respective teams would meet in the camp championship.

The pressure of a big game reveals character. Both Monet and Jamila had already led their high school teams to state championships. But in this championship game, a scholarship to the premier women's college program was on the line. There were other elite programs that were just as good with winning traditions; UConn, Stanford, Notre Dame, Duke, USC, or North Carolina. But both Jamila and Monet wanted to be Lady Vols.

They would settle the dispute of who was a better basketball player by playing head to head. The best wanted to leave no doubt. The scholarship to Tennessee was at stake; virtual automatic Final Four appearances and national championships were all part of the package. Monet wanted it. Jamila wanted it.

All elite athletes have a lot of diva in them. Divas get what they want.

The game was close. Through the first half Monet had more points from posting Jamila in the paint. She made sure the coaches jotted that down in their notebooks. Jamila had more assists. Monet went after every rebound she had a remote chance of getting and still managed to get back on defense,

With the game tied with five minutes remaining, whoever played well during the last two minutes would likely be rated higher.

Magic Johnson called it "winning time." It's the last two minutes of a close game where every possession is critical, every mistake is magnified, and every converted field goal cranks up the pressure on the opponent to respond. And that's just regular season games. Factor in a multiplier of ten for championship games. Everyone doesn't respond well. They think they can. They hope they can. But winning time in a championship game is where legends are created and only a few players are so blessed.

With two minutes remaining, Jamila and Monet had complete control over the game. Monet made a great block from behind, then finished the lay-up on the fast break. Seconds later, Jamila hit a player in stride with a sweet needle threading bounce pass after a backdoor cut.

With twenty seconds remaining and the score tied, Jamila rubbed off a high pick. The defenders didn't step out enough and she drove into the lane. She scored by lofting a high teardrop over a 6'6" player. It seemed like the dagger.

Monet's team didn't call time out. Monet brought the ball up the court while being hounded by Jamila. Monet protected the ball, but she still had to hurry. With ten seconds remaining and trailing by two, Monet knew she would go for the win. That was her style. A power forward and center set staggered picks at the top of the key and the right elbow of the free throw line extended. Monet faked left, then ran Jamila in the first screen and then past the second to make sure she had an open shot.

Monet stepped back behind the three-point line, squared up, set her feet, elbow in... shot... follow through. If she makes it they win. The shot rattled in and out. Monet was devastated. She couldn't believe it. She did everything she was supposed to do and she still missed. Given what was at stake, it took all of her willpower to acknowledge her opponents after the game. High-fiving Jamila Jetter hurt the most. But Monet understood that during winning time, Jamila produced and she did not. You can't get mad at that. Sports, as in life, is about what you produce.

Just as Monet feared, Jamila got the offer from Tennessee. Monet was out, so she chose The Ohio State. At least her parents would be able to see her play. She knew she would meet Jamila Jetter again. She vowed that next time she would be the victorious.

Chapter 15

Old Wounds

December Twelfth, Team meal

"What time are we leaving, eh?" Sonja asked.

"We're supposed to be in front of the Arena by eight o'clock. But the flight doesn't leave until ten."

"But that's in an hour and a half, I haven't packed yet," Sonja said.

"Well you better get on it then, eh?" Tamika said. "Nice nose stud." She was standing behind Jennifer and Sonja in the buffet line. Jennifer stuck out her tongue to show off her new tongue piercing. "Get that thing away from me... Hey, Sonja are you gonna eat that?" Tamika said.

The team was having its preflight team meal in the banquet room of the dorm cafeteria. They were going to the airport in an hour. It was going to be a long trip: Knoxville, Tennessee then Lexington, Kentucky.

Big women need to eat big. They were facing twelve hours of traveling which included several bus rides, a red-eye flight and a two-hour layover in Chicago before they caught a plane to Knoxville.

"Damn, girl," Sonja said, sounding more like Tamika with each passing day. Her perfectionist mother, the gymnast, would have been mortified.

"I know I usually don't eat this much, but I'm like hella hungry," Jennifer said.

"Do your thang," Tamika said, nudging Sonja who had served herself a respectable plate of food. "And you, all the runnin' you do, you need to be eating a whole lot more'n that."

Sonja looked up from her food then back down at her plate. There were dark circles under her eyes and her cheeks were sunken in.

"You gonna eat that?" Tamika pointed to the untouched roast beef on her plate. "How is it? It looks good."

"Take it," Sonja said, pushing her plate away.

"Watch out... You guys... take all this food... for granted," Tamika said, chewing and talking at the same time. Tamika always ate like the next big meal wasn't a certainty. By then everyone had become used to her gorging herself on the more delectable items on the menu. It was always the food she could never afford back home: mounds of shrimp, scallops, and salmon. Once, Lonnie had caught her stuffing popcorn shrimp into her pockets.

Sonja, Jennifer, and Tamika sat down with the team.

"Somebody is taking advantage of being away from home," Clio said.

Jennifer stuck out her tongue, showing off her new piercing. Her tongue ring clipped her tooth and she grabbed her mouth in pain. "Yoo-wantha-s'thee-my-tatoo?"

Sonja listened to her teammates ramble on as she cut her meat into bite-size morsels, scooped up her peas, and balanced them expertly on her fork. But the food never made it into her mouth. She merely moved her food from one part of her plate to another. She moved the peas from the two o'clock position down to the seven. The roast beef was moved from three o'clock to ten o'clock next to the rice, which she moved from four to nine. Since she appeared to bewas "eating" with the same rhythm as everyone else no one noticed that she wasn't eating much at all. She managed to eat some lettuce and a handful of grapes, which she washed down with apple juice. But she wasn't eating enough calories to support an eight-year old let alone a six-foot college basketball player who ran four miles a day on top of two-hour daily practices.

Shirlie said, "Tamika is going to lose a lot of weight during the summer when she goes back home."

"Maybe we could have a telethon for her during the summer while we're away," Clio joked.

"Or put her on a UNICEF milk carton," Roxy added, laughing. "Have Sally Struthers ask people to help. Please send this woman any popcorn shrimp you can spare."

"Are you still going out with that placekicker guy?" Monet asked Gina. "What's his name... Vince?"

"Yeah, why?"

"I saw you guys arguing the other day."

"Naw, we're cool."

"It didn't look like it. He was all in your face."

"He gets like that," Gina said.

"Guy that gets in my face, better look out below," Tamika said.

"You let a guy talk to you any 'ol way, soon he'll be treating you any 'ol way," Kendra said.

"True that," Roxy added.

"I swear I thought he was going to hit you," Monet said.

"Vince? No way."

"What were you arguing about?" Monet said.

"Some guy..." Gina exhaled. "Some guy was talking to me after class and Vince totally thought the guy was trying to hit on me. I told him he wasn't, but he wouldn't listen. It was a little scary for a moment, but he calmed down. He's fine."

Monet didn't believe the "he's fine" part, because when she had seen them that day there was more to it than just placekicker jealousy. She could see the veins in his neck bulging 50 years away.

Jennifer said, "I saw him the night after the football game. He threw a garbage can through a dorm window. The guy's a psycho."

"He's a placekicker," Clio said, to a chorus of umm-hmmms.

"All of you need to keep quiet," said Shirlie, the usual voice of reason. "All the bad decisions you guys make, none of you have room to judge Gina. Kendra, all I have to do is say Mo Ellis and you'll want to change the subject. Clio, you spent two months chasing that baseball player and you didn't catch the hint until he dated and broke up with three different girlfriends. And don't forget Jennifer, Ms. Table Dance."

"Hey, that was blown totally out of proportion," Jennifer said.

"Yeah, but you don't remember any of it, so how would you know?"

"Because Chad is my boyfriend now."

"And what kind of boyfriend gets on the practice squad to–."

"–Shhh, Coach doesn't know," Kendra said, looking down at the coach's end of table.

"He must really love yo' ass, 'cuz one whiff of you during that first practice and I would'a broke up with you and dropped out of school," Tamika said.

"My locker is next to yours, Tamika, and believe me I thought about it after smelling you," Jennifer said.

"How's your quest going?" Sonja said to Jennifer.

"What quest?" Clio said.

"Jennifer and Chad are on a quest to have sex in every building on campus."

"It'll never happen," Roxy said.

"Why not?" Jennifer said.

"Because the church is on campus."

"The priest's residence is on campus."

Jennifer hadn't thought about that.

"Forgive me father, for I have sinned... 'You did what... Where!?... I'm sorry lady, you're going straight to hell.'"

The entire table laughed.

"And you know what? You and Chad should stop with the holding hands and bumping up against each other in practice."

"Yeah, get a room, before you both get kicked off the team."

"Someone has a crush on Ray," Roxy said, opening up a whole new can of worms.

"Yeah, you!" Clio said. "The way you wanted a thorough background investigation for, wait a minute that was for–."

"–Chris Chamberlain. Now don't you feel stupid?" Roxy said.

"So why have you been flirting with Ray the last few weeks?" Shirlie said.

Roxy didn't answer, but she locked eyes with Monet.

The ticket line at Chicago's O'Hare airport doubled back over itself four times. The team's connecting flight to Knoxville had been canceled and they were scrambling to get on another flight. Normally, Renee or Stephanie would handle all the tickets, but this time quick executive decisions needed to be made which meant Lonnie was stuck standing in line.

"Make sure they don't scatter," Lonnie said. "I want to be ready in case we have to run to catch a flight."

Renee and Stephanie nodded, thankful they didn't have to stand in line. When they returned to the group, seven of the twelve players were gone.

Tamika had just lugged in the last of the bags. The victim of more freshman hazing, she dropped six duffel bags near the seating area. She wasn't pleased.

"Where is everyone?" Renee asked Monet, who just shrugged, didn't even look up from her book. Renee and Stephanie hoped it would take a while before Lonnie got their travel plans together. No such luck, since she was standing right behind them.

Lonnie said, "Okay, we're flying on American– Hey, where is everyone? I thought I said..."

"Lonnie, they were gone by the time we got back."

"The flight's in thirty minutes and it's all the way on the other side of the airport."

Kendra, Clio, and Roxy returned chomping on sandwiches. Not a care in the world. Shirlie was right behind them.

"Where are Sonja, Jennifer, and Gina?"

Shirlie said, "Jennifer stopped to buy some popcorn and ice cream. I think Sonja went to the rest room. Are we leaving?"

"Not if we miss our flight. I told everyone to stay here... I'll go get her myself," Lonnie said.

Only one stall in the ladies' room was occupied. Sonja walked to the stalls at the end. She waited a few minutes while two ladies finished up, washed their hands, and exited. It was silent for a moment.

Then someone else rushed into a stall and vomited.

Misery might like company, so Sonja pulled out her tooth brush and rammed it down her throat. It didn't take much for her gag reflex to kick in. She'd been doing it for years. The two women took turns vomiting several rounds together.

When Sonja was finished she asked, "You okay over there?"

"Yeah, I guess so. This never..." She stopped because they'd recognized each other's voices. Sonja and Jennifer stuck their heads slowly out of their stall's at the same time.

"Hey."

"Hey."

"What's the matter with you?" Jennifer asked.

"I think I had some bad fish on the plane," Sonja said.

"But you didn't have the fish, remember? You had chicken. Actually, you ordered chicken, but you didn't eat any of it."

Jennifer was interrupted by more convulsions. She ran back into the stall.

Sonja was starting to worry. It's one thing to purge yourself quite another to throw up involuntarily. "You okay?... You're not pregnant, are you?"

"Hell no, I better not be," Jennifer said, wiping her mouth. Her face was ashen.

"You sure? Cause..."

"I can't be pregnant, my parents would kill me."

They flushed their toilets and washed up in the sink.

"Only time women vomit like that is when they're pregnant," Sonja said.

"I am not pregnant! Okay? Maybe *you're* pregnant."

Just then Lonnie walked in and winced from the sour smell of vomit.

"There you are... What is that smell? You guys do that?"

Sonja and Jennifer were speechless for a moment. "There was some lady in here, I think she was pregnant," Jennifer said.

Nice save.

"Our flight is leaving in 20 minutes and you two are going to be the cause of us missing it. Let's go."

They scurried out.

"All right, let's get the hell out of here," Lonnie said, striding toward the team. Everyone scrambled to attention. Renee did a quick head count. As they were about to leave, a familiar voice called out to Lonnie. She immediately turned pale. It was her ex-husband, Merle.

"What are you doing in Chicago, I thought you hate to travel?" Lonnie said.

"Every now and then there's accounting to be done outside of Ohio. You would think they couldn't find someone in California to add and subtract but–."

"–You're going to California? We're coming from San Francisco," Lonnie said, trying to contain her surprise.

"It figures. How's the new job?" he asked.

"Good. I've got a good group of players. We're playing on ESPN2 tomorrow night.. We're you going to look me up?"

Being evasive, he said, "You still working 120 hours a week?"

"No. I learned my lesson. I'm just trying to fit in."

"A little late for that don't you think?"

"You couldn't wait for that, huh?" Lonnie said. "I couldn't get a job for three years after that stunt you pulled, serving divorce papers the night we won the national championship."

The players gasped.

"That wasn't my fault," he said.

"Of course it is."

"Besides, you divorced me long before that. You were never home."

"Was too."

"All you wanted to talk about was basketball."

"Did not."

"I just made it official." Merle grinned as he remembered the look on her face after she read the divorce papers in the locker room. Five seconds later ESPN stuck a microphone in her face.

It was sweet revenge. "You probably want to blame me for you not getting hired for three years."

"You know athletic directors want head coaches to be married."

"I never understood what one has to do with the other."

"Look, we said we were going to take some time and then try..."

Lonnie and Merle turned their heads to see the entire team engrossed in their conversation. They composed themselves.

Looking at his watch, he said, "It looks like you guys have a plane to catch."

Merle and Lonnie Delaney stared at each other for a moment before he reminded her she needed to go. As the team walked away, Monet heard Lonnie say, "You should call me."

Then she heard Merle say, "Why?"

December Thirteenth, 10:00 PM

Tamika lay on her hotel bed in Knoxville. She was watching SportsCenter and talking to Victor.

"This is it," Victor said. "The big time. If you wanna make a name for yourself you gotta have big games against the big teams."

"Yeah, but sometimes Coach be trippin'." Tamika said.

"Great players don't worry about the coach. Remember it's your talent that secures *her job*. You gotta start acting like the great player you think you are. That I *know* you are."

"Nah, but..."

"You wanna play in the ABL or WNBA right?"

"Yeah.," Tamika said.

"Then when the bright lights are on you have to play well enough so it shines on you. Let me give you a reality check. Your grades and that thing you got into–."

"–I didn't steal no car."

"Well, your grades kept you from going to Tennessee in the first place. You know that already. And you know Del Mar isn't exactly an elite basketball school. So you gotta have great games against the Tennessee's and UConn's of the world." Victor had given Tamika a lot of money over the last few weeks. He had a lot at stake. "Delaney did you a favor by scheduling all those great teams, but it's up to you to perform when you play them. If you don't play well against them, then you can forget it."

*　　　　*　　　　*　　　　*

December Thirteenth, 10:30 PM

Roxy was orchestrating her usual hotel room party. Clio was popping the popcorn. Roxy was mixing drinks. Jennifer and Sonja were sprawled across each of the double beds watching SportsCenter. Shirlie walked in wearing her usual road trip sleepwear; pink long-sleeve, one-piece pajamas complete with rubber-soled feet. The long zipper stretched from her crotch to her clavicle. She looked like an earless pink Easter Bunny. She could get away with this kind of fashion high jinks on the road with her teammates although a boyfriend had quickly become an ex-boyfriend when he saw her in her funny bunny jammies. She had caught him rummaging through her closet. He was high on mushrooms at the time and for a moment he thought he had shrunk. At any rate, Shirlie's big pink jammies brought out the kid in her.

"Who wants a Pina Colada?" Roxy announced. No hands went up. "Okay, who wants a Daiquiri?" Eight hands went up. "Okay, we only have Pina Colada mix and no strawberries. If you want a Daiquiri you'll have to go down to the hotel bar and buy one for twelve dollars. Now, who wants a Pina Colada?" This time everyone's hands went up.

"I see you stopped chasing Ray," Shirlie said to Roxy.

"Yeah, a spot opened up with Chris Chamberlain," Roxy said, smiling. "You know I like football player."

"She's still jealous of Monet and her game balls," Clio said.

"I am not," Roxy lied.

"De-nial," Clio said.

"Monet practice shorts are practically covered in game balls," Kendra said.

"I am not jealous."

"A little piece of you dies every time she gets another one. You can see it on your face."

"I am not jealous, I don't care what you say," Roxy said.

All eight players said it together, "De-nial."

"Fine, virgin Pina Colads for everyone, now,' Roxy said.

"Is it just me or are we playing better?" Kendra asked.

"We're playing better, but you don't have anything to do with it," Clio said. "Not from your seat on the bench." Everyone laughed.

"Truth or dare," Clio said. Everyone groaned.

"Come on Clio, you make us play this every time we go on the road."

"Truth or dare," she insisted.

"Next thing you know we'll be playing spin the bottle," Kendra said, which got Jennifer to look up from staring at SportsCenter. "I just want to say that I have a boyfriend and I am not going play spin the bottle with any of you."

Before she left Oroville for San Francisco, Jennifer's devout Catholic parents had warned her about girl on girl love. She hadn't seen it on the team, but she felt the need to state her position.

Roxy said, "Freshman, you'll play with another freshman when we say so."

Roxy said, "Make the freshmen go first."

Clio smiled, perfect. "Sonja, truth or dare?"

She hesitated, then said, "Truth."

"Is it true that you think Coach Delaney is a crimson and cream fashion catastrophe waiting for the next scheduled game?"

"Uhhhh..."

"What was that thing she wore to the last game?" Kendra said, still laughing.

"The cream suit with the flared pantlegs," Shirlie said.

"Coologs."

"Gauchos," Roxy said. "Those cream high-water pants. Pants ridin' so high they're afraid of heights."

"Aww, look who talkin', Miss Have-to-Have-a-Ground-Floor-Room because you can't walk on the balcony, because *you're afraid* of heights," Clio said to Roxy.

"I want to be on the ground floor if there's a fire. Sort of like where Coach's hemline needs to be, closer to the floor," Roxy said.

"I hate to say it, but coach could use a manicure," Kendra said.

"And a pedicure. You seen those toes, they're like twisted crusty shrimps."

"No, prawns. Little, twisted, ashy prawns," Clio said.

"Someone should tell her she's not obligated to wear the school colors at games."

"No white."

"Helloooooooo, no white or cream after Labor Day or before Memorial Day," Kendra said; even the freshman were laughing now.

"The VPL is embarrassing."

"Eeewwwww. Visible panty lines."

"If she wants to match with the players, she should put on a uniform."

"Like baseball managers."

"And if she's going to wear a skirt, she can't go kneeling during the game."

"Did you see all the guys across the court craning their necks?"

"Trying to get a peek."

"From a forty-five year old woman? That's just wrong."

"She's not forty-five."

Sonja stood up to change the channel. She was wearing her practice shorts. Roxy immediately noticed Sonja's three game-ball patches. "Nice shorts."

"Don't get on the freshman because she's got more patches than you," Shirlie said.

"All that damn running she does," Roxy said.

"Stop complaining. You're still playing, just not on the point. Frankly, I think we're a better team," Shirlie said.

"We've run more in two months than we did in three years with Coach Satcher."

Shirlie said, "Yeah, I hate it too, but she is a better coach. We beat Cal and now we're about to beat Tennessee. Call me crazy but I think we have a shot at winning."

"No more Pina Coladas for you, Big Girl, it's clouding your judgment," Roxy said.

"I think we might be pretty good and not even know it."

"Obviously, some of you have had too much to drink. Who's the designated driver?"

"What's up with Gina?"

"She's always standing right behind people in practice."

"She just don't want coach pickin' on her."

"No, she does that even when we're not in practice and–."

Tamika knocked on the door, saying, "Here you guys are," as she walked in.

"Jennifer. Truth or dare?" Clio said, changing the subject.

"Dare."

"You sure?"

"Dare."

"Okay, I dare you to run outside in the hallway and buy a Coke from the vending machine."

"What's so hard about that?"

"Butt naked."

Jennifer thought about it for a moment. The hotel wasn't crowded. She had heard the concierge say the team had the floor to themselves. "OK, I'll do it."

"OK, here's 50¢."

"Remember the table dance," Tamika said, reminding her what coach had said about conducting yourself with dignity and self-respect.

"Shut up, Tamika, or we'll make you go," Roxy said.

"Yeah, that's what yo' mouth say," Tamika said.

Jennifer felt a rush of adrenaline as she slipped off her T-shirt, shorts, and panties.

Kendra opened the door, and like a thoroughbred at Churchill Downs Jennifer sprang out of the gate. She turned right, and hit top speed when she passed the elevators.

"Where's she going?" Shirlie said.

Jennifer made it all the way to the end of hallway but when she turned into the area for the Coke machine she was standing in front of the ice machine. The soda machine was in the same spot at the other end of the hallway twenty feet from the hotel room.

Uh-oh. Jennifer turned around and sprinted back down the hallway, stark naked and bouncing. She heard the elevator bell ring.

"Oh, shit."

The entire team had stuck their heads out, but when they heard the elevator door ring everyone ducked back into the room and closed the door. Jennifer was in a flat-out sprint. She passed the bank of elevators in a blur, fortunately, a half second before the doors opened. Behind her, she heard Lonnie Delaney's voice, "You guys go ahead. I'm gonna check on the team real quick."

"Shit."

Jennifer was just a few feet from Roxy's room. She nearly fell trying to stop. The soles of her feet burned from the friction on the carpet. She pulled on the door. It was locked. LOCKED.

She knocked.

"Come on. Let me in quick." All she heard was giggling behind the door. The hallway was clear but it wouldn't be for much longer. Jennifer took off for the soda machine area four strides from the door just twenty feet up the hallway. To the left this time. It was going to be close.

"I'm going to check on Merle?" Lonnie said to Renee and Stephanie.

"Who?"

"I mean the girls," Lonnie said, embarrassed.

"See, there you go again," Stephanie said.

"Somebody get that woman a date."

"Don't start,"

"No, she's too far gone for that, she's gonna need a *big–*."

"–Heeeyyyyy! Easy now," Lonnie said, laughing at herself.

"I'm gonna go check-on-the-team. O-kaaay?" Renee and Stephanie laughed as they walked down the hallway.

Jennifer stood there breathing heavily, butt naked, pressed up against the vending machine, hoping Lonnie would just go to her room. In a few moments she would know if she saw her from down the hallway. The wait was excruciating.

Kendra let Lonnie into the room when she knocked. They had hidden the Pina Coladas.

"Whoa, what is that smell?" Lonnie asked, waving her hands in front of her face. "You guys need to cut down on the body splash. It's making you smell like Pina Coladas. Where are Monet and Jennifer?"

"They're around here somewhere," Kendra said with a huge grin.

"Barely," Clio said. Everyone started laughing. Lonnie looked at them.

"I'll go check on them. Are they feeling OK?"

Clio said, "Jennifer said something about getting *stripped* throat."

More laughter. Lonnie decided it was time to leave, because the jokes were going over her head. A roar of laughter erupted the moment she closed the door.

"By the way, who was that man at the airport?" Clio asked after Lonnie left.

"Renee said it was her ex-husband," Shirlie answered.

"Can you see coach gettin' some?"

"Yes. Yes. Yessss," Clio said.

"Damn it, Merle, show AND recover," Roxy said. "If you're gonna show it for three minutes the least you can do is recover quickly."

"You ever notice how she's always talking in threes?"

"–Together, together, together." Kendra said, mockingly.

"Hey, where's Jennifer?" Sonja said.

Jennifer was still standing, naked, in front of the Coke machine waiting for Lonnie to walk down the hallway. Fortunately, no businessmen or families with young children showed up looking for a frosty beverage. Lonnie Delaney passed the elevators on her way to her room. Jennifer thought she was going to make it back safely until the elevator door rang again. A bellhop delivering luggage got off the elevator bell. He was headed toward Jennifer and was about ten feet away, when suddenly he stopped. He had forgotten which door he was looking for and had to walk back to the elevators to call the concierge. Lonnie was almost at the end of the hallway. Jennifer scrambled to the door and knocked softly.

On the other side of the door, Clio said, "Password."

"Open the damn door!"

Lonnie heard Jennifer's voice, but when she turned around the hallway was empty.

After Jennifer closed the door behind her, everyone threw sheets and blankets at her. Within seconds she was buried under a mountain of linen. "Damn you guys, I could have been in big trouble."

Tamika shook her head. She wasn't impressed with college fun.

"Jennifer?" Clio said.

"What!?"

"Where's my Coke?"

As usual, Gina was in Vince's room. Vince liked the fact that Gina was a walk-on because she would never go on road trips with the team. Which meant he had her all to himself when they traveled. Besides class time, he liked her to spend all of her time in his room. He paid for meals, usually pizza, until she started to put on some extra weight and made him order Chinese food. It was like having her own butler, who gave his own orders. It was a strange relationship.

"So what do you want to do tonight?" Gina asked.

"I don't know, let's just stay in," Vince said.

Gina shook her head. "We're playing Tennessee tonight on ESPN2. And you don't have cable."

"So what are you saying? You wanna go out?" Vince said.

"Yeah, I want to go out."

"But I don't want to go out."

"And you don't have to."

"Yeah but..."

Gina said, "I'm just going to the Watering Hole Bar to watch the game. I'm going to be right back. Why don't you come with me?"

"I told you, I don't want to go."

"Okay, then I'll see you in–."

"And I don't want you to go, either."

Now she was stuck. She didn't know what to say; he had bought her Chinese food and now he just wanted her to stay. It was a reasonable request, she supposed. But she still really wanted to see her team play on television. He was starting to get angry.

Since meeting Vince, Gina had spent every Friday night in his room messaging his legs and whispering sweet "atta boys" in his ear. When he would complain that his teammates didn't appreciate him, she said, "That's the life of a placekicker. They love you only when you make the winning field goal and hate you if you miss an extra point."

He wanted her to be more sympathetic. He was quick to remind her that he had never missed an extra point in three years. She could tell he liked hearing himself say it.

He took care of everything for Gina, but Vince was very sensitive, and there was a long list of things she couldn't mention to him. He was going bald already, so jokes about his diminishing follicle count and steadily enlarging forehead were off-limits. She thought it was cute when he would get upset about something he couldn't control while looking in the mirror.

"You know, it makes me unhappy when you don't do what I say. Sometimes I think you're like all the rest," Vince said.

The guilt trip worked on Gina. He stood there looking like a sad puppy. Even though, she really wanted to see her team play, she decided to stay with Vince.

She knew the routine. She would do her homework for the weekend. He would watch television. Bored, she would do some advanced reading for her classes while Vince talked on the phone. Later, Vince would use some cornball line, then they would have sex.

Rough sex.

It didn't start off that way. In the beginning, sex with Vince was rather uninspired and pedestrian. He always had to be on top. At first, she didn't mind a little horseplay. But it wasn't long before a little push turned into a shove, which turned into a light slap. Once he suggested using handcuffs for one of his fantasies. It worried Gina a little, but he insisted. She justified it to herself by thinking how cute he was when he got his way. Vince's fantasies grew increasingly painful. Each time he wanted to increase the intensity he used another guilt trip. "You'd do it if you loved me. I'd do it for you." But they never switched roles and it always seemed to be her turn to play the submissive role in his fantasies.

Every week they broke through new thresholds of dominance

and sometimes new thresholds of pain. A pattern was forming–a dance. Vince wanted to see how far he could take her. He craved the new boundaries of control she surrendered, like Hitler marching through the France of her psyche. They had been dating only three weeks. Three weeks and she was allowing him to choke her while they had sex, teeth clenched, heaving on top of her. It was a rush for him.

One time she fainted. She was out cold–scared him to death. The pain Vince inflicted wasn't unbearable. Actually, the endorphins made the pain exciting, which both disturbed Gina and made her proud at the same time. She was disturbed by how far she had come in her submission to him. Submission meant trust. She felt her self-respect eroding. Just like her mother. Over time Gina became proud of the pain she could endure to please her man.

December Fourteenth, 7:30 PM EST
Thompson-Boling Arena
Knoxville, Tennessee

"Good evening and welcome to women's Runnin' Rhinos basketball. Tonight the 5-7 Lady Rhinos of Del Mar travel halfway across the country to play the 7-0 University of Tennessee Lady Volunteers, coached by Pat Summitt. It's a sellout crowd here in Knoxville. The band is blaring Rocky Top in our ears and we're just about ready to begin. I'm with my broadcast partner Courtney Heinz. Courtney, tell us some of the keys that the Rhinos will need to have a chance at beating the number one team in the country," Thalia Clark said.

"At 5-7 the Rhinos' season is sinking faster than the Titanic. This is a statement game for them. They're playing the number one team in their house and–."

"–Tip-off is in 20 seconds, what do they need to do win?"

"They have to do the little things. Make shots and play defense," Hienz said.

"That's it?"

"Yep."

"There you have it. In order to win the Runnin' Rhinos basically have to play basketball."

Monet had circled this date on her calendar the moment she

saw the schedule. It had been three years since Monet had played against her cross-country high school rival, Jamila Jetter. The memory of losing that championship game their freshman year was still vivid in her memory. Monet had lost the championship to Jamila and the Lady Volunteers in her freshman year. Since then, their careers had taken vastly different turns. Not only did Jetter win that championship game, she went on to win one more championship her sophomore year. Her junior year her team lost the semifinal game. Jetter redshirted her fourth year, after she tore her ACL. And now in her fifth year, she was on another Tennessee team that was expected to play Stanford in the final.

Jetter's basketball success annoyed Monet only because she knew she had the ability to play at Tennessee. Monet figured that she would have been hoisting all those championship trophies herself if she would have made the winning shot at the Nike camp. Instead, it was Jetter who got to expience the greatness of Tennessee women's basketball.

Now, Tennessee, ranked number one in the country, 7-0, was poised to win another NCAA championship. Del Mar, 3-2, realistically wasn't going to make it to the NCAA tournament. In fact, the only reason Tennessee was even playing Del Mar was the mutual admiration of their coaches. This would be Monet's only opportunity to avenge that championship game loss against Jamila Jetter. In effect, this was Monet's.

As the teams ran through their warm-up drills, Monet thought about her rivalry with Jamila, the missed shot at the Nike camp, the missed shot in the finals their freshman year. She had made seven game-winning shots during her high school career, one for a state championship. But she missed the two most important shots, both against Jamila Jetter's team.

Monet needed to shake the shroud of doubt that had enveloped her. She bounced back and forth on her toes at mid-court, repeating to herself, "*I'm the man. I'm the man. I'm the man. I'm the man.*"

Even if Del Mar beat the number one ranked Volunteers, it wouldn't equalize Monet and Jamila's rivalry. Jamila had won when it counted, when the stakes were greatest and championships were on the line.

"This is a big game. Big game players make big game plays. They find a way for their teams to win."

"The Rhinos win the tap." Clark said, doing the play-by-play.

210 **Under the Rim**

McCasner pounds the ball into the front court, big size advantage over the Tennessee All-American point guard, Jamila Jetter. Down to Hightower on the block, McCasner cuts to the basket for a lay-up. Nice cut by McCasner and an even better pass by Hightower." Monet was worried. She was trying to win the biggest game of the year against her old nemesis when she had no confidence in her teammates. They didn't want to win as badly as she did. They might even revert back to their old tricks just because they knew this game was important to Monet.

As the game took shape, Roxy, Clio, and Shirlie didn't go out of their way to freeze Monet out. They couldn't. Each time Tamika received a pass down on the low block, she wheeled around and scored. Tamika was hogging all the shots. She was determined to make sure the whole country got to see her play well against Tennessee. She needed to prove to Victor, her "unofficial" agent that his investment in her was solid gold.

Jetter stole the ball. Shirlie raced after her and was able to foul her on the way to the basket. "Going up, two shots," the referee said. Like many teams, the Rhinos formed a brief huddle before the free throw.

"Good foul." Roxy said.

"We have to box out on the shot and..." Monet added.

"What are you doing?" Roxy said.

"This game is important to me, I want to make sure..."

"That's fine and dandy, but who's the captain?"

Tamika, Sonja, and Shirlie looked at Monet. It was a tense moment. Renee nudged Lonnie to pay attention.

Monet knew the next thing she said would be pivotal... "You're right. My bad," smiling, trying to defuse any tension because she would need them to win the game.

The lead referee interrupted, "Okay, ladies. Line up,"

Roxy said, "Okay then. Shirlie, Tamika, Sonja rebound the ball."

"Ladies, line up or you'll get a technical foul."

"Wait." Monet said, making sure she didn't make eye contact with the referee to show him she was talking to her teammates and not to him. "Look, if we beat this team, it'll put us on the map. Maybe get us into the tournament, in March. So let's do it."

Everyone nodded, even Roxy. She put her hand in the middle. On the third beat they murmured, "together!" and then lined up for the free throw.

The referee said, "You guys aren't going to do this before every free throw, I hope."

"If we do, will you call fewer fouls?" Monet asked. The referee winked.

The Rhinos defended the Vols' fast break. They communicated. They rotated and switched on weak side picks. They contested every shot. Everything was fine until...

"Whoa, that was a perfectly executed pick and roll... There's another well executed pick and roll. The Volunteers may be on to something. Coach Delaney calls time-out," Clark said.

In the huddle, Lonnie remained calm. "Tamika, you have to step up on that pick so they can't shoot over the top. Come on now. Show and recover. You have to trust your teammates."

Tamika stared blankly at the clipboard Lonnie Delaney was drawing on.

During the game, Monet and Jamila Jetter were in a classic point guard battle. Monet had superior size but Jamila had better quickness. Monet scored by posting up the smaller Jamila, who responded by driving to the basket. In the first half, their personal battle was a stalemate. They had the same number of points and assists.

"At the half, Tennessee leads Del Mar by five, 38-33. So what does Del Mar have to do in the second half to beat Tennessee?" Clark said.

"They have to believe they can win." Heinz said.

"Is that it?"

"Well, they also have to make shots and play defense."

"There you have it..."

In the locker room, Lonnie was pleased but not satisfied with her team's performance.

"We're right there, ladies. Right there. They thought we would come in here and get blown out. Sonja and Shirlie, way to rebound. Tamika, you gotta step up and stop Jetter from driving all the way to the basket or shooting over the top. Monet needs help when they set that high pick on her. They're killing us on the pick and roll, and I'm sure we're gonna see a lot of it in the second half until we prove we can defend it..."

"11:50 remaining in the second half. Tennessee was making a push to blow the game wide open. They are really exploiting

Tamika's poor defense. She seems confused on the pick and roll," the play by play announcer said.

"She's forcing her shots too."

Monet could feel the game slipping away. The team was barely playing together. Jamila had that look in her eye and was confident she would make her team win the game. Monet didn't feel the same way about her team although she was confident in her own ability.

With two minutes remaining, the Rhinos were down by five. Tamika had been taken out by Lonnie, but when Tennessee scored four unanswered points she immediately sent her back in.

They needed stops but they also needed to score.

Monet and Tamika ran a pick and roll of their own. They scored each time and cut the lead down back to five. After Tennessee committed back-to-back turnovers, the Rhinos were back in the game.

With 20 seconds remaining, up by two points, Jamila milked the clock; Monet stepped up on defense. Jamila had the advantage; if she were fouled, she was assured of making free throws and putting the game out of reach. But there was a five-second difference between the game clock and shot clock. She couldn't just run out the clock. With eight seconds, Jamila started to drive; she actually got around Monet but Tamika stepped up to help, and she had to take a jump shot. Tamika's defense set Jamila up for Monet to come from behind and tip the ball away. Monet recovered the ball and called time out.

This time, Lonnie would not give Roxy, Shirlie, or Kendra a chance to decide the game. She diagramed the play. Tamika would set a screen for Monet, and depending on how the defense reacted, Monet would either drive to the basket or shoot a three to win the game.

Five years of frustration for Monet were riding on this play. Jamila had beaten her every time it mattered. It was likely this would be the last time they would play against each other, Monet at least wanted the satisfaction of knowing she won the last game.

Monet returned to the court repeating her mantra.

I'm the man, I'm the man, I'm the man, I'm the man.

Everything went according to plan. Monet received the inbound pass. Shirlie, Roxy, and Clio cleared out. It was Monet and Jamila on an island on the fringes of the mid-court Tennessee logo.

"Five seconds... Four."

Tamika moved to the top of the key to set the high screen; at the same time Monet started her drive down-court. They met just before the three-point line. Tamika effectively sealed off Jamila on the screen. The other Tennessee players didn't step up far enough to contest the shot. Monet had an open jumpshot.

"McCasner at the top of the key with an open nineteen footer. Two... One."

The referee checked her feet then raised her arm to signal the shot would count for three-points. It was in Monet's hands. Win or lose. Do or die. Just the way she wanted it.

The ball left her fingertips softly, with backspinning rotation. Her form was perfect, shoulders and feet square, elbow in, guide hand guiding, fingers splayed in follow-through.

"McCasner for the game... No good! No good! And Pat Summitt's Tennessee Volunteers survive a real scare from the upstart Del Mar Runnin' Rhinos and win 70-68. McCasner had a good look at the game winner but just couldn't knock it down."

Not again.

At the end of the game, the two teams met to acknowledge each other. When Monet's team lost, this was the most difficult part of the game for her. She hated to lose. Usually someone would make eye contact and say something innocuous like "good game" or "nice shooting." Monet hated it all. And now she had to acknowledge Jamila one more time.

Look at her all smug. She thinks she's so hot. Damn! I can't believe I missed that shot.

Monet and Jamila were last in their respective lines. Neither said, "Good game" or "Nice shooting." They had too much history for that. Knowing this would be their last meeting, Jamila couldn't resist one final dig. She winked at Monet just as they were high-fiving each other. It was the most personally painful trash talk she had ever felt on a basketball court.

Bitch.

Chapter **16**

Alpha Woman

December Sixteenth

"I am not good at this," Mbika said, as Monet retrieved her missed free throws. For the good of the team, she was giving Mbika free throw shooting lessons. Sonja and Jennifer were shooting, too.

"You better get good at it. People are tired of running extra laps because of you," Monet said. Jennifer and Sonja gave each other a look that said, "You got that right."

"Do you even like this game?" Monet asked.

"I love basketball."

"Then why don't you practice your free throws?"

"I have no time," Mbika said. "Too many classes."

"Seems to me, if you can't make time to do something you love for 30 minutes a day, then you don't love it as much as you think you do."

"You sound like Lonnie," Sonja said.

"That's how you elevate your game. You've got to work on it. Work before play." Monet finished, repeating one of Lonnie's mantras.

Ray watched from the tunnel. Monet pretended not to see him, preferring to make him wait until he showed himself. Cat and mouse. Besides, he was early.

"Nobody has run that many laps because of me," Mbika said.

"Lately," Jennifer added.

"But the potential is always there," Monet reminded her.

Ray stepped out of the shadows and onto the court. "You giving lessons in ass-whoppins too?"

Monet grinned then turned to Mbika, "Would you mind if we stopped here? I want to kick my friend's ass in a little one-on-one?"

As she walked past Ray, Sonja got up the nerve to look him in the eye, "You're going down, mister."

"Oh yeah?" Ray moved in closer to Sonja.

"Yeah."

"Oh yeah!?"

They were now forehead to forehead.

"Yeah!"

Ray pulled away shaking his head and Sonja took a seat in the front row of the bleachers. "Freshmen today. When I was a freshman we were seen and not heard," Ray said.

Sonja started up again from a distance, "Oh yeah?!"

"Yeah!" he yelled back

Monet said, "What's worse, being a freshman or being a senior who acts like a freshman?"

Ray picked up a ball.

"Nice Girl Scout patches," Ray said, referring to the game balls sewn on Monet's practice shorts. "Oh look, you've got Ironing. Cooking and Cleaning. Where's the 'Freaky wife In Training' patch?"

"Shut up."

"Nobody ever admits to getting that one–the Freaky Wife In Training Girl Scout patch. All the good girls go for map reading, camping, making fire. But that Freaky Wife In Training patch, they must hold secret meetings for that one."

"Are you ready yet?"

"Hey, what does that tattoo mean on your right leg again, with the hearts and the–what are those things?"

"Thorns. The thorns protect the heart," Monet said.

"Cute."

"I wish I'd been around when you were a freshman," Monet said.

"Why?"

"Because it would have been nice to see you but not have to hear you," she laughed.

"Real talk. Play you for it."

"For silence," she said.

"One week. Nothing. Zip and zzzzzpt. But if you lose."

Monet was really interested now. She snapped a chest pass at Ray which did shut him up. He caught it.

Ray said. "But if you lose, you have to tell me 'I'm the Man.'"

"Fine. You don't want to warm up?"

"I'm always warm. And ready to get down."

Monet rolled her eyes. She had enough incentive; winning would eliminate comments like that for a week. "Name the game."

"Let's see, three-point skins game, one-on-one, Horse, but I like to spell B-I-T-C-H."

"We are not going to spell that for obvious reasons."

Ray said, "Real talk. I like to play it with the fellas anyway. Of course, I won't have the added humiliation of kicking your butt on national television. But they'll do." He pointed to Sonja and Mbika then gave a big thumbs-down sign.

"Oh yeah?" Sonja said, from the distance.

"Yeah," Ray yelled back.

"Whatever. One game. One-on-one. Winners outs. Twelve straight, by ones. Clear 15 feet–accept air balls and blocks."

"You plan on shooting air balls?" he said.

"No outs. Check." Mouth set, eyes focused, Monet was ready to play. She snapped another chest pass at Ray; he smiled. "What are you smiling about?" Monet asked.

"I don't know. It's hard to take this female-competitive-intensity thing seriously. It's so cute."

"Keep taking it lightly," she said, before drilling an 18-footer in his face.

The game started off as a friendly game of basketball. Ray was confident he could take her off the dribble or back her down to the post. She was giving away 35 pounds and five inches. Ray started off cold and Monet got off to a 9-2 lead. Monet missed a shot, hustled, and beat the lackadaisical Ray to the loose ball. She was also beating the smile off his face.

"You can turn it on anytime, Big Daddy," she said. Trash talkers hate to have the tables turned.

Ray got serious. Monet was toast on the crossover. Frozen on the jab step. Faked out on the up and under. Overmatched on the power-up. She cut off the baseline nicely only to watch helplessly as Ray spun away, taking two steps on his way to soft reverse lay-up.

"Nice move."

Ray winked over his shoulder as he walked to the top of the key. Score: 9-9. Monet didn't quit. Ray took the ball out, took two hard dribbles, then rose up for a jump shot. Monet was totally off balance and realized what a simple but brilliant move it was. The defender wouldn't know if she was going to drive to the basket or stop and shoot a jump shot. It created a clear shot. She felt like a marionette reacting to the whims of the puppeteer. "You gotta get that move in your game. Especially in crunch time," he told her. Monet didn't dismiss the comment this time.

Ray continued, "If you're gonna be the go-to girl, down one with four seconds remaining, you gotta have an 'attack the rim' move and a pull-up move. Listen, if I see you playing up to contest the jumper, I'll ball fake you once, fake hard left then go right past you to the rack. But you gotta establish your willingness to attack the rim earlier in the game, otherwise they'll just play you straight up and you won't have an advantage," Ray said.

"I can do that move," Monet said confidently.

"But can you do it when the game is on the line, people hollerin' so loud you can't hear your coach, teammates gettin' out of the way because they're scared, and everybody in the building knows you're gonna take the shot, including the woman guarding you. Can you deliver with all that going on?" Ray asked.

Ray and Monet both knew she had been in that exact same situation many times, three times against Jamila Jetter alone. Each time, she didn't deliver.

"What's the secret?" Monet asked.

"Practice those two moves 500 times a day."

"500 times?" Monet asked.

"Do you want it or not? Because it seems to me that after every close game you always seemed to be on the crying, sulking, excuse-making side. Well, I've been on the other side. The screaming, hugging, laughing, net-cutting side, and I'll tell you, it's *way better*.

"500 each?"

"Thousand moves... Well, 250 during the season," Ray said.

Ray threw up a half-ass shot from beyond the three-point arc, Monet gobbled the rebound, head faked then went hard to the basket for lay-up. 10-9, Monet.

"That's what I'm talkin' about," Ray said. "In a close game, attack the basket."

The intensity was high. Monet wanted to make him eat his words about her not being a winner. Ray was sweating and had taken off his shirt. He was pure chiseled muscle with lats that could fly. Distracted, Monet missed her next shot. Ray scored, 10-10. Not to be outdone, Monet took off her T-shirt and was wearing only a sports bra and tight compression shorts. Ray immediately noticed her tight physique, among other things. This time he missed his next shot, an air ball Monet collected and put in for an easy score.

"No clear," he said.

"You didn't plan on shooting air balls did you?" Monet said.

"You gotta clear that," he said.

"Not air balls. That's me. 11-10." Monet said.

"You didn't have to take your shirt off...." he said.

You didn't have to, either.

"Check," she said, distracted by his six-pack abs and flyaway lats.

Monet stood at the top of the key, bent over, holding the ball with two hands, but protecting it against the steal. Ray was bent over pawing at the ball, getting mostly arm and wrist. The more Ray tried to steal the ball the more of Monet he clipped. They would have been fouls in a real game. After a few attempts, it became an excuse for Ray to touch her. She didn't get mad.

Monet started her move but Ray seemed to know which moves would be a fake or not. He was always right there, those hard thighs kneeing her in the butt. She couldn't get around him.

Monet gave him the same head fake, then drove to the basket again, Ray extended his left arm placing his hand on her hips, stepped around her like a matador while shooting his right hand around her back to tip the ball out. The ball was loose, but not far enough for him to recover it. As Monet went to retrieve the ball, Ray slid his right hand back around her waist, hips, and behind, copping a nice feel. Monet didn't mind; it felt good, plus it left him out of position so she could drive in for the game-winning lay-up. She collected the ball, then drove to the basket, but Ray came out of nowhere to block Monet's reverse lay-up, pinning it on the glass.

Down one, Ray took the ball at the top of the key, then crab dribbled to back Monet down in the paint. She swiped at the ball helplessly, but could only muster some nice feels of her own on his lats and obliques. He scored easily. 11-11. Game point. Ray walked the ball to the top of the key to reset.

They were bent over at the waist. Face to face. Close enough to kiss. He thought about it. So did she. Her lips were inviting– without even trying.

Ray held the ball and talked quietly to Monet as if he was her subconscious, "Damn, what should I do? I gotta stop him from going to the basket. But he rises too high to contest the jumper. I can't guard them both, but I'll stand a better chance if–."

"Shut up and play!" Monet yelled at his irritating monologue.

Ray saw she was back on her heels; he dribble-walked to the left side of the court, ball faked left, took two hard dribbles to the right, then pulled up for an open 15-footer at the free-throw line. Monet reeled back on her heels from the fake. She never got a hand up to contest the shot. Immediately after the release, but before the ball reached the rim Ray called, "Next."

Ch-kh.

When Monet turned back to Ray, he winked. "See."

Damn, he won again.

"Don't you have something you want to say?" he said.

Monet kept silent with dread.

"C'mon now, a bet's a bet," Ray said.

"You're the man," she said, reluctantly.

"That wasn't so bad, was it?" he said, beaming a winner's smile. "Just remember, I'm not one of those argyle-wearing geeks you can just beat up on. On the real, you gotta get two go-to moves in your game."

"Ball up..." she said.

"You just won't quit."

"I never quit. Check."

She snapped a chest pass at his head. Ray barely got his hands up in time to catch the ball inches from his face. He held the ball up in front of his face then peeked around the orange leather globe.

"And you know what?... I dig that about you," Ray said.

"Then let's go."

"I can't. I'm meeting someone in 20 minutes."

"The boom-shaka-la-ka?"

"Nooo. This guy down the hall is creating a demo tape."

"You're trying to become a rapper?"

"No, listen. He's in the school of broadcasting so he's putting together a demo tape, wants to have as many celebrities as possible. So, he's going to interview me."

"Yeah, right," she said, incredulously.

"Yeah, right what?"

"You're not going to help some guy down the hall–."

"Okay, whatever. Listen, I'd love to beat you again, but I really gotta go. I'll holla at you later." With that, Ray ran of out the arena.

        *   *   *   *

The shower felt good on Monet's body. Playing basketball with a man is hard on a woman. She was still annoyed about losing to Ray. No amount of water could make that feel better.

Taking off his shirt was cheating. Totally threw me off... Man, he's got a great body. The hands, the eyes, don't get me started on the lats. Ooh, la, la.

As attractive as Ray was to Monet she had lots of issues with him. Issues that prevented her from ever seeing him as a potential boyfriend. He was purposefully annoying. Women were constantly glomming onto him and he never seemed to say "No." Ever.

I mean, say "no" sometimes.

He always had something irritating to say. Monet felt compelled to compete with him on everything, just to take his perfect little life down a few notches.

Standing in the window of her room on the sixth floor, she could see most of the comings and going in the quad. There was Ray. She could smell his sweat on her pants and sports bra from their game. The combination of watching him from above and smelling his scent on her clothes was intoxicating. She was wet and aroused.

She watched Ray walk. Then he was immediately greeted by a guy. They shook hands and began walking together.

I guess he is going to do his interview.

Ray and the guy didn't walk twenty feet before Ray was stopped three times by three different groups of guys. First some football players, trying to get some tickets. They talked guy talk, laughing, and kidding each other. They gave each other a pound, that weird shake-hug thing guys do–really a chest bump that lasts long enough for them to put their chins on each others shoulders.

What is that?

Monet figured it was the closest thing to intimacy big tough guys allowed themselves to express toward each other. *Whatever.*

Ray's confidence was impressive. He was always poised. Cool. It was his sexiest attribute. Of course, he had a great body. She also had to admit that he was well-read, although she couldn't figure out why he tried so hard to hide it. When she thought about it, she realized that every time they were together she learned something new or he said something thought provoking. She liked that about him, too.

But damn, he could be irritating. Like he's going out of his way to be obnoxious and juvenile.

When he broke free of the football players, a freshman on the basketball team stopped him. Ray listened then showed him how to defend a spin move. That was the other thing she liked about him. He listened, really listened, and made time for everyone. He had been headed to do an interview, but fifteen minutes later he was still in the quad.

That's what was so infuriating about Ray. One minute he was helping others, the next minute he could be so irritating I could slap him. Okay, now he's on the move. Nope, Barbie attack. Three bogeys at nine o'clock.

Ray made time for them, too–a little too much time. He didn't go out of his way to take advantage. He never pestered women on campus. Didn't "Big Time" people by using the "Don't you know who I am?" line to capitalize on his notoriety. He just enjoyed the benefits of being a guaranteed NBA first round draft pick. Monet couldn't take her eyes off him.

Okay, get a grip.

She thought about what she wanted in a guy.

He has to be a tall and athletic, look good in jeans and a tuxedo. Ambitious. Respectful to women. Altruistic. Fun, with a sense of humor. He could have a little adventurous streak, but not too much. Modest but not a pushover. Confident but not all in the mirror admiring himself. He should also be smart but with common sense. Trustworthy... No Momma's boys.

Monet went over her list as she watched Ray. She couldn't put her finger on it, but there was something missing from her list.

As he disappeared around the corner, Monet pledged to follow Ray's advice and to reach out to her teammates. She had to do something; the Rhinos were 5-8 and still had to play Stanford, UConn, and their full WCCschedule. The way things were going, winning 15 games seemed unlikely.

December Eighteenth

"Over there, there's a parking space in front," Tamika said, pointing.

Sonja was confused. All she saw was a barred storefront with gigantic letters painted on the windows. Things like "Sale. Reduced. Half off." punctuated with exclamation marks. *Ereon Dress Emporium*, located in the heart of East Oakland, seemed like an unlikely place for *haute couture*, but Sonja was trying to keep an open mind. Tamika had asked her to help make her wardrobe more collegiate. It needed to be "de-skanked" was Sonja's first thought. It was a big task and she felt honored that Tamika had had the courage to ask her for help. Sonja had never shopped for a dress at a store with bars on the windows.

"It's closed, let's go," Sonja said, wanting no part of the fashion horrors that probably lay inside.

"They're open," Tamika said. "They buzz you in to keep out the bums wanting to use the restroom."

Just as Sonja suspected, it was a fashion hall of horrors. Loud colors. All synthetic fibers; rayon, Lycra, and the old staple–polyester. Tamika was attracted to faux fur and animal patterns like ants to sugar. Sonja shook her head and hoped the fashion police would shut the place down before Tamika bought anything. Then she reminded herself that her teammate was reaching out for help. This was a humanitarian mission.

"What about this?" Tamika asked, holding up yet another leopard print shirt.

"You know, you can still look like you're on safari without looking like one of the animals. A nice khaki pant with a white shirt is simple and classy. You'll look like Meryl Streep in *Out of Africa.*"

"I don't see any khaki here."

"Of course you don't, it's not flammable."

Tamika started laughing, "A leopard *is* flammable." She didn't know what the hell flammable meant.

"A leopard is a *mammal*... never mind," Sonja said.

Every time Tamika held up a garment, Sonja politely vetoed it. It was becoming difficult to not incenuate that she had bad taste. "Why aren't you picking something out for yourself?" she asked.

Sonja didn't take the bait. "We're here to make over *your* wardrobe not mine. Listen, you want me to help you, right? Well, it's going to be hard doing it in here. Close to impossible. Let me take you to a another store and you can tell me what you think."

Tamika was a little disappointed; after all, this was where she bought all of her clothes. But she was trying to be open-minded, plus she had money to spend, so after an hour in *Ereon Dress Emporium*, they drove back to San Francisco.

As they crossed the Bay Bridge, Sonja stared at the unique San Francisco skyline, the TransAmerica Pyramid, the Golden Gate Bridge, Coit Tower. She was in awe. "This city is so beautiful. Back in Minnesota we have lakes, the Metrodome, and the Mall of America."

Tamika had never thought about the beauty of the city. She had been too busy surviving on the streets to appreciate it. "I'm just glad Monet let you drive her car. Otherwise, this trip would have taken all day."

Sonja took Tamika somewhere safe, *Banana Republic*, where she could easily coordinate the safari look she craved. She was going to trade Tamika's animal print shirt, (and the polyester, thank God) for khaki and cotton. It was better to look like the hunter rather than the prey.

Tamika kept telling Sonja to pick out more clothes, so she did, until it dawned on her.

"How are you going to pay for all of this?"

December Eighteenth, 10:15 PM

Vince Fontainebleau passed Sonja in the dorm hallway. He had a head of steam going, blinded by another jealousy induced rage. He almost bumped into her as he passed. He turned around, "Hey. Have you seen Gina?"

"Uh, no. I think she said she was going to the library," Sonja said, sensing danger and hoping Gina wasn't in her room.

"Figures. I'm gonna check her room anyway, thanks." Vince turned and disappeared around the corner.

December Nineteenth, 5:30 AM

Monet spoke with Shirlie, Kendra, and Clio individually. She asked them what they thought the team needed to win more games. She couldn't make herself approach Roxy, who made it clear she didn't want any part of it. Monet sat at her locker feeling better about the possibility of putting aside their animosities.

"Mbika, you smack me on my ass one more time–." Clio screeched, while everyone got dressed for practice.

"I am supporting you," Mbika said. "I see it on football."

"It's okay. Okay? It's okay," Clio said.

"Damn, this happens every year," Shirlie said. "Around this time my cycle always changes,"

"Me, too, girl," Kendra said.

"There has to be a way I can play on a damn team without my period synchronizing with all of you knuckleheads," Shirlie said.

"Don't look at me, it's not my fault," Monet said.

"They say the one whose cycle doesn't change is the Alpha Woman," Roxy added.

"Who says that?" Kendra asked.

"Don't worry about it, your period changes every year. Live with it, you're a Beta," Roxy said.

Kendra knew, as did all of last year's players, that Roxy's cycle was never affected by the synchronous menstruation phenomenon. It was accepted that Roxy was the dominant female, The Woman of all the women. Even the coaches' cycles adjusted to hers.

"Wait a minute, Roxy. This isn't your week," Clio said.

"Yes, it is."

"Roxy, I've been playing with you for three years, yours was supposed to be last week."

"Wait a minute," Roxy said. She and Clio looked around the locker room to conduct a visual roll call. Big Shirlie, pad. Kendra, pad. Sonja, tampon. Tamika, pad. Each player shrugged or shook her head to indicate it wasn't her normal time either; their bodies had made an adjustment. Gina or Mbika, no. When Roxy got to Monet, she smiled and nodded her head.

"Yeah, it's me," Monet said, "Now what? Captain."

Roxy shook her head and bit her lip. Her cycle had adjusted as well.

Monet dismissed it as a nonissue. She didn't feel any stronger than she had five minutes before. But now, everyone knew, Monet was the Alpha Woman.

Chapter 17

Heed These Words

December Nineteenth, 5:50 AM
Players entered the arena one by one. The male tackling dummies were off to the side, stretching and yawning. Chad was the only male player sitting next to a female. Everyone was in a good mood for 5:50 in the morning.

When Lonnie Delaney entered, everyone got up and gathered at mid-court. Women in close, men on the perimeter of the circle. Monet caught Chad copping a feel on Jennifer. A few moments later she caught them hooking pinkies as they listened to Coach Delaney review the practice schedule. Monet nudged Jennifer and directed her to look up at the two video cameras that recorded every minute of every practice. Chad and Jennifer quickly unlocked fingers.

Gina was 15 minutes late for practice. An ominous silence descended on the arena when she walked in, everyone quickly calculating how many laps Coach would make her run. It was at least 360 laps or 21 miles. No way she could do them all at once, she would have to run the laps off in installments. More important, Gina was just a walk-on. Walk-ons don't have the security that scholarship players enjoy. She could be summarily dismissed from the team at any moment.

Gina had never been late. In fact, she did a good job of maintaining her anonymity. Now, she was not only late but came to practice wearing dark sunglasses. When she reached the court she stood behind everyone in the huddle.

"Uh, excuse me," Lonnie said. "I know you're young, getting good grades. Your future is bright. But in my practice, no one wears shades."

Gina didn't take off her sunglasses.

"Gina... No shades!"

Silence. The huddle parted as Lonnie Delaney walked toward Gina. Everyone gasped when Gina removed her sunglasses. It stopped Lonnie in her tracks.

"Who did this to you?" Lonnie Delaney asked, putting her arms around Gina's shoulder.

No response. Gina tried to hold it together, but shebegan to sob.

"Renee and Stephanie, you'll have to takew over."

Gina and Lonnie walked out of the arena. Gina told her how Vince had barged into her dorm room the night before. He accused her of cheating on him. Denying his accusations only made him angrier. That's when he hit her. Smacked her up pretty good.

"No one from the dorm came to help you?... Look at me."

"They did, but I told them we were just having an argument and we'd quiet down."

"Why would you say that?... Look at me! Why didn't you leave when you had the chance."

Gina paused for a long time confused by the question, "I don't know. He calmed down, but when we started talking about it some more he got mad again. That's when this happened."

Lonnie didn't know which was more infuriating, the fact that Gina didn't try to get out of there when she had the chance or that she turned down the help that came to her rescue. She did know what the next move should be.

"Did you two have sex after that?"

"He wanted to but when I told him I wouldn't, he thought about it for a minute, then he just left. I think he broke up with me."

"Wait a minute, he thought about it?" Lonnie picked up the phone to call the police station.

Gina was quick to say, "But he didn't, okay? He just left."

Lonnie hung up the phone. "Do you want to press charges?"

"Not really."

Vince had been doing unspeakable things to Gina and yet she protected him. Lonnie knew about his unreasonable jealousy and his controlling nature. But Gina didn't want to be saved.

Lonnie asked, "Why not? You have two black eyes. This is not ok. You let him get away with this and, you'll be putting ice on your face for the rest of your life."

"It's not like that."

"Gina, they all say that. Not the men, the women."

"But he loves me."

"But he hit you..."

"It's over, let's just drop it."

"See what I mean? It's not over. Look at me, God damn it!"

"I am."

Her eyes were so swollen she could barely see at all. Lonnie picked up the phone and dialed another number.

"What are you doing?"

"The least *you* should do," Lonnie said. It was still ringing.

"I don't want you to call the police," Gina said.

"I'm not." Lonnie stood up, phone sandwiched between her ear and shoulder. Hand on hip. Foot tapping impatiently.

"I just want this stuff to go away."

The phone was still ringing. Fed up, Lonnie Delaney walked out of her office. "You stay here."

As Lonnie walked down the hallway she didn't know exactly what room she was looking for but she was certain when she found it the person she was looking for would be in it. The doors whizzed by until she peeked her head into one. It was filled with mops, brooms, and cleaning liquid... that wasn't it.

Billy Joe Bivens, the head football coach, and seven assistant coaches were watching video tapes of the Georgia Bulldogs, their opponents in the Sugar Bowl. All heads turned when Lonnie stuck her head into the room.

Bivens was cool and calm, "Missy, this had better be good."

"Get up and meet me in Haneline's office. NOW!"

All the assistant coaches looked at Bivens. He contained his anger and took his time getting up. He pointed to the screen before he left, "We've got to find a way to stop their running attack. While I'm out, come up with some suggestions... Ok now missy, I'm *ahll* yours."

Billy Joe and Lonnie stormed past Forrest Haneline's secretary and into his office.

"Hey, he's on a conference call," Janice said, as they rushed passed her dcsk.

"Dutch, you better keep this crazy woman outta my tape room b'fore I–." Bivens started.

"What the hell is going on?" Haneline asked, putting the phone down.

"Tell him," Lonnie said.

"Tell'm what? Crazy woman. You never told me."

"I didn't?" Lonnie said.

"Naw, you didn't," Bivens said. They both turned to Haneline.
"Well, don't look at me." Forrest Haneline excused himself and ended his conference call.

"One of *his* players beat up one of *my* players," Lonnie said.

"Hold on," Haneline said, pushing back his chair.

"It's the first I've heard of it," Bivens said. "Which player?"

"Fontainebleau."

Bivens put his head down and shook his head. "Anyone but the place-kicker."

"You guys knew this would happen; it was just a matter of time," Lonnie said.

"Listen, I don't have time for this." Bivens started walking out knowing he couldn't win the argument.

"Where are you going?" Lonnie asked.

"I've got a bowl game to prepare for. A bowl game that pays 15 percent of this athletic department's budget, including your salary."

Lonnie Delaney turned to Forrest Haneline. "Aren't you gonna make him stay?"

"There's two sides to every story, missy," Bivens said over his shoulder.

"One of my players has two black eyes. Two! And stop calling me Missy."

"So what do you want us to do?" Haneline asked.

"Suspend him pending an investigation," Lonnie said.

"Placekickers don't grow on peach tress. We're playing in the 'Shuga in two weeks, I ain't cuttin' my place kicker." Bivens had paused at the door.

"Has she pressed charges?" Forrest Haneline asked.

"No, not yet."

"See," Bivens said.

"She hasn't pressed charges yet?" Haneline asked Lonnie.

"I'm outta here. Yawl, call me when you got more answers than questions." Bivens walked out. Lonnie just stood there.

"Don't worry, we'll get to the bottom of this. Let's find out what happened first," Haneline said, trying to calm her down.

"Yeah, we'll see," she said not believing him.

"These are serious charges."

"Yeah, well I already know how this works. She'll get blamed and the guy will get off."

"You're too cynical."

"Cynicism is born from experience." Then Lonnie turned and

walked out slamming the door. She wasn't gone for five seconds before Haneline was on the phone.

"Janice, connect me to the football tape room."

Bivens answered. "Yeah. What yawl think?"

"You think it's true?"

"It was just a matter of time; that kid is nuttier than a Snicker bar. But he's also the number one placekicker in the country. Hasn't missed a field goal or an extra point all year."

"Can't you run someone else out there?" Haneline asked, not happy about the situation.

"Dutch, this is the Shuga. If I run a wide-eyed freshman out there he'll pee his pants in front of a hunert thousand fans."

Haneline was thinking fast. He was barely listening to Bivens.

Bivens continued, "You gotta make this thing go away, for at least a month... Dutch. Dutch!"

Haneline answered, more thinking out loud than addressing Bivens, "I'll have Terry do the investigation."

"Gonna try to leverage her?" Bivens said.

"Everyone has a hot button. Terry is good at finding them."

"What about Delaney?"

"Just like my ex-wife. Let me handle her," Haneline said.

Bivens took solace in Haneline's confidence until he remembered Haneline's ex-wife had cleaned him out during their divorce.

Ray knocked on Monet's door. He had a big grin on his face when she opened the door.

"Wassup yo? I found this outside your door." He handed her an envelope. "Watch out. Someone went a little heavy on the cologne."

Monet took the letter but didn't open it. She didn't have to put it to her nose, she could smell it at arm's length. Ray saw how uneasy she looked.

"Domestic violence," Ray said, plopping onto her bed again, like he owned the place.

"What about domestic violence?" Monet said.

"It's a problem, a real bad problem in Brazil. Let's do our report on that."

"Hits a lot closer to home than that."

"Yeah, I heard. Did I tell you I got another Shakespeare assignment?" Ray said.

God help us.

"Don't get too comfortable. Let me grab my keys," Monet said.

"What's up with that funky-ass envelope?"

"You really want to know... I think the Stinky guy is sending them to me."

Ray opened the letter and read it. "You gotta tell the police and Coach Delaney."

"Naw," she said.

"Monet. Real talk."

"I'm always around people. My teammates. You–."

"You can't let this kind of thing slide," Ray said.

Monet didn't answer.

"I'm just sayin', bad shit happens to good people. You gotta tell the police and your coach," Ray said.

"Tch. Please, I'm six-one. Ain't no five-eight Napoleon going to approach me, and if he did, I know all the pressure points and defensive tactics," Monet said.

"All right, be hardheaded... Yo, you didn't tell me you went out with Chris Chamberlain," Ray said, still not liking what Monet told him.

"That was last month."

"I see my little girl is moving up the food chain. From argyle geeks to first round football players," he said.

They got up to leave. Monet stopped to lock the door while Ray continued walking down the hallway.

"It was awful. The guy was totally full of himself, just like someone else I know." She realized she was talking to herself. "Wait a minute. Can I ask you something without you making fun of me?"

"Depends on if it's really stupid; then I might not be able to help myself," Ray said.

"Well it kinda is, it's about guys... Anyway, I went out with this guy and he was, you know, always trying to get me to decide on what we were gonna do. Where we were gonna eat. Everything."

"So," Ray says, pushing the elevator button.

"Maybe it's me. But it really bothered me because he just wouldn't take charge."

"You Post-Feminista women will be the bane of us all," Ray said, Shakespeare rearing his ugly head.

"Please don't–."

"Gorging yourselves. Drunk... from the chalice of independence."

Monet said, "No chalice. No wine. No Shakespeare. C'mon I'm serious."

It was too late.

"Woman... You ask me and yet you try to winnow the jurisdiction of my rebuttal?"

Damn! I hate it when he...

"Take note, fair lady, and heed my words. For I predict that the great walls of civilization will soon crumble, as you, and women like you, continue to find strength by turning your back on chivalry. Chivalry, the very cement that bonds man to woman, woman... to man. For in your lust to have the independence of men you are fighting fire with fire! A tactic so woefully misguided–."

"What's woefully misguided?" Monet asked.

"Respectfully submitted, fair lass... You!" he said.

"I just think men can't handle it."

"Milady, you don't fight *fire* with *fire*."

"Sure you do."

"No, you babbling-decision-making-strumpet, you fight fire... *with water!* And alas, therein lies your folly. Think about it. Water ever bending. Ever flowing, ever adapting, water. Ever, dare I say it... Feminine. Water, the most feminine of elements–taking the path of least resistance yet never yielding to the brute force of men."

"Where do you get this stuff?" Monet asked.

"Like a woman, water gets where it wants to go. With time, water can turn a jagged rock into smooth marble. And here is my point. Women who fight fire with fire abdicate the *noblese oblige* that is the essence of femininity."

"The what?"

"They stop being women and become men," Ray said flatly, before resuming his Shakespearian monologue, "For as you women.–."

Lord, please make him stop.

"Stumbling like a drunkard on your own self-reliance. Later to whine – no pun intended – about your loneliness when there are no suitors at your beck and call. Ah, yes..."

Ray had struck a chord with Monet.

He continued, "So, I beseech you fair lady. Drink responsibly from the chalice of independence, for it is filled with wine that will leave the bitter taste of *contempt* and *indignation* on the palate of all men. Men who are weak! *And* men who are strong!"

Lord! Please! Make him stop!

"How so?" she said.

"Madame, you drink at our peril... For as long as the roles of men and women are blurred there will always be a constant struggle to see who will lead in the dance of romance."

Monet rolled her eyes. "And of course you think it should always be men."

"Apparently, you do, too. As your inquiry indicates."

Touché. But hold on.

Monet said, "I don't think it's too much to ask for a guy to be able to take the lead and yet be comfortable within himself to be able to let me lead when I want to."

"That's the problem," Ray said. "Half the time you don't even know when you want a guy to take the lead, so how's *he* supposed to know? Too many damn mixed signals. Keep it real, you don't even know what kind of guy you want, do you?"

"I do. But the Chris Chamberlains of the world ain't it."

"Why not?"

Monet sighed. "First of all, he wouldn't shut up about himself."

"Yeah, but how did it go afterward," Ray said with a wink.

"Please. He was trying to set up the booty all night."

"What do you mean?"

"You know what you guys do, or at least try to do."

"What?"

"Be all nice."

"I thought you liked it when we're nice."

"But he wanted to pay for everything," she said.

"Hold up. See, that's what I'm talkin' about."

"And sure enough at the end of the date he wanted some–."

"–You can't have it both ways."

"Well, I'm not going to let some guy, especially on the first date, think he can make a down payment on a happy ending just by buying me dinner and taking me to a movie."

"You wanna know something?" Ray asked, as they got on the elevator.

"Yeah."

"It's gonna piss you off. Actually it's a question."

"Go."

"Can you, a strong black woman, subordinate yourself to a strong man or will you choose a Milton and be eternally frustrated by a diminutive husband?"

"Diminutive. Nice word."

"See, and no Shakespeare," he said.

"Why do I have to choose?"

"Uhmmm... Polyandry? It's a tough choice. Dominate a weak man or constantly compete with a strong one. Struggle to see who can convince the other to give in," he said.

"You're oversimplifying it," Monet said.

"Am I? You challenge everything I say."

"That's different... You're an asshole."

"So, love will miraculously mediate your differences? I don't think so. Of course, you can be the "man" in the relationship."

"I don't have to. Ultimately, I just want a partner. Someone to share decisions with. Of course, you wouldn't know about that part of a relationship."

Ray shook his head. "I still think you want it both ways." They stepped out of the elevator and headed for the library.

They showed their student identification, took an elevator upstairs, then walked to a table.

"Let me ask you something? Why do you act all ghetto when you're around your friends?" Monet asked, as they walked the aisles.

"Shhhhhh, there's no talking in the library," Ray shushed her as he pulled out a chair for her.

In the library, Monet and Ray did more talking than studying.

"So, what were you thinking when you made the shot to win the national championship," Monet asked.

"Everything was quiet, which was a trip because it was hella loud in the Charlotte Coliseum," Ray said.

Monet listened closely. She wanted to learn how to perform well under pressure. She had reached out to her teammates and was practicing the two moves 250 times each and every day. "Were you nervous?"

"Everything was in slow motion. We were down one with ten seconds remaining. Coach didn't call time, and so I knew."

"Why you and not a senior?"

"Our main guy didn't want the ball with the game on the line. He'd get you 18 points, but his sphincter got tight in crunch time."

"So."

"I had been penetrating all game. So, this time down the court the defender thought I was going to penetrate. Nope. Two hard dribbles and a pull-up. He barely got his hand up. Shot, bottomed out. Game over. Thanks for playing. Hugs for everyone. Cut down the nets. Cue *One Shining Moment*. Good night now. "

"Damn, I want that."

"Five hundred shots each. I didn't feel nervous because I had practiced that shot so many times, I knew what he was thinking. I knew I would have space to shoot it because I set it up earlier in the game. All I had to do was focus and I knew I would make it. There was no reason to be nervous," Ray said.

I want that.

Monet was mesmerized. She wanted that one shining moment. She liked listening to his stories. The anxiety about the season's progress was swelling, so she changed the subject. "No more Shakespeare, okay?" Monet whispered. "But I still say you have to make room in your life for someone else."

"Why should I listen to someone who sabotages herself on every date she goes on?" Ray responded. "The first date at that."

"Oh, like you're really gonna find a good woman in the afterglow of having sex on the first date."

"Whole lot of sabotaging going on, huh? Difference is, I gets mine," Ray said.

"Don't start with that."

"Over your shoulder, Buffy and Kirsten at ten o'clock–don't look," Ray said.

Monet looked anyway, then stuck her tongue out at them before turning back to Ray.

"Why'd you do that?" Ray asked.

"I hate everything thing those two stand for."

"Hate them on your own time, when you're by yourself," he said.

"Let me ask you something?"

"What?" Ray said.

"How do you change the mind of two blondes?"

Ray looked over Monet's shoulder at Buffy and Kirsten, both blondes. "Okay, how?"

"Blow in their ears."

Ray laughed.

"Are we gonna work on this assignment or not? Ray... Ray?"

"... Too damned independent for your own good. And then you want to sabotage me. Ain't that about a blast," Ray said, watching the blondes.

"I've seen my friends spend all their time chasing after guys, buying them stuff, thinking that givin' them a little booty will make the good ones stay. They don't."

"That's because the good ones have options," he said, craning his neck to see past Monet. It was annoying her.

"Options," Monet said, with a dismissive tone.

"Danger: Educated Black man."

"That's debatable–."

"–Scariest thing in America. An educated black man," Ray said.

"One day you'll be the notch on some woman's belt."

"That'll never happen," Ray said, confidently.

"Being confident doesn't make you right," Monet said.

"Stop taking your frustrations out on me because you don't have the same options. Actually, you do; you just don't want to use all your skills to get yours." Ray said.

"All money ain't good money," Monet said.

"No, because what you do is stop the dance before the music starts just so *you* can be in charge."

"What dance?"

"The dance of romance."

"Oh, you mean the dance when a woman agrees with whatever a guy says when you know he's wrong, stupid, or both. *That* dance?" Monet said.

"I hate to keep saying it but that's your problem. Relationships are give and take," Ray said.

"Guys take, so I take. Wait a minute, that's all you do is take."

"Naw baby, I give. That's why women love me, I'm a giver. See, that's your problem. You need more give and less take," he said.

"A guy can't make a decision, but when I step up and fix the problem, I'm a diva. But when I sit back and let him lead and he screws it all up and I say something, then I'm a bitch," Monet said.

"You are a diva," Ray said.

"I am not."

"You're used to getting what you want."

"Why shouldn't I? I work hard," she said, getting angry.

"Don't get mad... That's what I dig about you. But you know what?" Ray said.

"What?"

"I'm a diva tamer, and deep down, that's what you dig about me."

"Shut up."

"You know I'll say 'no' to that ass–off-top." Ray chuckled to himself as he watched Monet grit her teeth.

"Shut up."

"You want it, but you fight against it. Don't want to take that bit. Rather be a wild and free mustang. Believe me, I understand."

"What am I fighting against, Mr. Diva Tamer?"

"Getting what you want. All you divas are used to getting what you want. Part of that ability to get what you want is why you are alone. Now, that's real. You need some 'No' in your life, keep you getting spoiled... Listen, I'm gonna work on the project a little later," Ray said.

Buffy and Kirsten were giving him the signal and he didn't want to make the wrong choice by choosing the feminist.

Ray stood up and picked up his binder. He said, "So, we agree on the domestic violence thing, right? Let me do some research about which country." Ray packed up his stuff and walked over to the coeds. All three were gone in moments. Ray still had his mojo working.

Monet studied for several hours before packing up her books to head back to her dorm. It was 12:45 AM, and the library would be closing soon. She got up and walked around an aisle of books to drink some water. The library was virtually empty. She smelled a funny odor, but didn't think anything of it.

When she returned to get her books the odor got stronger. She recognized it. There was a hint of *Old Spice* or was it *Aqua Velva*? Monet grabbed her books and walked toward the bookshelves toward the elevator. She noticed the scent again and tried to remember where she'd smelled it before. It was *High Karate* mixed with *Skin Bracer* and *Pierre Cardin* cologne. She looked through the books, left, then right. No one was on either side but the smell was getting stronger and she could hear footsteps.

She looked at her watch. The library would be closing in 10 minutes. All of a sudden the lights flashed off and on.

Oh man.

She had to get to the elevator. The smell was getting stronger. Then she remembered–it was the same as the scent from the letters. The scent of *High Karate*, *Skin Bracer*, and *Pierre Cardin* followed her like the whistling *Old Spice* sailor. It was getting stronger.

She started to panic and lost her way in the aisles of books. *Damn, the elevator is the other way.* Monet turned back and started running. "The library is closing in five minutes." *You just said ten minutes. Don't turn the–."* The library lights turned off for a moment and when they came back on a man was standing at the far end of the aisle. She couldn't make out his face, because the overhead lights casted a shadow. She thought she saw something shiny in his hand. She took off running down the aisle in the opposite direction, looking up to see the green exit signs. She heard his footsteps behind her. She thought about throwing her book bag at him but her dorm keys were inside.

Monet burst through the stairwell doors bounding down the stairs six at a time. She heard the stairwell slam open behind her, but didn't turn around. One wrong step and she'd sprain her ankle. She ran down three flights of steps when two men stepped into the stairwell. Monet ran past the two guys and then heard a door close two flights up.

Monet ran the rest of the way to her dorm. She knocked on Ray's door. Monet was heaving for air and looking over her shoulder down the hallway at the elevator. Ray had company, lots of company, but when he saw Monet's face he told Buffy and Kirsten to leave.

He pulled her into his room. "What happened?"

*   *   *   *

Monet sipped fruit punch as she watched the other kids dance. It was the first dance ever in the St. Ignatius Elementary School gym. The parents had lobbied hard to persuade the sisters of St. Mary's to allow the party. They had promised there would be no fornication. Consequently, parents stood guard every ten feet.

At five-feet nine Monet was the tallest girl in her eighth-grade class. It was great for basketball, terrible for a junior high school dance. None of the boys asked her to dance because they would have had to look up at her like a three-year-old talking to his mother. It was a bad visual better left alone.

Monet stood alone at the punch bowl drinking more than her share. She wished Miles Kincade would ask her to dance. She had a crush on him mainly because he was tall and had dreadlocks.

Leslie liked him, too. Leslie the cheerleader, the girlie-girl, former friend, now Monet's arch rival.. Monet's rivals. Leslie was jealous because Monet spent so much time with the boys playing sports.

When the song ended, Miles came over sipped some punch and asked Monet to dance. She couldn't believe it, they danced to four songs.

"Damn girl, yo big ass can move," he said. She took it as a compliment. Just guy talk. "Hey, you wanna see something?"

They left the gym and darted around the corner and down the hall way, Miles leading Monet by the hand. They stood in the hall, Miles' back against Karen Milken's locker. The coast was clear. He pulled Monet closer to him. She pulled back reflexively, but quickly relaxed. She wanted to be there with him. It was risky, given the no fornication stipulation. They were pressed against each other, chest to chest, their hands intertwined at their sides. Miles kissed Monet. A movie kiss, no tongue. Monet shivered.

"You cold?" he said.

"No. You?"

"No... You like it."

"Uh, yeah," she said, trying to sound experienced but the "uh" betrayed her.

They kissed again. He wriggled his fingers free of hers, working his hands to the small of her back. Moving slowly upward, he tried to cop a feel, but she pinned his wrists under her biceps.

"Don't."

He was cuffed. She relaxed a little and he tried again.

"I said, don't."

She moved in to kiss him while he guided her hands into his crotch.

"Stop."

"Why?"

"I don't wanna do that," she said, firmly, but trying not to break the mood. They stood with hands at their sides staring at each other.

Miles looked down the hall impatiently.

It was decision time, an internal clock was ticking in her head.

Ten, nine, eight...

That kiss, her first kiss, felt so good.

How come kissing wasn't enough?

She knew what she wanted, but she also knew he wanted more. She wanted to kiss. Just kiss. No hands.

Three, two, one...

Monet slowly backed away from Miles. She kept her head up to see his response. Miles didn't look at her, his mind was already back at the party. He shook his head twice, turned, and walked back to the dance. Just like that, gone.

It was quite a roller coaster ride for Monet.. The excitement of her first kiss, followed by the disappointment of watching Miles walk away. By the time Miles turned the corner she felt ambivalent. Monet wanted him to stay, but she was glad to see him go. She had never felt anything like it before.

Maybe that's what wanting your cake and eating it too, feels like.

The bottom line was she felt like she had done something wrong.

Wait a minute.

She replayed the last 15 minutes in her mind. They danced together. Drank punch together. Snuck off together. She was an equal partner all the way. And yet now, she couldn't explain why she was the one who felt vulnerable when Miles walked away.

Why should I feel bad? I didn't do anything wrong.

That was the problem. She didn't do anything wrong.

It was that look.

She kept thinking about the look on his face. She replayed it again in her mind. He was excited, then all of a sudden he was disappointed, like he was expecting something.

Ohhhh. I get it.

She was supposed to have said, "yes." She was supposed to say, "Yes, you can kiss me. Yes, I'll let you feel me up. Yes, I'll let you put my hands down your pants. Yes, we can do it in the hallway, get caught fornicating right here, so future generations of St. Ignatius 7th graders will never have a dance at their school again. Whatever you want Miles, the answer is yes."

Hell, no!

Miles was cute and even though she wanted to continue kissing, she decided she wasn't ready for more.

Walking back to the party, she wondered if that is what being a woman is about? When two people want sex, is it the woman's responsibility to say yes or no? Will she always have to decide which is more important, her ethics or his pleasure?

Monet didn't know this was only the beginning of navigating through the land mines of adult sexual politics.

Back at the party, Monet watched Miles dance with Leslie. They danced for three songs, then snuck off just as Monet had done 45 minutes earlier. The party was going to end soon. Her father would be there to pick her up. Twenty minutes later, she saw Miles and Leslie return to grab her coat. They were trying to look natural, but he had a grin that gave it all away. Monet knew what had happened. When it was Leslie's turn to decide, She had said, "Yes."

Monet's father picked her up at 11:30. While driving home he noticed how sad she looked. She hesitated, but told him what had happened between her and Miles. He was glad that she was comfortable enough to share her dilemma. But, he was seething at the thought of some little dreadlocked punk slobbering on his little girl. He exercised a lot of restraint maintaining control of the car.

"Sounds like you listened to me for a change. Remember we talked about this kind of thing. And I said the most important thing you can do as a young lady is to know yourself, define your values. Know what you will and will not stand for. That way, if you have to make a decision on the spot, you'll always be true to yourself. You can bet, you'll avoid a lot of regret in life, if you remain true to yourself."

He was right. Even though, she had wanted to continue kissing, she didn't tell her father that part. She didn't feel any regret.

That night she learned to trust her father's judgment and she gained a lot of confidence in herself and her decision making.

As they rode home in silence they were proud of each other.

Chapter 18

Damage Control

December Twenty-seventh, 11:15 PM
"Look at this." Lonnie reviewed the videotape with Renee and Stephanie. She stopped on a team drill during practice. "Is that what I think it is?"

Chad and Jennifer were hooking pinkies and brushing up against each other. Renee and Stephanie were speechless; they had known for a while that those two were dating, but had chosen to keep silent. They knew Lonnie wouldn't like it.

"What?" Renee said.

"They're rubbing against each other."

"I don't know; basketball is a physical game," Stephanie said. Renee gave Stephanie a look.

"How long did you two know?"

Both remained silent.

"Well, how long?" Lonnie insisted.

"Not that long, a few weeks."

"I want him off the team. Things break down when feelings get involved. The first thing to go is discipline."

"Heaven forbid," Stephanie said, barely audible. She thought their relationship was cute.

"What?"

"I said, I think. I still hate it when you make us practice during the Christmas break," Stephanie said. Lonnie ignored her comment.

"It was a good idea to give Gina some time off. She couldn't concentrate," Renee said.

"You'd be a basket case, too," Lonnie said.

"You talk to her?"

"No. You see anything in the paper yet?" Renee asked.

"I haven't," Stephanie said.

"Which means Haneline is up to something," Lonnie said. "Monet told me she thinks that Stinky guy is stalking her. She said she had received a couple of letters and then just last night someone followed her through the library."

"That's scary," Renee said.

"I contacted campus police and the police department. They're going to have Monet describe him to a police artist so we can post his picture around campus."

"I hope they find that guy before someone else gets hurt," Stephanie said, worried.

"I think Clio is still light in the ass to get a lot of minutes," Renee said, wanting to change the subject to basketball. "She's too slow to defend the small forwards and she'll get abused if we put her at the four spot."

"Who else then? Lonnie asked.

"Mbika," Renee said.

"Mbika? The girl has virtually no basketball IQ." Lonnie shook her head.

"But she's got good feet from playing soccer," Stephanie said.

"Football," Lonnie corrected.

"Whatever, she's twice as athletic as Clio and doesn't mind mixing it up in the paint."

"All right then, it's your project to make her a smarter basketball player if we are going to rely on her. How's Tamika?" Lonnie asked.

"You know 'Meek, she's like Rambo," Stephanie answered.

"Yeah, well, I wish she'd spend more time studying."

"She thinks you don't like her," Renee said.

"I yell at her, don't I?" Lonnie said.

"Maybe that's the problem."

"Do I yell at Monet?"

"Of course," Stephanie said.

"Exactly, I yell at all the good players. No one gets special treatment. Why should Tamika be any different?"

"You should ease up on Tamika."

"We're trying to win games. Our athletic director couldn't care less about our program and each of us makes less than half of what the men's coaches are making. I'm trying to fight real battles here, I don't have time to baby–sit Tamika."

Renee and Stephanie felt a lecture coming on.

"Tennessee torched us, on the most basic play in basketball because of Tamika. Remember? And now you want me to hold her hand?" Lonnie said.

"Well something's up with her," Stephanie said.

"We better figure it out before it's too late."

"You think she'll quit?"

"Worse, I think she'll become even more hardheaded and stubborn."

"Great, another Beamon."

"Pure cancer," Renee said

"I think you're scaring her," Stephanie said. She had always been the softest of Lonnie's assistant coaches.

"She doesn't understand what you're trying to do, because she's so used to getting her way on the court," Renee added. "You should talk to her."

"Maybe I should let her coach, too?" Lonnie said. "We haven't been out of coaching that long. The X's and O's don't change."

"But the kids do."

Lonnie thought about it then shook her head, "No they don't."

Renee said, "Speaking of being stubborn, I hope you eased up with Haneline."

"You promised him you wouldn't cause any trouble," Stephanie said, reminding Lonnie.

"Guess who called?" Lonnie said.

"Uh-Oh," Stephanie and Renee braced themselves.

"ESPN," Lonnie Delaney said smiling.

"Lon-nieee."

"You know I'm right."

"I'd rather be wrong and employed than right and unemployed," Stephanie sighed.

"Lonnie, please, don't do it."

"You know I'm right," Lonnie said.

"Please Lonnie. I just signed a twelve-month lease. I can't afford to get fired right now."

"You know I'm right, but relax, they called *me* about a story they're putting together," Lonnie said, pleased with herself.

"And did you bring *our story* to *their* attention?"

"They've got some good reporters over there at ESPN. It's the sports leader," Lonnie said, avoiding the subject.

"So. what's the story about? Salaries? Our locker room? Cold water?"

"It's getting late. Let's call it quits for the night," Lonnie said dodging the questions.

"So, what did you say?" Renee was undeterred.

"I talked about respect, I didn't talk about Title IX at all," Lonnie answered, turning off the VCR.

Stephanie and Renee looked at each other.

"God help us."

January Second, 1997 5:00 AM
One Nation Under A Groove played softly in the background. The CD was on repeat, so this was Funkadelic's thirty-fifth replay.

Lonnie slept, mouth open, on the couch among piles of VHS cassettes and empty Chinese food cartons. It was her usual resting place. The video remote rose and fell on her chest with each deep breath. She had canceled practice scheduled for New Year's day, more for her own sanity than for her players. There was no sense in forcing hung-over, sleep-deprived women to practice. They would only make her angry with their poor execution.

So, she spent all of New Year's day in her apartment, watching video tapes of upcoming opponents and checking on her Ohio State Buckeyes who played in the Rose Bowl against Arizona State.

Del Mar had played Georgia in the Sugar Bowl. Even though Del Mar was coached by her least favorite colleague she still made herself tune in periodically to check on the game. After all, it was a major bowl, and sure to be a topic of conversation at the office. She had watched a few plays before pressing "Play" on her VCR to watch game tapes of her team.

It was 5:05 AM. Mr. Fundamentals, her cat, groomed himself in the light of the television screen. When the phone rang Lonnie jumped. The remote went flying, bopping Mr. Fundamentals on the tail. Startled, he jumped onto the stacks of video cassettes on the coffee table, lost his footing on the slippery plastic, fell off the table, kicking the bottom of another towering stack of video cassettes, which knocked over a third tall stack of cassettes.

The phone kept ringing.

"What!" Lonnie barked, into the phone. Blurry-eyed, she surveyed her living room and wondered how a ringing phone and a scared cat could make such a mess .

"Did you see the sports page this morning?" Stephanie asked.

"What? Uh, no. I fell asleep on the Sugar Bowl. Did we win?"

"Yeah, Fontainebleau kicked the winning field goal with four seconds left. Fifty-two yards."

"Damn! You know he's gonna come back a hero and Haneline isn't going to do anything about him beating up Gina."

"Yeah, I know. I think they've already done something about it," Stephanie said.

"Yeah?"

"Yeah, Gina told me last night that Bivens gave her a scholarship."

"Bivens? What the hell is he doing giving... And I thought there wasn't any more money for scholarships." Lonnie was so mad she dropped the phone.

"Lonnie? Lonnie."

If you'd like to make a call please hang up and try your call again.

January Third, 6:00 AM

"I haven't seen him again." Monet walked into practice with Lonnie. They were talking about Stinky. "And he hasn't sent me any more letters."

"That's good," Lonnie said.

"I'm glad," Monet said, not liking the feeling of helplessness.

Lonnie took one whiff of the envelope and held it out at arm's length. "Unfortunately, all we can do is be security conscious and hope he makes a mistake so the police can catch him."

Great. I'm a sitting duck.

The team huddled around their coach at the jump circle in the Arena as she outlined how they were going to bolster their offense. As she reviewed the changes, she noticed how someone in the rear was sniffling every few seconds. It was annoying.

"First of all, where's Gina?" Lonniwe said.

"Over here, coach." Once again she was standing behind someone.

"Jennifer, please go blow your nose." Lonnie had located the culprit. But Jennifer didn't have a cold, she was crying.

"What's the matter?"

At first, Jennifer was reluctant to say anything.

"Here we go again," Clio whispered.

"Uhmm, I was wondering if, uhmm... Am I?...Would I lose my scholarship if..."

"Breathe. Freshman. Breathe," Kendra said.

"I missed my period," Jennifer blurted out.

"Welcome to the club," Kendra said.

"You sure you're not just... Synching with your teammates?" Lonnie asked.

Roxy let out a big sigh. "Damn, we go through this every year with freshmen."

"No, it's not that," Jennifer said, trying to contain herself. "Would I lose my scholarship if I got pregnant?"

Everyone gasped. It caught Lonnie off guard. "Let's talk about this," she said, putting her arm around Jennifer's shoulder and walking her off the court.

As they walked Lonnie asked Jennifer, "Are you sure?" Jennifer nodded. "Do you, uhmm, know who the father is?"

"Chad."

Lonnie was glad she knew who it was. Trying to figure out the identity of the father after diagnosis could be difficult. She had seen it devastate a young woman back at Ohio State after each one of her partners denied involvement. It left her in the awkward position of identifying a father who didn't want to be found. Lonnie was glad Jennifer was confident, but she wasn't pleased it was one of the tackling dummy.

"How do you think he is going to feel about you being pregnant?"

"I'm not sure. It's not the best news," Jennifer said.

"I would agree with that, but it's not the end of the world either... Why haven't you told him yet?" Jennifer didn't answer. "Having a baby is a beautiful thing. It'll probably cut in on your minutes though," Lonnie said, trying to get Jennifer to smile.

"What about my scholarship?"

"I'm not sure about that. I know the NCAA has rules against special treatment but we should be able to work something out. Can your parents help you with tuition?"

"Don't tell my parents! Promise me you won't tell my parents!" Jennifer was almost hysterical.

"Jennifer. I don't know if I can do that. I mean, how are you going to hide your pregnancy?"

"That's if I keep it."

"How far along do you think you are?"

"I don't know."

"How many periods have you missed?"

"Two."

"Two! What the hell were you waiting for? It's not the kind of thing that just goes away," Lonnie said, getting angry.

"I know. I know." Jennifer started crying again.

"The longer you wait the fewer options you have. Denial won't solve this problem... Okay, okay, you still have a little time. Let me find out about your scholarship. You go talk to Chad. He should be involved with whatever decision you make."

"Are you going to tell my folks?"

"I think they would rather hear it from you. But think about all your options. Talk to your friends. And even though you don't think your parents will understand, you still should tell them. Listen to them more than your friends. And–."

"–Coach... I'm scared," Jennifer said, when they reached Lonnie's office.

Wrapping her arms around her, Lonnie said, "You're a big girl now... Ready or not, these are adult decisions."

Forrest Haneline peeked into Lonnie's office. Just the sight of him made Lonnie mad. "Why are Stephanie and Renee running practice, something happen?" he asked.

"I see you guys found a scholarship for Gina," Lonnie said, disgusted.

"Usually, when you're not in practice something has happened."

"I thought there wasn't any more money for scholarships for walk-ons?" Lonnie repeated.

Jennifer looked from Haneline to Coach Delaney, then became the center of attention.

Haneline said, "Things change. Did something happen? Jennifer?"

"No... Uhmm, not that I know of," Jennifer said.

"Then why aren't you in practice?"

"Who me?" Jennifer looked at Coach Delaney for help.

"She needed to talk to me about something she needs for this afternoon," Lonnie said.

"So, will you, Coach?" Jennifer pleaded with her eyes.

"Let me work on it, OK," Lonnie said.

"What?" Jennifer said, not getting it.

Lonnie Delaney went bug-eyed. "You know. The thing with the tackling dummy."

"Ohhhhh. Yeah. I mean, thanks coach. Whatever you can find out, let me know." Jennifer excused herself.

"What was that about?" Haneline asked, suspiciously.

"Nothing, basketball stuff."

"Tackling dummies?–."

"–So where did the money come from or did you find it in one of your old suits?" Lonnie said. "How could you give one of my players a scholarship and not tell me?"

"She's a good kid. Single-parent family. First in her family to go to college," Haneline said, his story was already in place.

"And being beaten up by the placekicker that just won the Sugar Bowl had nothing to do with it? Sounds like bribery to me."

"Gina embodies what student-athletics is all about," Haneline said.

Lonnie said, "Stop right there! You know you wouldn't have *fouuund–*." making little quotation marks with her fingers around her head. "–A scholarship, if she hadn't had this incident with Vince. It's nothing more than hush money."

"Forgiveness."

"What?"

"Forgiveness. There isn't enough of that today, everyone wants to sue, which is the problem with this country. At Del Mar we keep our problems within the family. So, if a scholarship helps to mend hurt feelings–."

"–It's bribery."

"Don't you think it's a small price to pay?" Haneline said.

"Is that what you told her? Keep the problem within the family?"

"No, but the scholarship got her to focus on forgiveness. There really isn't enough of that in this world."

Lonnie pulled out photos of Gina with her swollen black eyes and bruised face. It was the first time he had seen them. They made him wince.

"I wonder if you would forgive the man who did something like this to *your* daughter?"

Chapter 19

The Concierge Factor

January Third, 4:30 PM
Wilma Dodd, the women's volleyball coach, peeked into Lonnie's office. She was forty-five and frumpy.

"Hey."

"Hey," Lonnie answered, looking up from Gina's file.

"Just wanted to let you know if there is anything I can do to help with Gina let me know, " Coach Dodd said.

"Can you convince Haneline that women's athletics don't exist so the university can have a football program?" Lonnie answered.

"You gotta watch Dutch. But, he'll do the right thing."

"The right thing would have been to suspend the kicker pending an investigation."

"Yeah, but Gina didn't even file a police report."

"How convenient! A week later, the guy kicks a game-winning field goal and comes back a hero. What are the chances of an investigation going anywhere now?"

"I heard Gina got a scholarship."

"Hush money–you mean."

"She really needs it, though," Dodd said.

"Do you think they would have given her the money if she hadn't gotten her ass kicked by the field goal kicker?"

"Well... probably–."

"–Hell, no! They wouldn't have found it."

"Calm down," Dodd said.

"You're talking about Haneline doing the right thing, but when it was time to do the right thing, he chose to buy his way out of the problem. Right is right, regardless of price."

"Well, that's not always true. But I think you're right. It could have been handled better. Hey, what did you do for New Years. I was expecting you to come by our house," Dodd said.

"I wasn't in the mood for a party."

"So, what did you do?"

"Broke down tape for New Year's Eve. New Year's Day, I watched bowl games and broke down more tape. Schemed for our game against UConn," Lonnie said.

"That's pretty pathetic and lonely," Dodd said, with a grin. "You were married once, right?"

"Yeah, I spent too much time focused on coaching and not enough time nurturing my marriage. Kept me from getting hired at least five times," Lonnie answered.

"It happens. Something's gotta give."

"Yeah, me."

"Know what you could use? A wife," Dodd said.

"Sorry, I know this is San Francisco, but–."

"A wife. Not in the lesbian sense, but you know, someone to be there for you while you develop your career. A man who's more nurturing than, say, a hard-driving coach."

"Not many men willing to take that assignment," Lonnie sighed, wishing it weren't true.

"Yeah, you're right, none worth keeping."

January Fifth, 9:45 PM EST,
Hartford, Connecticut

"Please, no truth or dare tonight," Kendra said to Clio while winking at Jennifer.

"I agree with that," Gina said.

"You should be glad you're even here," Roxy said to Gina.

The walk-ons were traveling with the team. Lonnie figured she might need them if any of the scholarship players were injured. But she had had to do some fast talking to get Haneline to foot the bill.

"What do they teach in those self-defense classes?" Kendra asked Gina.

"How to run," Clio joked.

For the first time, Gina felt like saying something in her defense. She was getting tired of people walking all over her. Still, she didn't say anything; just sat there.

Shirlie and Monet entered the crowded hotel room. Shirlie was wearing her pink pajamas. She looked like a giant Easter Bunny.

"Any of your boyfriends see what you sleep in?" Roxy asked.

"Them nerds Big Shirlie dates? Please!" Clio said. "They think that big fuzzy jumper is a camisole."

"I don't know what you're talkin' about, Big Shirlie throws away more men than all of us," Kendra said.

It was true. Shirlie, a premed major, dated a lot of "keepers"– guys with bright futures.

"Shirlie, how do you get these guys?"

"They think my bunny suit is sexy," Big Shirlie smiled.

"Speaking of sexy, you get any more letters?" Clio asked Monet. "Stinky's picture is all over campus. Everywhere you turn. It's like he's watching you."

"I tore down the one in the locker room. It was too creepy," Kendra said.

"Naw. I haven't received any new letters," Monet said.

"Thank God for that."

"Knowing someone like that is out there gives me the creeps," Sonja said.

"Yeah, well he's not the only one," Monet said.

"I see you guys started drinking without me and Monet," Shirlie said, changing the subject.

"Nobody has time to wait for you to finish five chapters of molecular biology," Roxy said.

Roxy handed Shirlie a drink

.   "I still don't see how you do it," Kendra said. "You go out with all these really smart guys, but you never go out with them very long. You just know some of them are going to be really successful one day," Roxy said. "But you dismiss them."

"What was wrong with Waylan?"

"Too artificial intelligence," Shirlie said.

"And David? Wasn't he premed?" Kendra said.

"Yeah, but he was way too into dead people."

"Can we talk about something else?" Monet said. "Clio, what's up with truth or dare?" Everyone ignored her.

"I feel sorry for Gina, poor thing."

"She needed to get away from that guy."

"Chad is the only keeper any of us has."

"I like Chad."

"Yeah, Chad is cool. A dork, but a cool dork."

"Yeah, they get on my nerves in practice, tuggin' on each other."

"Hooking pinkies."

"Yeah, get a room."

"Tamika, I thought your little makeover was cool. Considering

what you were wearing before. Where are you gettin' all this money?"
Tamika shrugged.

Lonnie knocked on the door. The room silenced. Clio opened the door.

"Hi, coach, we were, uh, just going over the defense," Clio lied. Lonnie stayed long enough to make a mental note of who was in the room. She hated walking in when they were obviously talking about her. It was awkward. When everyone was accounted for, she said, "Listen everyone, Sonja is not to do any more running."

"What?"

"I know it's doesn't seem fair, but she's too thin as it is. Anyone who catches her running and has proof will get something special."

The team got excited. It was just a matter of time before Sonja would go running again. They all wanted to collect the bounty. Lonnie closed the door behind her.

"I've known you for a long time and I've never been able to figure out how you get such great guys," Kendra said to Big Shirlie.

"And then just break it off after a few weeks," added Clio.

"She doesn't know what she's doin'. She throws the good ones back," Roxy laughed.

"No, really, I want to know. Because I think we all want a guy that has all the things those guys have," Kendra persisted. "For instance I want a guy who is smart, ambitious, fun–."

"–See, that's your problem right there. How many guys have you dated who were smart, ambitious, and fun?" Roxy asked.

Kendra's list got everyone thinking about what they wanted in their ideal man. Jennifer started writing a list.

"Smart, ambitious, fun."

"Cute butt."

Jennifer looked up to get a consensus. Everyone nodded.

"Okay, ambitious, fun. Cuuuuu'te... butt. What else?" she wrote. Each player contributed something to the list.

"Intelligent."

"Isn't that the same as being smart?"

"How 'bout good decision maker?"

"That's good."

"No mama's boys."

"No punks."

"What?"

"Punks. Pushovers."

"It's too hard to list what you want, let alone what you don't want," Shirlie said.

"Yeah, keep it simple, keep it in the positive."

Jennifer read the list. "Okay, I've got intelligent, ambitious, fun, *cute butt.*" Everyone laughed. "Good decision maker."

"Gotta have a good sense of humor."

"A guy that can make me laugh can take it to the house."

"Respectful."

"Oh, yeah, that's a good one."

"Gotta be confident."

"Altruistic," Clio said.

"What?" Tamika asked.

"Altruistic. It means to help others, genius."

"How many guys do you know who are altruistic?"

Silence.

"Exactly."

"But I want a guy who's altruistic," Clio said.

"How 'bout respectful."

"How about good to others?"

"How 'bout respectful."

"All right, fine. Respectful."

"Gotta be a good kisser."

"Work that tongue, too." Clio gave Roxy a high five.

"Monet?" Kendra posed.

"He doesn't have to make more money than I do," Sonja said.

"He better," Roxy said. "A four-bedroom house, private school and German engineered cars are expensive."

"Ambition will take care of that," Shirlie said. "That's on my list too."

"I could totally be with a guy whose life's work was working with kids or the environment," Sonja said.

"Yeah, right up until the time you realize you'll never able to afford a house because you're the one who is making all the money and his life's work only pays for utilities and cable," Roxy said.

"Tamika, you gonna add something?"

"All yawl need some thug in ya life," Tamika said. After a moment of silence everyone dismissed her comment, then turned back to the discussion.

Monet was silent. She, too, had a list of things she wanted in a man she would consider marrying. All of their traits were on her list as well. But something was still missing.

"I want a guy who can get stuff done," Monet said.

"What do you mean?" Kendra asked.

"You know, someone you can depend on."

"Depend on workin' that tongue," Clio said.

"That's what I'm talkin' about," Clio said.

"Flat tire? No problem. Sold out concert. No problem. Flowers delivered, BAMM! on your birthday," Monet said.

"A 'Go-to' guy," Clio said.

"Sounds like you want someone to take care of you," Roxy said.

"No. I can take care of myself. I just want a guy who can take over and get things done when there's a problem."

"A Go-To guy," Clio repeated.

"Nah, that doesn't quite sound right," Monet said.

"Yeah, and not get all flustered. I've been out with guys who are like that," Shirlie said.

"Me too."

"Soon as something doesn't go according to plan he'd call his mother," Shirlie laughed.

"Stop."

"No, really. He literally called his mother when his car over-heated," Shirlie said.

"Oh, hell no."

"So, what do you call a guy like that?" Jennifer said, taking notes. "Someone who remembers birthdays, sends flowers, gets concert tickets, and can change a tire all on the same date."

"A concierge," Shirlie said.

Everyone laughed.

That's it, a guy has to have the concierge factor.

"A concierge with a cute butt," Jennifer added.

"Now, that's what I want."

10:30 PM, EST
Storrs, Connecticut

"I am so glad Gina has been going to those self-defense classes I set up for her," Lonnie said to Renee.

"I noticed she's stopped standing behind people all the time."

The coaches were studying tapes of UConn's games in their hotel room. The Huskies were ranked number two in the country.

"Well, any suggestions?" Lonnie Delaney asked.

For a moment they were silent. Then Renee said, "They got some big girls in the backcourt. Look at how Timons and Wilcox slow down the fast break until their bigs can get down the court."

"Good rotation on defense, see? Here, when Timons gets beat they close the gaps and help out," Stephanie said.

"They can't guard everything," Lonnie Delaney said.

"They're doing the next best thing."

"I have to say I'm a little disappointed in your game strategy. With a big team like this you can draw and kick. Roxy should be able to penetrate to draw in their bigs to help, then kick it out to Monet or Clio."

"So, you're going to have Roxy play the point tomorrow."

"It might cause more trouble than it's worth, you know between the two of them," Lonnie said. She thought for moment. "Maybe we can do the same thing by pumping it into Tamika on the block"

"They won't be able to handle her," Renee said.

"But when they double-team she has to kick it out." Lonnie said.

Renee said, "She's like a roach motel. Balls go in, but they don't come out."

10:45 PM, EST

Monet thought about her list as the team tried to add more attributes to their perfect man.

Is it too much to ask for a guy to be intelligent, ambitious, confident, independent, funny, respectful, open-minded, introspective, appreciative of the arts, a concierge, tall, athletic, with a sense of style? And for the record, I'm willing to trade a cute butt for winged lats. That's compromise, isn't it?

"A concierge with a cute butt," Jennifer said.

Shirlie interrupted the laughter. "I hate to burst your bubbles, but that's you'll have a hard time finding what you're looking for."

Everyone fell silent. No one knew how a six-foot-five woman could be so successful in dating, but they knew she discarded a lot of seemingly good men.

Shirlie continued, "Your lists are too long."

"I'm not gonna marry a dumb concierge even if he has a cute butt," Clio said.

"You don't have to. But I'll tell you this. Every one of those traits makes the pool smaller so that by the tenth item you're down to two guys. One in Seattle and another in San Antonio."

"But I've never been to Seattle," Sonja whined.

"It's a big joke now, but you will have to deal with it sooner or later."

"Maybe we can get coach to schedule a game with Washington," Shirlie said. "Anyway, I have a long list too, but I have three deal breakers. Once I figure out that a guy isn't intelligent, or ambitious or hasn't got that concierge thing," Shirlie nodded to Monet for coining the phrase. "I end it right there. Done."

"You don't work with them?"

"For what? I'm not going to look for the goodness underneath his obsession with fart jokes. I won't make excuses for his need to watch football when his grades say he should be studying. And he can forget about it if he gets flustered by a sold-out movie."

"I like that," Monet said.

Shirlie continued, "If a guy isn't intelligent, there's nothing to work with. There is no future. And if there's no future, why invest more time when you know he's never going to have what it takes. You're wasting your time. So move on. The sooner you move on, the sooner you'll be available to meet the guy who has all the basic things you want."

"It's not that simple; sometimes it just feels really good."

"That's real," Roxy said.

"Yeah, and while you guys are wasting your time with losers that make you feel good, I'm moving on, getting that much closer to finding The One. Thing is, he might be your One before he ever meets you. And I'll find him faster than you because I'm focused and I have a plan."

"It's not that simple," Roxy said. "My cousin told me the same things. When she was 22, even 25 years old. But she started her own business and made it successful. Then, she said, she woke up on her 35th birthday and remembered she forgot to have kids. So, it's not that simple."

"Wait. What if he is intelligent and ambitious, but selfish?" Clio said.

"Yeah, what about that?"

"That's a tough call," Shirlie said. "Look, the point is, I don't waste time trying to turn a frog into a Prince. Soon as I realize they don't have my three deal breakers, I'm outta there. It just takes a couple of dates."

"And if he's got the three deal breakers?"

"Then I'll work with the rest," Shirlie said.

"Selfishness?" Clio said.

"Only selfishness that's within reason. Hell, I'm selfish myself." Monet elbowed Gina, who was transfixed by the conversation, "Now, that's senior leadership."

January Fifth, 1997
Harry A. Gampel Pavilion
University of Connecticut

"The number two ranked UConn Huskies are leading the Del Mar Runnin' Rhinos 23-17, with 5:45 remaining in the first half. The Rhinos seem to play well against ranked teams. We saw that at Tennessee and Stanford and now here at UConn," Thalia Clark said, the play by play announcer said.

It's just good coaching. The Rhinos are playing an in and out game where they get the ball into the paint either with Roxy's penetration or dumping it down to Tamika on the post. Then, when UConn collapses on them they kick it out for an open shot." Clark said.

During the time-out Lonnie instructed her team. "You're rushing. Be patient. Make good crisp passes. Remember the smelly practice?" Everyone nodded quickly, not wanting to revisit that moment again. "Kendra, you're in for Tamika."

"Why am I out?" Tamika challenged.

"Because you're forcing shots. Every time you've touched the ball you've shot it."

"But, I've made it."

"One more pass would have led to an easier score."

"But I made the shots."

"Let's see how many you make sitting next to me... We're playing the second best team in the country, ladies. They haven't made a run yet, but it's coming. Let's beat 'em to it. Let's try to get out and run. OK. 'Together' on three. One. Two. Three."

"Together!"

The team was coming together although there was still tension between Monet and Roxy. It was the kind of tension that hangs around when two people are looking for a way to take the other down. Roxy's ego still had not recovered from being usurped by Monet at point guard. Monet wouldn't admit it, but she was more than a little jealous of Roxy's popularity with men. On the court, they tolerated each other.

Pick and roll defense was still a mystery to Tamika. Despite the importance of the game, Lonnie sat Tamika on the bench. The Rhinos continued to play well without her scoring.

With the Rhinos leading, 36-32, with 22 seconds remaining in the first half, Roxy closed the passing lane and stole a pass. As she raced down the court, she had a two-on-one fast break with Monet. The defender ran flat out to get back and defend her goal. Roxy passed the ball to Monet before they reached half court. Monet passed it back to Roxy before they reached the sideline hash mark. The UConn defender stopped at the free throw line, she had to stop the person with the ball, but she had to guess correctly.

As they passed the three-point line, Roxy held the ball for half a second before she passed it back to Monet. Her hesitation allowed the defender to react to the pass instead of committing to stop Roxy with the ball. She stepped in the path of the charging Monet who had already made her move to the basket. Monet was in no-mans-land; unable to make a clean drive to the basket and unable to avoid a collision. She tried to salvage Roxy's pass by tipping it back to her but that only solved half the problem. Monet collided with the UConn defender and fell to the floor.

The demonstrative referee had the call all the way. She skipped a couple of times on one foot, grabbed the back of her head and punched the air with her right fist–offensive foul.

The UConn player got up, Monet did not. She writhed in pain clutching her knee. Lonnie, both coaches, and the trainer ran to her aid. Her knee was already starting to swell.

"Did you hear anything pop?"

"No, we banged knees, then I twisted it when I went down."

The ESPN broadcast replayed the collision over and over. It looked bad. The color announcer explained how Roxy's hesitation didn't fake out the defender and had left Monet defenseless when she switched to draw the offense foul on Monet. The defender had established position and Monet plowed right through her. It was an easy call.

Tamika and Shirlie carried Monet back to the bench. She was done for the night. She was worried that this might be how her college career would end.

Roxy's blunder was a four-point turnaround. Del Mar didn't score and because Del Mar was over the foul limit, UConn got to shoot two free throws. They made them both.

Roxy, on the other hand, was secretly happy to be able to play the point guard position again. She didn't want Monet to have a serious injury, but she wasn't mad about regaining the starting point guard position either.

When Shirlie returned to the court she nudged Roxy, "You wanted it back, now let's see what you do with it."

During the time out, Lonnie said, "We're still in the game. Roxy, we practiced this all season, you've got to hold the ball long enough to make the defender commit! This is what happens!.. Tamika you're back in. We're going to look for you on the post. We have an advantage there, let's work it."

Collectively, the team was disappointed in Roxy and she felt it. Monet was indifferent. Injuries happens, that's basketball.

As the team walked back onto the court, Lonnie Delaney pulled Tamika to the side, "You wanted the spotlight. Now's your time to shine. Let's see how far you can take us now that Monet is out. But you have to help your teammates help you, so keep them involved."

Tamika smiled. "Let's do it." Tamika felt vindicated. She was determined to show Lonnie that taking her out of the game was not a viable option. Lonnie had unleashed a beast. Tamika controlled the rebounds on defense and played within herself on offense. After she had scored eight straight points, UConn double-teamed her. She calmly made passes to Shirlie and Kendra for easy scores. UConn couldn't make a shot and Del Mar went on to win the game, 65-59.

The Runnin'Rhinos' record rose to 7-8. But it was a Pyrrhic victory; Monet was out indefinitely.

Chapter 20

Secrets

January Seventh, 3:15 PM
Monet sat on the trainer's table. She winced from the manipulations, Derek, one of Del Mar's trainers, was putting her through. She was amazed at how much pain he could inflict with just thumbs and fingers. After the massage, she sat there alone icing her knee before Lonnie walked in. "So, how's it coming?"

"Fine, I guess," Monet said, doing her best to hide her disappointment.

"I'm glad you're not mad," Lonnie said.

"It's not exactly the best way to end your college career."

"OK. Ice for 30 minutes," said the trainer, wiping the icy-hot gunk from his hands.

Lonnie said, "Let's see how you rehab. You might be able to come back. Thankfully, you didn't rip it up... We'll have to make do without you. Tamika said, she had first dibs on your shots."

"She can have 'em, as long as she makes 'em like I do."

Ray entered the trainer's room as Lonnie was leaving. Monet placed a huge ice bag on her knee. Her eyes followed Ray as he took a seat on the table facing her. They stared at each other until Monet broke the silence.

"Thanks for getting my assignments. It would have been impossible to go to all of my classes," Monet said. Ray sat there expressionless with two bags of ice on his knees. "And for the notes in Psych 430 and the Body Politic." More silence. "And for bringing me breakfast... Lunch... The pizza last night–Why are a you being so nice to me?"

"A brotha can't help a sista out?" he asked, finally.

Third-person references; he must be Ghetto Ray today. Right now, I'd prefer Shakespearian Ray. He's funnier.

"Being ranked number one go to your head yet?" Monet asked.

"Not yet, but give it time. We're gonna show Duke how to hold it down."

In his own the way, she knew Ray was trying to cheer her up. As they sat there staring at each other, again, a tear crawled down her cheek.

"Hey, hey. Don't cry... You'll violate the vulnerability clause of the Feminist Manifesto... You were supposed to laugh... Don't worry. You're going to be fine. You know what? I want to take you someplace," Ray said.

"Where?"

"It's a surprise... You know, you could at least be a little excited."

Ray watched her reaction. Her head was down. There was a lot at stake: the remainder of her college playing career, in fact. He watched Monet in silence, knowing what was on her mind.

Most people would have blamed Roxy for her injury. Not Monet. She believed in controling her own destiny–creating her own luck. Down one, with the ball, she wanted to take the shot while everyone else played hot potato. For Monet being out of control was what was so devastating about being injured.

When Monet looked up, Ray saw the fire in her eyes. He knew that look. He saw it when he looked in the mirror. That, I'm-the-Man look. He'd never seen it in a woman before. It was very sexy. He thought, "Me and a woman like that could conquer the world."

Ray looked up at the clock. "Oh man, I gotta go."

"You've only been here five minutes. And why aren't you in practice?" Monet said.

"Exactly, I told Coach I felt a little twitch in the hammy. And you know, he almost blew a gasket right there. Hold on... What do you mean? Ray, you go and get that checked out right now!'" Ray said.

"Yeah, but you have ice on your knees. Are you all right?"

"Girl, ain't nothin' wrong with me. I just wanted to get out of prectice and holla at you for a minute."

He finally got her to smile. Mission impossible turned into mission accomplished. He was out like a shot.

As she sat alone she thought again about the list of things she wanted in a man.

He had to be a tall athletic brother, ambitious, respectful, altruistic, fun, have a sense of humor, be a little adventurous, confident, and have the Concierge Factor.

As the list got longer, she knew a guy like that would already be taken by the time she met him. Monet decided to take Big Shirlie's advice and just look for three deal breakers when she evaluated a guy's potential.

The ice bag fell to the floor and she gingerly scooted down off the table to retrieve it.

Deal breakers. Deal breakers. What are my deal breakers? Intelligence is one. Ambition. Definitely, no lazy ass Negroes.

She struggled with the third deal breaker. It would be painful, but she could work with a guy who wasn't particularly funny or was so traditional he needed to be prodded to try new things. Monet was six-one but a guy didn't have to be six-three for her to talk to him. Altruism was important, but still not a deal breaker. Being respectful wasn't even a deal breaker, because like being trustworthy, it was a given. If they didn't have it, there would be no relationship. It was like saying she wouldn't consider a guy who would punch her in the face if he got mad. It went without saying.

She was stuck figuring out the third deal breaker.

The Concierge Factor, being able to get things done. Isn't that the same as being ambitious? Well, not really. You can be ambitious without getting stuff done. Of course, that would make you a dreamer. Plus, being able to change a tire or plan a surprise party doesn't require a lot of ambition, but it sure does make a girl feel safe and secure that my man can handle anything that comes his way. That's it. I'm done.

Monet felt good about her list: Intelligence, ambition and the Concierge Factor. With those three things in a guy, she figured the rest would take care of itself.

She had visions of saving months of dating time by limiting the number of dates she went on with guys who didn't have all three deal breakers.

She was definitely going to put her new strategy to the test. She applied the deal breaker criterion to Chris Chamberlain. He failed miserably. His conceit overpowered any intelligence he might have had. The breadth of his conversation literally revolved around himself and nothing else. Milton was different. He was intelligent, although she had forgotten if he was an engineering major or into molecular biology. Whatever it was, he was smart. His ambition didn't rock the charts, but he had plans for his life. However, Milton was no concierge. He didn't know how to get things done and he was awkward around women. That first date on the basketball court was proof enough. Milton did have a lot of potential; a white collar job was in his future, he was respectful, the argyle was offputting but he had a lot of potential. In basketball, it's called upside, which counts for a lot. The timer went off and the physical trainer returned to wrap up Monet's knee.

Monet had to use crutches to walk. One of the maintenance guys gave her a ride back to her dorm in a golf cart. But she had to take the scenic route to the basement to get a plunger for a stopped up toilet, over to the football field to turn off the water, and finally to her dorm room. A five minute walk, even on crutches, took 20 minutes. She didn't think it was worth it. She thanked him all the same, after enduring more than a few maintenance man horror stories.

When Monet returned to her room, she picked up an envelope that someone had slid under her door. It smelled bad. She read the contents in horror. "Your knees won't feel better if you don't hold on to your icebergs –You know who".

January Fifteenth, 4:30 PM

Lonnie sat at the desk in her office. A video tape of the morning practice was playing; she had a coffee mug in one hand and Tamika's grades in the other. They weren't pretty. She had an abysmal 1.75 grade point average. Lonnie figured you'd have to be catatonic, stupid or just not give a damn to get a 1.75 GPA. She had to somehow convince Tamika she was missing a valuable opportunity. Knowing Tamika, Lonnie knew she would probably view her scholarship as some kind of time card she needed to play basketball professionally.

Only quitters made Lonnie angrier than underachievers.

"Dan Cantrell on line four," the receptionist said on the intercom.

"Okay... Hi, Dan."

Lonnie could hear the exasperation in his voice. "You asked me to call you but you, never return my phone calls."

"I'm sorry, there isn't much time during the season," Lonnie said. "Remember?"

"You can't be that busy."

"No really. I am."

"How about dinner on Wednesday?" Dan said, sounding hopeful.

"I can't, we're going to be in Los Angeles playing Pepperdine and then Loyola-Marymount."

"We can eat in Los Angeles."

"I can't... Really. I have to prep, watch tapes, game plan with my coaches, review it with the team, there really isn't much time," Lonnie said, sitting back in her chair and using the remote to rewind a play on the VCR.

"We met back in September; now it's January and you still can't fit me in?"

"I told you I don't have much time during the season."

"You're making this very hard," he said.

"Don't say that, I really want to get together, but it's hard during the season," she said.

"People make time for what's important to them and besides..."

"Whassup? Coach," Tamika walked in and sat down apprehensively.

"Dan, I'm sorry, but I have to go. One of my players just stepped into my office. Let's have coffee in February," she said.

"Lonnie, it's January."

"I have to go. So are we on? Coffee, February 2nd at 10:30?"

Dan didn't answer.

"Call me later and–." But Dan had hung up. She turned to Tamika. "I was reviewing everyone's grades for the fall quarter. You want to tell me what's going on with yours?"

"Nothing."

"Ds and Cs is definitely something."

"Nothing."

"You need more than this to be eligible to play," Lonnie said, closing Tamika's file. They may pass players along on the men's teams, but it won't happen on mine."

"C'mon, Coach. I'm just trying to stay eligible anyway, maybe if I took your class you could give me an A and boost my GPA?"

"This isn't a joke. You're wasting my money."

"How is it your money?"

"$28,000 worth of tuition, room and board, books."

"I get that to play basketball," Tamika said.

"Who do you think decides who gets a scholarship? I control the budget on this team. I control who gets what. There are people on this team who deserve a scholarship, but I can't give them one because there isn't any more money. And here you are wasting money with a damn 1.65 GPA."

"1.75."

"Next quarter you had better have a 2.25 average," Lonnie said.

"2.25? The minimum is 2.0.'

"There are no minimums on my team," Lonnie corrected.

"Or what? You gonna cut me from the team?" Tamika challenged. "We're 9-9. Probably only need 8 or 9 wins to make it to the tournament and you're talking about cutting me? You're trippin."

"I've cut scholarship players before. Players who were more talented than you."

Tamika rolled her eyes. "Tch. Where you gonna find 20 points and 15 rebounds a game? Roxy? Clio? Don't say Kendra, 'cause I drag her ass up and down the court everyday."

"Somewhere." Lonnie caught herself before she lost her temper watching Tamika's obstinate scowl. Tamika rolled her eyes. Lonnie wanted to kick her off the team immediately. Tamika was bold and ghetto, which isn't a good combination. Lonnie tried another tact. "I know you want to play in the ABL or even the WNBA if they get it off the ground, but let me ask you something. What will you do if it doesn't workout?"

"Oh, it's gonna work out," Tamika said, arms crossed, with major attitude–working her neck.

"OK, but what if you get injured?"

"Stop hatin', coach."

"Hating? I've already done all the things you're trying to do. I played professionally in Europe, won two Olympic Gold Medals, won NCAA championships. So what can you tell me about basketball that I don't know firsthand? Players get hurt all the time. You can make a bad cut and blow out your knee tomorrow. Takes two seconds. Women are five times more susceptible to tearing their ACL than men. Then what'll you do?" asked Lonnie.

"Go to rehab and come back stronger," Tamika said.

Lonnie shook her head. She wasn't getting through to Tamika. "Just do me a favor and get your grades up to 2.25. OK?"

"Yeah, okay, Coach. Can I go now?"

Tamika was up and out of her chair before Lonnie could even answer.

The altercation with Tamika made Lonnie feel like a sellout. She tried to be philosophical about the predicament–dealing with stubborn 18 year olds with runaway egos and the talent to back them up was an unenviable, but common way of life for a college coach. The problem gets worse at the better programs because having talented players is job security. Lonnie knew that cutting her would have been like taking the first step toward firing herself.

266 Under the Rim

For coaches, winning is the cure-all. Winning puts butts in the seats. Winning inspires alumni to write checks. Winning gets teams on television. Winning sets up the program to recruit future high school stars. Winning provides job security for coaches because winning in college athletics makes money.

Jennifer walked into Lonnie's office next. Lonnie smiled.

"Coach, I decided to keep the baby," Jennifer said.

"That's wonderful news," said Lonnie, meaning it.

"Not that I have much choice; turns out I'm 14 weeks pregnant."

"That's a miracle, given all the running you've been doing. Would you have considered the alternatives?"

"No. I'm Catholic."

"Adoption is an option. Have you told your parents yet?"

"I can't."

"Jennifer," Lonnie sighed. "You have to tell your parents."

"My father will make me go back to Oroville–be like all my high school friends. I'm not going back to that."

"The truth should never get you into trouble."

"You don't know my parents; they're Catholic. I still want to play."

"Play? You're not playing another minute," Lonnie said.

"Will I lose my scholarship?" Looking like she was about to cry.

"I checked on it. Basically, the NCAA rule is that players can't get preferential treatment."

"What does that mean?" Jennifer asked.

"No child care or extra medical services. Stuff like that. The NCAA doesn't treat your pregnancy like an injury."

"Uh... Right. It isn't. I guess."

"As it relates to your scholarship, you can get an extra year, but if you quit, you'll lose it."

"I don't want to quit."

"I know, but we can't give you special treatment through the athletic department. The school has health coverage for all students through St.Mary's Hospital, so you're covered there."

"So, how am I supposed to keep my scholarship and take care of my baby?"

"Not that many women get pregnant, but when they do, they quit playing their sport to focus on school, so they can gradute, get a job and start supporting themselves," Lonnie said. "Unless your parents or a relative can help, they will quit. Why can't we help them stay?"

"They may as well take my scholarship. How many guys have to quit?"

"You know the answer to that. It's not fair, but let me see what I can do."

"What'll you do? Go up against the NCAA? You may as well fight the IRS," Jennifer said, slumping back in her chair.

"True, but I'm not the type to give up just because I might lose. Hey, What's that in your mouth?"

Jennifer stuck out her tongue to show her tongue stud.

"You know Jennifer, I know you are away from your parents for the first time, but you can't say 'yes' to every impulsive thought you have. I think that's one lesson to be learned from all of this."

January Sixteenth, 10:00 PM

Sonja sat at her desk in her dorm room. Fifty expressionless models on her wall stared back at her from the ripped out pages of fashion magazines. Looking at the photos brought out her inner Supermodel when she was alone. She would pout then turn to the left; pout, then turn to the right. She puckered her lips which hollowed out her already hollow cheeks. She liked the way it made her face look thinner. In Sonja's mind, thin girls ruled. They got first dibs on the cutest guys. Clothes always looked better when you were thin. Thefashion models on her wall were her ideal body image. All sharp angles, no curves.

Tamika saw something entirely different in Sonja. She saw the long strands of hair Sonja left in her combs and brush. Sonja had stopped having periods a month ago. While Tamika liked the notion of not having a period, she figured not having them at Sonja's age probably wasn't very healthy.

Tamika was on the phone with Victor. He told her that injuries are never a good thing, but that this was her time to show what she could do. The best way to get noticed would be to play well.

"Don't worry about playing defense, just make sure you remain eligible to play. Did you get the money I sent?" Victor asked.

"Yeah, thanks. Listen I gotta go... OK, bye." Tamika turned to Sonja and said, "For someone who is always in the mirror, you would think you would know what you look like by now."

"You think I gained some weight? I hate these uniforms, they make me look fat," Sonja said.

"You look fat because the uniform is too big. You've lost a bunch of weight. You look like one of those Shar-Pei dogs with elephant skin," Tamika said.

"I don't look fat."

"Sure you don't. You look like those skinny ass bitches on your wall." Tamika said, "How can the uniforms make you look fat? You eat five grapes, some lettuce, and apple juice for dinner. You get straight A's. Your class notes are better than the teacher's. It's like, damn girl, the Miss Perfection Pageant is next summer. Now, where you going?" Tamika asked, as Sonja grabbed her bag.

"Studying," Sonja said.

"Where?"

"UCSF library."

"That's a mile away."

"No, it's not. It's 1.7 miles away," Sonja said.

"Jennifer gonna give you a ride?"

"No."

"So, how are you gonna get there?" Tamika said.

Long pause.

"Ooooooooo. Coach said you can't run anymore," Tamika said.

"When you tell Lonnie about your agent then I'll tell her about my running... It's eleven o'clock, no one is going to see me."

"I'm just saying, it's on you. But you should see yourself."

"What?" Sonja said.

"To be honest, you look like a crack ho from my neighborhood. All skinny and..."

"I do not."

"Please. I normally wouldn't give a shit, but with Monet out we're gonna need yo' skinny ass to win some games."

"I gotta run to stay in shape."

"You keep runnin' and you're gonna disappear."

"You're hurting the team," Sonja said.

"*I'm* hurting the team? Oh, with my agent?" Tamika said.

"Yep."

"Here we go," Tamika crossed her arms.

"Everybody knows it. Ms. Ghetto Fabulous with an affinity for leopard, rayon and–."

"Watch your mouth, girl."

Sonya continued, "Last month you bought an entire wardrobe. You think people are stupid?... At least when I run I'm not putting the entire program in jeopardy."

"I ain't, either."

"If someone asks how you can you afford a diamond tennis bracelet, then one thing will leads to another," Sonja said. "This school is makin' way too much money off of us for that to happen. Trust me."

"You haven't gone to class in four months. You're already on academic probation. And, just so you know, they make a lot of money on football and men's basketball. They lose money on us."

"I'm gonna get my grades up," Tamika said.

"Not unless you're taking a class on soap opera appreciation."

"No you didn't," Tamika said. "Wit' yo' hair fallin' out. Pretty soon you'll be takin' Rogaine, like Karl Malone."

"You're still putting the entire program at risk," Sonja said, ignoring her remarks.

"No, you are. Every time you grab a rebound you look like a Spanish exclamation mark. What's gonna happen when yo' dumb ass dies after one of your 15-mile runs. Coach been tellin' you to stop runnin'. Have you stopped? *No.*"

Sonja heard enough. She slammed the door on the way out. They both knew their secrets were safe.

Forrest Haneline was waiting in the tunnel for practice to end.

"Well, well, well. That was a truly enlightening interview you gave to ESPN," he said, as Lonnie walked out. "And the part about how most schools are in violation of Title IX was especially good."

Lonnie stopped, "I think I gave a balanced interview."

"We don't want you to be balanced. Not when we sign your pay checks. We want you to sing the praises of the school, the program, and the team. And I specifically told you at the beginning of the year–."

"–What I said was the truth," interrupting him. "Women's coaches are not paid the same as men." I didn't say anything about here at Del Mar."

"You basically said it."

"Either way, it's true. The softball coach and the baseball coach don't make the same amount. I certainly don't make as much as Warlich. Is that true or false?"

"I distinctly remember telling you to fit in and not rock the boat like you did at Ohio State."

"I have."

"This interview isn't what I'd call 'not rocking the boat,'" Haneline said, angrily. "Do me a favor. No more interviews." He turned and walked away.

Lonnie knew she couldn't make that promise.

Lonnie saw Clint Warlich in the hallway that afternoon. She was already mad at Haneline and couldn't pass up the chance to throw a verbal dart at him. She walked up along side of him and pretended to read a newspaper article, "A six-figure contract for a guy who's only won a few WCC conference titles. All of his NCAA appearances ended prematurely. No Warlich team has ever reached the Sweet Sixteen and now he is going to make three times as much as the women's coach?"

Warlich was unfazed. "I have a good therapist you should go see."

"So tell me, what the hell *have* you ever won?" Lonnie asked. She'd been waiting a long time to ask him that.

"Look lady, I know you want more money, but communism doesn't work. Ronald Reagan proved that already," Warlich said.

"That's right, when you can't argue facts, argue the theory of how things should be."

That made him mad. "My team is the life's blood of the athletic department."

Lonnie said, "Yeah, that's the reason why you're coaching, to financially support the nonrevenue sports."

"Alumni give to this school because of two things, football and *men's basketball.* And whether you like it or not, it's through my success and *because* of my success that *you have a job."* He was jabbing his finger at Lonnie.

"You have to talk about money because you've never won anything. Talk to me about success when you win a national championship," Lonnie said. She could tell, he hated that.

"Talk to me when your salary is over five digits," he said.

Before walking away Lonnie held up her left hand and wiggled her fingers so Warlich would get a good look at her national championship ring.

Refusing to be outdone, he held up his left hand with his wedding band. "I've got the one that really matters. What about you?"

*   *   *   *

January Seventeenth

Ray and Monet talked about photographs as they walked through the Irwin Elliot exhibit in the Frankel Gallery on Geary Street. This was Ray's surprise.

Ray said, "You know what I like about Elliot's photographs? The cat had a sense of humor. The chihuahua standing next to the Great Dane. Look at his eyes. He knows he's gonna get eaten. Hat and all."

I can't believe he actually knows about these photographers.

"Every Chihuahua looks like that, it's probably a defense mechanism," Monet said.

"What? Don't eat me 'cause I'm scared to death?" Ray joked.

"Nature takes whatever you've got and uses it to your advantage."

They had been talking for 30 minutes, an hour if you included the ride over from school and the time they spent looking for a place to park. Ray talked a lot but was engaging and funny, not like that bore, Chris Chamberlain, who could only talk about himself.

"Have you ever seen that kind of fear in someone's eyes?" Ray said.

"Not really," Monet said.

"I have. When the game is on the line. You can tell who wants the ball."

"In the huddle, too."

"Yep," he agreed.

"Give me the damn ball," Monet said. Ray smiled. He loved it when she talked dirty.

He smells good. Come to think of it, he always smells good. He sure is sexy when he's not getting on my nerves.

After they had walked through the exhibit, Monet suggested they go to some of the other galleries. Ray turned his nose up at the idea. "C'mon, paintings don't have the range of photographs. Can't capture the true soul of man at his best and his worst."

"It's stupid to say one is better than the other."

"Van Gogh couldn't go from fashion to photojournalism like Avedon," Ray said.

"So what? There's abstract, classic portraiture, avant-garde, impressionism, that's range for yo' ass," Monet said.

"Real talk," Ray said.

"Take this painting by Dre Patterson," pointing to 'Adam and Eve' on the wall. "What do you see?"

"I see a blue-black brotha with a high yellow sista," Ray said.

"Adam and Eve."

"There's the devil in red reaching around the brotha offering the apple of knowledge."

"Yeah, but the bible blames it on Eve. What else?" Monet said.

"There's another face right behind them," Ray said.

"That's envy, your friends who smile in your face. The devil is your enemies, you know that already."

"Raight. Rai'ght. And the face on the tree?" Ray said.

"Those are evil deeds you know you shouldn't do, but you do them anyway."

"And that face, the purple block thing, what's that?"

"That's the evil that lurks in the world," Monet finished.

"The bad things that happen to good people," Ray said.

"You're funny. When I met you I never would have thought we'd be at an art gallery arguing about whether photography has more range than paintings. And I almost forgot about the poetry reading."

"Stop right there about the poetry reading."

"Why? Because you were in the homoerotic section?" Monet smiled.

"I don't want to talk abou it." Ray walked away in mock disgust.

They visited six exhibits in all. The galleries were like mazes, long hallways leading to large rooms. They moved slowly through the rooms taking in the art. They moved with the harmony of an old married couple. Smooth. Unhurried. When they unknowingly separated they returned to the spot they last made eye contact. Sure enough, within a few minutes they were reunited. They both noticed how comfortable they felt together.

January Seventeenth, 7:30 PM

Dan Cantrell stood outside Lonnie's door. It was their first real date after numerous talks on the phone and a few failed attempts at having coffee at Starbucks. As he stood in front of her door he checked his breath. Lonnie opened the door. She smile when she saw him.

"You look great," he said. She smiled again.

"I appreciate you squeezing me in and not making me wait until February 15th."

"So, what are we going to do?" she asked.

"A little dinner, ride a cable car to the wharf, let it flow from there."

"How do you know I haven't been on a cable car already?" she joked.

"You've been complaining about not having any time for the last four months. How would you have time to do something touristy like ride the cable cars?"

Lonnie liked Dan's confidence. It was the same attribute she wanted her players to have.

They had a wonderful dinner at *Masa's*– classic french. Lonnie surprised herself by letting him hold her hand as they walked up Bush Street to catch the cable car on Powell.

"Tell me again why this took so long to happen?" he asked.

"The date?"

"Yeah, I mean, it's the middle of January, we met in September."

"There's no time during the season. Right now, I'm thinking about basketball ninety percent of the time," she said.

"That's the short answer," Dan said.

Lonnie sighed. "The long answer is we have practice every day from six to eight in the morning. Wednesday nights and Saturday nights we play our games. So, that means Tuesday and Friday are travel "to" days and Thursday and Sunday are travel "from" days.

"What about during the day?"

"Every Monday I watch videotapes of the previous week's games with my assistants. Then we watch videotapes of our opponents for the upcoming games. THEN, we develop a game plan for those games based on what we think are our strengths and their weaknesses. Finally, we develop a plan for the week's practice, so we can teach the players what we want them to do in those upcoming games. Each of those steps can take from two to six hours and I haven't even included the time it takes to watch the videotapes of the practices."

Dan held up his hand, "C'mon, Lonnie..."

Lonnie continued. "That's during the day. At night, there are receptions with alumni and boosters."

"Wait, a minute–."

"Oh, and when there's a break in the schedule Renee, Stephanie, and I break away to watch recruits play. That's when we met, remember?"

"Sure, at the airport," Dan said.

"So, it's me and about 50 other coaches sitting in the same living rooms, telling the same kids how great they are and why they should come play for our program."

"No wonder their egos are out of control."

"It's mostly boys, but some girls too. They're just trying to act like boys," she said. "Which is understandable, since many of their role models are men."

"That's why you have girls wearing baggy clothes and pants down on their asses," he said.

"It's a hideous look on boys, too," she said. "Besides, it's not like there aren't any good athletic female, role models. Lisa Leslie, Mia Hamm, Dawn Staley."

"Lisa Fernandez, Brandi Chastain. Cheryl Swoops. Tough, competitive, and feminine," Dan added.

Lonnie was impressed with Dan's knowledge of female team sports players. "As a woman, you don't have to give up your femininity to be in our athletic culture. Some girls feel like they have to because we ingrain in our girls that being competitive is a masculine trait. But you certainly don't have to act like a man to be a serious athlete."

"It has to be confusing for a high school girl who's a great athlete. She knows she's female, but if she does what it takes to maximize her talent she has to be competitive, determined–."

"But then people will criticize her for acting like a boy. She'll say, 'No, I'm not. I'm playing basketball. I'm doing what winners do.' It's a lot of pressure, especially if it comes from your parents. That's why so many girls quit playing sports after high school."

"They don't quit if they are really good," Dan said.

"Yeah, they have a different set of problems. Usually it's a runaway ego. In a way, I can't blame them. By the time a good player gets to the tenth grade she has had 50 coaches contact her. If she's really good, three of them will be Hall of Famers and ten more will coach teams that are regularly on television. So the kid sees the coach that she's seen on television, not just sitting in her living room, but putting up with her crazy uncle insisting she take a few of his basketball plays drawn on three napkins. The coach is trying to impress the kid by spouting her stats at her last game. It might comes across as ass kissing."

"I would not kiss seventeen-year-old ass," Dan said, shaking his head.

"Seventeen? We've tracked kids as early as the seventh grade if I get a tip from someone I respect."

"Seventh grade. What is that, thirteen?"

"Yep."

"We're developing a relationship, sometimes as early as thirteen. We visit, we call, we send letters. We see them during summer camps to track their progress. It never ends."

"I'm sorry, I will not kiss a seventeen-year-old's ass," Dan said.

"What about a thirteen-year-old's?"

Dan shook his head, then looked at Lonnie as if she shouldn't either.

"Yeah, but I do it with dignity," she said.

Dan laughed out loud. "How can you? When both of you know your job depends on it."

"I get down to their level. I adapt. I've been in every kind of household. Suburbia; mom, dad, three daughters, a dog, and a mini-van out front, solid family. But I've also been in public housing tenements with a whacked out mom, no dad , where the kid is using basketball as a lifeline to get out of her neighborhood."

"That's gotta be tough to see."

"We talk about all the opportunity basketball can offer them. We talk about their education and a chance to change their future. I get on their level. You have to talk *to* kids, not *at* them. Biggest thing that surprises them is when I tell them I listen to hip-hop," Lonnie said.

"You do not–."

"The hell I don't. Take Ice-T and the Wu-Tang Clan straight to the dome," she said, with more than a little funk in the trunk.

"You are just full of surprises. So, what do you do with the remaining ten percent of your time?" Dan asked.

"I try to remember to take a shower, lock my apartment, and put gas in my car," she said.

"Doesn't leave time for much else."

"I told you," Lonnie said. A faraway look came over her. "Sometimes I wonder if it's worth it. Maybe it's me. Maybe I need to stop pushing so hard to get them to treat women equally."

"Lonnie."

Why do I need to be the one that makes these guys do what they're supposed to do?

"Lonnie."

"No one is stepping up."

"Lonnie! Do you want a family?" Dan said.

"What?"

"Do you want a family?"

"I do. But I can't keep a husband," Lonnie sighed. "You can tell from my schedule I'm still not making much room in my life time to find a replacement."

Dan squeezed her hand gently. "You seem to do okay at the airport," he said with a wink. They stood there in silence as the cable car approached. "I'm busy, too. All I need is a little bit to work with."

Lonnie turned to Dan, put her head in his chest, and gave him a big hug, "Have you ever considered being a wife?"

January Eighteenth

The Lady Runnin' Rhinos were playing the San Diego Toreros. They started league play with four straight wins. They were, 13-9, overall.

Shirlie whispered to Roxy as the starting players shook hands with their opponents at mid-court, "Keep doing what you're doing."

Thalia Clark said, describing the play-by-play, "After the injury to Monet McCasner, Lonnie Delaney starts Roxy Davidson at point guard, Clio Wysinger moved over to shooting guard, Kendra Washington moved over to small forward, Tamika Hightower stayed at power forward, and Shirlie Torretta remains at center.

"The Toreros are smaller and quicker but realistically not a very good women's basketball team. The absence Monet McCasner has changed the chemistry of the team. They are not running the fast break as often. Even though Roxy's much shorter than Monet, she doesn't push the ball on the fast break as relentlessly as Monet. Consequently, the Rhinos aren't scoring as many lay-ups. They're relying more on their half-court plays to score."

Kendra, Clio, Sonja, and even Roxy had come to accept Mbika's smacks on the behind as they checked into the game. Now, whenever they got up to check into the game, they put both hands, palms out, over their behind. After a few games, it had evolved into a Rhinos rallying ritual. Whenever they fell behind by more than five points, Mbika slapped her team-mates hands when they placed them behind their backs when a teammate checked into the game.

During the game, Kendra was open several times, twice coming off a screen and three times working off backdoor cuts to the basket. Roxy's passes never connected. They were either stolen, deflected out of bounds, or were too far out in front. On the fifth blown pass, Kendra yelled at Roxy to make better passes. She would never have done that in years past.

Tamika and Shirlie were upset as well. Shirlie didn't shoot much, but she took pride in setting up her teammates with her bone-crushing stealth picks. She continued to mash the Lady Toreros into the floor with her physical play. But it takes three people to score on screens away from the ball; Shirlie was setting the pick, the cutter, either Tamika or Kendra, and the passer who was Roxy. Shirlie, Tamika, and Kendra did their part but when it was time to receive the ball, Roxy couldn't deliver the ball consistently in a place where they could score. Tamika, Kendra, and even Roxy had gotten used to catching Monet's passes, which were always delivered in stride, chest high, right on time. All they had to do was catch it and lay it up softly. Monet's passes practically scored themselves. Even though, the Rhinos had been winning there was a big difference in how Monet and Roxy played the point guard position.

The Rhinos lost to the San Diego Toreros, 38-45. Shirlie couldn't believe it. In all her four years at Del Mar they had never lost to them. She blamed Roxy.

*   *   *   *

It was the first date with Alphonso Tisdale–THE hottest guy in high school. Monet stood guard at the living room window waiting for his arrival. She was hopeful but forlorn. There was a good chance the date wasn't going to happen. The date was in jeopardy because Alphonso liked to blow his horn and have his date run out to the car. Monet didn't object. She would gladly run out in a ballerina tutu doing grand jetes, *and spreading flower petals along the way if that's what it took for her to go out with Alphonso. It was her father, who had a problem with some pimple-faced kid blowing his horn for his high school daughter. It didn't matter if he was the cutest guy in school. It didn't matter if his 1976 Spider was immaculate. Who did he think he was–Cary Grant?*

Monet continued her vigil in the window. He was due at any moment. Alphonso was from a good family, always respectful of girls in class, funny, great boyfriend material. He just wouldn't get out of the car and came to the door.

When she told him what her father expected, he said, "They still do that?"

That was a deal breaker as far as her father was concerned. Pops didn't have a lot of rules, but he was firm on this one, "No meet, no date."

Here he comes.

Monet tried to sneak out.

"Where you going?" Her father asked looking up from the Lakers/Celtics game on CBS.

"I was going to..."

"Yeah, I know, but..." He didn't have to say any more.

Mac, her brother, laughed but thankfully kept his comments to himself. Mac knew about Alphonso, too, but that wouldn't save her.

Get out of the car. Get out of the car. Get out of the car.

Monet prayed. Alphonso blew the horn.

Damn.

"I know that kid didn't just blow his horn?" her father said, contemplating going over to the window.

"Maybe he hit the horn trying to take his keys out of the ignition," Mac said, trying to be helpful.

"Please. Mac. Don't help!" Monet said, looking out from behind the curtain. She went back into her mantra. "Get out of the car. Get out of the car. Get out of the car."

Alphonso got out of the car. But, then he leaned on the door of his car, arms folded with his legs crossed at the ankle. The top was

*down. He was lookin good. After a few seconds he blew the horn
again. Monet took a step toward the door.*

"Don't you dare!" Stopped her in her tracks.

*She took a few steps back, then walked to the window, hiding
the fact she was standing behind the curtain. She curled her finger
for him to come to the door. He didn't move. He curled his finger
in response, waited, then looked at his watch impatientl. He was a
guy with options. And so, it was a standoff. Soon, her father appeared in the window and ended it. Alphonso's body language
stayed cool, but his bug eyes gave away his fear.*

*"Mom! Daddy's scaring off my date!" Monet cried out to her
mother, who was in the kitchen.*

*With Monet's father standing in the window, Alphonso calmly
got into his car and drove off.*

Monet started to run to her the room.

*"Wait a minute," her father said. "Before you go slamming
doors and calling your girlfriends about how I'm ruining your
social life, sit down for a minute."*

Here it comes, the lecture.

"You gotta demand respect," he said.

*Monet rolled her eyes as any self-respecting teenager getting a
lecture would.*

*"I know it's hard for you to believe, but I was your age once
and you KNOW how your brother here acts around girls–."*

"I always go in and meet the Ogre, I mean the Dad," Mac said.

"Shut up. Mac," Monet said.

*"It's about respect. I'm not going to harass the guy. So, what's
the big deal?" Mr. McCasner said.*

"What about the guy you had your cop friends check out?"

"I don't do that all the time. That kid had driving issues."

*"Dad, you called the police on her boyfriend," Mac said.
"He got stopped two blocks from the house. They took his car."*

"This isn't about me," her father said.

*"Right, he's coming to see me. I don't see the big deal about
coming in to meet you," Monet said.*

*"Anybody you're going out with has to come in here and look
me in the eye. You know why? Because I want him to feel in the
core of his DNA that if anything happens to you while you're out,
he will live to regret it. You are precious to me and he won't know
how precious you are until he meets me. That's why it's a big deal."*

"Same goes for me," Mac said.

"Same goes for your brother. I better not hear how he wouldn't go in to meet a girl's parents."

Monet stuck her tongue out at Mac.

Her father continued. *"The convertible is nice, I'm sure all the girls like it. But I want you to understand, you set the standard of respect boys will have for you. It comes from you, not them. Demand respect, you'll get respect. Dismiss the importance of respect and you can expect to be disrespected."*

Monet stood there weathering the lecture. None of her father's words assuaged the hurt feelings from the missed date that never was with the finest boy in school.

Chapter 21

The Ray Scale

January Twenty-first

The Lady Runnin' Rhinos were playing Gonzaga at home. Since Roxy had taken over, the Rhinos had lost three of their last four games. The team was angry with Roxy because they believed they were a better team than their record indicated.

A shooting foul had been committed. The players took their places outside the key. After a Bulldog player missed the foul shot, one of her teammates dove for the rebound in front of Kendra. She missed the ball and landed in Kendra's lap. The problem was Kendra was still standing. As she fell to the floor, Kendra jackknifed around the diving Bulldog player, hyperextending both of her knees. It was a freak accident. Clio and Shirlie had to carry her off the court. Kendra wasn't one of the Rhinos' leading scorers but she was always good for six points, ten if she was really shooting well.

Mbika was now in the game. By November, she had the basics of the game, but Lonnie didn't trust her to do, so the Rhinos played a 2-3 zone the remainder of the game. They ran the clock out to secure the victory.

Mbika thanked God she didn't have to shoot any free throws.

With five weeks remaining in the season, the Lady Runnin' Rhinos faced some must-win games. Fortunately, they were winnable games against teams in the bottom of the WCC standings. They would have to win all their remaining games to have had a chance at getting into the NCAA tournament. At full strength, they would have a good chance. But with Monet and Kendra out of the lineup their chances were about 50-50.

Losing a close game at Tennessee, beating UConn at home and beating Stanford at home might persuade the NCAA selection committee that they deserved to be in the tournament.

In the locker room before a home game against Portland, Lonnie addressed the team, "We control our own destiny from here on out. We're 14-10, six wins from magic number 20 with seven games remaining. Over the next month and a half the true character of this team will be revealed."

Everyone interpreted Lonnie's words differently. Shirlie correctly saw it as a call to arms for the Big Four to show some leadership. Tamika saw it as a green light to shoot every time she touched the ball. Roxy thought it was just another canned pregame speech. Mbika figured it didn't apply to her because she rarely played.

Monet was still in street clothes. Her knee was feeling better, but she couldn't convince Coach to let her play. During Lonnie's speech, Monet looked over at Roxy with disdain. The feeling was mutual. Their relationship was still icy even though Monet hadn't played for a month.

As the team prepared for practice, Lonnie stood in front of Sonja's open locker. Sonja was in the bathroom and Tamika was a little nervous with Coach standing over her staring into Sonja's locker. Tamika knew Sonja had been running late at night. She also knew about the hair she lost every night, the diet pills, and the vomiting. Sonja used to purge her last meal sporadically. Now she was vomiting after every meal and before every practice.

Lonnie stood there, staring into Sonja's locker trying to cover for Sonja. Tamika stood up and asked the coach some innocuous question about defense.

"Since when are you interested in defense?" Lonnie asked. Then she looked around. "Where's Sonja?"

"I don't know, I think she went up already," Tamika lied. Everyone else shrugged.

Lonnie looked past Tamika and saw two feet, soles facing out, in one of the stalls in the bathroom. Sonja was on her hands and knees, vomiting what remained of her dinner when Lonnie burst into the stall. Sonja jumped and hit her head on the toilet paper holder.

"What the hell are you doing?"

"I always throw up before a game," Sonja said, nonchalantly.

"This is the first time I've seen it."

"A lot of great players threw up before a game."

"Name one."

"Bill Russell and he was the greatest winner of all time?"

Lonnie pulled Sonja up off her knees, "Get up. You've got to stop this."

*   *   *   *

Jackie Wilkerson stood before the class. For her report she used an authentic-sounding Indian accent, despite her Alabama twang. "I was cooking dinner. But I heard them whispering in the other room. My family... my husband's family, whispered a lot back then. I had gotten used to it.

"I was just cooking. Being a good Indian wife. I knew that my husband's father had asked my father for more gifts–Kanyandanam. They wanted a bigger dowry. Kanyandanam literally means bride and gift. As is the tradition, my family paid for the wedding and gave Rajeev's family many gifts as the price for taking care of me. They wanted more money even though my father had already given them 5,000 rupees, a refrigerator, a motor scooter, and other things for their house. Not my house. But my husband's family's house. And it still wasn't enough. My family is not rich.

"I went to school. I can work. I am not a burden for their family, but yet my family had to pay. It is our way.

"I didn't know what to do. I was 800 miles from my family. I begged my father to let me come back home. He refused. I had no place to go. He said, 'You will not bring shame on our family. You have two sisters and I don't know how I am going to pay for their Kanyandanam.' I stayed with Rajeev for my sisters and my family's honor.

"When I met my husband a few weeks before our wedding I hoped he would be a kind man. A decent man. After a while it seemed like he was only interested in the bride-price and getting more things from my family if I don't stay. My sisters would never get married.

"I was scared. They whispered a lot. And now I know why. They were wondering what they were going to do with me. So, I tried to please Rajeev in every way I know how. I am a good cook. I cooked for them, but something was wrong because they wouldn't talk to me. I am so lonely in my house, but I cannot go home. It would ruin my family.

"I was cooking dinner yesterday. Out of the corner of my eye I saw someone run past the kitchen. I smelled kerosene. My skin started burning. I was on fire. I screamed for someone to help me. For my family to help me. No one helped me. I smelled my skin burn. I knew I was going to die. Thank God, my husband's eight year old sister poured water on me. My Salwar Kameez melted on my skin. You can see the metallic pattern that was sewn into the fabric here on my arm.

"I am totally blind in my left eye from the kerosene and the fire. The doctors tell me I am burned on over seventy-five percent of my body. I do not want to see my face. My husband will marry again because they will say it was a cooking accident. I saw his mother throw the match. I saw her. Who will care for me now?

"Two days after the police interviewed Jivanta, she died of third degree burns on 75 percent of her body. Her death was classified as a cooking accident. Every year, there are approximately 4500 reported dowry-related deaths in India, although it is suspected the real number is closer to 25,000 deaths annually. Many are disguised as suicides or cooking accidents. Rarely is anyone prosecuted for these deaths. The practice of Kanyandanam was outlawed in India in 1961 but it still continues today, especially in rural and lower-class areas.

"As a result, prenatal sonograms form a $100 million dollar industry in India. Prospective Indian parents can determine the sex of a child before it is born. Often female fetuses are aborted. It is estimated, that at current trends, India will have 10 percent more men than women in three generations. With a population of approximately 1 billion people, India could have 100 million more men than women in sixty years.

"When there are no women to marry, maybe then, in India, the value of female life will be equal to that of a man."

February First

"So, how's it work again?" Monet asked. She was chillin' on the Quad with the fellas, during the lunch break. It was the usual cast: Snag, Flip Mode, Ray, and Chris Chamberlain. The weather was beautiful, unseasonably warm for San Francisco. The sky was crystal clear.

Snag started, "You break it down into three parts. Face, chest, and ass. Each area gets three points maximum, 1.5 being average.

Monet laughed, "But that only adds up to nine."

Flip Mode, "Right. There's a miscellaneous point for style, overall sexiness, or whatever."

Ray, "Actually it's for boosting the scores of ugly babes that are still sexy."

Monet shook her head, "That's terrible." Then she giggled. "But it sounds like fun."

"Don't go tellin' all your girlfriends, because it's not politically correct," Ray said.

"You mean the ogling and objectifying women part?" Monet asked.

Ray laughed, "Don't start with the Feminista stuff."

Chris said, "Yeah, don't start with–."

Monet cut him off, "You can't tell me to 'don't start'... Only Ray can tell me 'Don't start.'"

Monet was still pissed off about her date with Chris.

Snag gave Flip Mode a look. Ray looked at Chris and shrugged, apologizing for Monet, but knew Chris had brought it on himself.

Monet looked at the guys, "So, why is there a need for standardization?"

Snag said, "We're guys. That's reason enough."

"All that crap about Bo Derek being a ten? The Ray Scale says–."

"–Wait a minute, the Ray Scale?" Monet said.

"Richter scale, the scales of justice and now... the Ray Scale," Ray said.

"The Ray Scale says, she's a weak seven. Not enough ass," Flip mode said, high-fiving Ray.

A very attractive coed passed by. Ray turned to Monet for a score. "Judges?"

Playing again, Monet checked her out, then said, "With my guy goggles on, she's an eight."

From a distance Roxy, Clio, and Kendra watched as Monet laughed with the fellas. They were jealous because each liked one of the guys Monet was hanging with.

Clio said to Kendra, "Think she'll screw it up by going the friend route?"

Roxy looked at her manicure, "As long as she stays away from Chris, I'm cool."

"Hell yeah," Kendra said, "She'll go right past being a diva to being one of the fellas."

"That's the kiss of death," Clio said.

Kendra turned to Clio, "Can't get none being the friend, right Clio?" winking.

Clio looked away, "Shut up."

Ray shook his head at Monet's score, "See it's that kind of guess-work the Ray Scale eliminates."

"Ok, then what?"

"Judges?"

Snag started it off, "Face 2.0. Definitely above average."

Flip Mode added, "Agreed. Chest? 2.5. Wow!"

"But only a 1.0 on the ass," Snag adds.

Chris laughed, "Boy, those Russian judges are tough."

Flip Mode added, "It wasn't that bad, I'm givin' it a 1.5. That's an average ass."

"You're trippin'," Snag said, laughing.

"Miscellaneous?" Ray asked.

"Full point," Snag said.

"Full point," Flip Mode agreed.

Ray said, "Full point. I like the athletic female thang she's got going."

Monet was displeased. "Guys are so..." She couldn't even find the words.

Flip Mode, "Shhhh. 1.5... Carry the one. 7.00. That's a good score."

"Just as pretty as Bo Derek. That's the thing, you don't know until you run the numbers," Ray said. "That's why we need standardiztion."

"She's a six," Snag said.

"Who?" Flip Mode asks.

"Bo Derek. From the movie 'Ten.' Bo Derek was a six, even with the corn rows. Definitely *not* an eight, let alone a ten."

Ray turned to Monet, "See, the Ray Scale knows all."

"Okay, let's try it on men," Monet says, enthusiastically.

Chris warned her, "Be cool, girl. This is not a game. Placed in the wrong hands. Things could get ugly."

A handsome well-built guy walked by.

Monet checked him out, "Let's see if it works on men. Face 2.0 not fine but above average. Chest and arms 1.0."

Ray interrupted, "Excuse me. There's no category for arms in the Ray Scale."

Monet ignored him, "Chest and arms 1.5, about average. 1.0. and zero on the miscellaneous point."

Ray smacked his head, "Not the zero!"

"I went out with him. Not only was he an asshole I could tell he had a little."

"Whoa. WHOOOAAA!" Snag and Flip Mode both yelled
Ray laughed, "New rule. No women judges."

"No women judges," Flip Modes repeats.

Chris backs them up, "That's a good rule, no women judges."

"Why not?" Monet asked.

"Because women do what women do–that woman thing. They
try to fix us up," Ray said.

"Okay," Monet said, "What about Roxy, where is she on the
Ray Scale?"

Ray looks across the quad at Roxy, "Hmmmmm. 1.5, 2, 2.5
and 1. Hey, that's a seven. That's a good score." It wasn't the
response Monet was hoping for. She wanted Roxy to get a three.

"Wit her fine ass. What's up wit' that Chris? That girl's had
the hots for you since day one," Snag looked at Roxy.

Chris shrugged while looking at Monet, who rolled her eyes at
him.

Monet turned to Ray, "Okay, how 'bout me?"

Sensing danger, Snag and Flip Mode excuse themselves.

Monet laughed, "C'mon. You cowards, what do I get?"

"No way!" Ray said.

"What's the big deal?" she asked.

"Believe me, nothing good can come out of it, especially if you
don't get an eight," Ray answered.

"So you're saying you don't think I'm an eight?"

"No. See. I didn't say that."

"Yeah, but that's what you meant."

"No, what I meant was what I said," Ray said.

"No, you're right Roxy's prettier."

Ray shook his head, "I never said that."

"So, what's so great about her?" Monet asked.

Ray sighed, "That's what I'm talkin' about. I never said she
was prettier than you."

"You didn't have to. You said it by what you didn't say," Monet
said.

Chris said, "Give it up man, you blew it way back when you
told her about the Ray Scale in the first place. You know how women
are. You know they're going to change it around, then use it against
you later."

*   *   *   *

February Seventh

"You wanted to see me coach," Sonja said, standing in the doorway of Lonnie's Office. Sonja was worried. All her life she had striven for perfection. Now here she was summoned into the coach's office.

Lonnie turned off the VCR. "Have a seat."

"I keep getting reports that you're still running."

"Who told you that?"

"Stop. You and I both know, you've been running. I've told you not to."

"Running is good for you," Sonja said.

"Running is going to kill you. You're not eating well. You've lost about thirty pounds since the beginning of school. I'm worried. The way things are going you could vanish before the end of the season."

"I have not lost thirty pounds. It just looks like I've lost weight because the uniforms are so baggy they make me look thinner."

Lonnie held up a pink card. "Says right here, you weighed 165 when you got here and now you're down to 135."

"That's not right."

"Sonja, right now I can't put you in the game even though you could easily play twenty-five minutes."

"Why not?"

"You're too thin. You won't be able to hold your ground against anyone. If you get pushed around you won't be able to rebound or defend on the low block."

"You shouldn't have to be fat to play this game."

Lonnie sighed, "Sonja, listen to me. You're not fat... Look at me. Not some card. Look at me."

Sonja held out her rail thin arms. "Look at how fat I am right now."

"You're not fat... Sonja, you've gotten straight A's since elementary school. Everything seems to come easy for you. Have you ever thought about why you think you're so fat when everyone else keeps telling you you're thin? Everyone can't be wrong can they?"

"I thought about it."

"And."

"I still think I'm too big."

"Did you take those photos off your wall like I asked you too," Lonnie said.

"Uh... No."

"Why not?"

"You can't tell me what I can have on my wall," Sonja said. "You gonna take my scholarship because I have modeling pictures on my dorm walls."

"No, but I can take it for not meeting the minimum weight requirements for someone your height. We're going to develop a plan to get your weight up that will include taking those photos off your wall, counseling, and a couple of other things," Lonnie said.

"Like what?"

"You'll see."

Wilma Dodd, the women's volleyball coach, dropped into Lonnie Delaney's office. "Lonnie. We all know how you fought for equal treatment at your last college coaching job. Hell, anyone who wins two national championships *should* be the highest paid coach."

Lonnie said, "I know, that's why–."

"–Excuse me." Wilma cut her off. There was a long pause as she collected her thoughts. "We have a nice thing going here. Volleyball, softball, soccer."

"Yes, you do but–."

"–Field hockey–."

"–Yes, you've got a really nice thing going here. Cold showers. Community locker room for all the women's teams. Women's practices scheduled, around the men's teams. Is that what you're calling a good thing, Wilma?" Lonnie asked.

"Football and basketball carry all the real pressure," Wilma said.

"Whenever you give away your chance to contribute to the direction of the athletic department, then you had better get something in return. Because right now none of the women's coaches matter at all. It's all about football and basketball. That's not right," Lonnie said.

"Matter!? You know what matters to me? My husband loves me and doesn't mind all the traveling I have to do. My kids have been in the same school since kindergarten. And on top of all that, I get paid to coach a game I've played for 35 years. What do I care if I don't get to decide how many bench press machines there's going to be in the weight room?" Wilma said.

"If not you, then who? Who's going to improve the conditions of women's athletics now and into the future?" Lonnie asked.

"You don't see other women's coaches complaining."

"Yeah, it's better to just wait around hoping Haneline and the Chancellor will look out for the best interests of women's athletics. C'mon, you can't believe that, Wilma."

"Dutch has the women's program in his future plans."

"The past tells me where his real priorities are. In the ten years you've been here, have you ever had a say about your recruiting budget, or getting your own locker room, or making as much money as the men's volleyball coach?"

"No, because I found a place I can fit in. That's why I've never been fired. I fit in. I just don't understand why you insist on bringing so much attention to yourself."

Lonnie said, "Because people listen to coachs who've won national championships."

Wilma said, "Well,the bottom line is; money and revenue trumps championships."

"The women here deserve better facilities. Volleyball players, *your* players, deserve better facilities."

"I'm not going to get into a pissing contest with those guys! Every coach who's tried has lost, male or female."

"Don't you think its unfair that their recriting budget is $50,000 more than the women? If they want to see a potential recruit play in New York, they merely pay the $2200 for a last minute ticket, just like that. But because our budget is so much smaller, we have to plan our trips a month in advance. Those extra dollars means they have more flexibility in recruiting and running their program. None of that shows up in the Title IX compliance report.

"We get more scholarships. That's the bottom line."

"You still the resources to do your job effectively."

Wilma Dodd said, "I'm sorry, but I don't feel the need to speak up about locker rooms and practice times. I'm sorry, but I don't feel the need to make as much money as the men's volleyball coach. My mother taught me at an early age. When it comes to men, never show you're smarter or stronger than they are!"

"Where I come from that's called being a kept woman or a sellout," Lonnie said.

Before Wilma walked out she said, "Funny. Where I come from it's called penis envy."

*　　　　*　　　　*　　　　*

February Ninth, 4:00 PM

"I feel fine," Monet said, to Lonnie as the team rode in vans down highway 101. Sitting in the rear, Roxy kept a watchful eye on them.

"The trainer says you're still wincing when he moves your knee," Lonnie said. She was debating letting Monet play again.

"It's been a month since I got injured. So, who are you going to believe, him or me?" Monet asked.

Lonnie thought about it. "Him."

"About *my* knee?"

Lonnie said, "Yes." Even though the team really needed Monet's leadership.

Monet sighed, "The season is slipping away."

"I know, but you can't play injured."

"What if the trainer clears me."

Lonnie thought for moment, "If the trainer clears you, then you can play."

"Okay, call him," Monet said.

"It can wait."

"It can't wait," Monet begged. She had already talked to him ealier, so she knew the trainer would back her up. "Call him."

Lonnie called and spoke briefly with the trainer and just like that, Monet was off the injured list. Roxy watched them closely. Monet's broad smile let Roxy know her reign as the starting point guard was over.

Monet looked out the window. "Where are we going, coach?"

"It's a surprise."

Lonnie had canceled their 6:00 AM practice. The players didn't like Lonnie's surprises; anything could happen.

The players looked nervously at each other when the team pulled into the military training camp at Fort Ord in Monterey. Lonnie reassured them they would enjoy the change of scenery. No one believed her. Sure enough, the sprints they ran in the sand and the medicine ball they passed made everyone yearn for the suicide lines they ran back on campus.

Lonnie Delaney had the team run the military obstacle course. It was difficult, but manageable. The course ended between two platforms that stretched four stories high. Strung between the two platforms were four ropes. The upper two ropes were eight feet above the lower two ropes, which were about three feet apart.

"Can't the Army do a better job of figuring out how to dry their laundry," Tamika joked.

Monet looked up at the platform. This was a new twist even by Coach Delaney's standards. A lieutenant colonel stepped up to give safety instructions on traversing the wire bridge.

"I ain't walkin' across no clothesline even if the Army does call it a bridge," Tamika said.

Lonnie said, "The lieutenant colonel told me everyone falls the first time mainly because they don't trust their partner. So, if anyone makes it across on the first try they won't have to go again and they won't have to do any running next week."

That got everyone's attention.

It didn't solve Monet's problem. She was still afraid of heights. The usual cliques on the team paired up. Lonnie stopped them. "I'm going to choose partners. First is Monet and Roxy."

Monet and Roxy had learned to coexist peacefully, but that didn't mean they wanted to be partners. They both knew it would be futile to ask Lonnie to change partners, so they looked at each other with resignation. "Let's just get through this," Monet said.

On the platform they were fitted into their harnesses. When they looked up from the ground they thought they would be able to use the upper ropes for support, but the upper ropes were used to attach their harnesses. They would have to hold onto each other and side-step in unison.

Walking up to the platform they both had done a good job of appearing confident, but now, one hundred feet in the air, they saw the fear in each other's eyes.

Monet said, "You know I have something to tell you..."

"This is no time to start your 12-step program," Roxy said.

"I'm afraid of heights."

"...Me too," Roxy admitted.

"I was hoping you could guide us through this one," Monet said.

Lonnie yelled up to them, "C'mon let's go up there."

"Make us," Roxy said, under her breath grinning at Monet.

That ice breaker helped them face their fear of heights together. They inched out onto the ropes, holding each other's forearms, legs bent, sliding their feet in unison.

"Head up. Look your partner in the eyes. Face it, together," Lonnie shouted from below.

"Stop shaking," Roxy said.

"That's not me, that's you," Monet said.

"I don't want to do this again."

"We'll get through just don't–can't you make your legs stop shaking."

"Shhhhh."

The talking helped. They hadn't said more than 50 words to each other once the season began. And now four stories up when no one could hear them, they took the opportunity to vent what they disliked about each other. They had time, they were moving slowly. Once they got passed the petty disagreements, Roxy admitted she was a little envious of Monet coming to her school and basically taking over the team in her senior year. Monet apologized for being such a diva, but was still annoyed at Roxy for attempting to sabotage her relationship with Ray. Roxy didn't acknowledged the subterfuge, but they had made big strides toward improving their relationship and settling their differences.

As an added bonus they were the only pair to make it across the cable bridge on the first try.

Chapter 22

Holding Her Own

February Sixteenth
"When was the last time you went out with Dan?" Renee asked Lonnie at the end of practice.

"We're supposed to have dinner tonight–Oh, damn! I can't do it. I've got an alumni reception to go to, Haneline put me on the program at the last minute," Lonnie said.

"Isn't this the fourth date you've canceled?" Renee asked.

"That's why you can't keep anyone interested," Stephanie added.

"Especially at the beginning of a relationship," Renee said.

"I gotta call him. Damn!" Lonnie said, as they exited the gym.

Stephanie nudged Lonnie. "Haneline, at twelve o'clock."

Forrest Haneline waited in the tunnel for the women's practice to end. He hated being up at 8:00 in the morning, but immediately after practice was the only time he was certain to catch Lonnie.

"You see this?" he asked, marching up to Lonnie. Renee and Stephanie took the equipment and left them alone.

"I know, but I was wondering if there is any way I can get out of the reception tonight?" Lonnie said, switching the subject.

"No, why?"

"I have a... never mind."

Haneline went back to the original topic, "Why didn't you give me a heads-up about this?" He was holding a copy of *Time* magazine, Lonnie was on the cover.

"I did," Lonnie said. She wasn't in the mood to deal with Forrest Haneline, she was thinking about what to tell Dan.

"How dare you? *How dare you!!!* ESPN was bad enough. You didn't have to go to *Time* magazine."

"I didn't go to *Time* magazine. They wanted to ask me a few questions about the changes in women's athletics in the three years I've been out of coaching."

"Look at this!" he said, holding up the magazine again. She didn't tell him she had five copies in her desk already. The cover photo was a solemn head shot of Lonnie Delaney with her hands clasped under her chin. Her diamond crusted NCAA championship ring sparkled. The headline read: "Collegiate Sport's Public Enemy No. 1."

"It doesn't bother you?" Haneline asked. "Not to mention the fact you're biting the hands that feed you."

"The jobs are the same and you know it. And just because one brings in more money doesn't change that fact," Lonnie said.

"You know as well as I do, we've had to cut men's gymnastics, tennis, and wrestling in order to equalize the numbers to be in compliance with Title IX," Haneline replied.

"Don't get mad at me. If you don't want to comply, don't take Federal money. Do it your way. Just don't take the money,"

"You know that's not realistic."

"You're still paying the baseball coach more than the softball coach, and the men's volleyball coach makes more than the women's volleyball coach."

"We added women' s field hockey, golf, rowing. All with full scholarships."

"Because you have 85 football scholarships," Lonnie said.

"Look, Title IX allows you to comply three different ways: You can show the proportion of women in the athletic department is the same as the proportion in the general student body," Haneline said.

"That's one of the standards for compliance," Lonnie replied.

"But we still have a third fewer women on scholarship than men, when women are fifty percent of the student body."

"Or we can show consistent expansion of athletic opportunities for women," Haneline continued, undaunted. "Like adding field hockey, golf, rowing." He counted them off on his fingers.

"Yes, but you just added those sports; to comply you have to show expansion over time," Lonnie corrected him.

"So, you're saying it's better to add one sport every year for three years than to add three sports in one year?" Haneline asked.

"I know the rule. The third way to comply with Title IX is to show that the university has fully accommodated the interests and abilities of women. Well, we both know you haven't done that,"

"We've added three women's sports. At the same time, I had to cut men's wrestling or gymnastics next because the male-female scholarship number would be way off. Now, men who want to wrestle for this university, can't. Is that fair?" Haneline was now turning red which turned his tanned face into a dark shade of taupe. "That's what you men do. If there is a descreptancy, it's our fault when we use your rules against you. Notre Dame has the number one football program in the country and a very good basketball team. With all the great black athletes that have played and graduated from Notre Dame, they have never hired one, not *one,* African-American head coach in any sport. It's 1996. And do you mean to tell me there has never been one African -American qualified to be the head coach in football, basketbal,baseball, or any other sport?" Lonnie asked.

"This isn't Notre Dame and this isn't a race issue," he replied.

"But it's the same old shell game. The same old boy network where insiders get treated well and outsiders-women–are given separate but equal facilies, but only so government money can continue to flow into the university."

"Do you just conveniently forget that you're a part of the coaching fraternity or are you purposefully antisocial?" Haneline asked.

"What coaching fraternity? During my three years out of coaching no one spoke out in the media on my behalf. No one came to my defense. A few people called me personally to offer their support, but no one offered me a job. Basketball fraternity! Have you ever notice how they never call it a sorority?"

"You brought all of that on yourself," Haneline said.

"The same fraternity that keeps Black coaches from getting the premier coaching jobs is the same fraternity that doesn't spend equal resources on women's athletics as mandated by the law. Is that the fraternity you're talking about?"

"Things are changing."

"You might be able to get around not hiring a Black coach, but the law says you have to have equal resources for women to play collegiate athletics," Lonnie said.

"You know, when I hired you, you said you were 'on board.' You promised you wouldn't pull this crap," he said, reminding her.

Lonnie just stared at Haneline.

"At the end of the day, you know you'll lose in a court of law," Haneline said.

"You're probably right. So, what do you think my chances are in the court of public opinion? Like say *Time* magazine?"

That brought Haneline back to reality. He didn't want to be the face of the NCAA's good 'ole boy system the way segregationist

Theophilus Eugene "Bull" Connor became the face of Jim Crow laws in the South. Right now, Haneline was just one of many athletic directors who had a practice of giving higher priority to men's athletics. Lonnie was right; in the court of public opinion things could get out of control quickly. Instead of only addressing the issue of equal resources for women, paying athletes a stipend could also become part of the discussion. They will want to avoid that topic altogether.

Haneline wanted to defuse this problem before it got out of control. In addition, bringing bad publicity to the university was a good way for an athletic director to be fired. "You make it sound like the goal is to get a Congressional hearing."

Lonnie stopped herself from smiling. Haneline obviously hadn't received his subpoena yet.

February Eighteenth

As Monet and Ray walked through the Quad, Vince was arguing while Gina cowered. Vince and Gina were in the middle of a heated argument near the fountain.

"You would think she would stay away from him after what happened," Monet said to Ray. They watched Vince make a fist and pound it into his other hand. Gina looked at him, her eyes pleading for him to stop making a scene. She could feel everyone watching. Vince pointed at her, said something, then walked away. Gina didn't cry but she was clearly shaken up. Before she headed to class she saw Monet and Ray. Gina waved them off before they could come over to her.

"That girl needs a self-defense class," Ray said.

"Coach got her into one," Monet said. "Tell you this. You ever point at me like that and you won't get your finger back."

Ray shivered mockingly. "Please don't hurt me, Ms. Big Bad Ass Momma."

"I'm just saying, I can take care of myself."

"We've had this conversation already. And that same day you got chased in the library by a hooded smelly man. Did you get any more letters?"

"No."

"At least you told the coach and the police. You listened to your boy. For a feminista like you, that takes a lot of guts to admit."

By now they had reached Ray's car.

"Nothing is more resourceful than an independent black woman." Monet said.

"Yeah, okay."

"Name one."

"A knife or a gun would trump your resourcefulness."

"That's real. Where are we going?" she asked.

"You'll see," Ray smiled

They drove across the bay to Oakland's Mosswood park. The same park at the corner of MacArthur and Broadway where Gary Payton and Jason Kidd threw their first assists. Ray's childhood mentors sat in the shade near the horseshoe pen. Steppin' Charlie, Gatorback, Been Gone, and Buddy Bazel had played Spades, Dominoes, and Tonk in the shade of Mosswood's trees for 30 years. After the late night pimpin', boostin', and dealin' they always came back to Mosswood; that is, when they weren't on "vacation" at the county jail or state prison.

They greeted Monet warmly when Ray introduced her.

"What you got there?" asked Gatorback, the pimp wearing scuffed up brown alligator shoes with frayed tassels. Monet noted his dismissive tone, as if she were an inanimate object.

Maybe this is where Ray got it from, hangin' with these old dogs.

"She's a friend of mine from school. Brought her down here to play with some real players. Matter of fact, where is everybody?"

"Where you from, Monet?" asked Gatorback. "Monet. That's a pretty name. Mo'nay. I could say that name *all night long.*"

"Columbus, Ohio," Monet answered.

"You know how it is, hit or miss, sometimes youngstas wanna play ball, sometimes they don't," Buddy Bazel said to Ray.

"Twomp!" Steppin Charlie said, slammin' the dominoes.

"Damn nigga, why you always got to slam the damn dominoes," Been Gone said.

"I told you about calling me nigga, now you best to be cool."

"I guess I'm just gonna gonna beat you all by myself," Ray said to Monet. "We'll be back." Monet and Ray shot around on the court talking and warming up. After ten minutes no one showed up, so they played a game of one-on-one.

"I see you put that move in your game. Two hard dribbles and a pull-up jumper," Ray said. "I get people on that move all the time because they think you're going to the hole. It's there all day."

"Like now." Monet executed the move perfectly. It was so quick Ray barely got his hand up. *Ch-kh.* The ball went smoothly through the net. Ray let Monet get out to an 8-2 lead, then reeled her back in with nine unanswered points.

The men noted Monet's skills and competitive spirit while they played dominoes.

"Ain't no woman got no business out there playin' ball," Steppin' Charlie said.

Gatorback switched his toothpick from one side of his mouth to the other, "Let bitches get out of pocket and you'll never get 'em back in."

Buddy Bazel shook his head, "Both of you always talkin' bad about women."

Gatorback smiled, "Not me, I love women."

Been Gone laughed, "Ain't nobody choosin' yo' snaggletooth ass today."

Steppin' Charlie slammed his domino, "Fittle'een."

Been Gone pounded his fist on the table, "See nigga, stop slammin' the dominoes."

Steppin' Charlie said, "I see, I'm gon' have to cut yo' ass today."

They rose to their feet staring at each other.

"Sit down. Neither one of you is gonna do shit," Buddy Bazel said. "Here they come. Be nice to the girl. It's on you, Gator."

Steppin' Charlie and Been Gone sat down. Charlie said, "You best to be cool 'cause I ain't gon' take too much more of your lip today."

Ray and Monet returned to the park benches.

Gatorback said, "Ray, I was just telling this cat here it's their nature to please men."

"Whose nature?" Ray said, knowing the answer.

"Women, of course. These cats get mad at me 'cause I use a little pimp game to bring out those natural instincts. Let a woman be a woman. But turn it into a moneymaking enterprise. Take care of daddy along the way. What's wrong with that?" he asked. "That's the American way."

Gatorback stared at Monet, his broad smile showed his missing tooth. Monet returned the stare without blinking.

"You prey on women, snaggletooth and all. And I don't mean pray on your hands and knees. Twomp!" Buddy Bazel said.

"Same twomp," Been Gone followed.

"Young'sta bring a woman up here, eyeballin' me," Gatorback mumbled to himself.

"Shut up, and play," Been Gone said.

Monet and Ray sat down on the benches near the domino game. Buddy Bazel asked, "Who won?"

"I did, but it was close," Ray said.

"I always measure the strength of a woman by how fertile she is," Gatorback said, probing."

Gatorback glanced over at Monet, who rolled her eyes.

Been Gone said, "Gimme my twenty."

Gatorback turned to Monet, "So, how do you like the big city?"

"I like it."

"Gets lonely though... sometimes. You know, when you're a long way from home. Maybe need a little extra money... I can help."

Ray remained quiet to see how Monet would handle Gator.

"Stop mac'in and play, Gator," Steppin' Charlie said.

"I'm good," Monet smiled. "Ray's been showin' me around."

"Ray's a good kid. But he don't know the city like I know the city."

Everyone at the table shook their heads. Hey, let a playa play.

Steppin' Charlie pointed, "Play that 4-3 you got in your hand, Gator."

"I'm askin' the lady a question," he said, turning back to Monet.

"I'm sorry, what did you say?"

"I said, would you like a tour of the city one day, from a grown man's perspective? Ray's prob-ly taking you on cable cars and down to Fisherman's Warf. Kiddie shit. Grown man'll take you to the Top of the Mark.

"No! Now play, Gator," Steppin Charlie said.

"Shhhh, you gotta give the weaker sex more time to make a decision," Gator said, smiling at Monet.

Monet scrunched her face. "You got it all wrong, big daddy. Men are the weaker sex."

"Bitch! Don't get out of pocket. Men run this."

Ray stepped up "Hey! Don't talk to her like that or I'll kick you're old ass myself."

"Ray, it's okay. I got it," Monet said, putting her arm out to stop him.

"What you got? Men run this," Gator said.

"Play before you get your ass kicked, Gator," Been Gone said.

"Gonna get it kicked twice," Steppin' Charlie said.

"Men run this, God damn it. Youngsta bring some woman over here, loud talk me. Men run this! Bitch, talkin' crazy talk. Women are stronger than men? Got to prove that shit to me."

Steppin' Charlie said, "Stop mumblin'."

Monet said, "If men are stronger why do you die six years before women do?"

"Ooops, gotcha there," Been Gone said.

"Why are there more women than men on this planet?" Monet continued.

"There too." Been Gone shook his head with the momentum going against Gatorback.

"Because men go to war to provide and protect yo' weak ass, woman," Gator fired back.

"Why are there twice as many retarded men as women?"

"Yep, he is kinda slow," Been Gone whispered.

"Why are there three times as many dyslexic men as women? And twice as many color-blind men as women? I don't know. I'm just saying," Monet said.

"I used to tell him, you can't mix green gators with a pastel lavender suit. There it is, right there. Gator, you color-blind. Domino wit' twomp-five. Shake 'em up," Steppin' Charlie laughed.

Gatorback was quiet. There was no sense in talking. You can't turn out anyone when the entire table is against you.

Gatorback sat back in his chair. "Back in the day, I was a, what did they call Robert Duval in *Godfather*?"

"Consigliere?" Ray answered.

"Yeah. Back in the day, I was a consigliere."

"That's a lawyer," said Buddy Bazel.

"No, that ain't it, then," Gator said.

"Listen to yo' dumb ass, knowin' good and well you was just a tennis shoe pimp," Been Gone said. "And stop using words you don't know."

Gatorback ignored him. "Now, you know I treated all my bitches good. When they needed somethin'; new threads, get bailed out of jail, a ride to the clinic. I was right there. What's the guy called at the hotel that gets shit for you?"

"A concierge," Buddy Bazel replied.

"Yeah, a concierge. I was concierge to my bitches."

"You mean a bellhop," Steppin Charlie amended.

"Ask any of them. I was good to them," Gator said.

Buddy Bazel got up from the game and walked Ray away from the table. "What's up with you? You've never brought a woman to the park before?"

"What do you think?" Ray asked.

"Girl's got heart, that's for sure," Buddy says, "Tell you somethin' else–good woman like that? Come down here and hold her own with us old playas, hard to find that."

Ray nodded, "Yeah, she's cool."

"Tell you one other thing to look for–got this from Gator."

Ray frowned.

Buddy noticed and said, "Be cool, young blood. Don't discount wisdom because of the source. Truth is truth. Gator said, 'See how a woman argues. If they throw shit, wanna cut you when they get mad, get rid of 'em quick. But if she does stuff in moderation–.'"

"–Like what?"

"–Shopping and eating. If you can talk to 'em without them getting all upset, then she's got good sense. That's the one you keep. Kick the rest of the chicken-heads to the curb. That's good advice. Good advice from a pimp."

"Real talk."

Ray went to the vending machine and brought Monet back a soda. She was sitting at the table playing Buddy's hand in the domino game. She and Gator were jawing back and forth. She was giving as good as she was getting. As Ray stood off to the side, Monet looked up at him and winked. She was having a great time.

February Eighteenth

"Switch!"

"Eighteen footer... Good," said Thalia Clark.

I said switch," Tamika yelled at Shirlie, who totally ignored her.

"Yeah, you better call yo' mamma," said Brenda Peterson. She was the only good player who played for the Broncos of the University of Santa. The Broncos lost a lot more games than they won so Brenda amused herself by talking trash while scoring on the person who was guarding her.

"Switch!" yelled Tamika, on another play.

"Peterson on the block... nice fadeaway... Good."

"Girl, I'm gonna whop yo' freshman ass like yo momma caught you playing doctor," Brenda yelled at Tamika.

Tamika looked over at Lonnie, pleading for help.

"Think we should double-team Peterson, she's killing Tamika?" Renee asked Lonnie.

"We're up by 15. I'm going to let her ego see what its like to get abused. Maybe she'll learn playing professionally may not be as easy as she thinks." Lonnie answered.

"Torreta flashed in the middle, pass from McCasner. Two. The Broncos are small and soft in the middle. I suspect Lonnie Delaney will exploit the mismatches by pounding the ball into the Rhinos big front court, Hightower, Toretta, and maybe even Njai."

Gina was playing confidently, with a joy her teammates hadn't seen in her before. She was setting hard physical picks that set up scores for all of her teammates. She bashed one Bronco player in the mouth with her elbow while clearing a rebound. Gina felt sorry then, unexpectedly, she felt a rush of empowerment as the player had to be helped off the corrt.

Mbika was playing more due to Kendra's injury. She had a knack for getting open, but she got fouled more frequently as teams realized she couldn't shoot free throws. She was making 38 percent of her free throws which was tolerable in blowouts, but not in close games.

Peterson scored on three successive trips on offense. As Tamika worried about the pick and roll, Peterson beat her on a give-and-go. After the fourth basket, both Peterson and Tamika looked to Lonnie to make a change as they ran down the court. "Coach, you gotta do something," Peterson said to Lonnie. Lonnie ignored them both. The Rhinos led by 12 with four minutes remaining.

On the pick and roll, Tamika reached back and waved for her teammates to step up to challenge the shot, but when they didn't, it left Peterson open, and she scored again. Tamika was lost. She tried everything. When she tried to slow her down with a hand check she got called for three quick fouls and finally had to sit down because she was in foul trouble.

Roxy had improved her passes. Everyone was getting a chance to touch the ball, so they were happy. Everyone was happy except Tamika who got torched by Brenda Peterson's 40 points.

The final score was Del Mar 65-52. The Rhinos were 15-12, five wins away from 20 and a virtual guarantee to receive a tournament bid.

During the post-game high-five line Peterson said to Tamika, "Your team must really hate you to let me drop 40 on that ass like that."

It was the worst Tamika had ever felt after a winning a game. Even winning couldn't help her feel better. Knowing she couldn't stop Peterson from scoring was troubling. She also knew anyone who could get torched like that by a good college player, couldn't rightfully be considered a legitamate professional prospect.

*   *   *   *

February Twenty-third
Team meal
"Look, here she comes," Roxy said to Clio as Sonja approached the table. "Look at what's on her plate. Then watch what she does to her food."

"What's gonna happen to her food?"

"Just watch. I'll tell you later if–shhhh."

Sonja sat down quietly. Clio did an inventory of the food on Sonja's plate; mashed potatoes, chicken, peas, grapes, and three bags of Doritos on her tray. A large heap of carrots, a saucer of sliced oranges. Lots of orange food.

"How'd you do last quarter, Sonja?" Roxy asked.

Roxy made a point of ignoring freshmen all year, so her sudden concern about her grades made Sonja suspicious. Sonja answered guardedly. "I got a 3.85."

"Damn, girl."

Lonnie passed by Sonja, she took a quick inventory of the food on Sonja's plate, then sat down.

Everyone settled into their team meal routine. Roxy, Clio, and Kendra caught up on the constantly evolving dating scene of the athletic department. Monet talked basketball with Stephanie and Renee. Tamika ate in silence, almost inhaling the roast beef and pocketing the popcorn shrimp. Mbika and Shirlie talked about biology because they had premed classes.

Sonja could be so quiet she could almost disappear from the dinner table. Sonja ate all of the orange food; the Doritos, the oranges, and carrots. She then skinned the grapes and one by one plopped them into her mouth. Roxy nudged Clio just as Sonja hid the grape skins under her mashed potatoes. Lonnie was also watching. Sonja had no intention of eating all of the food on her plate. It was ruse. She pushed it around on her plate. She even scooped up some mashed potatoes and peas, but none of it made it into her mouth. She merely rearranged it, moving it from one part of the plate to the next, hiding almost all of her peas and some of her chicken under her mashed potatoes. Roxy and Clio watched the mound of mashed potatoes grow higher.

By the end of the meal Lonnie had seen enough. She had to do something. As the team meal ended Lonnie turned to Sonja, "I think we need to spend a lot more time together."

＊　　　　＊　　　　＊　　　　＊

"So, Mom, we were doing stuff, but I don't know, it wasn't right." Monet said.

Monet's mother was uncomfortable. She knew it was coming and had read all the books to prepare her for this moment. She had even encouraged Monet to ask her questions, but nothing truly prepares parents for talking about sex with their children.

"Honey, what happened?" asking gently.

"We were going to, you know," Monet whispered.

"Where?"

"We were at the Horse Shoe."

"In the stadium? Why would you?..."

"In the parking lot. But I didn't want to..."

"And what did he do?"

"He was cool with it, well sort of, I mean, I just didn't want to. Not in a car."

"Well–and I don't want to sound like I'm lecturing–."

"–Don't worry Mom, I'm listening."

"Your first time... I mean, you only get to be a virgin... Until you have sex. Wait, that didn't come out right."

They both laughed.

"I'm just thinking back to my first time. Not good. It was nothing like I wanted it to be. I really liked the guy too, but I was young, he was a sweet talker, I thought he really cared about me."

"And he didn't?"

"No, he just did his thing. I was like, 'Hey, this is my first time over here.' Really pissed me off because that's my story, my first-time story."

"That sucks," Monet said.

"What do you want your story to be?" her mother said.

"I want it to be nice. It's doesn't need to be leaping ballet dancers spreading flower petals."

"Remember Monet, you don't get a second chance to have first-time experiences. So, you should take your time and do what you can to create good ones. Of course, I think you should wait. Your virginity is not something to just get over with."

"Yeah, some of my girlfriends said they just want to get it over with. I don't understand that." Monet said.

"Let me tell you, there's no magic moment that happens afterward. You don't get a rush of adult wisdom. There's no sprinkling of magic dust. As far as I'm concerned you're a kid, just

a kid who's had sex. And I don't think you're ready for all the responsibilities that go with it."

"That's the lecture part?" Monet asked

"That's the lecture part. First-time experiences stick with you for the rest of your life. Your first kiss, losing your virginity, your first car, your first real job, marriage proposal. Be conscious of those moments. When they involve other people, let them know how important those things are to you. Your father knew he had to make his marriage proposal special. And he did, and now I love telling people how he proposed to me."

"Not like Uncle June when he proposed to Aunt Claudette in the parking lot at Safeway."

"You don't want that to be your story," her mother laughed.

"I have girlfriends who've done it in cars and the same thing happened to them, the guys turn out to be a-holes."

"I know your father has told you this but it's true, especially in this case. Know yourself. Know your standards. Then make people, especially boys, rise to that level. When you know yourself, you'll know when you are ready. And you won't have any regrets no matter how it turns out. I have very close friends who don't remember their first sexual experience because they're in denial about how bad it was. You don't want that to be you."

"That's their fault."

"Probably. Tell you something else. Nobody ever wishes they would have had sex sooner than they actually did."

"Guys do."

"Women. I'm talking about women. How many of your girlfriends wished they would have waited?"

"All of them."

"Well, that's part of the lecture, too."

Chapter 23

Getting What You Want

February Twenty-fourth, 10:30 PM
Shirlie told Monet she would be out studying all night, so she was free to gaze up at the ceiling of her dorm room with the light on all night.

The outing with Ray to Mosswood Park had made Monet think. She was proud of the way she held up. Kickin' the OGs butt with the Bones made it even sweeter. Ironically, Gatorback's talk about being a concierge made her think about her ideal man. The more she thought about it the clearer it became: she should ask Ray out– take the first steps toward changing their relationship.

He has all the deal breakers.

Intelligence. Check. Sure, the irksome comments, the Shakespearian diatribes, and the Ray Scale were very, very, very annoying, but you have to admit wit is the hallmark of intelligence. I just wished he'd use his superpowers for good and not evil.

Ambition? Check. The NBA career was a given. Even after the NBA, you can tell, Ray is going to be successful.

The concierge factor? Check. He was always helping people; Eric, Nigel, that knucklehead Flip Mode. Faked an injury to get out of practice just to cheer me up; graciously shared the spotlight with me at Midnight Madness. Brought me dinne, lunch, flowers and my week's assignments after I was injured.

He has lots of red flags though. My father told me to watch the traffic signs. Let's see, he loves art and poetry, but he won't tell his friends. He knows Shakespeare, but he's the same guy who created the Ray Scale. And yes, he's always been respectful to me, but he indulges bimbos.

Despite the womanizing, Ray had the basics. More disturbing was how good Monet felt with him. It was the little things about him. She loved his cologne–Givenchy Gentleman. He often rested his head playfully on her shoulder. She felt as if she knew him, and yet she knew there was a lot more to learn. He intrigued her.

*   *   *   *

February Twenty-fourth, 1:30 PM
Sonja and Lonnie walked side by side through the hallway of
the Athletic Department. Janice was coming toward them. She had
that look on her face.
"What now?" Lonnie asked.
Janice had confidential news, so she hesitated, looking at Sonja
quizzically.
Lonnie said, "Don't mind her. We're going to be spending a lot
of time together. Aren't we, Sonja." Sonja looked down as she
nodded her acknowledgment.
"You got your raise," Janice said.
Lonnie Delaney was surprised, but tried not to show it. "How
much of a raise?"
"I'm not supposed to tell you, it's equal to Clint's."
"$150,000?!" Lonnie gasped.
"Shhhhh," Janice put a finger to her lips.
"I got a $100,000 raise." Lonnie said. She was shocked.
"I'm not supposed to tell you."
"How much did Dodd and the others get?"
Janice said, "You're the only one. I just wanted to give you a
'heads up' so it wouldn't be a surprise. So you–."
"–So, I wouldn't say anything to screw it up?" Lonnie's mood
turned sour.
Janice frowned. She was starting to understand why Forrest
Haneline hated Lonnie so much. Her directness rubbed people the
wrong way. Janice noticed again that she was still standing oddly
close to Sonja.
"So, that's what Clint makes, right?" Lonnie asked. When she
raised her arm, Sonja's arm rose too. Janice saw they were
handcuffed. She gave Lonnie a questioning look. Tilting her head
toward Sonja, Lonnie said, "We have digestion issues."
Janice raise a brow, "What? Upset stomach?"
"Not exactly. She has problems not eating enough and keeping
down what she does eat, so we eat together and then spend the next
four hours handcuffed together," Lonnie said, as though it was not
a strange situation.
"Why four hours?" Janice asked.

"You want to take that one Sonja?" Lonnie said.

This was the seventy-sixth time Sonja had had to answer the question, "It takes four hours for food to digest past the stomach." Lonnie said, "I don't know who is suffering more. It's killing my social life. I had to cancel three dates with a guy I'm seeing. And that's a helluva sacrifice. Isn't it, Sonja?"

Sonja nodded like a prisoner. Then when Lonnie wasn't looking, she mouthed the words, "Help me," to Janice.

"Taking one for the team," Lonnie said, grinning proudly then she got serious again. "Why didn't any of the other coaches get raises?"

"You know why."

Lonnie didn't allow herself to bask in the victory. There was too much work to be done. When changes were made, Lonnie didn't stop to celebrate, she moved on to the next issue. To the administration her relentlessness came across as thanklessness, which made them unwilling to make further changes. This was the main reason Lonnie's contract had not been renewed at The Ohio State University.

Janice said, "Don't push your luck. These guys–."

"–Haneline and Warlich–."

"–And Bivens..."

"Lonnie, they don't like to lose," Janice said.

"Really. Well I don't like being patronized."

"Them giving you a raise like this in the middle of the season means they had some heavy pressure put on them, probably by the Chancellor. They're trying to avoid the bad publicity."

"Might be a little late for that."

"You should be nice, Lonnie. Be gracious. Dutch gave you a chance with the job. Don't rub his nose in it."

"Yeah, we'll see about the Duchess."

February Twenty-fourth, 11:45 PM
Exhale.
Monet was lying in her room thinking about Ray, again.

All her thoughts about Ray had been different since their trip to Mosswood. She couldn't get him out of her mind. He was right about her need to work on her game. He was right about reaching out to the Big Four. Those simple things turned their season around. And now they were in a position to make the tournament. She even took his advice and practiced setting up the pull-up jumper with the head-fake drive, repeating each move 250 times a day. She promised herself she would be ready at crunch time.

Monet thought about all he had done for her, which made her realize all the things he had done for others during the school year. Sure, he walked around with a princely aura. People constantly wanted to do things for him. But, instead of hoarding those favors, he served them up to friends and even acquaintances. He did it without wanting something in return. It was a beautiful thing, she just didn't understand why he didn't want anyone to know about his generosity.

Still staring at her ceiling, she counted the ways she had leaned on Ray. Being with Ray was fun and frustrating, stimulating and cerebral, all at the same time. She had really leaned on him and if she weren't careful she would fall for him.

Maybe it could work. He has all the deal breakers. We have good chemistry. He could even lead, as long as he didn't mind me leading at times. His ego could handle it. That is if he could see the value in having a strong woman in his corner.

She would have to work through the rest of his issues, and he might not even be interested in her, but the only way to find out was to dangle the possibility in front of him.

She was eager to get started, but if she called him now, at 11:45, he would think it was a booty call.

She thought about it for a moment, then picked up the phone.

She paused again after picking up the phone and thought about the advice about men her father had given her the morning she left to drive cross country.

"Follow the traffic signs," he had said.

She had just broken up with her boyfriend, whom she had caught cheating on her. She continued to wear his friendship ring laced into her shoe strings because back at Ohio University she had always had big scoring nights when she wore it. Now, the ring was more about her than about the guy who had given it to her.

As she lay in her dorm room, she was beginning to see the wisdom of her father's advice about men and relationships. He had told her, "Being with a man in his 20s, even if he's a good one, could lead to frustration and a broken heart. Chances are he wouldn't be ready to commit when she would be ready and that she shouldn't be in a hurry or try to hurry him into committing before he was ready. Most of all, you have to choose wisely. It's the most important decision you'll ever make because as rewarding having a good companion is, choosing poorly can set you back years in many unforeseen ways. A womanizer could jeopardize your health with a venereal disease which could prevent you from having children later. A guy who's physically abusive could permanently injure or even kill you. A slickster could take all your money and ruin your credit. So, that's why you have to follow the traffic signs in relationships to avoid making bad decisions."

Monet picked up the phone to dial Ray's number. *What the hell are you doing? You know what he's going to think. Remember, you have to choose wisely. Remember all the women? Do you really think you're going to be able to get him to settle down and turn his back on all that?*

Still, Monet wanted to go for it. That was her nature. To shoot when no one else wanted the ball. To put her will to succeed up against any challenge, that's what Monet was about–getting it done. She knew it wasn't wise to call Ray at this hour, but she couldn't get him out of her head. Instead of fighting it she gave in to the desire.

As she dialed his number, she promised herself that if he invited her up, she would control the urge to get physical. Being physical led to being sexual. She was there to tempt. To dangle. To see how he felt about her having sex so soon would confuse everything and put her in a category she didn't want to be in with him. She didn't want to be a chicken-head.

She called. Ray answered and invited her right up.

12:05 AM

"Hey," said Monet walking into Ray's dorm room.

"Wassup girl?" Ray was wearing basketball shorts, a skullcap, and a Wifebeater tank top.

The first thing Monet noticed about Ray's room was how clean and organized it was. She had been in his room only once, the night Stinky chased her, but she had been so upset she didn't remember anything about it. The second thing she noticed was a Gordon Parks photograph and a small section of poetry books on the shelf. Ray stood in front of the bookshelf, blocking her view of all the titles.

"What are you hiding back there?" she asked playfully. She reached behind him and grabbed what she thought were two poetry books. She opened it without looking and read aloud. "'Number two. There is greatness in a man who is five-foot, eight. The secret is not in the five, but in the eight.' What the–?" Monet looked at the cover of the book. *Doin' It: A Guide to Great Sex.*

Ray was embarrassed. "Give me that." He reached for the book, but she pulled away from him.

"Oh, this is a good one," she said, reading another passage and dodging Ray at the same time. "'Number nine. Guys want it to be good, but they don't want to know how it got that good.' Now, that's true."

"My favorite is number three hundred forty-one. 'Men reach their peak at 18 years old, women at 35. Do you ever get the feeling that God flunked math?'" They both laughed.

"How many are there?" she asked.

"Four hundred and seventy-five."

"Daaamn. Check this one out. Thirty-four. 'If you want your mail delivered, sometimes you have to lick the stamp,'"Monet said. *What do you think of that?*

Ray didn't respond to her reading number thirty-four.

Monet sat down at his desk. She was going to read more from the novelty book until she saw an open notebook of Ray's own poetry. Ray immediately tried to snatch it from her. Monet dodged Ray by getting up and running to the other side of the room. He was much more defensive, so she knew she touched a sensitive nerve. It was a face off.

"You don't invite many people to your room do you?" Monet asked, holding the notebook behind her back.

"Not unless I absolutely have to," Ray said.

"Why?"

"It's a good rule I've always used," he said, lunging to take the notebook away from her.

She dodged him again, facing him with the notebook behind her back. "Everything around here seems to be a big secret."

They stood in the middle of the floor.

"You're gonna make me take that from you, huh?" he said.

"I'd rather you just let me read it, but if you wanna fight, let's do it."

"I'm cool. I don't want any mysterious assault charges to be a part of my future."

"So, what are you saying?" Monet said.

"Nothing, my bad," he said, plopping backwards onto his bed.

Monet sat down at his desk and read a poem.

"So what brings you up here at... 12:15 in the morning? I hope you don't mind, but I keep my dorm lights on low. I hate those fluorescent lights up there," Ray said.

Monet didn't answer. She was reading Ray's poem. It was beautifully written.

"I'm sorry, what?" she said, looking up.

"Never mind."

"You should publish these," she said.

Ray ignored the comment.

There was an awkward moment of silence that Monet felt compelled to fill. She saw a map of the regional sites for the men's and women's NCAA tournaments. Iowa City caught Monet's eye.

"Did you know Iowa high school girls played six-on-six high school basketball," Monet said.

"Six-on-six? Basketball is played with five-on-five."

"Yeah, but back in the 20s when they didn't want women exercising, let alone playing basketball, they made up different rules for boys and girls."

"Six-on-six," Ray repeated still skeptical.

"Yeah, they played sixes because they wanted to decrease the amount of running girls would have to do. They probably thought too much exercise would make them burst into flames or something," Monet said.

Ray laughed.

"They just recently stopped playing six-on-six girls basketball. 1993 was Iowa's last six-on-six girls high school state championship."

"Naismith would roll over into his grave."

There was another long silence. This time Ray said, "Monet. Why are you here?"

"I came up to figure out what else we have to do for our domestic violence project."

"I just got off a plane. I don't feel like talking about school." Ray sat up. "Maybe you can answer this question for me about women. I went over to this girl's room and she says–."

"–Tonight?" she asked, hiding her disappointment and jealousy. "Why didn't you just invite her over here?" Monet said, as she stood up to look at his books.

"Escapeability. It's easier for me to leave than to convince someone to leave," Ray said.

"That figures."

"You know I know good figures when I see 'em."

Monet rolled her eyes.

Ray continued, "So when she starts kissing on me–and the girl can't kiss. She thinks she can, with the tongue and the grabbing my face. She thinks she's workin' up the passion, but it's too much."

"Too much kissing," Monet said, although she didn't like how he brought up the subject. "And what do you know about kissing?"

"I know that flicking my tonsils is not good kissing. But neither is one of those Hollywood kisses."

"Open mouth but no tongue."

"Right."

"I hate it when guys cup my cheeks," Monet said.

"Grab my ass or put your hands in my pockets. Just don't grab my face," he said.

Sade was playing. The lights were dim. It was a nice vibe. Easy to segue into something more intimate. She realized the atmosphere might have been planned. After studying his bookshelf, Monet sat at the foot of Ray's bed. He shot a Nerf ball into a hoop on the wall. He had it rigged so that after he made a shot the ball went through the net, hit a slope, and returned to him. Monet stopped counting after he made the thirteenth shot in a row. His T-shirt hiked up each time he raised his arms to shoot, exposing his rock-hard abs.

Hmmh-mmh-mmmh.

Ray noticed Monet watching him with a look that was far from platonic. The sexual tension was increasing.

"I wrote a poem about kissing, but it wasn't very good," he said, turning to face her.

"What do you know about kissing?"

"When you do a lot of it, you develop an opinion," he said.

She was curious and so was he. They'd agreed, although not verbally, that they would be friends. It was the reason they had become so close. So, even though Monet was sitting on his bed late at night, Ray was hesitant about making a move without a signal.

"You know if you were someone else–never mind," he said.

"What?"

"Nothing... Hey, you never told me the story about your tattoo," Ray said.

"You wouldn't get it."

"Why not?"

"Because it's about love."

Ray furrowed his brow. "The woman who's only gone on two dates the whole year is telling me, *me,* I wouldn't understand her tattoo because its about love. Does that even makes sense to you?"

"It's a symbol of the prickly nature of love," Monet said.

"That explains the thorns surrounding–."

"–The hearts. Right. Now, forget it."

"I like 'em even more now," he said, with a wry grin, watching for her response.

Monet played along. "My tattoo or my legs?"

"Both."

Monet was looking for an opening to give him the green light without being too obvious. Agreeing with his admiration of her tattoo wasn't enough to work with. Still thinking, she lay back on his bed. But as soon as Monet lay down, she regretted it and jerked herself back to a sitting position.

BOP! They butted heads just as Ray bent over to kiss her. They both sat up holding their foreheads.

"Hold on, I got some ice," Ray said. "I've only got one bag to put it in."

"One bag?"

"Don't worry, I have an idea."

Ray returned with the ice, sat next to Monet and put the ice pack on his forehead. Monet sat there for a moment wondering when he was going to give her the ice pack. Instead he leaned in and pulled her shoulders to him. He guided her head onto the ice pack on his forehead.

She didn't know which she liked more, his ingenious first aid or his inventive way of creating intimacy. They sat there staring at each other, condensation dripping off their noses. Then Ray licked a drop from Mouth lip.

Whoa. Now, that's a tongue. I wonder how skillful he is with that thing?

"How long should we stay like this?" Monet asked, not wanting to move.

"They say you should use ice to reduce swelling for the first 24 hours, but..."   Then he kissed her. They kissed tentatively at first, trying to balance the ice pack between them.

As their kisses became more passionate, the ice pack was tossed aside.

*   *   *   *

Gina had stopped going up to Vince's room, but it was common knowledge that they were still seeing each other even though everyone wished they wouldn't. Lonnie wasn't pleased about it either. Gina wouldn't talk about it when they probed, so they left her alone. They hadn't had any public fights recently, so everyone figured the problems were resolved. Lonnie knew better.

Since taking her self-defense classes, Gina had become more confident. She stopped standing behind her tall teammates in practice and she was practicing and playing with more confidence.

Vince, on the other hand, was smoldering. He got angry over the smallest things, usually things he thought he should control, like Gina. Once, he even had the nerve to complain that her bra was too small, that she had a little too much jiggle when she walked, which made guys stare. Other times he was very nice. Since their incident, he had tamed his anger somewhat. She still secretly visited him. She had stopped going to his room, but she allowed him to come to her room. If things got out of hand, she could at least say she wasn't to blame because she hadn't gone to his room.

"You gonna let me in?" Vince asked, banging on her door. He walked in without saying "Hello." "Did you pick up those notes from Kim for me?"

"No."

"What do you mean?"

"I couldn't go by there today. I got tied up with Jennifer and a class project."

"I need those notes to study tonight," Vince said.

"Well, maybe you should have taken better notes yourself."

"What the hell's gotten into you. This isn't about–."

"–No, why do you keep bringing it up?" she said.

"I just want us to get back to what we had before," he said.

"Me, too."

"We can. But it makes me mad when you don't come through for me."

"You mean, do what you want," Gina said.

"I didn't say that."

"I told you I couldn't go by Kim's today. So can we just drop it?"

Vince was pissed. She saw him make a fist at his side. They sat there staring at each other. Neither blinked. Gina stood her ground. He expected her to cower. Expected her to try to make it right, offer to get the notes now while he waited, or at least be frightened. When she didn't respond, it forced him to cool down.

"Where's your roommate?" he asked.

"She went home for something," she said. "She'll be back to-morrow for class."

"She never goes to class."

"True, but what can you do, she gets As and Bs?"

"So can I study with you?" Vince asked; his temper had cooled.

Gina studied psychology while Vince watched TV. After SportsCenter, Vince rubbed Gina's shoulders as she studied. She was a sucker for a good massage. They lay down on her bed and embraced. Vince wanted to be more intimate. When she rejected his advances, she saw the anger rise in him again. Vince made a fist again, but saw the resolution in Gina's eyes. There was no fear, no room for intimidation. He settled down again.

"Let me just take a nap and then I'll order some Chinese food," Vince said.

"That's fine," Gina said, getting up.

While Vince slept, she finished her reading assignment. She had read about the Stockholm Syndrome where, over time, hostages become empathetic with their captors. As Vince slept soundly, Gina felt like a captive. She took his abuse because he was the first popular guy to be interested in her. A sure sixth-round NFL draft choice was a big improvement over the skateboarding slackers who usually asked Gina out. But the more she thought about it the more she realized she deserved a better boyfriend.

Vince was lying on her bed with his legs open, snoring. A sharp pinch awakened him. When he opened his eyes his entire view was filled with Gina's face. He was still groggy but that sharp pinch he felt was the point of a knife Gina was holding was digging cautiously, but confidently into his perineum. He was wide awake now.

"I want you to leave," she said, whispering.

"But–."

"–I want you to leave now."

The sharp point just below his left testicle got him to focus on the seriousness of her request. Gina rose up a bit to make enough room for him to raise his head to see the business end of a four-inch knife lodged in his crotch. All he saw was her hand, a little bit of the handle, and even less of the sharp steel.

The pain made him inhale while he said, "Shhhhhhh."

"I want you to leave now," she repeated.

His anger was rising, but he could also feel a slight increase of pressure with each passing second. They both knew it wouldn't be long before a decision would have to be made. Gina gave him a hard stare. She'd learned it from Coach Delaney, and it was scaring the hell out of Vince.

"Okay, okay. I'll go," he said, knowing she couldn't walk him to the door with that knife in his crotch. The tables would turn and then she'd see who's in charge.

Monet knocked on the door. "Gina. It's me, you called."

Vince turned his head back to Gina. She was grinning.

"It's open," Gina said, as Monet walked in.

Vince got up, carefully. Gina and Monet watched him gather his things and leave.

Dejected and beaten , he rallied and said, "This ain't–."

"–Oh, it's over... Way over." Gina slammed the door in his face.

February Twenty-fifth
The home game against Portland was close. The teams were evenly matched. Kendra had returned to play, but wasn't totally confident in her knee. She played well, scoring eight points in the first half. Even Tamika was playing as if she were a part of the team, rather than the only player. To the consternation of Roxy, Monet was again the starting point guard. She just couldn't get past Monet being better in that position. She had played it for too long.

Roxy tried to assert her authority over the team by getting the Big Four to stop passing Monet the ball, just as they had done in the first game. Clio was willing. But Kendra was enjoying a career game largely because Monet was giving her the ball in position to score. She never got such sweet dimes from Roxy. Shirlie didn't cooperate because she saw the potential of the team and knew that with Monet they had a chance to get into the NCAA tournament.

"Just play the game," Shirlie said to Roxy.

Gina was playing a very physical game; setting hard picks, swinging her elbows after grabbing a rebound.

Stephanie turned to Lonnie, "What's gotten into Gina?"

"She's playing to keep her scholarship," Renee said.

"No, its those self-defense classes. She's learned to mix it up.

"She doesn't stand behind anyone anymore; she doesn't wave past picks."

"Even Roxy has been complaining she has been too physical lately," Stephanie said.

"Roxy's a crybaby," Lonnie said. "I knew those classes would change Gina's life for the better. She can actually go out and make life react to her now instead of the other way around."

"She's doing a good job of it; she has four fouls," Renee said.

Lonnie called time out.

"Gina, good job. You might play your way into a football scholarship from the basketball team after all. Keep playing physical. Take care of the ball; the way it's going, the one with the ball last may win this ball game... They are sagging on defense, so I want Monet to drive and kick. Roxy, be ready. Remember, we still have to play good defense. Okay, let's do this..."

"Together."

Clark had the play by play, "Rhinos down four, 49-45. McCasner penetrates, out to Davidson for three... Roxy Davidson knocks down a big three to get the Rhinos within one..."

"Rhinos down one, 49-48, with two minutes remaining. There have been fifteen lead changes in this game. The way it's shaping up, it's going to come down to the end."

In the huddle with five seconds remaining, 55-55, the Rhinos had the ball. Lonnie drew up a play that would inbound the ball to Roxy or Kendra. Monet would start on the low block, then run around a double pick set by Shirlie and Tamika at the free throw line. If there was time, she could drive down the lane or shoot the fifteen-footer. While Lonnie was drawing up the play, Roxy made eye contact with Kendra, Clio, and Shirlie. They all knew what she meant.

"Inbound to Kendra. Whoa, where's the foul? The refs aren't gonna call that now...Five seconds, four. Pilots play a physical man-to-man. McCasner around the pick at three seconds. Big Shirlie Torretta passes her the ball. Two. Shot is up... It's good! It's good! And Lonnie Delaney's Runnin' Rhinos beat the Portland Pilots by two, 57-55. What a finish!"

The team mobbed Monet after she made the game winning shot. Everyone except Roxy. One by one, Clio, Kendra, and Shirlie peeled themselves off the pile. When Monet could finally stand up, she punched her fists into the air and screamed. She had finally delivered. Now, the team was 16-13. They wouldn't make it to twenty games, but they could still be WCC champions. Monet was ecstatic about bringing the team one step closer to their goal. It felt good to win as a team. Monet made sure everyone contributed.

After that game, Roxy would never be considered one of the team leaders again.

Chapter 24

Sabotaging Yourself

Class: The Body Politic

Monet's note to Ray read, "Thanks for the ice pack the other night."

He read it without responding.

Monet then wrote, "Thanks for letting me read your poetry. Are you ready to do this report?"

"Please don't tell anyone about my poetry," Ray wrote.

"Ray, Monet, you're up," Lonnie said.

Ray and Monet walked to the front of the class. Ray sat on the floor with his hands on his head, fingers laced. He was in character, a prisoner in the all-female police precinct in Rio de Janeiro, Brazil.

"So what happened?" said Monet, the *Delegacias de Mulheres* (DEAM, or Women's Special Police Station). "We got a call that you were fighting with your wife again."

"I'm not going to tell you nothin'. You dragged me out of my house. What about her?!" said Ray, the accused.

"When we arrived you were fighting. Your wife had a black eye."

"Accuse me? You just beat me up. Look at this," Ray said, head tilted up pointing to one of his closed eyes. After a minute he was having trouble maintaining the long wink he was holding for effect. And he thought acting was easy..

"Your wife didn't do that," the policewoman said.

"Yeah, I know. You did," he said.

"I didn't," Monet said.

"She did," Ray said, pointing to an imaginary person, then flinching in fear.

"Who? Officer Michelle Lopes de Moura? She couldn't hurt anyone, especially a big macho man like you."

"She kicked me in the... you know... Three times," he said, with a pained look on his face.

"No way. *Mulheres das policias* are not allowed to beat people when they arrest them. So, what happened?"

"I am not telling you anything," he said.

"Maybe Officer Michelle should talk to you–."

"–Okay, okay," Ray said. "I saw her."

"Who?"

"My wife. I saw her dancing, talking to another man."

"It's Carnaval, there are a lot of people dancing and talking," Monet said.

"That's right, it's Carnaval, so you know. When we got home, I told her I saw her. She said she saw me dance, too."

"Were you dancing alone?"

The accused said, "No."

"–So what gives you the–I'm sorry, go on."

"I know what happens here at these all-female police precincts."

"We investigate when a man beats his wife–."

"–I was defending my honor," he said.

"Broken jaw. Fractured eye socket. Your wife said you dragged her by her hair."

"I did not."

"Let me see your fingers," she said. "You have hair under your fingernails. And you have teeth marks on your knuckles–."

"–I hurt myself at work," he lied.

"I hope you make enough at that job to afford a lawyer," she said.

"What do you mean? We've had arguments before."

"I know. Three years ago you kicked her in her face. The year after that you held her over a tenth floor balcony. Every year, 2,000 Brazilian women die at the hands of their husbands. Since the *mulheres das policias* began arresting and prosecuting domestic violence cases the numbers have decreased. You can't hide behind the regular police anymore, the *mulheres* will prosecute this case–."

"–Bring her in here. Bring Danita. Bring my wife," the accused said.

"You're under arrest–."

"–I know my wife. She won't bring charges," he said.

"She already has," the police woman said.

"Bring her in here. We will make up right here in front of you."

"Yes, that's a good idea."

"Thank you officer. I will show you. It'll be okay."

"Tell Officer Lopes de Moura she can come in here now."

The accused was struck with fear. "Noooooooooooo."

*   *   *   *

After class, Monet walked across campus to the library. She was going to stop at the bookstore then at Starbucks. While crossing the Quad she saw Ray giving a passionate kiss to a coed. It was just like the kisses she and Ray had shared the other night. Monet forgot about her errands and went straight to his dorm. *Oh, heeeell No! Kissin' on a Hoochie Momma after kissing me.* Monet waited outside the dorm for Ray to return. When he returned he was with the girl he had been kissing. Monet followed them into the building.

Ray had his arm around "Ms. Thang's" waist, sort of; she was short, about five-foot three, so it was almost a headlock. He saw Monet walking purposefully toward them. There was no place to hide.

"I thought you liked 'em tall?" Monet said.

Ms. Thang looked up at Ray. She then looked at the six-foot one Monet and realized she was standing in the land of giants.

"Kissin' on them shorties standing up has to be bad for your back," Monet said.

"If you want some, honey, you gotta stand in line like everyone else," Ms.Thang said, looking up at the tall people. Monet ignored her.

"Monet. We didn't do anything," Ray said.

"*Who* didn't?" Ms. Thang asked.

"*We* didn't," Ray said, pointing to himself and Monet.

"This is not okay," Monet said.

Ms. Thang started to say something, but seeing an angry six-foot one woman make a fist made her reconsider. She stepped behind Ray. "Ray, I'll talk to you when you get your issues resolved, baby. Call me." Then she walked quickly down the hallway, looking over her shoulder, just in case she needed to break into a full sprint to get away from Monet.

"See what you did," Ray said, opening his door. Monet walked in behind him.

"Well?" Monet said.

"You're puttin' way too much on it. We kissed a little."

"A little."

"A little more than a little. So what?" Ray said.

"You wouldn't know it, but that's how relationships start. Get to know each other a little at a time," she said.

"Yeah, in the fifties. In the nineties people don't have to do the soda pop thing to get to know each other. That went out with giving a girl your pin and going steady."

Monet pulled his poetry book from the shelf and gently flipped through the pages. She was looking for something in particular.

"See, look here. All this about wanting to find someone who will love you for you and not the future NBA player. That's all, bullshit..."

Ray had no answer. At the moment he was regretting breaking his rule of letting a woman into his room.

"Gotta go back to the fundamentals," he said, out loud.

Monet closed the book. "I should have seen this coming, especially the way you were wiggin' out."

"Wiggin' out," he said.

"Wiggin' O-U-T," she spelled.

"Over what?"

"People knowing you. Which is stupid," Monet said.

"You've known me for what four months and–."

"–You don't need to be Oprah to see it. I've never seen a guy work so hard at making himself appear so dumb."

"I don't do that," he said.

"Then why won't you let your teammates see that you're interested in poetry or art, or why it is such a big secret when you do stuff for people?"

"You think just because–."

"–What's up with the Shakespeare? Huh?"

"You think–."

"–Can't shut your ass up with the 'Drink responsibly from the chalice of independence.'"

"You divas hate it when a brotha won't shower you with yeses," Ray said.

"Everyone is so busy–."

"–I keep tellin' you–."

"–Kissing your ass–."

"–You need is some more 'no' in your life," Ray said.

"While you have all these women kissing your ass. Buyin' you chocolate when you can't stand it. Sexing it up and doing whatever else on the first date just so *they* can get a second date...I'll tell you straight up. I don't want nothing from you, okay, nothing!"

"You're just used to getting your way. So you get mad because you sabotage the dance of romance," Ray said.

"Talkin' 'bout you want to find a good woman," Monet said.

"I just want a girlfriend. Now, if you were my girlfriend–."

"–If I were your girlfriend?.." Monet said, "You wouldn't know a good woman if she came over and gave you a lap dance."

"Oh yes, I would."

"No, see that's just it. You wouldn't. Because after that lap dance, she stops being a 'good woman.' You're not going to want a woman who'll do all that stuff on the first date because in the back of your mind you'll be thinking she's doing lap dances for other guys too."

"Or professionally," Ray said.

"That's probably where you will go looking for a wife. At the strip club. The one who gives the best table gets to be the mother of your children."

Ray had thought about it. He didn't tell though.

"So, who's sabotaging the dance of romance?" she asked him.

Ray said, "I think, she protest too much."

"Yeah, maybe so. But at least I'm honest about it," she said.

"So why don't you just write it off as a lesson learned? We kissed, so what?" Ray said.

"We did more than kiss."

"We kissed with bonus coverage, how's that? So, why don't you just call it off? Don't mess with me anymore because I'm an a-hole. You're great. I'm missing out. You saved yourself from a broken heart. There it is, done deal," he said.

"I just did."

"But you didn't have to chase off my shortie."

Monet realized Ray would never understand how he was sabotaging himself. "You can run, but you can't hide from yourself."

After she left, Ray plopped onto his bed. He stared at the ceiling, reviewing. It had never mattered to him what a woman thougtht of him. He would never have allowed a woman to interfere with his hooking up with another. And yet he had allowed Monet to do it without a protest–twice.

Ray e smiled when he thought about how she argued. She was passionate, but not loud, resolute but willing to listen–sort of. She challenged him but remained respectful. She showed no signs of being violent which was a good thing. She didn't try to trash his room or rip up his poetry books. Didn't throw a glass, a book, or a punch. In fact, the argument went rather well.

"She might be The One.".

*   *   *   *

February Twenty-sixth

Tamika got her midterm grades. She was in trouble; two Bs and three Ds. A cumulative 2.125 grade point average. She panicked and called Victor Bitinour.

"What do you mean you'll get cut from the team?" Victor said.

"We're all supposed to have a 2.25," Tamika said.

"The minimum is only 2.0."

"Coach said everyone on the team has to get a 2.25. That's ridiculous."

"So, if you don't, you can't play?" he asked.

"Yeah."

"Your coach can't be that stupid, not two days before the tournament selection. What's she gonna do if you guys make it? If it's not one thing it's another." Victor was seriously thinking about getting out of the sports agency business; it required way too much baby-sitting.

"You don't know her," Tamika said.

Victor went into damage control mode. "All right, talk to your professors. All of them. See if you can get them to change your grades. But don't get greedy; ask for one click, D to D plus–."

"D plus!"

"Chances are you earned that D. You don't want to piss the guy off by asking for something you didn't earn. If it's just one click, you might catch him in a good mood. Grades are pretty subjective. If you ask nicely, he might give you the benefit of the doubt. But if you go in there asking to turn a C into B he'll throw you out for insulting his intelligence. Trust me. Try to raise them all a little instead of changing one or two dramatically," he said.

"Okay."

"What the hell have you been doing all quarter?" he asked.

"I don't know, just playing basketball."

"Let me give you a little dose of reality. You get yourself kicked out of school or off that basketball team, we're done as far as I'm concerned," Victor said.

"What do you mean?"

"How do you guys in the 'hood say it?... It's a wrap. You have no value if you're not playing."

"Wait–."

"–I can't represent your crappy report card."

"You said, 'As long as I keep putting up twenty and ten a game I won't have to worry about grades.'"

"True, but you still need grades good enough to remain eligible to play. To play, you have to be in school," he said.

"I am eligible to play."

"Not according to your coach," Victor said, then hung up.

Tamika's professors were unsympathetic. One complained about how she never came to class and when she did she read *Sports Illustrated.* He dismissed her request as if he were waving off dessert. She got word that one of her professors was sympathetic to athletes and regularly changed their grades. Tamika rushed to see him, but he politely reminded her that she was not a football player and that she should have foreseen this while she was reading about the WNBA. Another professor snickered in her face when she pleaded her case. Moments after she closed the office, door she heard the professor say, "Revenge is mine!" with a sinister laugh.

Professors gossip, too. By the time Tamika tracked down her other professors, they had reviewed her tests and remembered how distracted and inattentive she had been during their lectures. None of them changed her grades.

February Twenty-seventh

The team ran through their usual early-morning practice drills. Although Jennifer didn't have to attend practice, she was there at 6:00.

During a four on four drill, Gina set a hard back pick on Clio. Crushed her. "Damn, just because you got a scholarship doesn't mean you get to play like a football player," Clio said.

"Blame your teammates for not talking," Lonnie said. The very next play, Mbika laid out Kendra while fighting through her attempt to set a screen. Kendra didn't like it.

"Coach I'm supposed to fight through, right?," Mbika said. Both of them looked back at Coach, who purposely turned her back to talk to Stephanie. The team was getting testy. All year, Lonnie had been trying to get them to put aside their petty personal animosities and become more competitive with each other in basketball. It was finally taking hold. The walk-ons were leading the way.

Sonja was dragging the entire practice. Lonnie had given the team two days off since their game on Saturday night. During those two days Sonja ran ten miles each day, ate a total of thirty grapes, three bags of Cheetos and four carrot sticks. She drank a quart of white grape juice. By Tuesday morning's practice she was pale and rail thin. An hour into practice, Sonja collapsed. Lonnie stopped practice immediately. They called the trainer, who called an ambulance. Practice was over.

At 5:30 PM, Sonja woke up to a fuzzy figure sitting at the foot of her bed. She tried to focus, but couldn't. She felt the burning icey-hot of intravenous tubes in the back of her wrist.

"Where am I?" Sonja asked, recognizing Lonnie Delaney.

"St. Mary's Hospital," Lonnie answered.

"What happened?"

"You passed out."

"I gotta pee."

"That's the IV. You were totally dehydrated."

Lonnie assisted her to the bathroom. On the way back to the bed, Lonnie paused at the wall mirror. She stood behind Sonja with her hands on Sonja's shoulders.

"I called your folks; they'll be here tomorrow," she paused before continuing.

"So what happened? We were doing so well with the handcuffs?" Lonnie said, smiling.

Sonja stared at her feet. "Look at me," Lonnie said. "Look at me!" When she didn't, Lonnie turned her face to the mirror.

"Look at you, Sonja. You're strong, you're tough. I used to sulk after every loss when I was kid. I had probably scored half of my team's points, but if we didn't win, I was mad for days. My mother used to tell me, 'Lonnie, you're not perfect. There's only one person who is and that's God Almighty. So, cut yourself some slack,'" Lonnie said.

"I don't sulk after we lose, and I don't think I'm perfect," Sonja whined.

"We all noticed a change in you right after you broke up with your boyfriend." When she said boyfriend Lonnie remembered she'd made a date with Dan. He was supposed to pick her up an hour ago. She had completely forgotten.

"What about my boyfriend?" Sonja said, bringing Lonnie back to the moment.

"You can't let people influence your sense of self."

"When we broke up it wasn't like we had gone out for a year."

"Something happened that set you off. Have you ever heard of something called the *'Female Athletes Triad'*?"

"No."

"It's like *Anorexia Nervosa* because women who have it tend to be perfectionists. The person they see in the mirror is overweight, even though she may only weight one hundred pounds. Women who have the Triad are also hyperexercisers and perfectionists."

"I only run a few miles to keep my weight down."

"Your weight is already in the basement. You have all the makings of a perfectionist whether you like the description or not. You've got straight "A's" and you're running yourself into the ground because you see a fat person in the mirror. Everyone else sees a smart, determined, attractive young woman. I don't know who you see, but it's probably not the woman who's losing her hair, is bone thin, and has exercised her period away, maybe for good. Who do you see when you look in the mirror?"

"I don't know."

Sonja tried to look away, but Lonnie wouldn't let her.

"Let me see your teeth..." Lonnie said.

Sonja reluctantly opened her mouth.

"At least the acid from your stomach hasn't started to break down the enamel yet," Lonnie told her.

"From what?"

"From throwing up. You've gotta stop doing this to yourself. The doctor said you have the beginning stages of osteoporosis."

"What's that?"

"Your bones are becoming brittle from a lack of nutrients. Brittle like toffee. If you keep it up, you'll have the bone density of an old woman in a few years. If you don't stop now, it may be irreversible."

As they looked into the mirror, Lonnie could see the fear surfacing in Sonja's eyes. She tried to put her head down. Lonnie pulled her head and up. "Keep your head! You're gonna face this. You're not going to feel sorry for yourself. You're gonna face this with your head up."

"I can't."

"You can, and you will. You're not gonna do it alone. We're gonna get you through this together." Then Lonnie took a deep breath. "One, you're off the team."

"What!?" Sonja yelled, turning to face Lonnie.

"Off the team. Two, we're gonna take down all those photos of skinny women from your walls. No mirrors either."

"No mirrors?"

"Well except this one," Lonnie said. She placed a handle in Sonja's hand which were at her side. "I want you to meet someone; she's really special. She's not having a good day today, but she's gonna get better. You two have a lot in common." Lonnie guided Sonja's hand up to her face. She was holding a mirror. They stared in the mirror for a few moments. Tears welled up in Sonja's eyes. They both studied Sonja face. A tear streaked down Lonnie's face when Sonja said, "It's nice to meet you."

Then Lonnie turned the mirror around. The back of the mirror was engraved with the words, *"Look to your future."*

March First
Toso Pavilion
Santa Clara, California

The Rhinos were playing at the University of Santa Clara Broncos. Brenda Peterson stood at mid-court, staring at Tamika as she ran through the lay-up line. When she finished her lay-up and ran to the end of the line, Brenda said, "Hightower burgers on the grill tonight."

A lot had changed since their first meeting back in San Francisco. Tamika had seen the light on defense, and she knew her teammates would help shut Brenda Peterson down.

At the beginning of the game, the Rhinos played such great defense Brenda Peterson got into foul trouble and had to sit out with three early fouls.

Monet talked the whole game, "Come on, run with me... Go get it... Outlet... Here we go." The team played better when she talked.

Thalia Clark called the play-by-play, "Long rebound to McCasner, she's off and running... Coast to coast, finger roll... Good... The Broncos are searching for answers. They switch to a zone defense...

Looking to somehow rattle the Rhinos, a Broncos fan sitting directly across from the players' bench held up a sign, "Jennifer, who's the daddy?"

There is a thin line between clever trash talk and mean-spirited insults. Anything related to hoe you play the game or your appearance, or the school is fair game, but personal insults are off limits. Jennifer was three months pregnant and beginning to show.

Lonnie called a time-out and complained to the referees, who explained that if the fans were not writing obscenities, their hands were tied by the First Amendment. Lonnie said, she would forfeit the game if something wasn't done immediately. The sign was removed, but it unleashed a torrent of verbal insults toward Lonnie and Jennifer, none of which were very clever.

It was a big distraction for the team. The first half ended with the Broncos leading 23-17.

In the locker room, Lonnie Delaney implored her team to step up, play better, and win. If they did, she promised it would be the most satisfying win of the year.

The Rhinos hung a thirty-two point asskicking on Santa Clara that night. Blew them out. It is rare when walk-ons play six continues minutes. Gina and Mbika were thankful Garbage Time had started early.

In the locker room, Lonnie praised her players. "See, winning is the best revenge."

Chapter 25

Tsunami Feminists

March Sixth

With 30 seconds remaining in the game against St. Mary's, Lonnie Delaney saw Forrest Haneline waiting to ambush her through the tunnel. He rarely came to women's games, so his presence was an ominous sign.

It was bad timing. Lonnie was in a bad mood. Her team had played flawlessly against the Gaels and still lost, so she wasn't in the mood to hear Haneline complain about all the national attention she had brought on NCAA and Del Mar University Athletics. After shaking hands with the Gaels' coach and making sure all the players had gone to the locker room, she took a deep breath and headed toward the tunnel.

"I'm getting lots of complaints about Jennifer sitting on the bench," Haneline said.

"Really, why?" Lonnie responded.

"She's obviously pregnant."

"So?"

"But she's not married."

"And..."

"This is a Catholic university. Parents are up in arms, not to mention the Jesuits. It's a bad example for the young girls who come to our games," said Haneline.

"What's bad? She made the decision to keep her child."

"This is a Catholic university."

"I thought Catholics are supposed to unconditionally support the decision to keep a baby."

"Nothing is unconditional."

"You're obviously not Catholic," Lonnie said.

"She's not married."

"If she were married, it would be okay? But since she's not, she can't be on the team?" Lonnie asked.

"She *can* be on the team, but she can't sit on the bench and represent the university. Come on, Lonnie, stop drawing a line in the sand on every damn issue."

"There have been a lot of male players who have fathered children while playing for this university. Not one of them was married. To my knowledge, you haven't kicked any of them off their teams."

"We'd prefer that she just not sit on the bench," Haneline emphasized.

"So tell me how many male athletes, football players, have you 'preferred' not sit on the bench when their girlfriends got pregnant?"

"None," he admitted.

"The NCAA should treat pregnancy as an injury," she said.

"All she has to do is apply to get another year of eligibility. She'll get six years to play five, instead of five years to play four," said Haneline.

"You know that's not what I'm talking about. If a player is injured, *he* gets all the resources of the athletic department's medical resources–acute and therapeutic."

"Women do too."

"Yes, women, too," Lonnie agreed. "But, if *he* needs surgery, the athletic department pays for it. We have a list of specialists that we use. When *he* needs physical therapy, we not only provide it but we supervise it. If it's career-ending, we'll even arrange counseling. True?"

"True."

"But, if a woman gets pregnant, *she* gets turned over to the general university health coverage. Ever wonder why that is?" Lonnie asked.

"What more do you think she should get?" Haneline asked. "Anyway, you're changing the subject. We just want Jennifer to not sit on the bench, that's all."

"You guys are nothing but a bunch of hypocrites."

"Here we go again," he sighed.

"You're damn right, here we go again. You can't name one male athlete who couldn't sit on the bench because his girlfriend was pregnant. But when a female athlete gets pregnant there are all these rules about what we can and can not do."

"C'mon, Lonnie."

"We're supposed to be helping young people, not turning our backs on them when they make decisions that don't suit our politics."

"Not even you can find politics in this," Haneline said.

"It's right there on the surface."

"Where? It's a distraction for her to sit on the bench," he said.

"Who's distracted? Father Maloney? The NCAA? You?"

"I'm not Catholic," Haneline said.

"Is the other team distracted, because one of *our* players is pregnant?" she asked.

"No, but parents have complained. Boosters have complained. Catholic-Booster-Parents have complained," he recited. "That's not politics. Catholics are just funny about unmarried mothers representing their university."

"Let me ask you. Why do you think the NCAA wants scholarship players who get pregnant to use the university health care facilities and not provide resources through the athletics department?" Lonnie asked.

"How many times do I have to tell you? Pregnancy is not an injury," Haneline said.

"But it is conceivable a scholarship player who gets pregnant might seek counseling to deal with her emotions, right? Or, maybe she's just confused about what to do and as her coach I see that she needs counseling. By your rules–by NCAA rules– I can't do anything."

"Oh, come on, Lonnie! That's a bunch of bullshit."

"All I'm saying is, if we're about leading young people, then, why would the NCAA prevent me from getting a player all the help she needs so she can make the best decision about her pregnancy? It just seems the NCAA wants to stay as far away from the issue of birth control as possible."

"They do not," Haneline said.

"They have no problem raising the banner of female independence through sports. They want young girls to aspire to become strong, confident women who play NCAA sports. They celebrate it on national television. But they know they would be seen as hypocrites if their official position is against a woman's right to choose."

"But that isn't their official position," Haneline said.

"Having no position or putting it off for someone else to deal with it, *is* taking a position, by omission. They also know they would be targeted by the Religious Right for supporting abortion if they allowed schools to offer counseling that presented abortion as an option."

"*There's the politics!* I knew it was in there somewhere," Haneline said. "Look, we just don't want her sitting on the bench. She'll still have her $25,000-a-year scholarship." Haneline was getting frustrated.

"So what? She can keep her scholarship."

"$25,000 is not a 'so what,'" he said.

"If she needs special arrangements to take care of her child so she can practice and go to games, then what? The rules say we can't help."

"Is the athletic department supposed to arrange for child care, too?"

"No, but the NCAA could make it so it would not be a violation if an enlightened school wants to arrange it."

"They won't allow it. So we don't do it. You gotta make choices in life," Haneline shrugged.

"And that's why Congress should hear what you guys are doing."

"What you guys?"

"You, the Chancellor, the NCAA. You're penalizing women for having the ability to bear children. Treating women differently, while it's not a direct violation of the Title IX, it violates the *spirit* of the law."

"By your perspective, we violate Title IX by having stand-up urinals for men and not for women," Haneline shook his head. "The NCAA is just a governing body, they can't mandate a change in the culture of this university."

"Bullshit! They do it all the time with their player eligibility rules and sanctions preventing post-season play. If a school wants to get TV money, bowl money or tournament money, they will comply with the NCAA. So, let's stop playing dumb," Lonnie said. "What makes me mad is you still want to get federal money even though you're not providing equal resources for female athletes. You want it both ways."

"This is a Catholic university. What's to stop a female athlete from getting a scholarship her freshman year, like Jennifer, getting pregnant, and putting the university on the hook for the cost of her scholarship, prenatal care, and child care after she's had the baby?" Haneline asked.

"How many female scholarship athletes get pregnant every year?"Lonnie asked.

"Nationwide?" Haneline said.

Lonnie answered her own question. "Maybe five. If the NCAA changed its rules, pregnancies would not go up dramatically. We're not talking about a large amount of money when you compare it to the billions of dollars the NCAA generates. And, we all know, that's the bottom line. No. What this really shows is your–."

"–You keep saying it's me."

"You're on the eligibility committee. So, why don't you try to make it easier for women?" Lonnie asked, arms folded.

Haneline was fed up. "You can't have it both ways."

"Men do."

"Well, not on our dime."

March Eighth, Saturday
Spokane, Washington

The Rhinos sat quietly in Gonzaga's visitors' team locker room. Ankles were taped. Shoes were laced tight. It was quiet. Sonja was on everyone's mind. This was the time Sonja usually vomitted before the game.

"Remember how she would peel her grapes?" Clio said.

"Or how she would rotate her food from one end to another?"

Monet missed Sonja too, but she was also worried about getting into the tournament.

"What's up with you? I've never seen you look this sad before a game," Shirlie said to Monet.

"I just want to get into the tournament," Monet answered. Monet sat at her locker head down, wondering why she felt so uncertain minutes before one of the biggest games of the year.

Lonnie entered the locker room with Renee and Stephanie. "Listen, I know you all are worried about Sonja. I talked with her a few minutes ago and she's feeling much better. She's getting stronger," Lonnie smiled. "Tamika, she wanted me to tell you to pass the ball... I agree with her."

Everyone laughed.

"Listen, I don't have to tell you this is an important game. We're 17-14. So, we have to win this league if we're going to get into the NCAA tournament. It's the next to the last game; two wins and we're in. We control our own destiny here. I know it sounds corny, but let's win this one for Sonja."

Lonnie then reviewed the strategy for the game. The team was as ready as they would ever be. When the team filed out, Lonnie stopped Monet.

"You okay? You look lost and that's not like you."

"Yeah, I'll be fine when I hit the court."

"I hope so, or you'll be sitting next to me," Lonnie told her. "We need you to play well." She put her arm around Monet's shoulders, and walked her out of the locker room.

The game was close. The Lady Bulldogs knew they could end the tournament hopes of the Rhinos, and were doing a good job of being spoilers. With 12:15 remaining in the first half, the Lady Bulldogs were leading, 23-15.

The Rhinos were down to tewlve players. With Kendra again out of the lineup, Mbika played in her place. Mbika was an offensive liability but her stifling defense earned her more playing minutes. Watching her shoot, though, was still an adventure. On offense it was like playing five on four. The scoring burden fell on Monet, who was languishing. She wasn't her usual talkive self, which meant trouble. She was 1-8 with three assists during the first half. Her teammates kept waiting and waiting for her to break out and take over the game as she had done so many times before. Instead, Tamika carried the team, scoring 15 points. At halftime, the Lady Bulldogs had a commanding lead, 45-31.

Lonnie screamed and hollered as expected in the locker room. She was particularly hard on Monet, calling her out to lead or step aside for Roxy. Monet knew that meant she would be on a short leash for the second half.

During the second-half warm up, Roxy cornered Monet, "What's going on with you? You're acting like you got man problems."

Monet laughed it off, but Roxy was right. Worse yet, Monet was in denial about her feelings for Ray. Acknowledging those feelings, in her mind, would give Ray the upper hand. She wasn't willing to admit he could have that kind of affect on her, even if he didn't know she felt that way.

"All right then, get it together, we got twenty minutes of basketball," Roxy said "I don't want our season to end tomorrow."

Lonnie switched Mbika to guard the Lady Bulldog's leading scorer. She also told Gina to look for her shot. Those two adjustments turned the game around. The Rhinos cut the deficit down to four points with five minutes remaining. The Rhinos might have led if Tamika had not hoisted up so many bad shots.

Lonnie called time out.

As the team walked over to the bench, Monet yelled at her. "Pass the ball."

"Make a shot first," Tamika yelled back.

In Tamika's mind, she was doing all she could to help. But in close games, getting any shot is not the same as getting a good shot.

"With one minute remaining, the Lady Bulldogs have settled down and scored on successive trips down the court. The Rhinos cut the Bulldogs' 18 point lead down to four. And now it's anyone's game," Thalia Clark said, the play-by-play announcer.

"So far, Lonnie Delaney's Rhinos have not been able to execute consistently on both ends of the floor. And they really need Monet McCasner to wake up. She's been asleep for 38 minutes.

"Okay, here we go. Gonzaga 66, Del Mar 64. One minute remaining. Monet dribbles up the court. Over to Hightower, back to McCasner, Lady Bulldogs play man to man, over to Wysinger, Njai sets a bone-crushing pick. McCasner is wide open from fifteen. Oh, she passed up the shot, over to Hightower, who forces up a terrible shot, rebound Tomcoe for the Lady Bulldogs. McCasner does not look confident tonight.

"Bulldogs outlet to Williamson over to Billingsley for a lay-up...Blocked by Njai! What a play by the Kenyan! 66-64 Gonzaga, ten seconds remaining. Time out, Rhinos."

"Monet, shoot the ball," Roxy said. "C'mon now, we've come too far!" Shirlie, Kendra, and Clio each gave a look of support.

In the huddle, Lonnie drew up a play for Monet to take the last shot. No one was confident Monet would make it, not even Monet.

They broke the huddle.

Lonnie pulled Monet to the side, "C'mon now. This is why you drove across the country. This is the first step toward getting into the tournament. You're gonna make it. Block out whatever is on your mind for these next few seconds. OK?"

Lonnie sent Monet out onto the floor. She didn't feel confident, but with the game on the line, Lonnie trusted Monet more on her worst day than anyone else on their best.

"This is it ladies, do something special," Lonnie yelled.

Thalia Clark, the play-by-play announcer, called the game. "Inbound to McCasner. McCasner dribbles over to the left hash mark, Njai sets a pick for Roxy Davidson on the weak-side, she's open at the foul line, McCasner passes to Davidson who gets off an off-balance shot, no good, Njai with an incredible rebound, one second, she puts up a shot, no good, but she's fouled... Mbika Njai is fouled with one half second remaining. With one-half second remaining, the Bulldogs are leading 66-64, Njai has to hit both free throws to send the game into overtime.

"Njai is a 45 percent free throw shooter, but some people rise to the occasion," Clark said.

Mbika couldn't believe the situation she was in. She'd spent the entire season making her teammates run extra laps because of her lousy shooting. And now their whole season would come down to whether she made these two shots or not. She had been practicing. But practice isn't the same as a game, especially when the entire season is on the line.

"Njai steps up to shoot two crucial free throws. She squares up and shoots... She makes the first one. She's gotta make the second one to tie. The crowd is screaming and her second shot is... No good! Rebound Gonzaga. And the Lady Bulldogs run out the clock. More importantly they spoiled the Del Mar Runnin' Rhinos chance to win the WCC, and get an automatic bid to the NCAA Tournament; 17-15 probably won't be enough to get an invitation to the Big Dance.

"I know Mbika Njai feels terrible right now."

March Eighth, Saturday night

A late winter blizzard blanketed the Pacific Northwest after the game. It snowed Saturday night and all day Sunday. The team could not fly out of Spokane to play their final game in Portland Sunday night. Lonnie thought about renting cars, but Haneline had already talked to the athletic director at Portland, and they decided they would postpone Sunday afternoon's game until Monday.

Lonnie figured the loss against Gonzaga virtually ended their chances of getting an NCAA tournament bid because the Rhinos had not won their conference, and their 17-15 record was not strong enough for consideration. She was hopeful the selection committee would take into account they only lost by one point to the number one ranked Tennessee Lady Volunteers *in Knoxville*. In addition, they beat two other top ten schools, UConn and Stanford, on their home courts. Often the tournament selection committee will choose teams because they are playing well at the end of the season. But with a loss to the Gonzaga Bulldogs the Rhinos couldn't make that case. It wasn't a good last impression. The airports wouldn't be clear until late Sunday night. Team morale was low. So low, Lonnie gave everyone Sunday off to do whatever they wanted. They were still in Spokane, so the options were limited. The players scattered Sunday morning but after a walking tour of Washington State University, the mall, and the movie theater, they all found themselves back in their hotel rooms by three' o'clock, just in time for CBS's *Road to March Madness* selection show.

While everyone else was wandering the streets of Spokane, Gina stayed in her hotel room. Tamika noticed her fastidiously addressing a stack of letters to National Football League teams.

"You switching sports?" Tamika asked.

"Not exactly. Vince is probably going to get drafted into the NFL."

"So?"

"I thought they should know what kind of guy he is."

"Yeah, but you didn't even file a police report."

"You saw what he did to me." Gina said, as she held up a color copy of the photos of her swollen eyes. Tamika winced. "My point exactly. He's projected to go in the fourth round, which is high for kicker."

"It ain't gonna do no good. If a team needs a kicker, they're gonna draft a kicker," Tamika said.

"Yeah, well I'm still going to send them to every single team. The letter with me describing the circumstances, the photos–."

"–The fact you got a scholarship and didn't file a police report... Not to hate on you or anything, but are you gonna tell them that too?"

"I'm still sending them."

"And if a team drafts him anyway?" Tamika said.

"I'll never watch that team again," Gina said, resolutely.

Roxy fired up the Daiquiris blender before settling down with the rest of the Big Four to watch the show that was certain to leave them out of the NCAA tournament. Mbika and Gina watched in Monet's room. Lonnie, Renee, and Stephanie settled down to watch as well in their hotel room.

The segment began by breaking down the four men's regions comprehensively. The commentators made their predictions on which men's teams would get into the Final Four. They predicted The Del Mar Men would rank number one in the West.

"Come on," Lonnie said, as the women had to suffer again through Jim Nance and Clark Kellogg's review of the men's brackets. They recapped the bubble teams that didn't make it. They reviewed the selection committee's sense of humor by discussing games in which head coaches were matched up against former assistants. They even showed reaction shots of four men's teams which had a fifty percent chance of making the tournament. They showed all of that *before* the women's brackets.

With five minutes remaining in the broadcast, the women's brackets were shown. The network showed each regional bracket once for what seemed like just a few seconds, then moved on to the next region. The show's producers didn't budget enough time, so they had to rush through the women's section so they could end the broadcast in time for *60 Minutes* in the Eastern and Central time zones.

The women's East regional bracket was shown: sixteen capillaries flowed toward the veins of the Sweet Sixteen, the aorta of the Final Four and the heart of it all, the Final Four logo, Cincinnati, Ohio. The interlocking "ND" logo of Notre Dame sat on top as the number one seed in the East. The Stanford "S" with the Redwood tree was at the top of the West Region. The blocked "T" of Tennessee, and crowned Lion of Old Dominion sat atop the Midwest and Mideast regions, respectively.

All four regions were then displayed. The Rhino players stared at the television screen hoping they would see the Rhinos' logo. Even on a 27" television screen, the brackets were too small to find one team.

Roxy gave up looking, and had already fired up the blender to make more daiquiris. Everybody moved away from the television set one by one. It wasn't long before they were having six different conversations, and Clio was thinking about questions and challenges for another game of "Truth or Dare."

The party was about to get started when Shirlie screamed, "Look!"

When they turned around, Shirlie was jumping up and down pointing to the TV.

"Number 13. Midwest bracket. Del Mar Runnin' Rhinos!" she yelled.

The Runnin' Rhinos were buried in the middle of the Midwest, bracket, but there they were in the Big Dance. Roxy heard Monet scream from next door.

Kendra popped her head out from underneath a pillow. It was right there on national television. The number thirteen seed of the Midwest, the Del Mar University Runnin' Rhinos. Roxy, Clio, Shirlie, Kendra, Gina; all of them couldn't believe it. They all started jumping up and down. Shirlie called Monet's room.

"Aaaahhhhhhhhhhhhh!"

"Aaaahhhhhhhhhhhhh! Get over here!"

Clio grabbed a pillow and hit Kendra on the head. By the time Monet knocked at the door, there was a full-blown pillow fight brewing. They all bashed each other. Heavy-handed Tamika nearly knocked Gina through the wall.

Someone hit Monet in the back of the head with a pillow. Monet turned around to see that it was Roxy. They stood there for a moment amidst the pandemonium. When Monet raised her pillow to hit Roxy back, Roxy didn't try to block her. She just stood there, willing to trust her teammate. They had been through a lot during the season and it was Roxy's way of calling an armistice.

Monet clobbered her. Hit her so hard that Roxy's feet came off the carpet as she flopped back onto the bed. When she got to her feet she was woozy. The entire team waited to see if Roxy would get mad. She didn't. She held it together, figuring she deserved what she got, given how truculent she had been to Monet all year. Everyone was happy to see them resolve their differences.

With Monet and Roxy declaring a truce, maybe now they could finally play as a team.

The next day they blew out the Portland Pilots by 25 points.

Class: The Body Politic

"I do not know why she would do this... Our children have no mother now."

A student sobbed intermittently as he performed his report in front of the class. Tears streamed down his cheeks.

"Mihri committed suicide yesterday. My wife! Mihri! My wife!...

"She hanged herself in our living room with her scarf, her burqa... Other wives have killed themselves over the months, probably two or three a week in southern Iran. But I never thought it would be my Mihri.

"Her sister, Nihani, said Mihri couldn't live with such restrictions any more. I thought it was because I sold Mihri's sewing machine... She used it to make extra money by sewing. But there is no work for me, none for six months now, and we needed money. I didn't like it when she made money and I couldn't find work. We needed the extra money but I wouldn't take it. She used the money to feed the children. I would not eat any of the food she bought with her sewing machine money. Two months like this, I couldn't take it, so I sold the sewing machine.

"Her sister said, 'No, she hated the burqa.' I talked to Mihri about it. Right there, I ended this talk of nonsense. There can be no disobedience. This is God's way. Besides, I told her we are more liberal than the Afghanis, their *burqas* cover their entire face. This is Muslim law that governs women's behavior; her dress, how she must act in public. I cannot give her permission to disobey God's law. It teaches that a woman's place has less value than that which is under foot. That she should never go out alone. This is God's law. Not mine, but God's... And now my children have no mother.

"Women here live with the duties of God's law as they always have. We live a spiritual life, not like the infidels with their immodesty and disobedient women. Women here live by God's law because that is their place. I don't understand why Mihri chose not to... When I found her, she was facing the photos of my children, our children, on the shelf. My picture was broken on the floor. Her eyes were still open. My children were the last thing she saw before she died."

As the student sat down the class remained respectfully silent.

Monet raised her hand, "What is the difference between the Afghani burka and the burqas worn in southern Iran?"

The student stood up and said, "The Afghani burqas are generally a long light blue silk garment that is draped over a woman's head, sort of like a round parachute with a square five inch mesh window to see through. The southern Iranian hijab is like you see in other Muslim countries where the face is totally exposed, but there is also a face plate that wraps around the forehead. An aluminum bar that extends down the bridge of the nose that connects to a another piece that stretches around the upper lip and mouth. Some of them resemble mustaches. But–."

"–With all due respect, what is it that women have?"

"Have?"

"What do women have that is so powerful that Muslim men must be protected from it at all costs? I mean, what is it about women that is so dangerous to men that women must completely cover themselves in a silk sheet or wear a football mask that makes them look like men? That part can't be in the Qur'an." Monet asked.

"A Muslim would say, 'It is God's teaching and isn't for Americans to judge,'" he said.

"Okay, I get that. But why can't men take more responsibility for the problem–protecting themselves from whatever that thing is that women have that is so dangerous."

"Like, so dangerous that men can't be trusted to even see it and then only in the privacy of their own home," Sarah said.

"Right, it just seems to be all on the women. I mean, am I missing something?" Monet asked.

Lonnie intervened, "Monet touches on a broader issue. What can be done to help the Mihris, Jivantas, even the Mbikas of the world? Women who live oppressed lives every single day."

"Do what Americans do best, send money," Ray said.

"There has to be more we can do," Lonnie said.

"What, like go there and buy up all the burqas?"

"Then burn them as a symbol of their oppression."

"A bonfire of the burqas."

"Just like the 70's."

"But for women around the world."

"We'll need a boardwalk, like the one in Atlantic City."

"We're Americans, we'll build one," Ray said.

"Hey, hey, hey. Settle down," Lonnie said, reeling the class back in from their gallows humor. It was a relief from the heavy tension of the subject. "Seriously, what could you do?"

"Communicate somehow," one student said.

"Information is power."

"Ideas can move mountains," Lonnie said. "But unfortunately, rural communities don't have a lot of access to outside information, let alone the internet."

There were no other suggestions, the class fell silent.

"You can vote," Lonnie said.

Everyone looked puzzled.

"Vote for representatives in the United States that support governments that work toward addressing the cultural problems of women around the world," Lonnie continued.

"But the people running those countries are men and they seem to like it that way," Monet said.

"With the right effort to win their hearts and minds, we and there rest of the world could help them discover that their most valuable asset has been living with them all along."

"Sharing thier beds."

"Never happen," Ray said.

"Why not?" Monet asked.

"They hate us," Rays said.

"They hate Americans," Monet said.

"They hate us because we're cowboys. Cowboys aren't very culturally sensitive," Lonnie said.

"Yeah, but we get shit done," Ray said. "Maybe they hate us because they're jeolous."

Monet wrote Ray a note, "Thanks for adding some good ole' American arrogance to the conversation."

"Its true, isn't it?" he wrote back.

"Winning the hearts and minds of men on behalf of rural women will take a feminine approach, not the cowboy way," Lonnie said.

"Never gonna happen," Ray said.

"These women need education, which will provide resources and independence."

"That's why it won't happen; the men don't want women to be independent. That's just men justifying their dominance of women. The Qur'an doesn't say anything about women being less valuable than men. Men are vested in keeping women dependent. It seems the only way they can justify it is through religion. But let me tell you, game recognize game. That's all part of the hustle. That's why it'll never happen.   It's not written but they justify it with religion. When religion is involved, it's a battle no one can win," Ray said.

"You all must make sure you vote," Lonnie said, sternly.

"I can't vote in India, China, or Iran," Ray said.

"But you can elect representatives that can see the wisdom in helping rural communities by building schools. Hell, we could build schools and teachers salaries. In exchange for aid, we should only require that girls must be able to go to the same schools as boys and for just as long. The U.S. gets hung up when our foreign aid comes with too many strings, like banning condom distribution and birth control counseling. We sabotage ourselves when we try to superimpose our country's value system onto other cultures' regardless of what they need or want. If we would be more open-minded and less controlling, we could have had a greater impact by letting peopleget it for themselves. All that's left are missed opportunities."

"Where do you start?"

"It starts with people. People empower government and government changes society."

Most of the students shook their heads; they weren't that confident in their government.

"That solution is too big a
nd too complex," Monet said.

Lonnie pressed on. "Slavery didn't just end in this country. There was a groundswell of popular support that said slavery would not be tolerated. People elected representatives to change it."

"Then came Jim Crow laws and 'separate but equal' in the South," Sarah said.

Lonnie said, "True, but Congressmen, Senators, and even Presidents passed laws to make them illegal. Most of the time those politicians were reelected after they took a difficult position on race. Now, government sanctioned racism is a thing of the past in this country. And I'm sure everyone in the early 1800s thought slavery would be an eternal way of life. Well, that change came from the people."

Mbika said, "Men in those countries, my country, will not give up those traditions, because it gives them a lot of power over women. So, that even men with the lowest status have greater status than most women. And when they wrap their control over women in religion, it's impossible to get it out. So, anyone who wants to help women, they see it as an attack on their religion."

Lonnie said, "I respect your feelings, especially since you know it first hand. But, changes won't happen over night. Just because it's may look like the unthinkable now, doesn't mean feelings can't be changed in the future. It may not seem like it, but you can make a difference, even halfway across the world."

"But racism still exists in this country."

"So does sexism, age discrimination, sexual harassment, and a lot of other prejudices, but now they're punishable by law. Those laws were passed in response to the demands of the people. Those laws changed our society. All I'm saying is the world community should embrace these cultures that mistreat women and get them to understand that the world community will not allow them to treat people in this way. We must help them change. The challenge will be doing it in a culturally sensitive way."

"But like Ray said, when men can justify their oppression of women with religion you can't win."

"Yes, it'll be difficult, but given how some women are treated around the world, isn't it worth it?" Lonnie took a deep breath. "Do you know that the women of the Women's Liberation movement, my mother's generation, are still proud of the gift they left to their daughters. *To us*. Women of completely different backgrounds were determined to change society so their daughters would have equal opportunities and a right to control their bodies.

"They had to go through men to get what they wanted. They had to convince men that it was the right thing to do for women and the country. They had to convince men that treating women equally was in their interest too. They met a lot of resistance. The odds were against them. They didn't quit because the odds weren't favorable. They pressed on and won—sometimes in court, sometimes by passing laws, sometimes but electing representatives who would later pass favorable laws. Whether you were Gloria Steinem or the first woman to become a firefighter, those women still feel a strong connection with the history they helped write. That history and those victories are the shoulders you stand on today.

"Now, *you* have the same opportunity to write history and create a whole new platform for future generations of women to stand on. Will you reach out to the oppressed women of the world and help them change their lives? Will you help bring them into our sisterhood? Will you help them enjoy the freedoms and choices that you take for granted? Or will you leave it to another generation to become Tsunami Feminists—Fourth Wave Global Feminists who leave no woman behind.

Chapter 26

I Know

March Thirteenth, Thursday
Monet had been in a funk for a week and a half since her argument with Ray.

She knew he was looking for her, but she had a been avoiding him. The spring quarter had begun, so they no longer had class together. Each night since she had returned from Portland, Monet stayed with a different friend or teammate. She only went to her room to change her clothes and even then it was only for ten minutes. Whenever she returned to her room, she found notes on her door from Ray. She balled them up without reading them.

Her teammates helped not only by letting Monet sleep in their rooms they also provided misinformation to Ray. He looked for Monet in the library when she was in the gym, or looked for her in the Quad when she was really in studying in Kendra's room.

Ray persevered. It became especially difficult once word spread on campus that he was looking for Monet and that she was avoiding him. He started getting propositioned by other women at every turn. One coed who knew the situation stood next to him and said, "You know you're not getting any. Why chase after her when you can get all you need right here?"

"You babes are cold-blooded," Ray said.

"All you have to say is 'yes', big daddy."

Ray shook his head. "Should've caught me three months ago, girl."

"I did. That's how I know what works with you."

Ray barely remembered her.

"Well, not anymore," he said, taking her hand off his arm.

"Yeah, we'll see," she said, walking away.

The women of Del Mar were making it hard on Ray, but he kept looking for Monet between classes, at meals, in the gym. He stopped by her room several times a day, but never ran into her.

Shirlie was tired of the game Monet was playing. It's tough living with a lovesick roommate. The way Shirlie plowed through engineers and other future millionaires, she didn't have much sympathy or patience. There are plenty of men out there to make a connection.

"You need to move on and get a grip," Shirlie said.

Monet was working on a poem, a love letter–to herself–at least that's how it started.

"Nothing worse than liking someone when they don't like you back. And that's why I looked for my deal breakers hard and fast. If they don't have them, I don't waste my time," Shirlie said.

"What are your deal breakers?" Monet asked.

"Well, liking me is pretty important," Shirlie said. "Kissing other women isn't on my list but it's definitely a deal breaker."

"What about when–."

"–Will you stop! Look at you, making excuses, sulking around, writing poems. For what? Because of some guy? A guy that doesn't even like you. Catch the hint. Well, not enough to stop kissing on other women."

Monet said, "I know, that's what it looks like, but–."

"–Didn't your father tell you something about reading the traffic signs of relationships. I'm no expert, but when a guy who is dating me–."

"–We were not really dating."

"That's another issue. But like I was saying, when a guy who's dating me kisses another woman, that's a big red 'DO NOT ENTER'. Isn't that worse than a red light? With a 'Do Not Enter' sign you know you're going the wrong way. Right?" Shirlie said.

"You're right, but–."

"–Listen to your father, heed the traffic signs."

Shirlie wasn't getting through. Monet handed her the poem that Ray had inspired her write.

I know
I know who you are.
I know you by your posture when you're sitting or standing,
*   when listening or speaking.*
I know you by your poise, your purposefulness, your confidence
*   in a crowd or when we're alone.*

I know who you are.
Every turn of your head, your every movement tells me
   something about you.

I know who you are by the sound of your voice, your passion
   for art and your willingness to share what you know.
I know who you are by the way you listen, alert for the meaning
   behind words.
I know who you are even though you do your best to hide it
   from everyone else.

You know I do.
I know you hold your arms open but let no one come close.
I know it's frustrating and unsatisfying because you're hungry
   for someone to share it all with.
I know because I, too, have opened my arms but let no one
   come close.
I know because I know you.
I also know because, like you, I am frustrated and unsatisfied.

I know you know me too.
Your eyes follow me seeking proof that I am who you think I am.
You know I am.
You know because when our eyes meet you see into my soul.
You know because I am bare before your gaze that lights up all
   my dark corners, places hungry for the light of you.
I rise up to meet your touch.
Meeting the light of you beaming down on me.
Basking in the light of intimacy and friendship.
I am known.

And yet, we both know
There can be no real intimacy without trust.
Fear is our first line of defense in the dance of romance.
We must set aside our fear of being known before we lose the
   chance to know each other.
Others will come into your life, but will they really know you?

Shirlie finished reading the poem, looked at Monet and said,
"You have got to be kidding."

*   *   *   *

Tamika had been summoned into Lonnie Delaney's office. When she walked in, Lonnie was looking at her grades for the winter quarter.

"Sit down," Lonnie said, holding up her file. "I got the report on your grades today... 2.15?!"

"The minimum is 2.0 to be eligible to play," Tamika said, quickly.

"No minimums on my team," Lonnie said.

"Why can't you just fix it like the other coaches?" Tamika said.

"I probably could, but I won't."

"Why not?"

"Because the world is unkind to a young black woman whose only skill is scoring, and rebounding."

"Warlich would."

"Last time I checked, you're not playing on the men's team."

"Yeah, but–."

"–I hate to do this but... you're off the team."

"What?"

"You're off the team," Lonnie repeated.

Tamika couldn't believe her ears.

"Coach, all I need to have is a 2.0 to be eligible to play."

"And like *I said*, no minimums on my team. I'm not going to take your scholarship, but you're gonna buckle down and make school a priority if you want to play next year."

Tamika stood up. "You are not going to ruin my chances to play on the Olympic team and the ABL."

"The way you play defense? I'm doing you a favor. You don't think so now, but you're going to need a degree after you're done playing basketball."

"Who do you think you are?"

"Tamika, you've got three more years to play. You can do both. Play *and* get your degree."

Tamika headed for the door. "Yeah, I got three more years, but it won't be playing for you."

*   *   *   *

"What do you mean you're off the team?" Victor said, on the phone.

"I know," Tamika said

"You guys are playing in the NCAA tournament."

"I know, you gotta do something."

"What do you think I can do, write you a note?" Victor sneered.

"You can't call her?" Tamika asked.

"Yeah, okay, 'Hello, Coach Delaney... yeah, this is Victor Bitinour... Yeah, *the sports agent*. Hey, listen, I really need you to reinstate Tamika because I've already given her a lot of money and not allowing her to play really screws up my investment.' You mean like that?"

"What about–."

"–What the hell were you doing all quarter?" Victor asked, shaking his head.

"You said, get 20 and 10. I got 20 and 15," Tamika reasoned.

"But you knew you had to stay in school to play."

"I got a 2.15," Tamika said. "Can't I sue or something?"

"She hasn't taken away your scholarship. You'll never win that argument," Victor said.

"She's not taking me on any of the trips," Tamika said.

"Well, why didn't you just get the 2.25"

"I got my grades up. Plus, I did just what you said."

"I'm sorry, then," Victor said.

"What do you mean?"

"I can't do anything with a player who's not playing. It would be different if you were injured."

"I'm not injured."

"It would be better if you were. You getting kicked off the team questions your character–."

"–I didn't get kicked off the team," Tamika said.

"You got kicked off something. Bottom line is you're not playing. All the best college players are playing come tournament time. Remember what I told you, you're playing in a terrible league on what used to be a terrible team."

"I'm the reason we're not terrible anymore," Tamika said.

"You had some good games against some good teams and you got lucky by getting into the tournament," Victor said.

"Because of me," Tamika yelled.

"Yeah, but you gotta be there to take your team deep into the tournament if not all the way. That's what great players do. That's what great players who play for good coaches do. You may not like Coach Delaney, but she's done a lot in this game. And so, she'll always get the benefit of the doubt."

"So, what are you saying?"

"If you're not playing with your team during the tournament, we're through."

"What about the money?"

"Keep it, but if I were you, I wouldn't tell anyone about it. Otherwise, you'll be the cause of that program getting shut down. I'll deny everything and you'll be left out in the cold."

"I should do it because that bitch won't let me play when I got my grades up." Tamika had never been so mad in her life.

"Don't do it. Bad things will happen and you still won't get what you want. You should listen to Delaney and get your degree while you're at Del Mar. You can do both."

"So you're dropping me, just like that?"

"Tamika, I'm not your agent. I never was your agent. We don't have a signed agreement. I'm just a basketball fan who gave a college friend a little extra spending money," he said.

"... So, that's it?"

"That's the reality."

Lonnie Delaney sat in her office scanning the sports pages. On page seven was the headline, *Del Mar Extends Warlich Contract.* Lonnie couldn't believe it. Not only had Warlich been given a five-year extension on top of the three years remaining on his current contract but he'd also gotten an extra $350,000 a year. He was now making $500,000 a year.

Lonnie shook her head, thinking, "These guys are always trying to hide the ball."

Then she noticed an envelope on her desk. She opened it and read the note: "One of your players is in violation. See me. Dutch."

Damn.

"You wanted to see me," Lonnie said, standing in Forrest Haneline office.

"You get my note?"

"Cut to it," she said. "I have tape to break down."

Haneline's voice was barely a whisper, "Who do you think you're talking to?"

.

Lonnie caught herself. "Listen, I have lot of tape to look at, I'm dead tired. I'm sorry. Ok? Yes, I got your note."

"Then you know who I'm talking about it."

"No, I don't."

"So you can dissect a two-two-one press, but you can't see when one of your players in taking money from an agent?"

"So, who is it?"

"Tamika Hightower. I heard from a good source that she's been getting money from an agent.

"Tamika."

"Yes, Tamika," he repeated. "Haven't you noticed her clothes? No more tiger skins pants."

"Is that your proof? Tamika bought some new clothes, so she must be taking money from an agent? You're kidding, right?" Lonnie said.

"No, I'm not," Haneline said, sitting forward in his seat.

"And who are these sources, probably unnamed sources right?" Lonnie asked.

"Reliable sources."

"Oh, reliable *unnamed* sources."

"I don't like your tone."

"My tone. You tell me this crap like you hope it's true."

"You're not going to bring this university's athletic program down. I'll fire you first!" he said.

"Me? Even if it's true. Football and basketball players get thousands of dollars. Thousands. Not to mention phantom jobs, cash in Federal Express envelopes, sneakers, shopping sprees, airline tickets, money shakes. C'mon, you can't be serious?" Lonnie said.

"So you're admitting it?"

"No, I didn't say that. I have not seen her take anything and I haven't seen any proof."

"But you have noticed the clothes right?" he said.

"To be honest, I was happy she'd gotten a makeover," she said.

"Well, I just want you to know I'll turn you in myself. You're not going to bring this university down," he said, pointing at Lonnie.

"Ohhhh. That's what you really want to keep me quiet. Make me toe the line," she said.

"If you want to coach, you'll toe it. Otherwise, you'll be out." Haneline said. "I built up a lot of goodwill when I gave you that raise–."

"–Without an extension beyond this year."

"Thing is, it should never have come to this. If you just would have listened to me," he said.

"Do what you want me to." Lonnie said.

"Right now, I want you to make all of this go away.."

"I can't make Congress go away."

"You can change your tune. If you change the tune, the party stops. They may still have Congressional hearings, but as long as there is no public pressure, this whole Title IX thing will fade away. Go from being a lead story to an afterthought. Then our lobbyists will do what they do behind the scenes and the whole thing extinguishes itself."

"You think so?" Lonnie said.

"Yes. Now, if you say what I think you're going to say, you'll get some grandstanding Senator, who'll try to impress women voters in home his state. Calling everyone in, demanding assessments and subpoenaing records. It'll get messy. We don't want that. And when you think about it, you don't want that to happen either. So, do us all a favor and change the tune."

"Okay, Dutch," she said.

"Promise me."

"What am I in kindergarten?"

"Promise..."

"I promise," Lonnie said. "There. You happy?"

Flip Mode and Ray were sitting in the Quad doing their usual noon thing, watching women go by. Flip Mode wanted some help in meeting a coed.

"Agent, Shy Guy, Lot on your mind, or Tattoo?" Flip Mode said to Ray. Ray wasn't paying attention. "Agent, Shy Guy, Lot on your mind, or Tattoo?... Ray. Ray."

"Huh?"

"Yo' man, what's up with you?"

"The Utah Jazz are strong."

"Brah, I've been talking to you about them shorties over there for the past five minutes. You're talkin' about Karl Malone. It's four of 'em over there."

"Where?"

"Two o'clock, across the grass, which stunt you wanna pull to meet them. Tattoo, Agent, or Lot on Your Mind?"

"Nah, I'm cool," Ray said.

Ray was preoccupied. He wanted to believe it was the anxiety of his college career coming to an end, pretournament jitters, the upcoming NBA draft season. There was a lot that could have been on his mind. He was watching couples cross the Quad, fixated on their displays of affection. It was spring. They were everywhere. One couple held hands. A guy laid his head on his girlfriend's lap as they talked on the grass. Another couple shared their lunch. Ray watched them laugh and share small intimacies. Watched how they looked at each other and their silent communication. Ray had never had a relationship where he could finish his girlfriend's sentences. He remembered all his encounters during the past school year and not one was worthy of a long-term commitment. Then, again, he wasn't following his mother's advice to treat a girlfriend like a wife, either. He treated them more like playthings, something to be discarded after the novelty wore off. Lately, the novelty wasn't lasting as long as it used to. He didn't know why.

Flip Mode gave up trying to talk to Ray and left. Ray didn't notice him leave. He sat alone in the Quad, enjoying the unseasonably warm sun. A woman cast a shadow as she stood over him. She smiled. He smiled. They both knew what was up. Sometimes that's all it takes. It was good timing. He needed something new to fill the void he was feeling. He'd left another note for Monet but had given up looking for her. Ray knew she didn't want him to find her. So for Ray, The Shadow was in the right spot at the right time.

It was 3:30 in the afternoon when Ray walked to The Shadow's apartment. He didn't know her name and he didn't care. He was going back to the fundamentals, starting with insisting on going to her apartment instead of his room.

That's how to get out of a slump, rely on the fundamentals.

They did their thing. Ray was in first-impression mode, so he put a little extra into his performance to leave no doubt that he was good at making love. When they were done he smiled to himself as he stared at the ceiling of her apartment. She was fast asleep. Snoring like a grizzly bear.

His smile faded as he watched her sleep. Although they had just had sex he felt no attachment to her. The melancholy feeling from the Quad was creeping up on him again. He couldn't make it go away. Ray lifted the Shadow's arm from his chest and rolled her off him. He swung his feet onto the floor and noticed a photo in her purse. It was the basketball team photo. His heart sank.

There were circled X's on the faces of eleven of the fifteen players on the basketball team and four of the six coaches. Ray's smiling face was circled but not x'd. Soon it would be. He stared at each face of the photo. He recalled stories of teammates' locker room conquests. Bits and pieces here and there. Then whole legends. He knew now they weren't legends. The Shadow was the common denominator. Sitting there on her bed, he was embarrassed that he was no better than anyone else who'd fallen for the chance to have easy anonymous sex. The hunter was now the hunted. He hated the thought of being complicit in his own stalking. It made him sick to his stomach.

*   *   *   *

"So how do you know when to cut it off?" Monet said to her father, her cell phone cradled next to her ear. She was driving across the country to San Francisco to play for Lonnie Delaney for her fifth year year of eligibility. She was taking a few weeks to drive cross country, and every few days she called home whenever she felt lonely. It's a blessing any time your young adult child calls home to talk, get advice, or share their feelings. Monet's parents considered themselves extremely lucky.

"I think you should have cut him off a long time ago," her father said.

"Why didn't you say something?" she said.

"Would you have listened?"

"I would have listened, I just might not have done what you said."

"I know," her father said.

"Dad, he was so nice to me. We always had fun together. He made me laugh. He was smart... A little too smart sometimes," she said.

"But."

"I caught him with another woman."

"Yeah, but you saw that coming," he said.

"How was I supposed to see that coming?"

"Traffic signals. People expose their true intentions. It's rare when things just happen out of the clear blue sky," he said.

"It was out of the blue."

"If you watched the traffic signals, you would have seen it coming. The other thing is sometimes even good guys aren't ready for a relationship."

"Tell me about it," Monet sighed.

"That's not to say all of them aren't, but if you meet a great guy in his twenties you may have to go through a lot of heartache until he finds himself," he said.

"Didn't you meet mom when you guys were in your twenties?"

"Yes."

"And?"

"We don't need to get into that," he said.

Monet smiled; she would ask her mother about it some other time.

"So I meet a great guy but like you said, he's got options and issues. What should I do?" she asked.

*"When the time comes, you'll have to answer that for yourself.
But you should ask yourself are you willing to see him through those
years when he's trying to find himself and be the guy you think he
has the potential to be? When he's screwing around, wasting money,
or whatever, that's when it gets tough. It's not going to be easy."*

"Is that what happened with you and mom?"

"This isn't about your mother and me," he said.

"I just want to know."

"What if I don't want to spoil your impression of me?"

*"Dad, I'm twenty-one years old. The damage has already been
done," she said with a smile. He didn't answer. "Dad, it doesn't
make you a bad person."*

*"Your mother saw something in me that I didn't see in myself at
the time, but eventually I became the person she thought I was," he
said.*

"Yeah, you turned 30," Monet laughed.

*"That's the dilemma. Your mother took a big chance on me
because there was no guarantee it would work out for the best."*

"But it did."

*"But I could have easily stayed what I was in my twenties–a
skirt-chasing thirty-year-old on my way to becoming a skirt chasing
forty-year-old."*

"That's not you, dad."

*"Choosing a husband or a wife–I told your brother the same thing–
is the most important decision you'll make. Chose poorly and it could
take you under in many different ways. Money, drugs, infidelity, HIV/
AIDS. Those are big glaring 'Do Not Enter, You are Going the Wrong
Way' signs. Whereas a guy who shows he has a temper, you'll see it as
a yellow 'Caution' sign. You gotta judge everyone individually for
yourself.*

"How am I supposed to see all that coming?"

*"Follow the traffic signs. They tell you when to 'stop' and when
to 'go'. I know you hate listening to me, especially when I'm right,
but just follow the traffic signs. They'll let you know," her father
said.*

"OK. Daddy."

*"No, promise me. Promise you'll watch the signals. I won't be
able to bail you out if you're careless."*

"I promise."

"As long as you do that, you'll be fine."

Chapter 27

Make or Break

March Eighteenth

Ray only had a few days before Monet would be flying off to Iowa City to play the Midwest regional third round game. The Lady Runnin' Rhinos surprised and upset the number four seeded Fighting Illini of Illinois. Then they advanced to the Sweet Sixteen by beating the fifth seeded Duke Blue Devils. Ray and the men had lost in the second round, upset by the Michigan Wolverines. Both teams returned to school late Sunday night but the women would be leaving for Iowa City on Tuesday so they could have a full day and half to prepare for Tennessee.

Ray called Monet's room, knocked on her door, even talked to her teammates, who didn't help him at all. He tried to get a message to her. He even began the message with, "You were right," thinking that would at least get her to call him. It didn't.

Ray had had an epiphany while he was looking at the team photo in The Shadow's purse. He was weary of his past relationships and afraid of what he suspected was self-inflicted desensitizing. He was tired of talking with people who wouldn't tell him the truth about himself. He was ready to hear it now. Monet was the only woman on campus who had been honest with him.

Ray was frustrated. He wanted to tell Monet she was right, but you couldn't find her. He went by her dorm room every 45 minutes. He went to the weight room, library, trainer's room. He waited until after practice, but she slipped out when he wasn't looking.

The more time he spent looking for Monet the more he thought about the way their relationship had evolved over the past six months. He liked Monet's self-confidence, her self-reliance, and her willingness to be herself. She had told him where to get off a couple of times. Told him she didn't want anything from him. At the time, he thought it was just a little reverse psychology, a strategy to distinguish herself from the pack. He realized now, she meant it.

He trusted Monet; she didn't tell Flip Mode, Snag, or any of the fellas about his love for art and poetry. She had even kept quiet about seeing him, book open and all, in the homoerotic section of the bookstore. That would have been disastrous to his all-important image.

Ray liked the fact Monet was principled and wouldn't put up with his mind games to spend more time with him.

Ultimately, he came to understand her point when she told him was telling him he was sabotaging himself by making all of those demands of women.

He saw the character flaws of the women who pursued him. He would never consider them as girlfriends, let alone his wife. He saw now that taking advantage and degrading them had become a defensemechanism. But then he realized that not only was he degrading himself but he was setting himself up to be incapable of having a meaningful and lasting relationship.

He realized Monet wasn't willing to trade her self-respect for his attention. She wouldn't submit to his tests. She stood alone. As a wife and partner she would make her own contribution, have her own identity. He hadn't appreciated the value of that kind of partner until now. The notion had blind-sided him, but he liked it. Monet was also smart, confident, a good kisser... It all had him thinking.

"Hey wait a minute."

Ray knew women where on their best behavior around him so he not only made them women jump through a lot of hoops to spend any time with him but he also started started small disagreements to see how they responded when things got testy.

He wanted to see their personalities in the extreme. So, he paid close attention when women were angry, ecstatic, intoxicated, hungry, disappointed, frustrated, in mourning, or even bored. He wanted to see how they handled themselves because he figured it would be a window into their true personality.

Ray wanted to know if a woman shopped when she got bored, or ate excessively when she was upset? Did she know her limits with alcohol or throw the first thing she got her hands on when she was angry?

Ray remembered all the emotional situations with Monet; when they were mad at each other, when she had had a little too much to drink at the Horney Rhino Bar, and when she was sad and frustrated after a loss. He remembered how she argued with him after she caught him kissing that other that woman. And that was the day *after* she had come up to his room. She didn't throw anything, didn't take a swing at him. He remembered that the argument had gone rather well.

Ray realized Monet was The One.

Monet had all the attributes he was looking for in a girlfriend so he would practice treating her like his wife. Just as his mother said.

He was trying to find Monet to tell her he was ready. He would even be monogamous because he knew it was a sticking point for her.

He wasn't going to propose, but he wanted to ask her if she would allow him to practice on her how he would treat his future wife.

March Eighteenth
Media room, Del Mar University
Press conference

"... At the beginning of the year, none of you thought this team would make it to the NCAA tournament," Lonnie said, to a small throng of reporters.

"Coach, you play Tennessee on Thursday. They're the number one seed and have been in the top three most of the year. How are you going to beat them given all the injuries and the fact you won't let Tamika Hightower play?" said one reporter.

"First of all, Tamika is going to be a great player. She contributed greatly to our success this year, but she violated some team rules–."

"–She's still academically eligible to play, right?" said another reporter.

"Yes, she is," Lonnie answered.

"So, why isn't she playing?"

"Like I was saying, she violated some team rules that she understood could jeopardize her eligibility to play."

"But what did she do?"

"That's between Tamika, me, and the team."

"So she's not academically ineligible and she's not injured."

"No... Any other questions?" Lonnie asked, wanting to move on.

"Yes. Coach, how do you feel about Coach Warlich getting such a huge raise?"

"I think it sends the wrong message, that weeks after a university equalizes the pay of the men's and women's coaches they then

more than double the salary of the men's coach," Lonnie answered.
"It was okay with you when you got the first raise, wasn't it?"
"I don't begrudge Warlich his pay raise, but this university is
not in compliance with Title IX."

"But you've heard the argument that men's basketball and
football earn a lot more money than any of the women's sports."

"We'll never get around that economic reality," Lonnie said.
"But the law still addresses resources, and resources are
supposed to be equal."

"Since when are salaries considered Title IX resources?"

"Listen, I'm not going to debate the merits of the law with you,"
she said. "His salary isn't a direct violation of Title IX, but it is an
example of the inequity between men's and women's college
athletics."

"So, are you saying you should get a raise or they should lower
the men's salary?"

"That extra $350,000 the school pays Coach Warlich could fund
more scholarships for women, improve our locker rooms and buy
better equipment. This isn't about me. So, no, I would not accept
the raise," Lonnie said.

"But you already accepted a raise just last month," the reporter
said.

Lonnie was fed up. She looked around the room. "Anyone
here want to talk about basketball?"

Another reporter said, "The ESPN piece, *Time* magazine,
Disparaging your employer, keeping a talented player off the team
because she didn't reach some arbitrary grade point average,
demanding higher salaries for women and better locker rooms, isn't
that the same kind of sanctimonious decision making that got you
fired and blackballed from coaching three years ago?"

Lonnie stared at the reporter as she struggled to maintain her
composure. Before she answered Lonnie she took a deep breath to
collect her thoughts.

"I promise every parent of every player I recruit, that if their
daughter plays for me, she will graduate. I take that promise very
seriously. In fact, in eight years of coaching college basketball,
102 of 103 of my players have graduated. I know you guys are
writers, so I'll do the math for you, that's 99 percent. How many
men's coaches have that kind of graduation record?" Lonnie looked
around the room and answered for them. "None. How many does
Warlich graduate, 65 percent, which is good. But I've had players

from the South Side of Chicago, the Bronx, Harlem, Compton, West Oakland, The Hill in Pittsburgh, East St. Louis. You want me to go on? Bottom line is, my players graduate because graduating comes *before* basketball... Now does anyone want to talk about basketball?" Lonnie looked around the room.

"What about the rumor that you'll be fired if you don't get to the Final Four?"

"I hadn't heard that," Lonnie Delaney said.

"Well, it comes from a reliable source."

Haneline smiled to himself as he stood at the back of the press conference.

"I expect my teams to make the NCAA tournament every year. When we get there, some times we win it all."

"Yes, but if you don't and you are fired, will you look back on this year and think maybe I shouldn't have brought so much attention to myself with the ESPN interview and the *Time* magazine cover story?"

"I will continue to speak up for women's athletics as long as I am coaching. By the way, the magic number is two-zero."

"What's magical about two-zero?" the reporter asked.

"It's the number of championships my teams have won versus the number Warlich's teams have won." With that, she stepped off the podium and left the room.

March Twenty-first
Carver Hawkeye Arena
Iowa City, Iowa

Monet sat in front of her locker, staring blankly at the photo of Magic Johnson hugging the Larry O'Brien trophy. The look on his face was pure bliss. Monet wanted that feeling. The locker room was unusually quiet. The starters, Monet, Roxy, Clio, Kendra, and Shirlie were all quiet. They had a big challenge ahead of them, beating the number one seeded University of Tennessee Lady Volunteers. The Rhinos had lost to them earlier in the year.

Clio spoke softly to Kendra as they changed clothes. "You hear about Vince Fountainbleu?"

"No, what happened?" Kendra said.

"I was talking with Jeff about the guys who would probably get drafted, right? And there are about four people who have a shot. They're all getting called to schedule workout appointments with teams before the draft. Guess who had all of his appointments canceled?"

Gina was sitting two lockers down. She looked over at Tamika.

"Vince Fountainbleu," Kendra said.

"Yeah? How'd you know?"

"Jeff said he talked to him. And he said he had had like five workouts already scheduled."

"They all canceled?" Clio asked.

"Yep. Jeff said, not only did all the teams cancel on him but when he tried to call other teams, none of them wanted to schedule a workout."

"That's gotta hurt."

"Gonna hurt his wallet."

Gina smiled to herself.

Monet sat quietly, thinking about her last five years, and her battles against Jamila Jetter, in AAU camps and in high school. She thought about losing to Jamila's team in the NCAA championship game their freshman year, then falling off the basketball map for three years. She thought about all her missed shots when the game was on the line and it was up to her to deliver the winning shot.

Monet hated to lose.

That's why she practiced so hard. Shot 200 free throws a day, worked on her game for hours in the off-season in order to be successful in crunch time.

Work before play.

In the three games Monet had played against Jamila Jetter, she hadn't delivered. Those past failures weighed heavily on her mind.

Before the game, Lonnie Delaney gave a short speech, reminding them that the pressure was on the Volunteers to beat the Rhinos. They were the number one seed. It was their season that would be a failure if they didn't get to the Final Four. Nevertheless, they shouldn't be happy just to be in the tournament.

"We play as a team and we'll win." Then Lonnie looked around the locker room.

The players shook hands at mid-court. Jamila Jetter grinned and said to Monet, "Here we go again."

Monet forced a grin in response.

The game was fast paced. Up and down. Turnovers led to points. During the television-mandated time-out, Lonnie Delaney cautioned her team to take care of the ball and value each possession. Midway through the first half, the score was 18-16.

Usually bigger players guards Monet, but this time Jetter had the defensive assignment. Anxious to exploit the size mismatch, Roxy took over the point while Monet posted up Jetter in the paint. Monet missed a jump hook then missed a two-foot lay-up after sealing Jetter nicely with a drop step.

"Another miss by McCasner. It's a bad time to go cold. Tennessee by eight, 24-16. Time out Del Mar," said Thalia Clark, the play-by-play announcer.

In the huddle, Lonnie said, "We've got to take our time. Monet, you're rushing your shot; if Jetter's playing good 'D', just kick it out and reset."

Monet was discouraged. Roxy put her arms around her and told her to cheer up so they could win this game.

It didn't help. Del Mar fell further behind. They really missed Tamika's scoring. They had to rely on Shirlie, Clio, and Kendra to score, but was never their forte. The first half ended with Tennessee leading, 34-22.

Lonnie was calm in the locker room. She figured there was no sense chastising her team when they already looked as if they were beaten. Her calm surprised the team.

Lonnie said, "Look, maybe we should just be glad to be here. That's how you're playing... You guys want to win this or what? We're only down twelve points. *We* can win this game. They're a better team than us. But we can win this game. We've only got nine players, but we can win this game."

The team didn't believe her.

"We'll do it together. Play together. Make some shots. Get some stops. Play together. Rebound. Get out and run. Play together. Cut the lead down to seven by ten minutes. Play together. It all begins with us playing together... Together. Together. Together. Together."

Roxy caught Monet's eye. They both looked at each other for a moment, then to each of their teammates around the locker room. They all made a silent committment to each other.

When the second half started, Tennessee added four more points to their lead, 42-26. Monet was still cold and Kendra was playing tentatively. Lonnie sent in Gina and Mbika to provide some energy. They were a shot in the arm for the team.

Gina set several hard stealth picks crumbling two Volunteer players. Her physical style rattled the Volunteers, who missed several open shots after a few hard fouls. The reserves brought energy. Problem was, they weren't scorers, so the turnovers they created were wasted when they couldn't find a way score.

Monet sat on the bench hoping the game wouldn't slip away. But she wasn't helping with her 2-9 shooting.

Lonnie knelt down in front of her, "Remember, when I told you never take over a game unless I said so?"

"Yeah."

"Well, it's time."

Lonnie sent Monet back into the game. Mbika smacked Monet's hands covering her backside on her way to the scorer's table. Gina and Mbika helped cut Tennessee's lead to 50-42. Roxy put her hand on Monet's shoulder and said, "If we're gonna do this, you gotta shake off Ray, like right now."

Shirlie nodded.

"Let it go, sister girl," Clio added.

Monet put her hand out and they placed theirs on top.

"Together!" they shouted.

Monet was energized. She pushed the tempo and the Rhinos scored six quick points on fast breaks. She guided the team like a general. The chatter was back. "Right there... Yeah, wait for it, it's coming... That's what I'm talkin' about... Nice steal... Run with me. Run with me. Finish that!" Monet's direction gave the team confidence. The more she talked, the better they played.

With 2:25 remaining, Monet brought the ball up the court. She head-faked as if she was going to shoot a jump shot, but when Jamila put her hand up to contest the shot, Monet drove hard to the basket to score a lay-up.

Two minutes remained, the score was Tennessee 59, Rhinos 56 the Volunteers had the ball. Jamila Jetter dribbled the ball around and used most of the forty-five-second shot clock to shorten the game and limit Del Mar's scoring opportunities. Lonnie told her team not to foul. It was frustrating for Monet because the game was slipping away and she couldn't do anything about it. With a minute and twenty seconds remaining Jamila Jetter took a shot. She missed, but the Volunteers got the offensive rebound. The shot clock was reset. Lonnie Delaney told the team not to foul.

"Sixty seconds.... Fifty five... The Rhinos are not going to foul..." Clark said.

Jamila made a pass and Roxy stole it. They were off to the races on the fast break, Roxy was flanked by Monet and Mbika. Roxy passed it to Mbika who passed it back, running a textbook three-on-one fast break. Roxy passed to Monet, who passed the ball back. The ball never touched the floor.

Deja' vu.

As they passed the three-point line, the defender would have to make a decision. She had to choose one out of the three. The Volunteer defender remembered from watching video tape that Roxy tended to pass on fast breaks, so she had to guess if the pass would be to Monet on the left or Mbika streaking in from the right.

Roxy faked a pass to Monet then threw a no-look pass to Mbika, who was coming in for the lay-up. The Volunteer defender guessed correctly, and challenged Mbika. She missed the lay-up but was fouled. Mbika didn't make the lay-up so she would shoot two free throws. There were 48 seconds remaining. Tennessee 59, Rhinos 57.

Monet wasn't confident Mbika would make the free throws. She was right. Mbika missed them both.

The Rhinos were down two points. The Volunteers had the ball. The Rhinos didn't foul. At twenty seconds, Mbika was trying to get into position for a rebound, and a Volunteer player elbowed her in the throat. The good news: The Rhinos were in the bonus, so it was a turnover, the bad news was Mbika would have to shoot the one-and-one free throws. If she didn't make the first one she wouldn't get a second.

The last person Monet wanted to shoot free throws was Mbika. Monet wanted the ball, but couldn't get her hands on it.

Mbika was nervous as she crept up to the foul line. The pressure was enormous. Her teammates were depending on her. Her university was depending on her. The Volunteers were looking at her, putting on the hex.

The referee bounce passed her the ball. She took three dribbles, looked up at the rim, raised the ball to shoot and... *Ch-kh.* Tennessee 59, Del Mar 58. Second shot: Mbika crept to the foul line again, received the bounce pass, three dribbles, raised to shoot... *Ch-kh.*

"Tennessee is up one, 59-59. Twenty seconds. Tennessee wants to hold it for the last shot. Rhinos need a quick steal but no fouls."

The Rhinos put on a full-court press. The well-coached Volunteers broke the press with composed passing. When they crossed half-court, there were thirteen seconds left.

Jamila Jetter was guarded by Monet. This was it. Just like old times. The two best players on the court going at it.

"Jamila Jetter starts her move at the top of the key. Seems a little early. Dribble drive through the lane. Spin move, fade awaaay. Blocked by McCasner!"

Monet scooped up the ball, took one quick peek at Lonnie, who was pointing up the court. She knew what that meant–don't call time-out.

Play-by-play: "Rhinos up the court, seven seconds, McCasner pushing it on the break. McCasner, half-court. Tennessee gets back on defense. Five seconds. McCasner and Jetter, *mano a mano*. McCasner, top of the key, drifts to the left wing. Gotta go! Three seconds. McCasner fakes left then dribbles right. Two. At the free throw, one second, fifteen-foot pull-up jumperrrrrr... Good! IT'S GOOD! IT'S GOOD!!! Monet McCasner makes the biggest shot of her college career with a last-second jump shot over the outstretched arms of Jamila Jetter. Jetter played good defense, but sometimes the offense makes an even better play. The Del Mar Runnin' Rhinos upset the heavily favored and number one seeded Tennessee Lady Volunteers ,61-59.

"Jetter was right there, but in the end she was too small, as McCasner shot over the top of Jetter's outstretched arms. This is the kind of win that can put a program on the map. Beating a heavily favored Lady Vol team that most people picked to go to the Final Four and win it all."

Thalia Clark said, "Let's go to Courtney Heinz to talk with Monet McCasner.

"Monet, great shot, what were you thinking when you blocked Jetters' shot with seven seconds left."

"I knew I needed to get it up the court in a hurry. Six seconds is a lot of time after a turnover."

"Why didn't you call time-out?"

"We've practiced this many times before; by not calling time-out we didn't give the defense a chance to set up. So, my first thought was to get it up-court as fast as possible. I've been working on this move a friend of mine taught me where I dribble hard to the goal, then pull up for the shot. I got a good look and knocked it down."

"Well whoever that friend is, they deserve a big hug when you get back to Del Mar. Back to you..."

Chapter 28

Holding Court

April Ninth, Wednesday
Lonnie and Monet stood in the Hall of Champions perusing the trophy cases. The team had played their last game the night before and just returned from the airport. It had been a roller coaster year; pregnancy, domestic violence, the longest cat fight they had ever seen. Lonnie had been on the cover of *Time* magazine and subpoenaed by Congress. Monet never made a love connection. Lonnie received a $100,000 raise, then watched her male counterpart get a $350,000 raise and a five-year contract extension. As they stood staring in front of one particular trophy, they felt it was all worth it.

"We did it," Lonnie said.

"We did it," Monet said. "I still don't know how."

"I was so proud of you after the Tennessee game. I know how much that win meant to you. It was a real breakthrough," Lonnie said.

"What are you going to do now?" Monet asked.

"Look at some offers."

"I hope you, make 'em sweat for not treating you better," Monet said. "You should take some time, go on a date, or something."

Lonnie laughed, "Dan and I are working on somethings."

"Ohhh, okay. Do your thang, coach," Monet said.

"What are you going to do?" Lonnie asked.

"Take a little time, I'm thinking about staying here in San Francisco after graduation."

"If you do, I've got a job for you."

"I still can't believe we did it," Monet said, hugging Lonnie.

"You have been calling them losers since September."

Jennifer poked her head in. "There you are. People are looking all over for you." Monet said good-bye to Lonnie.

"Figures. The phone has been ringing off the hook," Lonnie said, waving Jennifer in.

"Are you leaving?"

"I don't know. You know I only had a one-year contract."

"But you got a raise," Jennifer said, raising an eyebrow.

"A raise, but no extension."

"They'd be pretty stupid to let you go."

"Thanks, Jenn." Lonnie knew Jennifer's sentiments were unrealistic, but it felt good to hear it.

"Thank you for being there for me," Jennifer said.

"I just told you to think about it... and tell your parents."

"It's going to be tough, but I'm gonna make it work."

"I'll make sure the school is there for you, so you can keep your scholarship, play basketball, *and* be a mom."

Jennifer paused then said, "Gina tell you about her letter writing campaign against Vince Fountainbleau?"

"She did," Lonnie answered.

"None of the teams invited him to work out. Not one."

"I have to admit, it made me smile when the sports information director told me, the Pittsburgh Steelers, his favorite team, told him his character was in question and he would never represent the Steelers, not even as a mascot. If he doesn't make it, this'll be the kind of thing that could haunt him for the rest of his life," Lonnie said.

"After what he did to Gina, it's probably a fair trade."

"There you are," Forrest Haneline said, possitively giddy. "I've been looking all over for you. I'm looking forward to the big check from the NCAA tournament win. So how does it feel?"

"Coach, I'll talk to you later," Jennifer said.

"Yeah, thanks Jenn," Lonnie waved goodbye. "Now, what did you say?" turning back to Forrest Haneline.

"NCAA. National Champions. Big Check," Haneline said.

"You know, it's been a rough year, Dutch."

"Sure, but how does it feel to win the national championship? I mean, with these players. It must be really satisfying. I hate to say I told you so, but–."

"–You told me what?"

"That you're a winner."

"A winner with a one year contract?" Lonnie looked at him quizzically. "Maybe we should extend it for five years," he said.

"You can keep that contract and–."

"–You think about it."

"I've got some offers," she said.

"Already?"

"News travels fast when athletic directors see you cut down the nets on television, hoise the trophy, and they know you don't have a long-term contract. Let's face it, that's what changed your tune."

"Speaking of that, are you still going to play down the Title IX stuff when you go before Congress, like you promised?"

Haneline had come to recognize that look in Lonnie Delaney's eyes. Bad things happened shortly thereafter.

"You get our subpoena yet?" she asked.

"Don't do it Lonnie. Believe me, Congress won't stop with equal resources. You know the questions they'll ask."

"You're afraid then," Lonnie said. "Because you won't have good answers. So, why can't student-athletes get a stipend when coaches can get hundreds of thousands of dollars to make their athletes wear certain sneakers or endorse products?"

"Okay Lonnie, you're right. But along the way you could bring the whole thing down. Is that what you want?" Haneline asked.

"The NCAA should do what's right."

"And what good would it do?"

"When I go before Congress, you guys just want me to act like the tobacco executives, tell lies with a straight face. You need to ask yourself, how will you answer when the Senator from California asks you 'Aren't NCAA eligibility rules un-American? As the president of the NCAA eligibility committee, how can you justify exploiting young people like this?' How will you answer that question, Dutch?"

Haneline was silent as he tried to find an answer.

"Your answer had better be better than that," Lonnie said.

"Be reasonable Lonnie, if the NCAA is bankrupt, what will you do?"

"As I see it, the NCAA is nothing more than a big scheduler of games between universities of similar size athletic programs and even then most schools belong to regional leagues. We don't even really need the NCAA," she said.

"Don't be surprised if women's team sports are the first to go because they are not profitable in a free market system. The NCAA facilitates women's athletics so they are not ignored."

"We can avoid all of this," Lonnie said.

"Name what you want. A five year deal. A ten year deal."

"Is the money going to come from the same hush money pot you used to give Gina a scholarship?"

"No, this is coming from the Chancellor, Father Maloney."

"That's a big blank check," Lonnie said.

"We don't want this to get ugly, Lonnie. Let's sit down and talk about it," Haneline said, almost pleading.

"Lots of changes would have to be made," Lonnie said, not budging.

"We want to do what's right," Haneline hedged.

"Practice times and scholarships?" Lonnie asked.

"Fifty-fifty."

"Locker rooms?"

"We'll budget for eight brand-new individual women's team locker rooms. Now that we have the cash."

"Radio contract?"

"I'll work on it." Haneline could tell Lonnie didn't like his answer. "Okay, okay. The season's ratings were much better than anyone expected. But who knew?"

"I knew."

"Okay. Okay. You were right," Haneline said.

"Again," she said.

"I'll try to get a commercial station to pick up the games. I even heard the woman doing your games got an offer to do WNBA games this summer," Haneline said.

"What about women's coach's salaries."

Haneline swallowed hard. "We'll make them equal."

"What happened to supply and demand?"

"Four million dollars buys me some time to find more money. Anything else, while you've got me over a barrel."

"Doesn't Warlich have an escape clause that says he can leave for any school on his elite list?"

"Uh, yeah, but–."

"–I'll give you my list in a couple of days." Lonnie cut him off.

"So you'll stay?" Haneline sounded hopeful.

"First, I want to see the plans for the new women's locker rooms, in writing. We can talk in a couple of day."

"Good, I'm glad we could reach an agreement. I told you when you first arrived here, this could be a good situation for you. I'm glad I was able to help you get back into coaching," Haneline said.

Lonnie had begun to walk out of the room. She looked over her shoulder and said, "You put it together, then we'll see."

*   *   *   *

Monet shot a round, alone, in the arena. Ray heard the bouncing ball and took a peek to see who was shooting. He was hoping it was Monet. He hadn't seen her since her team had won the national championship.

"If I didn't know better, I would swear you were are avoiding me," Ray said.

"I've been a little busy. You know, winning the national championship,"

"You couldn't wait for that, huh?" huh said.

"You deserve it, calling me a loser."

"'I said you were not a winner, there's a difference."

"Don't try to be all cool about it, because I know it's killin' you inside," Monet said.

"I'm happy for you. You listened to The Man, followed The Man's plan, and now look at you. You had to go about it in your own spoiled diva way, but you still came through. No one can take credit for that. That's all you."

Monet smiled. "You were right, it does feel way better than losing."

"The NBA draft is in June. Believe me, I'm feeling good too."

"Yeah well, you're still an a–."

"–How long are you gonna hold that against a brotha?"

"You don't get to just walk up, say 'Ah, baby I knew you were a winner all along and it will be okay."

"I said I was happy for you winning the national championship."

"But you still kissed her and whatever else," Monet said.

"Please let me know when you're changing the subject."

"I changed it."

"I see. You sure you don't want me to bask in your glory some more? I can do it in Shakespeare?"

"No!"

"What can I do that's more significant than an apology? How 'bout a proclamation. 'I proclaim that from this day forth'..."

"It happened two weeks ago."

"Retroactive to the tenth day, of the third month, in the year of our Lord–."

"Begging is effective, too," she smiled; he was getting through.

Ray looked around the arena to see if the coast was clear. He got on his knees, bowed, and kissed the laces of her shoes. Monet looked around, a little embarrassed for him but still impressed by the display.

Like a benevolent monarch she bent over and lifted his chin from the floor. "I don't like it when you're on your knees."

He stood up, and they embraced. She looked into his eyes searching for the truth.

"What are you looking for?" Ray said.

"Traffic signals."

"What?"

"Never mind," Monet said.

"Hey, you ever get any more letters from that guy?"

"No, thank God. I think all the photos around campus scared him off."

"Yeah. Can I admit something without you getting mad?" Ray asked.

"Are you going to confess to being the rapist?" Monet teased.

"No." Ray laughed.

"Then go ahead," she said.

"I was worried about you. Especially after the incident in the library. So..."

"So what?"

"So, I've been discreetly following you around. You know to make sure you get to where you're going," he said. That is until you started ditching me."

"Awwwwwww. How sweet is that? My thoughtful stalker protector," Monet said, hugging him again. "You know, if you weren't such an a-hole you might be good boyfriend material."

It took Ray a couple of seconds to comprehend her back handed compliment.

"You don't believe I can be a great boyfriend, do you?"

"You want the truth?"

"Yeah," he said, bracing for a reality check.

Monet shrugged. She was torn. As much as she liked the idea, his history made her proceed with caution. It felt wrong and right at the same time. The Do Not Enter sign was flashing.

"Let's play for it then," Ray said.

"Play for what? Your sincerity?" Monet asked.

"Uh, yeah?... Name the game."

"Strip."

Ray looked around. "Here?"

"S-T-R-I-P. It's like Horse, but we'll spell strip," Monet said.

"All right."

"By the way, after every letter *you* have to take off one piece of clothing."

Ray looked himself over. He wasn't wearing much. He had on shorts, a tank top, a jockstrap, shoes, and socks.

Monet shot a twenty footer.

Ch-kh.

Ray missed. "Damn!"

"'S.'"

"Do shoe strings count?"

Glossary

ABL
American Basketball League. Women professional league which functioned from in fall of 1996 to 1999. Now defunct.

ACL
Anterior Cruciate Ligament. A stabilizing ligament under the knee cap. Common injury among female athletes in sports that require jumping, quick acceleration and quick changes of direction. Women are 2 to 8 times more likely than men to sustain this injury.

Aight   *Slang.* "All right." Used by urban hipsters.

Air ball   A shot that entirely misses the backboard, rim, and net.

Alley-oop
A pass thrown with a high arc near the basket so a teammate can make a leaping catch and score in a single motion.

Assist
The last *pass* to a teammate that leads directly to a *field goal*; the scorer must move immediately toward the *basket* for the passer to be credited with an assist; only one assist can be credited per field goal.

Back cut   See *Backdoor cut*

Back pick
To set a screen behind the defender who is guarding the screener's teammate.

Backboard
A 6-by-4-foot rectangular wood or fiberglass structure that holds the basket.

Backcourt
1. The area from the centerline to the baseline nearest the basket being defended by the team.
2. A team's point and shooting guards, considered as a unit, as in, "Del Mar has an excellent backcourt."

Backdoor play/cut
A play on which an offensive player slips behind the defense along the baseline, usually from the weak side, to receive a pass.

Backdoor pass A pass thrown to a player after making a backdoor cut.

Baseline
1. One of the two lines that mark the lengthwise boundaries of the court.
2. A loosely defined area just inside the baseline; used in phrases such as, "He drove the baseline and made a lay-up."

Basket
1. The goal in basketball, made up of a metal rim 18 inches in diameter, suspended 10 feet above the floor, with a corded net 15 to 18 inches long.
2. A field goal.

Big Dance   See *NCAA Tournament.*

Bigs   See *frontcourt, definition 2.*

B.M.O.C
Abbrv. Big Men On Campus. Acknowledged social elite of university.

Blocked shot
A shot that is deflected from its course toward the basket by a defensive player before it has reached its highest point, thus preventing a field goal.

Blocking
Using any part of the body or impede an opponent's progress; a personal foul. Compare *charging.* See *established position.*

Blowout A double-digit scoring lead of 15 or more points.

Boom-shaka-la-ka   *Slang.* Intimate relations.

Bounce pass   A pass thrown to a teammate on one bounce.

Bootie
Gluteus Maximus. Used to bump other players to create space to rebound and/or score.

Box out
To position oneself between the basket and an opposing player in order to get a rebound, usually by a defensive player. Use of *Bootie* is required.

Brick
A poor shot, usually thrown on a low trajectory, that bounces hard off the rim or backboard.

Bucket   Another name for the basket or a field goal.

Burqa
Traditional women's clothing worn by Afghani women. It covers her entire body, with only a square five-inch mesh opening allowing her to see.

Buttonhook
Football term. A route run by wide receivers where they run straight then quickly turn left or right toward the quarterback to receive a pass.

Center
A player who is generally in the center of the offense, usually the tallest player on a team, who takes the tip-off and is usually stationed in a post position on offense. The Five position.

Center line
Line in middle of the court, 47 feet from the baseline. Divides the front court from the backcourt. Also called *midcourt* or *halfcourt*.

Chicken-head An undesirable woman.

Ch-kh
Sound. The sound a ball makes when it through the net. Also *swish.*

Charging
An offensive foul committed when a player runs into a defender who has established position and is essentially motionless. If the defender has not established position, and there is contact, it is blocking, a defensive foul. See *established position.*

Chest pass
A two-handed pass starting from the chest with elbows out.

Choke
1. To be unsuccessful in a close game, a game a team is expected to win or shooting the game winning shot/free throw.
2. To succumb to the pressure of not performing well in a close game.

Close the passing lane
To intercept or deflect a would-be pass. Considered good defense. See *passing lane.*

Coast to coast
The entire length of the court; used to describe a player's movement on the court. E.g., "He grabbed the rebound and went coast to coast for a lay-up at the other end."

Come to the ball
When the receiver of a pass moves toward the ball to prevent a defender from stealing it away. Compare *shielding a pass.*

Composed passing
Passing the ball with care to avoid a steal or turnover.

Cornerback   A football player who defends wide receivers.

Court
The playing area for a game of basketball. College and NBA courts are 94 feet long by 50 feet wide. The court is bounded by baselines and sidelines and is divided in half by a center line.

Court vision
A player's ability to see everything on the *court* during play—such as where his teammates and defenders are set up—which enables him to make better choices in *passing*; the best point guards have good court vision.

Crab dribble
Post player dribble used to back into the defender to get closer to the basket, taking one step backwards by alternately pivoting off each foot while dribbling.

Crossover dribble
A dribble on which the ball is moved across the body, from one hand to the other.

Crunch time　See *Winning time.*

Cut
A quick change in direction, to elude a defender or find an open area on the floor. As a verb, to make a cut to the basket.

Cutoff man
Baseball term. An infielder an outfielder should relay the ball to when throwing to the infield.

Dagger
Game deciding shot. Also, a shot that significantly increases the probability of that team winning the game.

Dap
A hand greeting or acknowledgment of something good. One person gently pounds his closed fist over the top of another's closed fist.

Dime　An excellent pass leading to a score. An assist with flair.
　　　ie., She dropped a sweet dime on the fast break.

Diva
A woman who requires constant attention and service of her whims. High-maintenance woman.

Diva Tamer
A man in a relationship (platonic or intimate) with a diva who can delicately navigate her whims, while not becoming a sycophant. He has the condifence and ability to tell a diva the truth without worry about the consequences or her temper. A required confidant fordivas in order to keep her egomaniacal sensibilities under control.

Double-team
To guard one player with two defenders. Also used as a noun.

Down pick
When a player starts from the free throw or wing to set a screen for a player on the low block.

Dream team
The name given by the media to the U.S. basketball team that won the gold medal at the 1992 Barcelona Olympics; it was the first time non-amateurs were permitted to represent the country; the members of this team were Charles Barkley, Larry Bird, Clyde Drexler, Patrick Ewing, Magic Johnson, Michael Jordan, Christian Laettner, Karl Malone, Chris Mullin, Scottie Pippen, David Robinson and John Stockton. In the 1996 Olympics, the U.S. team was called Dream Team II and in 2000, Dream Team III.

Dribble To bounce the ball repeatedly with one hand, while moving or standing still. Also as a noun, the act of dribbling.

Drive
An aggressive move toward the basket with the ball with the intent to make a lay-up. As a verb, to make a drive to the basket.

Drive and kick
A decoy move, where a player drives to the basket but with the intent to draw in defenders so he/she can pass the ball out to the wing or corner for a jumpshot-usually a three-point attempt.

Drop step
A move on which a player, back to the basket, takes a step back on the side of a defender behind him, then turns and drives past him on that side.

Drop-off pass
A pass made to a teammate after driving to the basket. Usually made in response to a defender, well positioned, to block the lay-up. Also, *Dime*.

Elite Eight
Teams that play in the fourth round of the NCAA tournament.

Established position
To have the feet firmly planted on the floor, occupying an area, before the offensive player arrives in that area. The difference between blocking and charging is whether the defender has established position.

Fadeaway
A jump shot on which the player jumps somewhat backward as well as up before launching the shot, to make it more difficult to block.

Fake
A deceptive move to throw a defender off balance and allow an offensive player to *shoot* or receive a *pass*; players use their eyes, head, shoulders, or any other part of the body to trick an opponent. Also done with a ball.

Fast break
1. A play on which a team moves the ball quickly down court toward the opposing basket in an attempt to get a quick, open shot outnumbering the defense.
2. An overall strategy in which a team seeks to get as many fast breaks as possible in the course of a game.

Field goal
A score made from the field during the course of play, worth two or three points, depending on the shooter's position. See also three-point field goal.

Final Four
The fifth round of the NCAA tournament. The four regional champions (formerly West, East, Midwest and Southeast) remaining from the 64 college teams that compete in the annual *NCAA Tournament*; play one another to determine the national champion.

Finger roll
A close-range shot on which the shooter lets the ball roll gently off his/her flicking fingertips toward the basket.

Finish   To score as planned. To make a lay-up on a fastbreak or make an open jumpshot.

Fittle'een   Fifteen Points. Domino scoring term.

Flare out
When a player starts on the baseline then quickly runs to the corner or wing to receive a pass. Compare *run out*.

Flash
When a player starts from outside the free throw lane then moves quickly through the free throw lane in order to receive a pass close to the basket for a shot. Players move through with their hands up and facing out, shoulder height, to be ready to receive the pass.

Flossin'   *Slang.* To show off. Not related to dental hygiene.

Forward
One of two players who usually operate near a corner, on both offense and defense. See *power and small forward.*

Four-point turnaround
When a team will likely score a field goal, but makes a turnover or violation that leads to the immediate score of their opponent.

Four-point play
A three-point field goal on which the player is fouled in the act of shooting and makes the consequent free throw. Compare *three-point play.*

Free throw
An undefended shot taken from the free throw line. Players from the two teams line up alternately on both sides of the free throw lane, with two players from the team that committed the foul closest to the basket. They aren't allowed to enter the lane or the free throw circle until the ball is released from the shooter's hand. A successful free throw is worth one point.

Free throw lane
One of two painted areas between the baseline and the free throw line. 12 feet wide in college and high school play. Players must stay outside the lane during a free throw attempt and an offensive player cannot spend more than three seconds in the lane. See also *paint.*

Free throw line
One of two lines, 12 feet long and 2 inches wide, marked 19 feet from and parallel to the baseline (15 feet from the backboard), from which a player attempts a free throw.

Free throw line extended
An imaginary line, through the free throw line to the sidelines, which determines the location for some throw-ins. Used also for player positioning. Also *wing*.

Frontcourt
1. The area from the centerline to the baseline nearest the basket being attacked by a team.
2. A team's center and forwards, as a unit.

Frosh First year students or players at a university. Alternative term for freshman.

Full court press
A swarming defense where players frantically pester the offense from the moment they put the ball in play with the goal of stealing the ball or causing a turnover.

Garbage time
Time in the game where the outcome is certain–when the lead is insurmountable within the time remaining. The best players are substituted for significantly less talented players. Time in a game that is usually marred by poor and frequent shot selection.

Gear(s)
1. Personnel management technique. Different response approaches to handling personnel, problems, and situations. As in, *when managing people you need lots of gears.*
2. The ability to run at different speeds while playing. Usually refers to a player who can run faster than everyone when needed. As in, *he reached for an extra gear on the fast break.*

Give-and-go
A play on which a player passes to a teammate, then cuts toward the basket, ready to receive a return pass.

Go-to Guy
The player the team depends on to score in a close game with time running out. See *The Man* and *PTPer.*

Guard
1. One of two players who usually operate from somewhere behind the free throw line in the frontcourt when on offense. They are typically responsible for bringing the ball out of the backcourt, setting up plays, and taking outside shots. Compare *point guard* and *shooting guard*.
2. To follow an opposing player while on defense with the intent of preventing him/her from scoring.

Half-court   See *centerline.* Also called *midcourt.*

Half-court press
A defense that's applied as soon as the opposing team gets the ball across the centerline.

Hand check
To use one or both hands, intermittently or continuously, on an opposing player, especially the ball handler. A personal foul.

Handles
To have exceptional dribbling control of the basketball. Used as an adjective, as in, she had *handles.*

High post
An area near the free throw line, where the center is often positioned.

Hook shot
A one-handed shot on which the player is sideways to the basket and the ball is released above the head from the hand farthest from the basket. Also see *Jump hook.*

Hurdler's stretch
Sitting stretch where one leg is forward and straight and the other leg is bent and angled at 90 degrees.

Inbound pass
To pass the ball into the court from out of bounds. Starts game action. Game clock is started when the ball is touched by a player on the court. Occurs often e.g., after violations, made free throws and field goals.

Inlet pass
A pass made, usually from the wing, to a center or forward in the post on the low block.

Jab step
A deceptive move made with the ball (before dribbling) by extending one foot toward one side of the defender to elicit a reaction then moving quickly in the opposite direction before the defender can get back into position

Juke　　See *fake.*

Jump ball
Two opposing players jump for a ball that an *official* tosses above and between them, to tap it to their teammates and gain *possession*; used to start the game (*tip-off*) and all *overtime periods*, and sometimes to restart play.

Jump hook
A hook shot launched while jumping. Compare *Hook shot.*

Jump shot
A shot on which the shooter jumps into the air and releases the ball from above the head before landing, making it difficult to block.

Key
The area encompassing the free throw circle and free throw lane; so named because it was shaped like a keyhole when the lane was narrower than the free throw circle. See *free throw lane.*

Lay-up
A shot on which the shooter leaps up from near the basket and banks the ball off the backboard gently with one hand.

Lay-up line
Two lines of players formed, usually before the beginning of each half, where players in one line shoot lay-ups and the players in the other line grab the rebound and passes the ball to the players in line to shoot lay-ups.

Lead pass
When a *passer* throws the ball toward the place where he thinks a *receiver* is headed.

Lineup
1. Player positions around the free throw lane during a free throw. Team players are positioned alternately with the defensive players being closest to the basket in the low block position.
2. The starting players.

Low block/low post
An area near the basket, just outside the free throw lane where the defense on a free throw lines up. Marked by a twelve-inch by five inch block near the lower portion of the outside free throw lane closest to the basket. *Centers* and Power forwards are often positioned here. Similar to *low post*.

Man-to-man defense
A defense in which each player is responsible for guarding a specific opponent.

March Madness   See *NCAA tournament.*

Matchup problem
Any pairing of two players on opposing teams where one player has a significant advantage of size, quickness, or talent.

Midcourt   See *center line.* Also called *half-court.*

Mismatch   See *Match up problem.*

Naismith, James
Inventor of the game of basketball. Canadian, clergyman, educator, and physician who formulated the game of basketball in 1891 at the Young Men's Christian Training Association School (now Springfield College) in Springfield, Massachusetts. Teams originally had nine players and used a soccer ball and peach baskets for goals.

NBA
National Basketball Association. A professional basketball league, created in 1946 with 11 teams, that now has 30 teams in the U.S. and Canada.

NCAA
National Collegiate Athletic Association. A voluntary association of 1,251 colleges and universities in the United States whose role is to establish standards and protect the integrity of amateurism for student-athletes. There are three division I, II, and III with Division Ia considered to be the top.

NCAA Tournament
Annual competition for 64 college teams to crown a national collegiate basketball champion. First tournament held in 1939. Also called *March Madness* because the three-week-long event is held during March.

NIT National Invitational Tournament.
The oldest college tournament, first held in 1938, in which 32 teams not selected for the *NCAA Tournament* compete each year.

Needle-threading pass
Pass that *narrowly* travels between two defenders. See *passing lane.*

No-man's-land
1. On defense, the area on the court where a defender can neither effectively guard the player with the ball nor guard another player who could receive a pass.
2. On offense, when players cannot avoid a collision because they jumped into the air and a defender has established position. Usually results in a foul.

Offensive foul
A personal foul committed by an offensive player.

Offensive rebound
A rebound of a teammate's shot, or of one's own shot. Compare *put back.*

Off-top   *Slang.* "From the beginning."

OG
Abbrv. for *Original Gangster.*
1. Older member of an urban, primarily, African-American gang.
2. Someone who has been around a long time.

On the block Player positioned on the low block.

One-on-one A free throw attempt awarded in certain situations in high school and college basketball in which the player gets a second free throw only if the first attempt is successful.

Open When a player is unguarded by a defender.

Open jump shot
When a player has clear space to shoot an uncontested jump shot.

Opposite side pick Also *weak side screen*

Outlet pass or Outlet
A pass made immediately after a defensive rebound, typically to a teammate who is starting a fast break. Compare *inlet pass.*

Paint, or, in the paint
Descriptive of a location in the free throw lane, because it's painted a different color from the rest of the court. Also see *free throw lane.*

Pass To throw the ball to a teammate. Also see *bounce pass, chest pass, inlet pass, outlet pass, needle threading pass and passing lane.*

Passing lane
An opening between defenders through which the ball can be passed to a teammate.

Personal foul
A foul that involves physical contact between
opposing players. Among the most common personal fouls are blocking, charging, elbowing, hacking, and holding. A player is disqualified from the game after committing five fouls.

Pick Same as *Screen.*
Informal, *a steal*

Pick and roll
Offensive play on which a player sets a screen, then pivots and heads toward the basket to receive a pass. Same as *screen/roll*

Pickup game Impromptu game played among players who just met.

Playmaker
1. The player who usually works to set up plays for his teammates; almost always the point guard.
2. A player who consistently comes up with big plays when needed. See *The Man* and *PTPer.*

Play within yourself
To consciously play fundamentally sound basketball. To do the skills one is proficient in and avoid those he/she isn't.

Point guard
The player who usually brings the ball upcourt for his team and runs the offense. Usually a good dribbler. The One position. Compare *shooting guard.*

Poo' nani power
Persuasive technique used by women to get men to acquiesce to their needs, suggestions or desires using intimacy as a motivator.

Post
A position just outside the free throw lane, either near the basket or near the foul line. See *high post*; *low post.*

Post up
To establish a position in the low post, usually in order to take advantage of a smaller defender.

Pound
A greeting or acknowledgment of something positive by lightly hitting the top of one another's fists. A noun. See *dap.*

Power forward
A tall, strong, and bulky forward who can score from near the basket and get rebounds. The Four position. Compare *small forward.*

Power up
A shot attempted near the basket where a player jumps off two feet, extending up to the basket. Used in anticipation of heavy contact from a defender.

Princeton backdoor
See *backdoor play*. Named after the offense used by longtime Princeton coach Pete Carrill.

PTPer
Prime Time Player. Term made popular by college basketball analyst, Dick Vitale. See *The Man* or *Go-to Guy*

Pull-up jumper
A shot when a player who is dribbling toward the basket stops and shoots a jump shot.

Put back
A shot when a player grabs an offensive rebound then shoots a lay-up to score a field goal.

Real talk
Slang. Veracity. A statement used to affirm that something is true. Also, *true that* and *that's real.*

Rebound
1. A carom of the ball off the backboard after a missed shot.
2. Gaining possession of the ball after it has come off the backboard. As a verb, e.g., To get a rebound.

Red shirt
An *NCAA* eligibility classification for a player who is officially on the team but cannot play in games. Generally, collegiate players have five years to play four, the red shirt year being the classification of the nonplaying year. Red shirt players may practice with the team.

Release
1. The moment the ball leaves a *shooter's* hands.
2. The moment the defensive player stops rebounding and begins to run on up the court on offense.

Reverse lay-up
A lay-up made when the shooter crosses under the basket to lay the ball in on the other side, usually to avoid the shot being blocked on the original side of attack.

Role player
A player on the team who has a specific assignment(s) during games that is essential to winning, but is usually not glamorous, e.g., rebounding and playing solid defense while leaving the scoring duties to other players.

Roll
When a player, starting with their back to the basket, makes a quick turning motion around a defender, followed by a break to the basket. See also *pick and roll.*

Run out
To contest a jump shot and then, without rebounding or boxing out the shooter, run down the court ahead of the other player. Strategy used by the defense to get a quick lay-up in transition if the shooter misses. The defense gets the rebound and makes a quick outlet pass upcourt.

Run, a
Occurs when one team scores several *field goals* in quick succession while its opponents score few or none.

Salwar Kameez   Traditional Indian women's clothing.

Scissors stretch   Seated opened-leg stretch.

Screen
Offensive play. To take a position in the anticipated path of the defensive player guarding a teammate in order to free the teammate to take an open shot or go to the basket. Also used as a noun.

Screen/roll   See *pick and roll.*

Set a screen   The act of screening. See *screen.*

Seed
Tournament ranking. 1-16 position in the *NCAA tournament's* regional brackets. Teams are ranked in descending order, generally, according to their national ranking. In each bracket, the highest ranked teams play the lowest ranked teams. The winners continue to play until one team remains to represent that bracket in the Final Four championship games. Used as noun, ie., *Del Mar was seeded thirteenth in the tournament.* Different usage include *seeded and seeding.*

Shield a pass
Technique used by an offensive player, usually in the post, who positions his body between the defensive player guarding him/her to create a passing lane to receive a pass. Adjustments are constantly needed to counter the movements of the defender.

Shirts and Skins
Expedient "uniforms" used in pickup games to differentiate opposing players where there is an absence of uniforms. One team wears shirts, while their opponents do not wear any shirts. Female players makes this solution problematic.

Shoo'bee da-bang
Slang. Affirmation. Used for acknowledgment or agreement, ie.g., Very good.

Shooting guard
A guard who is depended on to shoot more and handle the ball less than the point guard; often a good three-point shooter. The Two position. Compare *point guard.*

Show and recover
Defensive strategy of the defender who is guarding the screener. When the screener sets the screen, the defender takes two steps up, along side the screener, (the show) to prevent the dribbler from taking an open shot or driving to the basket. This allows his/her teammate (guarding the player with the ball) to get around the screen and return to their position. Then, the defender must get back to the player he/she is guarding (the recover) so a *matchup problem* is not created. Also see *matchup problem* and *pick and roll.*

Sideline hash mark
Mark on the sideline of the court. See diagram.

Six-on-six
Iowa brand of girl's basketball where teams played with 12 players (six-on-six) on the court at one time. The last Iowa State girls six-on-six basketball championship was played in 1993.

Skank
Floozy or Hussy. A vulgar promiscuous woman who flouts propriety.

Small forward
A forward who is typically smaller and quicker than the power forward, therefore more likely to play facing the basket and shooting jump shots. The Three position. Compare *power forward.*

Spaz   A socially awkward person.

Spin move
A reactionary move while dribbling or driving to the basket where a player starts in one direction then pivots backwards on one foot into the opposite direction in order to avoid a defender.

Square up
When a player's shoulders are facing the *basket* as he/she *releases* the ball for a jump shot; considered good shooting position.

Stack /Stacked up
An offensive alignment in which two players set up in a low post position on one side of the lane and a third player is in the low post on the other side. Most commonly used for throw-ins from behind the baseline.

Steal   To take the ball away from an opponent.

Stealth Pick
To set a screen unbeknownst to the defender, often the one who is guarding the person with the ball, with the intent to create space for an open shot or by rolling to the basket. See *pick and roll.* Very effective at creating an opening. Effectively defended when the defense communicates to one another to make the player to be screened aware of the imminent screen. Also see *show and recover.*

Strong side
The side of the court on which the ball is located. Opposite of *weak side*.

Sweet Sixteen
Teams that play in the third round of the *NCAA tournament*.

Swish   See *ch-kh*.

Switch To temporarily swap defensive assignments with a teammate.

Tch
Sound made when sucking front teeth. A nonverbal dismissive expression.

Teardrop
A shot. When a player, driving to the basket, lofts a high arching shot several feet away from the basket. Used by smaller players to avoid a blocked shot when attempting a lay-up.

The Man
A team's most valuable player. Depended upon to play well every game in order for the team to succeed. Also see *Go-to Guy*, *PTPer*, and *Playmaker*.

Three-point field goal
A field goal made from outside the three-point line (19'9") and therefore worth three points. The shooter must have both feet entirely behind the line before shooting or jumping to attempt the shot.

Three-point line/arc
A semicircle drawn around the center of the basket, with a radius of 23 feet, 9 inches in the NBA; and 19 feet, 9 inches in college basketball.

Three-point play
A two-point field goal followed by a successful free throw. Occurs after a player scores and is fouled in the act of shooting.

Trailer
An offensive player who runs behind teammates on a fast break.

Transition
The shift from defense to offense when a team has gained possession of the ball in its own backcourt.

Trap A sudden double-team on the ball handler. Also used as a verb.

Trey   A three-point shot. See *three-point field goal.*

Tsunami Feminist(s)
Fourth Wave Global Feminists. Any group or individual that works
to advocate for and educate women in rural parts of countries where
women are subjected to traditions that physically or emotionally
prevent them from free and unencumbered expression of their whole
selves while remaining sensitive to the local culture.
Motto: Leave no woman behind.

Turnover
A generic term for when the offense losses possession through a
bad pass, violation or steal. Turnovers limit opportunities to score
and thus are avoided.

Twomp   Twenty points. Domino scoring term. See *fittle'een.*

Two-on-one fast break
When two players are ahead of the rest of the team, moving quickly
toward the basket and only one defender is back to defend the basket.

Up and Under
An offensive move where a player fakes a *power up* shot from close
range, then if the defender jumps to block the shot, the offensive player
ducks beneath the airborne defender, takes one step to shoot a lay-up.

Upset
When a higher-seeded team (considered superior) loses to a lower-
seeded (inferior) one.

Upside
Having great potential to improve. Used as a noun, e.g., The point
guard was young and thus had lots of upside.

Walk-on

A non-scholarship player who usually plays very few minutes. Walk-ons usually play at the end of games when the outcome is certain. See *Garbage Time.*

Walk-on tryout

A workout conducted by coaches to evaluate unidentified players at the university who may have the talent to play for the team. Can be open or by invitation only for students who do not have athletic scholarships.

WASP

Abbv. White Anglo-Saxon Protestant. A white, usually Protestant member of the American upper social class.

Weak side

The side of the court away from the ball. Opposite of *strong* side.

Weak side pick

A screen on a defender that is set on the opposite side of the ball.

Whole Wop   *Slang.* All. Everything. The sum total.

Wing

Area on the court between the sideline and the middle of closest line of the free-throw lane, up to the hash mark. See diagram.

Winning time

The moment, late, in a close game where effectiveness will decide the outcome. Coined by Earvin "Magic" Johnson. Compare *choke.*

WNBA

Women's National Basketball Association. Professional women's basketball league created in June of 1997 with eight teams. WNBA games are played in the summer. As of 2005, there are 14 WNBA teams.

Zone defense   A defense in which each player is responsible for a specific area of the court and must guard any offensive player who enters that area. Compare *man-to-man defense.*

Acknowlegements

First and foremost, I am indebted to my wife, Tracy, who amazes me by seamlessly incorporating the competitive, feminine, and independent parts of her personality. She has contributed to my maturity and been patient with my progress. There have been triumphs and failures, but it is her unconditional love that is the foundation of my confidence and my safety net.

Thanks Mom, Joyce, for being my staunchest critic and supporter. I knew I was onto something big when you said, "I think you have a nice little story." To my mother-in-law, Mary Harrison, thanks for believing in and facilitating the dreams of Tracy and I. We can't thank you enough.

Thanks Dad, John, for showing me the value of serving others, while allowing me the freedom to do it my own way. Through the civil law you help a small number of people in a large way. My path, hopefully, will help a large number of people in a small way—with wisdom and perspectives, maybe even move humanity forward by one increment.

To Tonya Blanchard, thanks for reading all of the different drafts of this story dating back to 1996 when it was called *Title IX* and was a screenplay. Only a true friend would put up with all of the bad grammar, omitted words, and horrific punctuation.

Thank you, my grandmothers, Alice and Imogene, for being the foundation of our families. Thanks, Grandma Burris, for teaching me the value of hard work with your entrepreneurial spirit. Thanks, Grandma Harrell, for lighting the flame of creativity in all of us.

To my sister, Carole Gardner, thank you for debating the meaning of your dating stories. You deserve half the credit for coining "concierge factor." Conquer the world, but make time to have a family.

To my friends, Malia Cohen and Deanna Champion, thank you for sharing your dating frustrations, conundrums, and triumphs. It is my hope that many young women will be empowered by your experiences, sprinkled with a little male perspective, of course.

Thank you to the first readers of *Under the Rim*. Your comments, especially about the areas that needed the most work, were extremely helpful in reshaping and improving this story. Thank you Armando Sandoval, Steve Mitchel, Nancy Marks, Amarita King, Gidget Uda, Cheryl Amana, Courtney Burris, Monique Barron, Daren Barron, Dan McLaughlin, Debra Bill and Benita Kim.

Jonathan Burris, Jovonne Smith, Monique Ambers, Ken Vierra, Mark Massay, Ndidi Massay, Denzel McCollum, Randy Raven, Luis Recinos, Derek Tullis, Todd Thomas, Cedric Armstrong, Matt Steinmetz, Bryan Thomasson, Maurice Ellis, Bobby Upal, Damien Semien, Rueben Gibson, Troy Hines, Tanyel Deterovian, Al Fleck, Ahmad Mansur, Sereptha & Terrance Thompson, Oliver Harrision, Jr., Everette Burns, Chris Griffin, Carl Sullivan, Barry Young, Fred Nelson, Shawn Loucks, Carole Shea, Omar Khalif, Charles Satcher, Justin Brown,

Dwayne Curry, Joe Tanner, Dave Penny, Bruce Woodard, Malcolm McLaughlin, John Ross, Stephanie Scanlon, Marlon Brown, Steve Mitchell, Eddy Taylor, Ralph McGill, and Doris Batiste–you all contributed with thoughts that I expanded, in some cases, into whole story lines. Thank you.

To my friends and colleagues at Youth Guidance Center, thank you for your support. This is what I've been working on for so long. Thanks for covering for me. I love my job, so I won't be leaving any time soon. Sorry.

Thank you, editors Carol Taylor for taking this story to the next level and Ruth Weine, Editorial, for John C. Diamante, Editorial Services, for cleaning up my mess and adding all those commas. **www.proofreader.com**

Thank you to Dre Patterson for contributing *Adam and Eve (see back cover and described in chapter twenty)*. You have been like a brother to me. You're a true renaissance man of artistic expression. We've come a long way since that first photo shoot for *Ebony Man Magazine*. Go to **www.menobodyknows.com** to see more of Dre's art.

Thanks to Luther Knox for laying out the cover, **www. knoxdesign.com.**

Thanks to David Freeman's, "Beyond Structure" writing workshop. It was instrumental in decoding the advanced writing techniques of professional fiction/entertainment writers. To take your writing to the next level go to **www.beyondstructure.com.**

To the readers, thank you for taking the time to read this little story. Please join me in becoming a Tsunami Feminist–a Fourth Wave Feminist. Together we can change the world. Go to **www.leavenowomanbehind.com** to visit our web log. To see what we're up to and how you can help go to **www.fourthwavefeminists.com.**

Also in the Goatee Graphics family of products:

Showyourmemories.com: We create personal documentaries for weddings, birthdays, church and wedding anniversaries or any other special occasion. We use your photos, interview your family and friends to create a personalize documentary. Go to **www.showyourmemories.com** to see examples and learn more.

Doin' It: A Guide to Great Sex is a novelty book with 475 observations about sex. Examples on page 321. It is not pornographic, but merely pokes a little fun at a huge American "preoccupation."

About the Author

Damon A. Burris' love of basketball comes second only to his love of his family. He has been a counselor in the maximum-security unit of San Francisco's Juvenile Hall for ten years. Burris lives in San Francisco with his wife Tracy, his college sweetheart, and their two children. He hopes to, one day, be able to call himself a successful Tsunami Feminist.

Quick Order Form

Internet orders: **www.undertherimbook.com** (secured server)

Postal orders: **Goatee Graphics,
PO Box 591840,
San Francisco, CA 94159-1840**

Please send the following book: *Under the Rim*
I understand that I may return any of them for a full refund for any reason, no questions asked.

Please send more FREE information on: circle those that apply
     Other books   Mailing list   Email about other books

Name:

Address:

City: State: Zip Code

Telephone
Email address

Sales price   **$15.95 per book**

Sales tax: Add 7.75% for products shipped to California address only.

Shipping:
U.S.: $2.50 for first book and $1.00 for each additional book.
International: $9.00 for first book and $5.00 for each additional book.

Payment: Cheque (include with order) or   Credit card

   (Circle one)   Visa   MasterCard

Card number

Name on Card   Ex date